Momaya Short Story Review 2020

Outsiders

A Momaya Press Publication
London, U.K. & Wallingford, VT, U.S.A

All Rights Reserved.

Copyright © 2020 Momaya Press and the Authors

Cover, Interior Design and Layout by Maya Cointreau

Editing by Maya Cointreau & Monisha Saldanha

This book is sold subject to the condition that it shall not, by way of trade or otherwise, be lent, resold, hired out, or otherwise circulated without the publisher's prior consent in any form of binding or cover other than that in which it was published and without a similar condition including this condition being imposed on the subsequent publisher.

Published in 2020 by Momaya Press.

The moral right of Momaya Press has been asserted.

ISBN 978-1-951843-13-7

Table of Contents

1	Foreword
3	The Rage, Angela DiLella *
14	Ripples, Connie Ramsay Bott
20	A Button Torn from My Yellow Dress, D.R.D. Bruton
26	The Ancestors, Niall Buchanan
36	It Just Wouldn't Do, Michael G. Casey
44	The Great Sea of Summer, Russell George *
52	Watching the Aurora, Mona Dash
63	Appetite, Madeleine Dunnigan
68	The Leaf Beetle, Mary Fox
76	Bridges, Jacquie Franks
86	The Outsider, Kevin David Joinville *
94	Parka Billy, Juliet Hill
100	Not Like Me But Just the Same, Taria Karillion
105	My Friend Ros, Jan Keegan
115	When I Was a Boy, Colin Kerr
124	The Initiate, Alan McClure *
133	Breathing Backwards, Yasmine Lever
145	Through a Keyhole, Katie Lewis
160	Volte-Face, Alison Lock
168	What You Know, Melissa Morrison
177	A Fresh Start, Catherine Ogston *
184	An Ordinary Life, Margaret Morey
195	Rewilding, Lucy Palmer
201	The Little House of Death, Ian Plenderleith
208	Ferhana, Sam Szanto

217	Born of Angels, Joan Taylor-Rowan
226	The Happiness Equation, Christine Powell *
231	Go, Amigo, Go!, Joan Taylor-Rowan
241	Charlene and the Fountain of Youth, Sarah Thomas
252	When a Caged-Bird Flies, Rima Totah
260	Everything That Means Anything, Maggie Veness
271	Bog Biddy, MacKenzie Tastan *
278	Left Hanging, Natalie White
290	Third Place, Engrained, Antony Dunford
300	Second Place, Leftovers, Kat Y. Tang
308	First Place, A Lesson in Love and Hate, D.R.D. Bruton
313	About the Authors
347	About the Judges
349	About Momaya

** Honourable Mention*

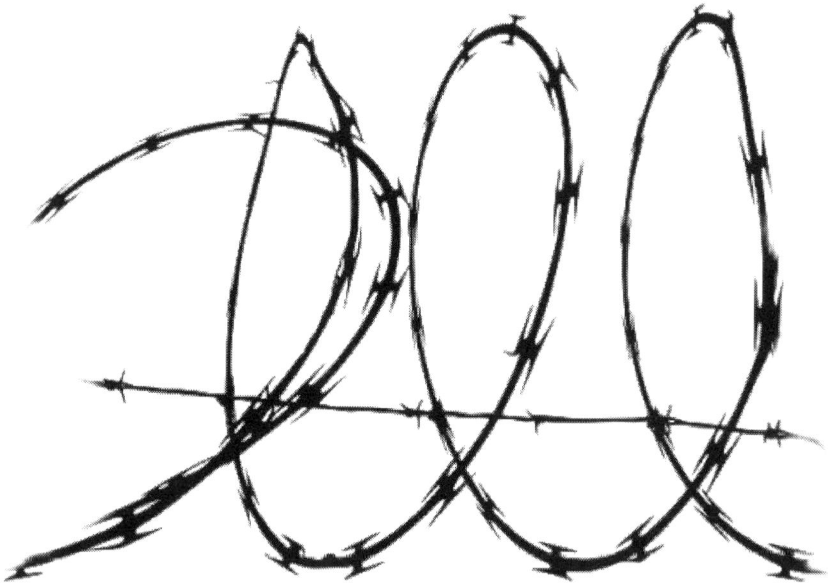

Short Story Review 2020

Foreword

Welcome to the 17th edition of the Momaya Short Story Review

Momaya Press has been giving writers a forum to express themselves and be heard since 2004. Our mission is to build the global audience for short stories and to inspire people all over the world to unlock their creative potential. Each year, Momaya receives short story submissions from all over the world and we bring the best of them together for publication in the Momaya Short Story Review. Our panel of judges spend the summer determining which stories will win. It is never easy. Each voice is unique, special, and appreciated. But in the end, only a handful will make it into the Momaya Short Story Review.

Outsiders

'Outsiders' is the theme for the Momaya Short Story Competition 2020. The stories in this volume tackled this theme in a number of different ways: social, political, economic. As the coronavirus pandemic gathered momentum, countries across Europe, Asia and North America sealed their borders against outsiders, enhancing the relevance to the theme we had already chosen. The global shutdowns seemed to give many writers a boost in creativity: this year, we received an outstanding crop of entries from 10 countries (Australia, France, Germany, India, Ireland, South Africa, Spain, Sweden, United Kingdom, United States).

Momaya Press

Our sincere thanks to the judges who reserve time in their busy schedules to read the entries, the writers who have honoured us by sharing their work, and the readers who give purpose to our efforts. Our judging panel included Meredith DePaolo (Screenwriter), Mikaela Pedlow (Editor, Random House), Gillian Pink (Research Editor, Voltaire Press, University of Oxford), and Alice Shepherd (Former Assistant Editor, Penguin).

Encouraging your contributions

While it may be true that we all have a novel to write, most of us won't find the time to do so. Our 3,000 word limit is about five pages typed – it's something you can write over a few lunch breaks, instead of watching TV after dinner, or by getting up a bit earlier on the weekend. Submit your story to Momaya Press and an experienced judge will read your story, reflect upon it, and make a considered judgment on whether your story should be published in this year's annual review. It's an incredible validation of your ability. It is an act of courage to share your words with the world.

We thank the thousands of readers and writers who support Momaya Press, and we encourage everyone who reads these words to submit their short story to our competition. The theme for 2021 is 'Harmony' and we are accepting entries on momayapress.com until 30th April 2021. We hope we will have the pleasure of reading your submission!

Happy writing!

Maya Cointreau and Monisha Saldanha

Co-Founders

Momaya Press

www.momayapress.com

Short Story Review 2020

The Rage

Angela DiLella

Honourable Mention

We women call it 'the Rage.' Or at least we did, when we were all still allowed to interact with each other. Well, I still call it the Rage, anyways.

Like almost every other sexually transmitted disease, nobody has been able to track it that closely to the moment of its discovery and documentation. It wasn't here, and then it was, and then it was already everywhere. We first heard whisperings at home up north, in New England. Some bug going around. Making people act oddly. Maybe the summer people brought it. And Jack announced that he wanted to go on a road trip, change the scenery. Why not? Then we were in our ugly little teak sedan in the Nevadan desert, after driving thousands of miles, I'd guess. I never look at the odometer.

I've had my suspicions of Jack. I don't have any reason to believe he's ever been unfaithful but – it's like getting bit by a dog that's had its shots. Even if you have confirmation that the dog has a clean bill of health and your wound has been treated perfectly and professionally... You're still thinking about it and chalking every slip of the tongue or trip up as a warning sign.

So, I watch him; in the car, I watch with – perhaps suspicion isn't the right word; a better one may be superstition. I saved myself for marriage. It wasn't on purpose and it wasn't hard. I was sort of homely in high school and not much better in college. I moved in with Jack after college, and there, with real privacy, it finally happened. So that whole time, men, and the things that health class and my classmates suggested made them men, were regarded with superstition. Health class and TV and magazines made clear the idea of sex and its consequences and gains, but there was still the actual sensation and the act. I look at my husband now when he drives the same way I'd look at boys leaving the locker room after changing for 2C PE, mythologizing to stand in for understanding.

The last place we stopped, really stopped, was one of those Motel Eights, the kind where you can't tell if the thumps through the door some poor sap is bedding a prostitute or beating her, or maybe some junky struggling through his death throes. That night we were lucky; nobody on the other side of our nicotine-yellow walls. I watched the TV late at night, while Jack was in the shower. He was shoeless in there and I wouldn't lay on the bed without the picnic tablecloth from our car.

'Only men can actively transmit the disease during sexual encounters during the incubation period of the disease. It appears to show symptoms in women earlier, and there have been reports of women running at cars or other humans much earlier in the disease's life cycle than men. If they reach their targets unimpeded, they will behave aggressively; it is important to keep your face, especially your eyes, well-protected.' I sat up straight and scrambled limb over limb to the edge of the bed, pulling the nubby, crackling plastic tablecloth with me.

Transfixed, I sat like a dumb child as I listened to the newscaster, and I jumped when I saw Jack's arm move in my peripheral vision. I hadn't heard him come back in from the bathroom. I bumped backwards and scooted away from him as he snapped the dial of the TV off, tangling and untangling my legs from the tablecloth, pausing long enough to slide it between me and the motel's thousand-year-old blankets.

'Some woman gets upset and decides to make a mess for everyone else. Nancy Neighbor insults Good Wife's quiche one too many times, and Good Wife decides she's had enough.'

I scooted across the pitted plastic to give him room on the bed. I could already tell that the tablecloth was going to be puckering against my skin all night.

'Husband forgets that Good Wife wants vacations once in a while, need 'em for the pressure valve. So, he gets it. That's all it is, some pent-up... Not everybody has it this nice, huh?' Jack continued. He reached over and snapped off the room light--the room was small enough, the switch was right there, the door out was right there, everything was close enough to be kicked.

I was quiet that night, my mind on other things, thinking: how would Jack know if he was infected? Certain sexually transmitted diseases can also be passed through blood. Was running at humans, cars, animals, or anything else that moved the first symptom? Would there be hydrophobia first? Lesions? Mysterious, lingering bruises?

'Forget the TV.' Maybe Jack heard me feeling for the remote on the nightstand.

I lay there, too in my head, and although it wasn't like him, he seemed to not be overly bothered by my bitten-back silence and just kept on going, plastic cloth scrunching and dragging, sticking and unsticking to every uncomfortable part of my body that I'd rather not have to know of. Everything could be washed. So, it didn't matter.

I held onto the noise of the flies crackling outside the window in one of those electric blue lanterns far into dawn.

***

The next day in the car I was quiet too. We drove a little--maybe a lot--we could have been going in circles for all I knew. A rock is a rock is a rock, a cactus is a cactus is a cactus, there's only so many times you can say 'Look, a roadrunner!' with enthusiasm, and the Acme jokes get older even faster than that.

'You don't look so good,' Jack said, like it was the kind of thing he knew he was supposed to say. I don't think he looked at me since I rolled the still-damp tablecloth up and carried it out to put back into the trunk. That was the first time I thought: the symptoms show in women earlier.

'I didn't sleep that well.'

We stopped at one of those rest stops that look nice from the outside, but the inside just has a sad gift shop, a Subway, a McDonald's, a Pizza Hut, and other cheap fast foods inside. It was just out there, in the desert. I always wonder where the sad teenagers that work at those kinds of places live. Near the state border there was actually a Dunkin Donuts and I brushed the cashier's hand and it was so dry, I thought that he crawled right out of a rocky crag, and I jumped like I had really touched a lizard. After I kept on looking at the spot below the ball of my thumb and I knew Jack noticed me looking, but I couldn't stop glancing over at the spot.

At that next stop, Jack gave me the same quick look.

'Stay in the car.'

'Get me chips?'

Jack shrugged as he slammed the door shut, like he didn't think he'd be able to find a single bag of chips in the whole of the western United States.

***

That's the way it's been. I think I last used plumbing a few days later, after we had stopped sleeping in motels and hotels and just slept in the car and slept with each other in the car. It hurts my back, but Jack has the keys. And our wallets. I keep my mouth shut and again, although it isn't like him, he isn't bothered, in fact, he gets annoyed when I shift--no matter how far your seat can go back it's not comfortable or fun if you're on the receiving end.

After we had left modern plumbing behind it was just in the desert, behind dunes and rocks and cacti. You'd be surprised at how quickly you get used to it. The crouching and kneeling is good for my joints. All the sitting is tough on my knees and my lower back. Since we've been out in the desert, I've sort of, well, dried up myself, so there's no worry about any discomfort there, but I've also kind of lost my internal calendar in that.

For all I know, we could be in New Mexico by now, or Arizona, or somewhere else that's – mostly desert? Or makes me think of the desert. We drove through those states to get to Nevada, but I couldn't remember if they all blended into one desert or if there was a difference in environment and region. I think I'd have seen more succulents by now if we had passed into Arizona. I don't know why I'd think that.

***

We saw a woman by the road, a few miles out from a rest stop. She was in khakis and a white polo shirt, somehow spotless, like she had wandered off a tennis court out in the desert somewhere. When she turned to the noise of our engine, we saw that she had a little blue visor, so that her face wasn't even sunburnt.

She waved at the car in a weird, angular way: her arm and hand stayed straight as it moved, obtuse, acute, right angles, 1, 2, 3. Then she stepped to the road tentatively, the toes of one of her Keds just on the tar, up out of the dust. Her little white Keds were stained tan from all the grime and dust and sand.

Jack's eyes went wide as if she was a ghost of someone he knew, and his mouth fell at the corners. His cigarette hung down out of the left corner like a cartoon character's might.

He was slowing cautiously, and my eyes locked on the muscles in his leg moving underneath his blue jeans. I knew he was worrying about the damage a human could do to the hood of our sedan.

'Jack.' He straightened and looked at me, same dumb look of surprise at my voice. Beyond 'ahs' and whimpers from me, he hadn't really heard my voice in days, and maybe even, I suppose, weeks. It seemed, and still seems, useless.

He knows my likes and dislikes, so it doesn't matter.

'Jack, the news anchor said running, she's just standing there. Maybe she needs help.'

Jack recovered and pulled to the shoulder. He made a minor introduction as she got in and let me try to do the same. The lady, Kay, bubbled, tried to make small talk about the Rage – only she said the R Simplex Virus. Still, her report matched the anchor's report and I knew. I knew.

'It's good to be out here, though. I knew I had to get out of that cramped apartment complex, so I had a friend drive me out, and I just kept walking... It wasn't my best plan.' She giggled and smiled self-consciously. The corners of her eyes crinkled in the mirror and my chest fluttered. She had all freckles on the apples of her cheeks and across the bridge of her nose. How dare a man try to infect her with the Rage.

'It was so precautionary, though, I haven't touched a man in--' She tilted her head back, her eyes crinkling so endearingly again. Then she got a look at Jack's face: I glanced at him too and it was unreadable, to me at least. There was something in his expression that made her uneasy. 'Or a woman,' she added weakly, her smile taut. She grunted a laugh: I'm friendly, hey, no problem here, I don't have a problem with men, we're buddies.

I understood the urge.

I tried a laugh. It was awkward. Jack looked at me as if he couldn't believe who was in his car with him, but I imagined that Kay understood my attempt to show camaraderie as well as I understood her deflection.

An hour later, Jack pulled over at a rest stop. He got out of the car with something like regret, looking back on us like an anxious mother willing bad kids to be good. Jack and I don't have kids, but Jack's mother still gives her sons, especially Jack, the same look around the table for Sunday dinner. It's nearly funny.

When Kay started to move to get up too, he said, 'No.'

'Sunflower seeds, please?'

Jack thumped the door shut.

'Stoic guy, huh?' Kay seemed a little cowed by the quiet of the car ride.

I pulled my lips into a tight smile for the rearview mirror.

'I bet he's just shocked by all of this,' Kay added, perhaps worried that she had offended me. 'It must be reassuring to have each other, though, you've got clean tests back and you don't have to worry about anybody else...'

'Clean tests?' I peeked over my shoulder to get a good look at her real face.

'Right? The tests. If you're a registered couple they would've just delivered them to you, no matter where you are. It looks like this little swipe card...'

Jack wears a wedding ring; I wear a wedding ring. Like purebred dogs, we have papers: we're registered.

Kay fished around in her satchel and came up with a small, thick plastic card, about the same size as an ID card, but thicker.

'This test, silly!'

She reached over the arm rest to show me the 'card': it had directions in microscopic font, and there were ten narrow plastic tubes embedded in the card. Eight were clear and showed nothing, two were a vivid green. There was a round, blue rubber button that said 'TEST' on it in huge, blocky letters.

At this moment, Jack came back in with all his usual pomp. He slammed the door and almost tossed the bag of sunflower seeds back before he noticed the card.

'Oh--Jack, do you have the tests on you?' I asked, feigning high spirits as best I could.

'Tests?' Jack's eyebrow arced in the mirror at Kay.

'It's just a little finger prick, and then the little device analyzes your blood, that's it. Red is...' The cute crinkles were going away. She might've thought I was absentminded, but I could tell that she had a feeling about Jack. 'Green means clean.'

Jack got the car started without another word. At the same moment, Kay was pressing the blue button to show me how the needle slid out of the top of the card for the pricking. Jack revved up and Kay's hand jerked to the side, burying the inch-long needle deep into Jack's bicep.

'CHRIST--' Jack swerved reflexively, and we all went knocking around. He braked, turned around, and roared into the backseat.

Kay pressed herself into the backseat as far as she could go, holding the card in front of her in shaking hands, as if that would keep her safe. I melded into the space between the door and seat.

'GET OUT, GET OUT, GET OUT!' he screeched, clutching the wound. Blood oozed from between his fingers lazily.

'W-wait,' Kay whimpered. There were tears in her eyes, and then she was distracted by the card in front of her, which was emitting a soft peeping noise. The back which faced us was a plain, smooth white, unreadable, but whatever the other side was showing had absorbed Kay completely. She glanced at me through the gap between my seat and the headrest, eyes huge.

'OUT!'

'It needs another minute--' she protested, but she was already sliding towards the door on my side. 'One more minute to be sure...' I craned my neck, but I couldn't see the results forming.

Jack reached for her and, yelping, she was gone--I half-prayed his fingers would get stuck in the slamming door, it's what he deserved for groping after her, but of course his arm wasn't long enough for that. Only her little blue visor got stuck and stayed with us when Jack revved up again and sped down the road. He let his blood run freely down his arm and onto the sedan's arm rest to trace canals in the pitted pleather.

'Crazy bitch. Walking around with a needle. I could die.' When I appeared unresponsive, he added, 'Disease, babe. You hear about it all the time.'

Do I?

'Some poor bastard swabs a coin return for a quarter and BAM, there's a used a needle in there, and then it's welcome to the wonderful world of...'

'She said they were issued by the g-government, f-for registered couples...'

'You're always falling for scams, remember that telephone thing? We had to cancel all of our cards.' He shook his head and clicked his tongue, some repentant televangelist ready to show me the error of my ways and help me however he saw fit, for a small fee. I knew what he was going to say next before he said it: 'What would you do without me?'

Maybe it shows in women first, like the lady on TV said, but I feel the same. I wish I had seen Kay's card with the results. Maybe he has the Rage, but he's had it longer than me. Way back in New England, for years and years and years: maybe Kay's card could have told me if he was patient zero.

That was days ago, and I'm still wishing for sixty more seconds. If only Kay hadn't said anything about the tests right away. If only Jack had tripped walking back to the car or had thought to hold open a door for some nice old lady. If only something had happened to prolong Kay's stay, even just a few seconds longer. Just long enough to see if the tube turned green or red.

We're still driving through the sand, past the roadrunners and the rest stops, and the endless faces whose eyes I won't meet, on and on, and on. Twisting and worrying Kay's half-crushed visor in my lap, I think: Maybe we'll drive forever.

Ripples

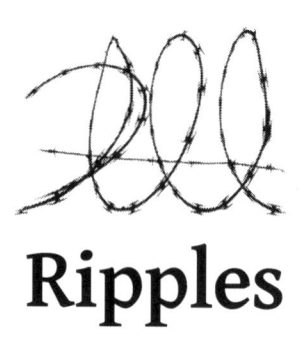

Connie Ramsay Bott

We'd all heard about the accident. It had been on the local news on Saturday, and then again on Sunday. Four sixteen year olds, two boys and two girls, had been out on Lake St Clair in a motorboat. Something had happened and they all had drowned.

Mrs. Thornton, my fifth grade teacher was like a kind mother. She wore shirtwaist dresses and her hair was in careful dark curls. I was new at the school. We'd moved from Detroit out to the suburbs in February, and I had a new best friend called Terry. I was the sort of girl who needed one good friend, so once Terry and I were amigos, I didn't think much about the other twenty-eight kids in the class.

There was whispering in the classroom first thing on Monday morning. Mrs. Thornton asked us all to quiet down. She said that we had probably heard about the boating accident over the weekend out on Lake Saint Clair, and she was sorry to tell us that one of the children (she didn't call them teenagers) was Cynthia's big sister. Cynthia would be away from school for a while, but when she came back we were to be nice to her, and we mustn't ask her any questions.

I was surprised by Mrs. Thornton's voice when she told us. She sounded upset in a very quiet way, like she wanted to cry but was being brave. I tried to think about Cynthia, what she had been like in class, but I couldn't remember much about her. She had mousy hair and her ears were pierced. She had a Polish last name.

She was away from school for more than a week, getting over not having a sister any more. While she was gone I spent a lot of time thinking about my own sister Pamela. She's two years older than me, not eight, like Cynthia's sister. She thought of me as an embarrassing nuisance. First I thought she'd be happy if I died. Then I imagined Pamela had died. Everyone would think I was brave at her funeral, but I would secretly be glad that she wasn't around to make fun of me. I wondered if Mom would let me move into her bedroom because it was bigger, and painted sky blue. I was thinking about that one night at dinner.

'What are you staring at me for?' Pamela asked. 'Mom, tell Leanne to stop staring at me. She's giving me the creeps.'

'Both of you, just eat.'

'I'm eating,' I said as I shoveled corn into my mouth. I give Pamela a big-mouthful smile and turned back to my plate.

'Weirdo,' she said under her breath. I was just learning my own way of fighting back. I knew I'd tell Terry about this little scene on the way to school the next day, maybe exaggerate it into a bigger story.

At first I thought Terry was Nice, with a capital N. She always followed the rules and showed respect to grown-ups. Sometimes it made me angry, she appeared to be such a goody-goody. When she came over to my house the first time she was really polite. She called my mom 'ma'am' and told her our living room curtains were pretty. We had tuna fish casserole for lunch, the kind you make from a can of tuna, a can of soup and some macaroni. My mom put crushed potato chips on top to make it crusty. To hear Terry rave about it, you'd think she never had hot food before.

'Mrs. O'Malley, this is so good. You must give me the recipe so I can give it to my mom. How did you make the top so crispy?' You should have seen my mother beam. She wasn't used to getting compliments on her cooking.

Upstairs in my room I asked Terry if she really liked the casserole. She wrinkled her nose.

'Tuna? Yuck!' was all she said. When she left to go home my mom gave her the recipe, copied out on one of her 'Here's what's cookin'' index cards.

'This is for your mother,' my mom said. Terry thanked her for the recipe, and thanked her again for the delicious lunch. I'm sure the recipe card was never delivered.

The day Cynthia was due back at school was hot, even though it was early May. I was wearing a cotton dress I'd worn the year before. I loved it. It had little cherries in bunches here and there, but it was tight under my arms, and I knew Mom wouldn't let me wear it again once she noticed.

'I wonder, if you paid close attention, if you could feel yourself grow.' I stopped right there on the sidewalk and closed my eyes. I could feel the sun shining down, even though it was before nine o'clock.

'You'll have to stop to feel yourself grow later, Leanne. We're going to be late if we don't hurry,' Terry said. 'Cynthia is back today. Remember?'

My dress had started to rub under my arms. We walked the rest of the way without talking.

I'd thought Terry was like me, one best friend, forget everyone else. We had talked about Cynthia a lot since the accident. I don't like to admit it, but when Terry talked about Cynthia I felt a little flash of jealousy hot in my chest. Neither of us had ever been to a funeral, so we had to imagine what it would have been like. Terry said in Europe people howl like dogs at the graveside. She'd seen it on the news. It sounded scary.

'They wouldn't do that in America,' I said, but I wasn't sure.

I had wondered if Cynthia would be wearing black, and if her eyes would be red from crying. She looked normal. She was quiet, but she was always quiet. She had more than a week of work to make up, but she spent a lot of time looking out the window.

At lunchtime Terry steered me to the table where Cynthia was sitting and started unpacking her lunch.

'Well, this is wonderful,' Terry said in a weary voice. 'Another baloney sandwich with mustard. I'm so excited. What have you got, Cynthia?'

Cynthia didn't answer right away. Then she said, 'Cheese.'

'Just cheese? Nothing else to make it super special?'

'Just a cheese sandwich. And an apple.'

'Wow,' Terry said, her voice still sounding bored. It was the stupidest conversation ever. I wondered what Terry was up to.

'I've got ham and cheese,' I said. No one was listening.

'I hope you don't mind me asking about your lunch, Cynthia,' Terry said. 'I know Mrs. Thornton told us not to ask you any questions.'

'She did?'

'Yeah. I don't know what she meant. There's nothing wrong with being friendly. If you want you can walk home with us tonight. My house is on the way to yours.'

'Okay. Maybe,' she said. She got up and threw her sandwich in the garbage and left the lunchroom.

'What was that all about?' I asked Terry.

'Just being friendly.'

I didn't see Terry leave after school. I thought she must have gone to the girl's room, so I waited. After a few minutes Mrs. Thornton asked why I hadn't left. She wanted to close up the classroom and go home. I went to the girl's room but all the cubicles were empty. The halls were empty, too. Mrs. Thornton walked me to the front of the school.

'Are you looking for Terry, Leanne?' she asked. Everyone knew Terry and me were best friends. 'I think I saw her leave with Cynthia.'

I walked home by myself. The skin at the top of my arms was rubbed raw from my dress and my throat hurt from wanting to cry.

When I got home I phoned Terry. I asked her why she hadn't waited for me. She said she couldn't talk because her mother wanted her to help fold the laundry. She sounded bored. I asked her if she had walked home with Cynthia, but she just said, 'Got to go' and hung up.

In the morning she called at my door to walk to school like she always did. She said she thought I had left for home without her the day before. I knew she was lying. She said yes, she had walked home with Cynthia, and Cynthia had told her about the funeral and that her mother still cried at the drop of a hat. I asked her what Cynthia said about the funeral.

'I can't tell you about that because it's private,' she said. It felt like she was looking down at me. I didn't want to believe it, but I knew right then that I had lost my best friend.

After that Terry made sure Cynthia had lunch and walked home with us every day. Terry didn't talk to me. She and Cynthia pretended like I wasn't even there. A week later I was almost late for school because I waited for Terry to call for me in the morning, but she never came.

I should have made more friends, but it seemed everyone already had best friends. When school finished in June, I thought it was going to be a long miserable summer.

To my surprise within a week Terry knocked on the screen door.

'Aren't you spending all your time with Cynthia?' I asked. I tried to sound bored and casual like I'd heard Terry do.

'No, no,' she said. 'We're not friends any more. Aren't you going to ask me in? I'll tell you all about the funeral and Cynthia's weird family.'

I opened the door.

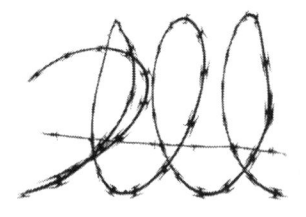

A Button Torn from My Yellow Dress

D.R.D. Bruton

I remember that day – I think I do. The one from the picture, a black and white photograph of the three of us in the same room with shafted sunlight breaking through the windows and falling on the floor in bright slabs, and dust like flecked gold in that light, and the air as still as a held breath – or still in the picture at least. And Julia, balanced on one leg, was singing, that I recall, too. She was always singing back then and still is when I think of her.

It was an easy day and a slow day, if it's the one that I think it is, by which I mean school was out and it was summer, though I cannot say if it was the start or the end or somewhere in the middle. Mam was at work at the grocery store, doing an extra shift for no reason, sitting at the checkout and getting heavy, and smiling at Mr. Gupta across the counter, winking at him like he was maybe on a promise. And da was no place – that's what he said when he was drinking at Purdie's Bar, the tv turned up so loud in there you couldn't think and Mary Laidlaw serving and her tits all pushed up and begging for attention. It was just us in the house and the cat sleeping somewhere and bees caught behind the glass and looking for a way out.

'You mind each other, now,' mam had said.

Jen, she's the oldest, and she announced straight out that she was gonna let Kenny Tucker put his hand underneath her dress if that's what he wanted. And Julia stopped her singing then and she put her two feet flat to the floor and her mouth was open and no sound coming out. Like a landed fish, I thought. I pretended to be shocked too at what Jen had said, though I'd already let Stevie Martin do just that with me. He'd promised not to tell no one and he swore on his baby sister's life and she only had one arm so I believed him. Just as long as he warmed his hands first, I'd said.

Stevie Martin was in a breathless hurry, that I remember also, and he was a little clumsy in his haste and he tore a button on my yellow dress, which bothered me more than Stevie squeezing my diddies like he was testing for ripe fruit. It was yellow like sunflowers, that dress, and mam had ordered it specially through a catalogue and the buttons were yellow, too, like little rounds of stamped butter.

Jen began describing Kenny Tucker's kisses, all hot and wet and urgent, and his tongue in her mouth soft as a pink slug and searching. And Julia said that was just plain disgusting and she made noises in the back of her throat like she was being sick or like she was the cat trying to bring up a hairball.

I remember that day, not just because of the picture. The things that we said, I remember, too, and Julia still so young – ever young and no getting away from that. And Jen going on and on about Kenny Tucker's kisses. In the dark behind the church they'd kissed. Right under the stained-glass window of the Mother of Jesus in her blue shawl and a gold ring about her head and one hand held up in a gentle blessing. Jen said Kenny's kisses tasted of toothpaste and salt and whisky. She said he was a little drunk and she was, too, and kissing Kenny was like licking – like the cat sipping milk and its bubblegum tongue lapping and lapping, making a noise like slurping. Mam disapproved of that noise if we was drinking milk the same.

Maybe that's why Julia took herself off. Maybe. That, or the disgust at Kenny's tongue and his spit in Jen's mouth. Like I said, Julia was still young and she didn't understand like I did.

It's all so long ago now. More than twenty years and nearer thirty. I can't really believe it, all that time having slipped through our fingers, like water scooped from the river and carried into the house and nothing in the hand when I tried to show mam the stickleback swimming, nothing 'cept the stickleback lying on its side and wriggling like a silver kissed worm and its fright-full face and its staring eye and mam saying it was just cruel and I should put it in water right away. And time has slipped through my hands the same and it's twenty and some years ago now. But the funny thing is, if I close my eyes I can still hear the back door falling shut and the small and smaller sound of Julia singing once again and Julia taking her song away with her.

'She won't never grow up,' said Jen, and she ran her fingers through her sun-coloured hair and she pinched her cheeks till they was pink and she stood on dancers' tip-toe so she could look at herself in the mirror on the wall and she asked me if I thought she was pretty enough.

I told Jen then about Stevie Martin and his fingers sticky with the juice of pears he'd filched from the orchard up on Greenacre farm, and his kisses sticky, too, and wet and sugar-sweet. And Stevie swearing on his sister's life and snorting like a bull and blowing warm breaths into the closed cup of his hands before touching me.

'Really?' Jen said, and I think she was a little jealous that it had happened to me first.

She wanted to know what it was like. Everything. 'Don't leave out a thing,' she said. 'Tell me it all – every dot and dimple.'

I shrugged and said it was ok. I wanted to tell her about the button on my dress, the one that had burst from under Stevie's too-quick, too-thick fingers and that button now lost in Brooker's field someplace and it'd maybe be found in years to come by some team of archaeologists as proof that I'd once been there, and they'd be at a loss to explain why there was just the one yellow button. I wanted to tell Jen about the dress and the button, but I thought she might then tell mam and I could not bear the cross that mam would be.

'It was ok,' I said.

And Jen asked me if I loved Stevie – which I laughed and said was stupid. Stevie Martin and his smile was gap-toothed and crooked and he had a squint in one pale eye and his feet were different sizes, and no I didn't love him. As if.

And Jen said maybe it was different when it was someone you loved who was touching under your clothes. She so wanted it to be special what she was planning to do with Kenny Tucker that I said maybe she was right and I said how it was better when Sissy's hands were doing what Stevie's hands did. Sissy who wore her hair in plaits and ribbons and she was the prettiest girl in our year and she thought boys was just dirty and they smelled of milk when it has been left out in the sun too long and it's sour. And I loved Sissy. It said so on my arm, high up and under the sleeve of my yellow dress so mam never knew; it says so still. In ink it says it, beneath the skin, scratched with a hot needle so it's permanent. 'I love Sissy'. And Sissy and me, we kissed most every secret day back then and she touched my diddies sometimes under my dress and she touched 'em slow as summer days and butterfly-gentle, and it took all my breath away when she did. So

I said maybe Jen was right and I said I was sure she was.

I pushed up the sash window to set free the bee that was lost and fizzing like a lit firework against the glass. And I remember thinking, when the bee was gone, how quiet the world could be and I remember thinking it was strange – like something was missing that should have been there. I know now, all these water-dripping-through-my-fingers years later, it was Julia singing that was not where it should be.

'Kenny Tucker's eyes are as blue as the sky with bits of the sun adrift in 'em, small pretty orange shards. And he's got a scar like a sickle moon on one cheek, like a smear of pearl. It's the most beautiful thing and I could look at it all day and never tire. And his hands are clean and they smell of lemon soap, and his hair, too.'

Later in the day, that easy and slow summer day, Jen was sleeping on a blanket thrown flat on the grass out back, lying with her top off and she was face down with her bra unfastened so the sun could run the smooth and warm of its hands evenly over her skin; and I was eating honey from a jar, scooping it up with two fingers and sucking, and sucking loud enough for mam's disapproval, and suddenly the police recruit was in the house somewhere and calling.

His name was Michael and he always looked as though he was surprised or lost even when he wasn't. I quickly put the lid on the honey and slipped the jar back in the cupboard in case he caught me – quick as lickety split. Then I went to find Michael.

In his arms he carried Julia, like a pale limp wet fish he'd pulled from the river, like that wide-eyed stickleback I brought in for mam to see, 'cept Julia's eyes was closed, as if she was sleeping, and she wasn't wriggling like any worm. And river water dripped from her hair and her dress, pooling in glassy puddles on mam's polished floor in the front room, and the cat was mewling at my feet and rubbing itself against my legs for comfort.

The whole world was dripping after that.

Mam was fetched from her work straight away and she cried every day from that day. And Mr. Gupta brought her flowers wrapped in purple cellophane and a brown paper bag of broken biscuits, and he said not to come into work for the rest of the week, and he said she could take as long as she liked, and he pressed her hand in his and he did not smile.

And da shook his head, and when they was alone he stroked mam's hair like she was a cat or clapped her shoulder like she was a horse, and he did not have any words for what he felt or what mam felt, and he never did find words again.

And Jen did not let Kenny Tucker touch her under her dress after all, not that summer or any other, not with her sister laid in a dark hole in the ground and a hole in all the summers that came after, a hole that is the absence of Julia singing.

I have that last picture of us, of me and Julia and Jen, and we are in the house and in sunlight and Julia is balancing on one leg and Jen is saying about kissing with tongues; and even though I am looking straight at the camera, I don't now recall who it was who took that picture, and after nearly thirty years it is that small detail that bothers me – like a button torn from my yellow dress when Stevie Martin was pressing his pear-juice-sticky fingers into my flesh, and that button still not found and still lying lost somewhere in Brooker's field.

The Ancestors

Niall Buchanan

Marek cut across the football pitch that day to avoid Hinch and Bell who he knew were waiting in ambush somewhere on the only road from the school gates up to town. Luckily Zoltan, his sole ally in Year Seven had warned him of the plan. They seemed to hate anyone with a foreign name, and even though he spoke like everyone else having been born here, the rough boys would talk to him in pretend heavily accented English that sounded more Russian than Polish. Not that they'd know the difference.

The pitch had a white line running round the edge, and as he came close to it, he saw a circle of different sized mole-hills just inside the boundary. That'll annoy Stephenson the groundsman he thought as he counted twelve. A busy mole. On the second one along from the outer edge he spotted a curious reddish stone that gleamed as it caught the late afternoon light. He had just started the Prehistory course and they'd been looking at flint tools, so he was on the alert and went in to get a closer look just in case. The sun must have warmed the stone for as he picked it up he had a sudden feeling it was like a piece of meat and he nearly dropped it. Looking closely after recovering from the shock, he saw it was about the length of his middle finger and in the shape of Africa. The North African 'coast' was bulbous and un-worked but the southern edge felt sharp as a craft knife with regular chip marks as if it had been knapped with some precision for some unknown purpose. He tried to remember where he'd seen such a thing before, and he set off with it nestled comfortably in the palm of his hand as if it had been made to measure. What could he do with such a sharp object? Scare the bullies with a sweep of his arm clutching this? They'd never expect such a thing. No, he'd get arrested and his mother would be livid. She always said the best revenge was to do well with your life.

As he began to crawl along the badger run under the blackthorns to get to Mill Lane and safety, he remembered the very first time he'd ever seen such a thing. It was the trip in year five to the Horniman Museum in London and the glazed displays of hand chipped flints from the stone ages all laid out in cabinets and labelled. But now he had one in his hand all to himself and he kneaded it with great satisfaction as he made progress through the snaggy branches.

Half way through, on impulse, Marek began to strip some bark off a low hanging elder branch blocking the path but the tool flipped sideways on the slippy underbark and the edge cut the side of his palm surprisingly deeply.

'Owya!' he cried. Blood trickled down his fingers, so he licked them as he walked tasting iron. To be so sharp after all those centuries. Perhaps it was a tool for scraping flesh off hides. He'd heard about this from Mr. High, the popular and very serious history teacher who always dressed in an embroidered waistcoat with a fresh pressed shirt and different tie each day. He noticed these things as his mother was a freelance designer.

***

'You're a bit late. And have you cut yourself again? Make sure you wash it. Well, how was it?' she asked meaning something to do with the trouble he'd been having with the thugs. Why had some fool gone and told her? He could mind read his mother which was his only superpower.

On the two computer screens on either side of her desk he could see the clothes patterns she was currently working on. It was weird she was always designing stuff at least a season ahead. He could see that she was working on a winter collection.

'Oh it was okay,' he said and let the stone fall into his pocket. They'd been worse than ever. In the last few months he'd stopped sharing everything with her but the side effect was the constant questions. She could mind read too apparently which was annoying.

'Can you put your clothes in the wash before you have your snack?' she shouted as he closed the door.

'Yeah,' he called from the bathroom.

When he changed before his shower, he took The Stone out of his pocket and concealed it inside a box of plasters which he'd smuggle to his room afterwards ostensibly for the cut to his hand. The warm water seemed to wash the contagion of school from his body along with the dried blood so he felt more cheerful on towelling himself before slipping on his jeans and tee shirt trying to keep his fresh wound from opening.

That night he took the tool to bed with him, and before putting out the light, he looked carefully at the pitted surface. It looked like someone had struck the stone several times with great skill to create this very effective cutting implement, and he looked forward to taking it in next day to show to Mr. High at the end of the lesson. He fell asleep with it in his plastered hand.

***

The wound on his palm still hurt but he bound it with some sphagnum moss and a small piece of leather he cut from his leggings with the sharp end of the Lodestone. He followed the fresh tracks of a yearling elk this time, and could smell its musky scent, so he knew it had to be just ahead on the widest forest path. The shame of failing the climax of the Quest was too much for Katlam to contemplate, and he really could not bear the idea of one more hungry night sleeping in some brushwood. The Stone swung from a thong around his neck always outwards so he knew his target must be ahead. Then he caught a glimpse of the animal's rump and saw the mud being churned up by its hooves as it sprang forwards in greater alarm. The spooked deer was now heading straight down the fenced run on the final stretch to the village. It shied and stopped when it saw the buildings, so Katlam made himself look as large as possible and roared out loud. It finally continued forwards and dashed to the end of the fencing before running headlong past the carved ancestor post and through the huddle of thatched buildings. Finally it leaped to safety over the far boundary and was gone. He'd done it.

Standing like a sentinel in the centre of the village, a tall man turned and entered a roundhouse after the animal disappeared. He was too far away to recognise but it had to be Aklash.

So he'd done it and would eat properly tonight for the first time in a month.

An hour later he sat cross legged in the centre of the twelve. They all had eyes closed and were humming a discord and their voices rose and fell as they summoned The Spirit. Time seemed to lose all meaning. He should close his eyes too but he could not resist glancing from one wizened face to another: The six elder men and six elder women were all sitting round him, while herb smoke scented the air of the Spirit House. It drifted upwards to disappear into the straw of the thatch above. Then the singing stopped when Aklash the medicine man banged a hollow stick on a log three times and they all looked at Katlam together. Ganka, the oldest looking woman with the three black spot tattoos of her rank on each cheek said she was ready and the others murmured assent.

'Who is this outsider that comes and disturbs the gathering of the elders?' she said in a strong voice.

'It is me Katlam son of Garoda and I am returned from a moon of Fast Days,' he replied as he'd memorised before the ordeal.

'Which animal have you brought within sight of our Spirit Man?' she asked.

'I have driven Elk to within sight of Aklash,' he said. There was a moment of silence and he could hear the steady breathing of The Twelve. Nothing was ever hurried in such gatherings but he was near to breaking point.

'So it is done. It is good,' said Chief Ganka with finality and she may have smiled but her face was so lined it was hard to tell. The woman leaned forward, took the stone from his neck, and made a nick in her finger to draw a bead of blood. She passed it to her neighbour who did the same, and the stone did the round till it was given back to him. Then one by one they leaned forwards and shook their bloody hands with his.

Ganka then spoke once more.

'Welcome Brother. Katlam the Child is no longer with us. Your new self is to be called Leaping Elk for that was the animal that came before you from your quest which the Spirit has answered. So Leaping Elk we welcome you to us the People of the Woods but first you must bury your Quest Stone and with it your old heart. First drink this,' she said and handed him a wooden bowl with some whitish liquid in it. She gestured for him to drink, and he obeyed. It tasted fermented like fruit gone off and it made him feel sick, although he was so ravenous it was better than nothing.

Go now before you eat your coming of age feast and may The Spirit be your Guide.

These words of the Wise Woman rang like the beauty of birdsong in his ears as he walked back into the forest and the path he'd run back on. The boy who'd once been Katlam found a flat anonymous spot way off the maze of trackways under some pines where no one was likely ever to venture, and he scratched a hole with his good hand. He laid the Lodestone carved on the week of his birth by his long dead father into the hole with reverence. A few hot tears fell on its surface for it had become so much his consolation and only comfort in the last lonely month of Quest. After solemnly thanking this magical stone for leading him to adulthood he took one last look before covering it in soil, then fir needles and a gale damaged aspen branch still with a few twirling leaves attached. He stood up in a ray of sun in which hoverflies and bees droned and smelled the sweet scent of emerging birch leaves hushing above in the spring breeze.

'Stay safe and sleep long and deep,' he murmured as he turned to go a little reluctantly.

But soon filled with a sense of renewed energy and purpose he set off for home humming to himself hoping the Stone would never found in his lifetime.

***

'Here he is Maarek. God he looks like one of those cavemen that 'His Highness' was talking about,' said Hinch, who had doubtlessly been hiding with Bell inside the drive of Meadow House Care Home on the way down to the school entrance and had fallen in behind him as he walked. He ignored them as usual, although he suspected they were imitating his gait again. Marek's's posture was much improved after an initial corrective operation but he was not as straight as he'd be one day.

'Yeah I mean that low brow and that stoop. Have you had your DNA checked to see how you are ninety percent Neanderthal?' said Bell who cackled like a goose.

'I think he's deaf as well as a foreign throwback,' said Hinch.

'And he's scared again' said Bell.

'Well actually I hate to disappoint you but I'm not,' said Marek turning round and standing like a stone in a stream while various children walked past avoiding eye contact on their way to the school.

The boys looked askance at each other and laughed.

'Going to do something about it Monkey Boy?' said Hinch shoving him with the heel of his palm on the chest. Marek stood firm and was very tempted to surprise them with that sweep of sharp flint in their faces. He could feel the stone in his pocket and asked it what he should do next. Then he heard a voice which surprised him as it was his own.

'Actually I feel sorry for you. You are too lazy to work and spend all your time fooling around in class so basically you are ruining your own future,' he said. Hinch looked sideways for a couple of seconds to an invisible mocking audience, his face a mask of outrage.

The blow when it came seconds later missed its target as Marek in new found hunter mode suddenly ducked and moved nimbly sideways at the same time. An unbalanced heavy Hinch nearly fell over and lurched into the path of Mr. Garside the scary English teacher who had to take avoiding action and dropped his briefcase.

'Watch out boy. What are you doing? Fooling about as usual Hinch. You nearly knocked me over,' said the teacher looking angry. Hinch had to try to look apologetic and bullshit about showing off a rugby move while Bell loyally melted into the stream of students hurrying towards the front gates.

With a barely mollified staff member just ahead, the boys fell in behind, and when Marek could see Hinch mouthing obscenities at him like an angry ventriloquist he almost laughed.

***

'So what was I saying about the Mousterian phase of the Palaeolithic? asked Mr. High holding his thumbs behind the edges of his waistcoat. Marek looked up from staring blankly at his desk.

'That it was a step change in technology towards hafted weapons?' he suggested.

'That's a good answer or it would have been if I'd asked it five minutes ago. Keep up Ostas I'm surprised at you,' said Mr. High who'd never had cause to tell him off before.

The Stone had distracted him so much. He wanted to show it to the teacher but now he'd been chided in public it would seem wrong.

Then the bell rang and the students all began to get up noisily.

'You can all go. Don't forget to read the second chapter of Renfrew about the ice age environment,' said Mr. High holding up the classic text on British prehistory. Less loudly, he asked Marek to stay behind. When the class had gone, he came and sat on a desk some distance away, and looked at him with concern in his face.

'So Marek Ostas, something up? You're usually on the ball but I can see something is bothering you. Can I help?' he asked.

'Well Mr. High actually yes. It's this' he handed the stone to the teacher who didn't say anything but spent some time looking at it with barely concealed wonder.

'Where'd you get this?' he asked at last.

'Can you guess?' asked the boy.

'Not really. It could be from anywhere in northern Europe although it might be from the British Isles.

Looks Acheulian. Scraper maybe judging by the shape but there is a groove here so I wonder if it was strung from something. Very relevant to today's lesson. You should have shown it to me sooner. Go on, put me out of my misery,' he said.

'The football pitch,' he said.

Mr. High looked inscrutable. He's not going to believe me, thought Marek.

As he explained about the molehill, High began to look impressed, then he stood up and began to pace back and fore in front of the white- board which he usually did when he was fired up about something to do with his subject.

'Good work Mr. Ostas. Good work. I've been wanting an excuse to dig that pitch up for a while as flint flakes do turn up from time to time and I've long had my suspicions there may be more exciting things under that turf. Now, with something as impressive as this find we can persuade the powers that be to let us get an archaeologist to come in and have the class dig up the pitch where you found that and neither Stephenson nor the Head will be able to block it. We might find an old hunting camp. What do you think of that?' he asked.

'That would be great' said Marek who was up for something outdoors for a change.

'I think this could really bring the subject alive for your class and the whole school so thanks for bringing this in,' he said and reaching forwards gave him a firm handshake he famously dispensed rarely and only for distinguished class work.

'Ouch,' said Marek who still couldn't help smiling.

'Oh sorry, is something wrong with your hand?' he asked.

'It's just a small cut. It's healing already,' said Marek who'd almost forgotten all about it.

'Can you leave the tool with me? Just for a few days?' asked the teacher.

'Yes. Of course. That will be fine,' said the boy who was enjoying the warmth of the reaction.

When he set off for home ten minutes later, he chose the front way and this time noticed less of the pavements and much more of the trees and through them the full moon beginning to rise.

… Momaya Press

It Just Wouldn't Do

Michael G. Casey

Jim had inherited the sixty-five acres from his father. He started out as a conscientious, hard-working farmer, but over the years, EU regulations wore him down and now he depended more on the postman who delivered his set-aside cheques from Brussels, than he did on cattle or tillage. He kept some cows mainly for breeding purposes, but that was little more than a hobby.

His younger brother had emigrated to America almost twenty years ago. They didn't keep in touch and Jim wouldn't recognise him now if he passed him in the main street of Manorhamilton. He had got used to living on his own but sometimes fell into a brown study which he thought had something to do with loneliness.

As well as depending on the postman, Jim also depended on the Metaforic Company of Illinois who delivered a crate to his farm-house one day in September 2009. When he took possession of the crate and started to unscrew the lid he didn't fully realise how his life would be changed.

Some months after the delivery Jim sat into his Ford Estate one Saturday and drove into Manorhamilton to get a few items for the week ahead. In the local Spar shop he couldn't find the washing-up liquid and had to ask the girl. She couldn't find it either; it wasn't in its usual place between the shoe polish and the toothpaste.

'Your mother would know,' Jim offered.

'She's away for a few days,' the girl said. 'I'll ask my aunt.' She disappeared into the back through a curtain of hanging plastic straps--the kind found in Italian chip-shops.

Jim had picked up onions and cabbage and a packet of back-rashers when the woman appeared. A younger sister but attractive, Jim couldn't help noticing, with long reddish hair and blue eyes, the kind that teetered on the verge of smiling. She had a good figure too, unlike her sister who had let herself go a bit. She pointed out the new location for the washing-up liquid--and the other detergents.

'Thanks,' Jim said, and then offered, 'I'd sort of...know you from your sister.'

'I didn't think we were all that alike.' She gave him a smile that rocked him on his heels. It was as if the door of a furnace had suddenly been opened.

'Oh no...I mean...just a family resemblance...a general one....'

'I'm Kay by the way.' She held out her hand.

'Jim, Jim McKeown.' He offered his hand, having rubbed it on the side of his trousers.

'Ballinvogue direction?'

'Yes, how did you know?' Without realising it, Jim had started to shred the outer leaves of the cabbage in his basket.

'We used to play together. In the convent school in Senior Infants.'

'God Almighty, you're right. Kay Maloney. Sister Benedictus's class.'

'That's not what we called her.'

'No.' He laughed and blushed at the same time. Her nickname was Sister Big Knickers. He had trouble making the figure '8'--one loop always much bigger than the other--- and she gave him a hard time over it. Sister Big Knickers---and Kay Maloney. Imagine that.

They chatted for a while longer. For some reason he didn't ask her if the shop stocked the last item on his list---hemorrhoid cream. He paid for his groceries and left.

That might have been the end of it except for mass on Sunday. He noticed her on the left hand side of the church, five pews ahead of him. She wore the sort of flying-saucer hat you'd see at a wedding. After receiving communion he looked through splayed fingers and saw her walking down from the altar-rail. She stared straight ahead and didn't put on the martyred ecstasy look of the other women. He waited for her in the churchyard.

'You're still here?' It was a daft opening, he realised.

'I'm back for good.'

'Oh, I thought....just while your sister was away.'

'No. After my marriage broke up I decided to come home. No children. There was nothing to keep me in the UK.'

'I see.'

'Yes.'

'I see.' He racked his brains but couldn't think of anything else to say. He had cross-bred a Charolais with a Limousin cow but she'd hardly be interested in that. Or in the recent milk quota directive from Brussels.   She came to the rescue, 'There's a good film on in the Grand, 'Valkyrie'. It's about an attempt to kill Hitler.'

'Do you tell me so?'

'Very good, I hear. Tom Cruise. Great suspense. Shots of the war.

Very accurate historically.'

'Imagine that. It sounds great....It's years since I went to the pictures....'

'Well,' she said with a slight note of impatience, 'I'm going to-night. If you want to come you'd be more than welcome.' She made it sound matter-of-fact, like a man asking him to go to a cattle mart or pub.

So, their first date was 'Valkyrie' in the Grand Cinema of Manorhamilton. It was like running the gauntlet. The locals looked at them in the queue, the lobby and the auditorium, and looked away as quickly. Jim only relaxed when the house lights went down and the images appeared on the screen. But he didn't dare hold her hand or touch her in any way. With any luck people might think they just ran into each other on the street and sauntered into the cinema on a fluke.

On another evening they had dinner in the hotel in Carrick. Two mixed grills piled high on the plates and a smell of boiled cabbage and furniture polish drifting into the dining-room from the hall. He noticed that she left most of her chips even though they were well salted and drenched in brown vinegar. When he drove her back to Manorhamilton he parked midway between two street lights; in the dim yellowish light they stayed for a long time in the car chatting and courting.

For the third date she insisted on cooking him a meal in her flat over the shop. He brought wine and a box of Quality Street sweets. She provided stout which he hadn't tasted in years. After the roast beef and a stint of grappling on the sofa they ended up in bed. Before they made love he warned her that it had been a long time. He'd been on his own forever and a day. Were they, he wondered, a bit long in the tooth for that class of thing? She took over and led him gently through the age-old ritual in a way that spared his blushes and was mutually satisfying.   'Do you think I'm too forward?' she asked afterwards.

'Ah, no. Sure, you've lived in London. Maybe I was too backward?'

'Not at all. You were...fine....just right.' Again, he was caught up in the force-field of her smile.

He asked her out to the farm-house to sample his cooking on the following Wednesday. He spent days cleaning and painting and tidying things away. He threw out seven black plastic sacks of old newspapers, empty bottles and left-over cures for liver fluke and mastitis. His plan was a simple chicken dinner, nothing too fancy, but he could hardly shop in Manorhamilton, not in Spar anyway, and if he went to the other shop and was seen, he wouldn't be able to explain. It could be taken amiss. He drove to Carrick and bought the chicken, tins of peas and beans, and a bottle of wine---white to go with the chicken. There was plenty of tea in the house but he bought a large tin of fresh fruit for dessert. Women liked sweet things.

 He went to the drapery shop and bought some new underwear. There was no point in washing the old stuff; it had all gone a bit grey. He recalled the night in her flat; he had just managed, in the nick of time, to hook his toe into the underwear and flick it out of sight under the bed. The rub of the green might not be with him the second time. He wondered if he should also visit the Chemist's shop.

Whenever he felt nervous about the upcoming meal he reminded himself that Kay wouldn't be expecting a feast. With women, he reassured himself, it was more the thought that counted.

The big day arrived, a crisp Spring day. A small cluster of daffodils had sprung up overnight near the front door. They reminded him that Easter wasn't far away. He had a bath early and couldn't do much work on the farm for fear of sweating into his new shirt. He put a white cloth over the table; it was a cloth his mother used for the altar when they held the Stations in the house all those years ago. She used it for the May altar as well, he seemed to recall. He put out the best crockery – Beleek with tiny shamrocks – which had been given to her on her wedding day. She would be watching from on high; he hoped she wouldn't object to a young woman coming into the house. He tidied up the bedroom, giving careful attention to the big brown wardrobe that reached up to the ceiling.

His anxieties were allayed when Kay told him how charming the house was and how she loved the view of the cattle sheds from the kitchen window. He gave her a quick tour of the farm-yard but didn't bring her into any of the sheds for fear of slurry smells, and carefully avoided the ash pit. She said that it a reminded her of the farm she'd been brought up on. But he couldn't relax completely. Her presence was a little overpowering. Once indoors, her perfume enveloped him and she looked really good in the candle-light. She wore a black flouncy dress that set off her red hair. There was no dandruff on her shoulders, not one speck. Whenever he served her a plate and his face came close to her neck, he could hardly speak for the lump in his throat. He couldn't wait for dinner to be over.

Towards the end of the meal she excused herself and went to the bathroom which he had of course scoured from top to bottom, adding a blue perfumed cube to the water closet. It was only about eight or nine years since he had installed indoor plumbing; some houses further up the hill still didn't have it. Imagine if he had to show Kay out to the chicken-house with a lighted candle. It didn't bear thinking about. He was clearing the table when he heard a scream followed by a crash. He rushed to investigate.

For some reason Kay had gone into his bedroom and opened the wardrobe. A hundred-pound life-size composite-rubber doll with perfect anatomical detailing, had fallen out on top of her. Kay had jumped back and the doll had fallen to the ground.

'You've met Breege.' Jim tried to make light of it. To his relief he noted that Breege at least had her bikini on---the blue one that he liked.

'God Almighty....' Kay passed a hand across her forehead. One of the doll's arms still lay across her shoe and she kicked it away. She held her own hands, palms facing away, as if to ward off imminent evil. 'And what's that?' She pointed a quivering finger at a much smaller object which had also fallen out of the wardrobe.

'That's her toothbrush,' Jim answered.

'A toothbrush,' Kay repeated dumbly. Then she started to moan. 'You...Who....What kind of pervert are you....?'

Jim was dumbfounded---although the Metaforic brochure had warned of the possibility of this kind of reaction from people who didn't understand. But Kay had lived in London for years. London, of all places. After a while he said, 'I've been on my own...for a long....'

'Shut up!' She showed him her palms, then covered her ears.

'I'm just trying to explain....' He felt like adding that she had no business sneaking into his bedroom and going through his stuff. But he had an instinct that this was not a good time to make that kind of point.

'Take me home immediately'

He tried to remonstrate, to calm her down but she pushed past him and got her coat. On the drive into town he tried again to explain but she covered her ears even more firmly and shook her head. She didn't want to listen or hear.

Over the next two weeks he tried phoning and calling to the shop but it was no good. Whenever their paths crossed she was glacial. She wanted nothing more to do with him.

'We're better off without her,' he confided to Breege one night as spring eased into summer. He had been to Dublin and bought her a new outfit and wig. He had carefully done her make up---greenish mascara and a new shade of lipstick called 'lavender twilight'. They watched The Late Late Show together even though he was a little jealous of the way she looked at the new host, Ryan Tubridy. After that he brought her to bed.

Breege was no trouble, no trouble at all, and she accepted him for what he was. She never complained or nagged---even about his 'affair' with Kay. He didn't have to watch his 'p's and 'q's. And he never had to go to the Chemist's. Breege looked as young as ever. There were no dimples in her thighs and she didn't have to shave her legs. The only thing was that her limbs were becoming a little loose and needed to be tightened up. He hoped that her joints were sound because he couldn't bear the thought of trading her in. It wouldn't be fair to either of them. He felt sure that a general service was all that was required. He sneaked out of bed and went to the garage where he found the crate she had come in. He would send her back for some work to the service department of the Metaforic Company of Illinois.

As they sat at the table for breakfast she looked wonderful even in the strong sunlight that streamed through the window. He took her hand and said, 'How about a little holiday, Breege? To Illinois. That's where you come from. Yes. I can meet your parents at last. Won't that be great?'

She smiled her agreement and he felt his heart melt.

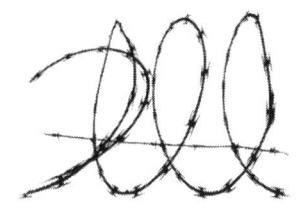

The Great Sea of Summer

Russell George

Honourable Mention

We always seemed to play in the narrow spaces. There were corridors that echoed to the chase, and hallways where you'd stretch across with hands and feet, make a bridge like Spiderman suctioned onto shiny, flock wallpaper. There were balance beams to cling to; there were thin, single beds. And the gardens felt like bowling lanes, a shed falling down at one end and the sides cordoned off with stinging nettles, so that the ball would keep sailing into next door's garden as if guided by an evil god. You'd see it snagged among the rose bushes, smirking, daring you to jump the fence.

Only somehow the neighbours were always there. Fumbling with washing or watering their flower beds, they hovered in your peripheral vision even when you imagined a different world entirely - spaceships and longboats, cops and robbers – as if they were listening, or trying to listen. But like the toys you'd pined for at Christmas, and the girls who sidled off in silent conference, they were getting older; sometimes you could see their backs arching to the tug of the earth's core, wrinkles inching deeper, uglier as they waved 'hello'. Next door was a reminder of the rules.

Or else you were in the alleyways. Those long dark caves where the afternoons drew in tightly, from grey to blue to black, where people took short cuts while you waited, waited until the coast was clear. They were frightening at first, the alleyways. There was a reek of piss and creosote, graffiti scrawled on dirty concrete, while the kids had scratches on their faces and scowled at strangers as if the place was under siege. Maybe it was. One or two of them would scale the garages, peering across the town while the rest of us squatted down until a signal was given - this fervent, urgent whisper - an all-clear to let the games begin again.

But it was the way they'd designed it; we were suburban kids and we played within certain boundaries. The rest of it was left to your imagination.

Only then, on a summer's day in June, you're taken somewhere new; a car trip to the country, an aunt with floury hands who lives alone. In a hallway beneath a winding staircase you stand there looking up at a row of wooden doors, each shut tight against prying eyes – yes, and didn't some of them even have bolts, and padlocks? You imagine searching through abandoned rooms where silent voices hang breathless, suspended; to peer behind disused wardrobes, under bathroom cabinets turning yellow since the war. You sense that something's hidden, though it's a secret that will only be discovered if they leave you alone to find it.

But instead you are led away. A darkened room of heavy curtains where the air tastes of furniture polish, where cakes and sandwiches are arranged on a long table to the side. They find a stool for you to sit on. But then the other adults, the ones slouched on sofas and easy chairs, strangers all, start to drift towards you like oncoming traffic. Some of them are wearing suits. Like a gaggle of policemen they take it in turns to ask questions that you cannot answer but the women, oh the women fuss and coddle until soon you want to scream, until all you can do is take another bun, another cake, hiding crumbs in case they see the mess. It's just all so embarrassing.

But this aunt is lonely; the truth of that is in the way she gazes at you across the room, the puffy face smiling like a waxwork come to life. Somehow you know that kindness is required, and so with every mouthful you allow yourself to disappear a little more, retreating one step further until it feels like you're barely there at all.

Then the patio doors are flung open. A bright rectangle of light appears as if someone has turned on a television, reawakening a forgotten day. There is the scent of cut grass, the distant hum of a mower and soon you are being coaxed forwards; it is your mother's voice, this aunt's as well, and for a moment you stand bleary eyed at the edge of darkness, blinking into a glaring void beyond.

But the world outside seems different somehow. There is a sense of something about to shatter, a wave a sickness that will pitch you forwards onto a blistering surface that you cannot fully see. Yes, even then you preferred to play it safe, sensing how indifferent the world could be. You turn back towards the room, almost frightened, but now the faces are lost in velvet shadow, burbling voices draining away like someone else's bathwater.

How long did you stand like that, waiting; what felt so disturbing in a summer's day? When, at last, you venture out it all feels strangely quiet, like falling onto the surface of the moon. There is a clean, depthless sky above and a patio with brightly coloured chairs, fabric pulsing with the morning heat. Then there are some steps and then – broad and flat and lush – the greenest lawn you've ever seen. For a while you stand there bathing in the sticky heat of summer, alone, not quite believing everything around you; it all looks so oddly perfect, the colours glowing in a way that reminds you of cartoons you've seen. There is birdsong, blossom, the quiet drone of insects. There is an apple tree hung with bright red fruit. It's as if this garden has been drawn as a picture somewhere, the scene from a long-forgotten fairy tale while beneath it all an unfamiliar presence as if the earth itself is moving, vibrating with a hidden current.

Things begin to move quickly then, as if a tape has spooled forwards and you're required to catch up. At the end of the lawn, wearing pastel dresses and stripy shirts, a ring of children with keen, tanned faces. They appear like adults only smaller, not really like children at all, and as you go towards them – as you know you must – every muscle is taut with anticipation. It is the same sensation you have whenever you are held at arm's length to the world, when there's something new to overcome and you wonder if you're going to make it home. It's the familiar call to flee.

One of the children, a boy with sandy hair and leather shoes, watches you slope into view. He is stood on some sort of box, elevated against the sun, silhouetted so that the closer you get to him the harder he is to see. But you stare at this boy anyway, squinting through the brightness, until you see him raise a sword. He swipes it through the air with a sweet, piercing cry but it doesn't stop you, and though your eyes prick with tears it feels like he is dragging you towards him, his face half-wild and contorted in a sneer.

But it is curious to think how quickly things changed that day - each minute seems almost like a day itself. These children, with their pretty clothes and bright, agile smiles, give you passage into their world so that, without any pause at all, you find yourself inside their circle. The games begin and they are new games and they're giving you the rules. Soon you are laughing, chasing across a boundless lawn with a smell that catches like something half-remembered, as clean and satisfying as a jigsaw piece that finally finds a home. Something new has started and you roll in the grass like it's some great sea of summer, the tickling warmth of it fresh and warm and young.

These are the moments, the minutes, the hours, that you will struggle to recall; in the years to come they will spin and fade like fragments of a dream, almost like memories to someone else's life and not your own.

So maybe the boy, his sword, wasn't real at all. Often, or so it seemed, there were demons that would disappear the closer you got to them. And yet the dog, surely the dog was real; it appears from nowhere, a great bumbling thing with eyes hidden beneath a shaggy coat, and it's so big that you keep your distance while the others seem not to mind. But you're running anyway, dancing even, calling out and that voice of yours like a speck of joy with the whole world above it; this freedom, this joy – how long did we stay out there? The sun blazed above us, its light unflinching and the heat lapping in waves. It all seems now so unlikely, the way we played in the sun that day.

But it must have got later, much later. You find yourself crouching down in a sort of gulley, stalking through long grass where insects cling beyond that vast, perfect lawn. Then, scuttling into a copse of trees where sunshine splinters and they're looking for you in the cool, delicious shade. No doubt it was hide and seek with you the hunted prey – and so in a crater that falls away you drag branches, bracken, make a camp to hide in. Panting, laughing, you lie there surrounded by the guttural smell of earth and everything that lives within it, a canopy of branches above. Still, silent, waiting. Waiting for them to come and find you.

Perhaps you fall asleep. Or maybe you just like the peace you've found, the fresh tang of conifers and the darkness of nesting inside, cocooned. There is an art to being alone, to re-making the world as you'd like it to be and so you stay there, drifting away in this alien quiet. At home, of course, you are never alone. There is always some crisis rattling through the house so that even when you draw those flags, hundreds of flags on sheets of foolscap paper and the colours so neat inside the lines, still they come and get you. The spell is always broken and they take you away.

But then you hear something; a whisper in the branches above, and when you open your eyes the sky has darkened. It is a scrapbook of swirling clouds, black and grey and cold, and as you watch them drift across you can feel your skin puckering, shivering. It's then that you realize that everyone else is now inside: you're on your own at last.

And so carefully you crawl out, push away your camouflage and look towards the garden beyond. Its colours are muted as if someone has turned the volume down, toys scattered like fallen soldiers. The place has been abandoned, and for a while you consider retreating to the warmth of your bunker, to wait until the world has reset itself again. But then it comes: a distant clip of thunder followed, almost at once, by the first dabs of rain.

At home the rain trickles down window-panes. It pools in dirty puddles and keeps you inside with board games, or old re-runs on the television. But here the rain is alive. You listen to its symphony falling through the trees above, watch droplets ricochet between branches, leaves. The rain is breathing, dancing. And since it falls around you, besides you, it is only when the thunder starts to move closer, a giant wardrobe dragged across the sky, that you think to move.

It's exciting at first. Leaping over roots and fallen trees, jinking through the darkening shapes. Instinct pushes you forwards even as the branches seem to drag you back, scratching and yanking at your t-shirt, the soft, pale skin beneath. Your heart is clattering but it's just like playing another game, trying to win another race, so that it's only when you reach the open ground, the house shrouded in a grey mist and so far away that it could be in another country, that you sense the rules have changed. Between you and safety, the rain sweeps down almost like a monsoon.

Did the rain get suddenly heavier, or beneath the trees had you just not noticed? Immediately your t-shirt is soaked, pressed tight against your back and chest. And there are streams of water sluicing across the lawn so that, even before you start to run, you slip into a morass of grass and mud. Tumbling forwards, sideways, your mouth fills with earth before another clap of thunder, booming like cannon at a battlefield, echoes from behind. The storm is chasing you down across that perfect lawn, relentless rain swarming until you find your feet, try to stumble on. \It is then, like a ghostly apparition, that once more the dog appears. At first there is the fear of it - you call out, try to shout the thing away. But the fear quickly turns to terror, tastes like blood bubbling up at the back of your throat. The dog is running alongside you, its mad eyes laughing before it leaps up, those huge paws pushing you backwards so that you're down again. Falling and sliding on the slick grass as the world spins and the dog stands over you. It is barking, taunting.

But just as it's about to gouge an eye out, or to trample you into the quaking soil, something changes. There is a second or two where the rain falls lighter, when it seems as if the storm becomes oddly quiet, and in that space you feel alive in a way that you've never felt before. It almost seems, as the storm gathers itself and the rain pounds heavier once more, that finally you are separate, unaffected by the chaos unfurling around you.

And so when you get to your feet, and the dog makes to leap up again, you throw an arm out to push the beast away. It gives a yelp of surprise, pain perhaps, but now there is just the storm and you running through it so that by the time you reach the set of steps, the patio with its colourful chairs now almost under water, the dog has disappeared. It's almost as if you've willed it to be so. You are at the house, safe again. Soon that door will open up and swallow you back inside.

But when you try to slide the door across the handle is wet and your hands are numb and cold. It is then that you peer inside and see a row of faces looking past you. They are flushed, star-struck, gazing at the storm. Your mother is among them, and you want to bang on the glass to get her attention only something stops you; your mother looks younger somehow, and when one of the men says something she smiles in a way you've not seen before, pushing a lock of hair behind her ear. It stops you calling out.

It is then that you notice the small boy stood beside her, a shallow reflection in the glass. He is streaked with mud and grass. How grave he looks as the rain pours down; how different from the people nestled in those soft, velvet sofas. It's hard to look at him like that, t-shirt torn and sopping wet, and so you turn your back to the window, the house, your mother staring out and you watch the storm instead. Another sweep of rain across the garden, the snap of thunder echoing above. And as the heavens heave in violent disarray there is something which feels like wonder, as if all the fear has been washed away. It is these moments - the chaos, the noise - that will stay with you the longest.

Watching the Aurora

Mona Dash

The water squelched when I sat down. The steam condensing, water accumulating in the crevices of the shiny blue tiles, so that when I shifted a little, trapped under my white swimsuit, it squelched louder. I was the only one in the steam room, I sat back and stretched my legs. The heat rose, it calmed my face, it stroked my body. I slipped the straps off my shoulders, right down, to feel the warmth on my bare skin. I could feel the sweat drops forming on my chest, on my back. I would have slipped off the swimsuit if I could, but the rules were strict, in this Reykjavik hotel's spa where I worked ¬- steam room with swimsuits, sauna without.

The door opened and a man entered, two shadowy children shapes behind him. I pulled the straps up quickly. What was he thinking of, wasn't there a rule that children below six weren't meant to enter? The boy looked four or five at the most. I wondered if I should say something, but I wasn't on duty , having finished for the day. I was just another guest now. The children squirmed as they sat down. The girl squelched, the dad squelched, and the boy laughed.

'Daddy, you farted!'

'I didn't. It's just the water,' the dad said.

'It's too hot here. I want to go out,' the little boy stamped his feet.

'Toby, please can you sit still for at least five minutes,' the dad said.

The children sat still on either side of him. They looked at their feet. They inspected their hands. The steam grew shapes around their faces, and they shut their eyes, smarting.

I leaned back, I shut my eyes. The vapour made me feel sexier. It made me think yet again about those days in London, with Mark. It made me think of his hands, which would always start by stroking my back.

I would let him, and then twist the ring off. Sometimes it was tight on his finger.

'It isn't coming off. Can you let it be?'

I wouldn't, sometimes I let it rub sharp on his skin, twisting and turning. 'At least be ring free,' I would say. Free of the bond, if not of guilt. He would smile.

The moisture swirled around me, in a haze. I watched the blood drop. A perfect red globule from my left arm, splat on the wet floor, then a second drop close to it, shapeless immediately. I looked up to check if the man and the children, especially the children had noticed, but they weren't looking at me. I'd done it two days ago, with the red-handled knife I used to cut vegetables. A quick wash of the knife, and then I'd sliced cucumber into circles, stacked them nicely on the middle of the plate, and ate them one by one, sucking the soft middle, letting the blood drip from the cut. It was almost healed, but the steam had eased it open.

***

Mark had set the rules clear and stark from the start. I wasn't meant to make any contact – call, text, WhatsApp – unless he initiated it. I had to be reactive, since you never knew who may have his phone. His wife, that long haired brunette. One of his three boys; the little buck toothed one, or the one with the long black hair, or the one with the thick eyelashes and dimples, so much like Mark's. His phone, like his self, became their property the minute he entered through the door.

Then he got a pre-paid number for me to contact him. The rules changed a little, I could WhatsApp when I wanted, but I couldn't expect an immediate reply. I would have to wait for the sun to stake its claim on the skies and the wife and children to go on the school run, though I might have spent all night messaging. I wasn't allowed to call, and even if I did, I couldn't expect he would answer as he had the phone on silent.

I'd met Mark in the Costa on the Chiswick high street where I worked. He came in every Saturday at about ten in the morning, casually dressed in a t-shirt and ripped jeans, hair floppy on his forehead, eyes very distant. He sat on the brown sofa in the corner, typing on his laptop, coffee cup drained. Once I brought him another, and he smiled without asking why I had. He paid for the extra of course.

'Hi, are you a writer?' I asked the fourth time I met him.

'Hey,' he smiled, 'Why do you think I am?'

'Well, you come here every Saturday, you type continuously...sometimes you look around but without really seeing anyone. What else can you be?!'

He nodded as if I had said something profound. 'Not a real writer, well, I am a banker in the week, but I try to write in the weekend!'

'That's impressive.' I had noticed his ring but didn't mention it. I could imagine his life. The terraced house set away from the high street, but not too far from it. The bay windows, the family, the chaise lounges, the dog – 'no, we don't have a dog' – he'd said later. We chatted again the next week. We exchanged numbers the third week. It is funny how easily you can bare when the medium isn't voice. It wasn't long before we were asking each other blush-inducing questions; the first fuck, the best positions. And it wasn't long afterwards, maybe a week or so of active messaging, when he came over. I lived in a tiny room, on top of a two-storied house, three stops away from Chiswick. Even then he was gracious. He complimented me on the couch, an overused soft cream sofa, into which we both sank. The narrow bed we managed to squash ourselves into. He had only two hours, but we made the best of it. After that day, he spent less and less time in the café. I changed my shifts to Sunday. Saturdays were our days, sometimes he wrote a little while I slept. I liked to nap knowing he would be there when I woke. He'd thought I was a writer as well. I wasn't one for words. I liked to dance, I loved music. I dabbled with colours, yes. I used to paint as a child but hadn't in a while. I was pretty much like every other person.

'Maybe you should try. I can sense you have an artist's soul,' he said. We sat on my little bed, sipping the wine he had brought for me, our toes interlaced.

I had my back tattooed that weekend. Monet's lilies trailed down to the base of my spine, and he followed them with his fingers, once my tattoo had healed.

One Saturday, his wife and the boys came by to the café, and not finding him there, called. His face froze when he answered his mobile.

'I couldn't write today, darling, I took a walk. I will be back soon.'

Later, he said she didn't encourage his writing. She couldn't understand why a grown man would hunch over a laptop, instead of playing golf, or taking the kids to football like his mates did. She had deleted an entire folder of his stories off the family computer in anger. He never wrote at home now; since she didn't want to see him engaged in this senseless pursuit.

That day, he'd left a bit earlier, since they were going out for dinner to the local Italian. I took myself out as well. I sat in the corner table by the door, and watched them come in, the children trooping after the parents, arguing, at times laughing. I watched them as they ordered, as he tasted the wine, swirling the redness expertly, nodding his head in acceptance. He acknowledged me, the faintest of smiles, a special look only for me.

He messaged late at night to say he had been distracted all evening. He'd wanted to come over to me, looking so beautiful in a light-gold off-shoulder dress, with my rose-gold flower pendant shining on my clavicle. So I did it again. I went to the park for a run at the same time as them. I was in the swimming pool in the leisure centre, sharing the same pool. I shopped in Waitrose on the weekends like they did.

That's when he said I must stop stalking him.

'I am not stalking you! I thought you liked seeing me around.'

'I do like to see you, but on my time. Not when I have family with me.'

I promised I would stop. 'I am sorry. Do you know how hard it is to not see you always?'

He smiled helplessly.

But he didn't come to the café on Saturday. Neither on Sunday. He didn't answer my WhatsApp on the special phone. On Sunday evening I went to his house. I stood on the opposite side of the road, just behind the large English-plane tree, willing him to show up. I stood in the darkness for more than an hour. Eventually the lights were switched on in the kitchen, and he stood there, at the sink, washing something. I saw him turn, saw her come in, get something from the fridge and come up to him. They looked at each other, she leaned against him. I had a vision of horror that he would slip her jeans off, and take her suddenly, on those polished granite tops. But she was only reaching out for something. She left.

Then he noticed me, I had left the refuge of the tree and was standing on the sidewalk. I saw the shock on his face, the furtive look around. He left the kitchen. Minutes later he was outside, looking over his shoulder at the house.

He crossed over, 'Just why are you here?' the anger in him hissed. I could see it, like the smoke from the instant noodles we had shared once, hungry from lovemaking. 'I haven't had this since uni,' he had laughed. You are such a child!' He had kissed me again, the noodles dripping into my mouth.

I tried to explain, I had missed him, but he looked a different man. I grabbed his hand. And that made him angrier. His face close to my ear, he said, 'Just go home. Now. Out of here.'

I left. All night I cried. I waited for his text.

***

Once, he had told me the story he was writing, about a girl who lived in the Arctic Circle, brought up by people she didn't know. Was she from the heat of the plains, from the waves in the seas, or from the highest mountains? No one knew, least of all her. But as she grew older, she belonged less and less in the world. The dancing lights of the Aurora was the only place she felt home.

'How does she find home? Her journey, the beasts she meets...that's what my book is all about.'

'A fantasy for young adults?' I asked. I'd assumed he wrote crime.

'Kind of... what do you think?'

He never answered directly, he often asked the same question back.

'Name her after me!'

'Maya! Why not?'

'Write about me,' I said imperiously.

'Always,' he kissed me.

Nothing from him, even three days later.

There were ways out. There were a dozen single men on Tinder. I would find someone else; I would forget Mark and move on. When he'd come begging me to have sex, I wouldn't. That night, I went out, I met some friends, we got stone drunk. My eyes met a cute boy's, greenish brown eyes, the way I liked them. I gestured, and soon we were dancing. We went back to his, a few of us in a group. I sent Mark clips of the heavy breathing, orgasmic screams, made louder through editing. He didn't respond.

I had been through worse before. I'd moved back to London from Rome, after Giovanni and I broke up. Giovanni said he needed to fly, but I apparently needed a cage and wanted to imprison him. He moved out of the flat. He changed his numbers and blocked me from all his social media. That's when I knew I had to leave. I went back to Cornwall, where my parents lived. Then I left their house and came to London, to get back on my feet, study further, get a job. I started waitressing for some quick cash, though my parents helped with my rent. I had meant to start applying for courses, but then I'd met Mark and he took over my days.

The next morning, I followed Mark all the way from his home to the station. If he noticed, he didn't react. After a few days of this forced invisibility, I waited until the wife and children were on the school run and stood right in front of him.

He said he would file a restraining order and tell the police I was stalking him. He explained why I would qualify for one.

'But why am I 'stalking you,' do you think?' I asked.

He didn't care he said. He wanted me out of the way.

'I can expose you! I can tell everyone! 'I shouted.

I could have, surely I could have torn apart that entire home with its facade and its curtains and its cream-beige blinds, the perfect shift dresses of his wife and the football kits on those boys. It was all in my hands, to tear and ruin.

Instead, I left, not to my parents, but to Reykjavik. My first real home, where unrestrained nature had stitched itself onto me. We used to live here, until my parents moved to England when I was six, and we had come back a few times on holiday. The sting of the cold, brutal, fresh air had stayed with me. I got a job in the spa, cleaning and keeping things in order in the steam and sauna room. But after Mark, it wasn't easy being on my own, even here. That's how I'd gone back to the cutting, the criss-crossing, the delight of the blood falling in drops around me. I said his name as I cut myself, in spidery lines, thick solid ones.

By hurting myself, I was trying to heal.

I wondered if he had healed.

I had been quick in the darkness. Every Thursday, he stepped out with the bin bags, between nine and ten in the night. I knew since I had been watching. Such a creature of habit, despite all his so-called creative impulses. Always the banker, never the writer. I hid behind the English-plane tree, its branches expanding into the skies, until the kitchen door opened, and he stepped out, bags in hand. I approached silently, swiftly, then broke into a run. I was wearing my black hoodie. He looked up only when I was right there, only a few yards away. Without looking into those eyes, I continued running, and lashed out just as I crossed him. The knife was sharp, I had focused on how it would feel, how it would dig into his side, making sure it wasn't fatal but just a nice deep cut, enough to make him bleed. I glanced only for a second to see the shock, the sudden gasp which rose in his eyes, the terror which almost solidified in the whites. The rest I had to visualise. I was off. I assume he staggered and fell, perhaps he shouted my name, or screamed for help. I imagined the thickness of the blood, the redness on his legs, his clothes. Did he know it was my hand, did he suspect?

***

I spent most of the night half expecting someone would come for me. I left very early for the airport in an Uber, still wondering if anyone would find me. Just like I had done in Rome, only that time, I had aimed a stone at Giovanni, and caught him on the head, nice and square, as he walked back to his flat. In the darkness, he had never known.

It's already a month since I have been in Reykjavik. No one had found me yet. Did Mark not suspect, or did he not tell?

The last time I was in Iceland with my parents, we had tried to see the Northern lights. Every night, Dad would drive far out of Reykjavik, every night the clouds shrouded over..

I had arrived in their homes and hearts, from India, when I was four. The orphanage had arrangements with airlines to send children like me, who had no one to call their own. My light skin didn't seem Indian, I heard them say at times. It's as if she always belonged here, they said.

'You belong here, with me,' Mark had said, when we lay together. Many say that, so loosely, but I had never wanted to belong. The outside was comfortable, where I stood and observed. Where I could be as much or as less of myself.

***

Tonight, I would drive myself far away, along the snow-filled embankments, into the forests rife with frosted red berries, reindeer and wild bird songs. Once there, I would sit still and look up at the skies, waiting for the lights to break loose with abandon. I would stretch out on the bare earth, and push my body into it, the soil taking my shape. Above me I would see the Aurora flash, dance. The outsider. But with the lights, the earth, the sky, I would be one.

Appetite

Madeleine Dunnigan

1.

The house is dirty and the garden overgrown. At the back is a patch of rhubarb. 'It's been there forever, won't go away.' I hack off the bright pink stalks with a bread knife, exposing their lime green centres. Carefully I remove the poisonous leaves and discard them in a pile by the patch of fruit I have not cut away. They are huge and floppy. It is getting dark and the evenings still have bite to them. Inside where it is warm, I sift flour into a bowl and chop in chunks of yellow butter. The butter is cool and firm from the fridge but as I rub, squeeze and roll it between my fingers it softens, joining with the flour to form tiny misshapen balls. Add brown sugar and the mixture turns to sand – soft, grainy, and golden. Rhubarb in a baking dish – no need to cook beforehand. For a fruit that is so tough it contains a lot of water. I think of it weeping in the oven, turning to a hot, squishy mess. There are also black currants, dark purple, almost black, which stain my fingers and leave a bitter taste on my tongue. More butter, more sugar and the dry goods on top, patted down to seal in the fruit. Another sprinkling of sugar crystals so it caramelises in the oven and then – forget about it. Five of us sit around the table, sipping Jameson's with ice, making jokes to fill the space. 'How long do you think it will it be?' 'Just another few minutes.' 'What? I don't mean the food.' While the others talk I slip out and return with the piping hot dish, silencing the conversation. The top is crisp and dark with burnt sugar. We cut through the crust to reveal the fleshy insides, purple, pink, green, sweet and sharp and soft. The heat runs through our bodies, comforting, reassuring. We eat the whole thing.

2.

The three of us work methodically. First, the fire: stacking the black briquettes of charcoal. It needs to get hot, black turning to grey to white to red. Next the food: aubergines on, the flames blackening their skins. Slices of courgettes, slick with olive oil and flecked with salt. Pillars of corn. A whole cauliflower, covered in tahini and dusted with paprika. Shallots on a stick. Spring onions, unpeeled. At the table I slice tomatoes into cubes and place them in a bowl, scooping up all the delicious tomato-ey water that escapes. Lots of olive oil and finely chopped garlic. In another bowl lightly pickled fennel with bright circles of orange. We do not talk except for the occasional, 'Pass me' or 'Give me' or 'Watch out'. We peel the aubergines quickly, their softened insides spill out and are mixed with sesame, garlic and oil. The courgettes are placed in a dish and covered in sharp lemon juice. And the cauliflower, we're not quite sure what to do with the cauliflower. Someone finds a jug and it sits there, tahini sliding down its sides. It is dark by the time we eat and we cannot see the food. Still we do not speak. This is not a holiday any longer. This is definitely not a holiday. We make a start. The spring onions are sweet and soft, melting in the mouth. The aubergine is rich, the courgettes light, the onions caramelised and the cauliflower nutty. The tomato salad, peppery and fresh, cuts through it all. We are exhausted, full, and a little sad. We eat more. We eat until we feel sick, but still there is food. Despair weighs down our already heavy stomachs. Then, smack! A piece of courgette lands on my cheek. A blob of baba ganoush in my eye. Kernels of corn in my ear. I pick up an onion and fling it across the table. Laughter grows around the table as vegetables fly through the night air.

3.

The cheeks are huge, as big as breasts, marbled with collagen and covered in a milky film on one side. This is the mucous membrane of the mouth and needs to be removed, along with excess fat before cooking. They will take hours to cook, for the collagen to break down and infuse the stew with a rich meaty flavour. 'Doesn't matter! We've got all day!' we laugh hysterically. There are only us now – whittled down from five, to three, to two. The two carnivores of the house. I begin to cut the membrane off but none of the knives are sharp enough. I get through four before I work out my technique, tearing the membrane upwards and allowing the weight of the cheek to pull downwards. Once the cheeks are trimmed they are covered in crushed salt and browned, the dark caramelised meat sealing in the bloody sinew. We fry onion, carrot and celery until they are translucent. The meat goes back in the pan along with a bottle of wine (save the glass or two we have already drunk). A can of chopped tomatoes and some stock, along with bay leaves, pepper, and salt. The trick is to leave a little of the cheek poking out, the rest of it submerged, like an iceberg, in the sauce. Into the oven and now we wait. I read recipes and make notes for future meals even though I am eating so much I have a permanent pain in my stomach and my piles have returned. Rice pudding, baked onions in cream and tallegio sauce, homemade cinnamon danishes, black pudding with crisp potatoes and sautéed cabbage. I read them aloud as the kitchen fills with the smell of rich, spicy, meat. It is hot and we peel away layers of clothing. We have been waiting for hours and anticipation slides into frustration. We pace the small kitchen and snarl at each other. 'What about the polenta?' 'I thought you said you were doing it.' 'No you!' I pour yellow grains of corn into boiling water and whisk, ignoring the ache in my arm as the polenta thickens. I stir in butter and cheese and spoon the velvety mixture into bowls. Finally the cheeks are ready. We're down to our pants now, sweat dripping from our concentrated faces as we lift the heavy pan from the oven. A whole cheek each, billowing steam, falling apart in our bowls. I'm not sure which one of us discards the cutlery first but I find myself plunging my fingers deep into the meat, scooping handfuls of flesh and sauce and polenta. Sauce streams along my arms and drips from my elbows onto the floor. And then we are not even using our hands. It just seems more practical to tip our mouths to the bowl and eat directly from it. Afterward we lie panting and naked, covered in flecks of sinew and smudges of tomato, avoiding each other's eyes.

4.

We had to take a break. It all got a bit much. We were vomiting after every meal, into plastic bags and once we ran out of those, into our shoes. The fridge was filled with pickles we weren't eating, chutney that had turned and tubs of hummus that were fizzy. We saved the aqua faba and made vegan whiskey sours, drinking so much we passed out and awoke, vomiting, again. We didn't leave the kitchen any longer, but had made a bed from packed down cardboard boxes and bin bags filled with old coffee grains. When the sun went down we went to dark places, using food in ways that thrilled and disgusted us. We didn't talk about the things we did, before or after, but each interaction was more elaborate than the night before. Our bodies were sticky and bruised, covered in and filled with food. Our breath smelt sharp of ginger and we were turning yellow from all the turmeric. It was hard to let go, but after last night, with the trifle, we were so sick and sickened – both of us curled on the floor, evidence of what we'd done smeared over ourselves and up the walls – we packed everything away in a frenzy, throwing away rotting food, sweeping the floor and covering the surfaces in bleach to mask the other fragrant and intoxicating smells. We showered and put on clothes and now we sit, side by side, in the gleaming, sterile-smelling kitchen. For the first time in weeks we look at each other. We're not sure what to do or how to cook anymore. We can't trust ourselves so we start small. 'Potato waffle?' We eat slowly, the crisp golden lattice bringing colour back to our cheeks and calming our beating hearts.

# The Leaf Beetle

Mary Fox

Kate and Ed sat at a battered metal table and gazed out at the ocean which, on this particular night, was the colour of mercury and seemed to be much further away than on previous evenings. As the light drained from the sky, Kate turned the ring on her middle finger. It had been a surprise Christmas gift from Ed: tasteful and expensive, emeralds and yellow topaz mounted in a white gold setting held in the form of a small leaf beetle. She loved it and stroked it protectively. She had only owned it for a few hours but within a day her middle finger would be bare, not through an act of carelessness or in a fit of pique: she would have given it away but, for the moment, it was still hers.

A little girl, probably no older than four, stood near Kate's chair. She watched as she continued to turn the ring, mesmerised by Kate' white fingers. She had a head of black curls crusted with sea-salt, a huge grin and one missing tooth at the front of her mouth. Her name was Lila. Kate turned to her.

'Would you like to try it on?' She proffered the ring on her outstretched palm. Saucer-eyed, Lila smiled and ran to hide behind her mother who was frying fish on a make-shift barbecue outside the hut which served as their home. It was the only hut with a thatched roof on the whole stretch of the bay. Inside was a small kitchen, three camp beds covered in crumpled bedclothes and a simple shrine with a squatting statue of Buddha surrounded by burning incense sticks.

Outside was a sink with a hosepipe attached, presumably where they all washed themselves and a bamboo screen for privacy. Although they were Buddhists they had strung up some coloured lights and a 'Happy Christmas' banner outside their glassless window. The mother whispered something in Lila's ear and they both approached the table.

'Thank you.' The little girl lisped through the gap in her teeth as she tugged on her mother's sarong.

'I hope you are enjoying your meal.' The mother bowed and then bent down to light the candle. 'The ocean is a little wild tonight, no?' She covered the flame with a clear plastic cylinder, cut from the bottom of a fizzy drinks bottle.

'Yes. We were just saying how far out the tide is tonight. Much further than yesterday. And the winds are stronger.' Ed took another sip of beer and gazed out towards the water.

'Yes. The ocean is unpredictable. But at least the fishing will be good tonight in these shallow waters.' She nodded towards her husband who was mending his lobster pot with some orange nylon thread and a large needle. Anyway, enjoy your meal and thank you for spending your Christmas with us.' Mother and child went back to the shack and continued turning the fish on the barbecue.

'So here we are then. Kate cupped her hands round the plastic candle-holder for warmth. 'Another idyllic setting. But there's still the elephant in the room. Or should I say the elephant on the beach as we're in Sri Lanka?'

'Ha, bloody Ha.' Ed looked out towards the ocean. 'It's really rough tonight. Even the cool dude crusty surfer has called it a day. Boy the water is beautiful at dusk isn't it?'

'Yep. This is definitely the way to spend Christmas evening. No wading through mountains of burned sprouts, watching 'The Prisoner of Azkaban' for the fourteenth time, listening to your mother argue over whose team she wants to be on for trivial pursuit. Here's to spending every Christmas on a beach in southern Sri Lanka.' They clinked beer bottles. 'Anyhow stop ducking the subject.'

'Which is?'

'The thing we keep avoiding. The 'baby' thing or rather the 'no baby' thing. Kate held up two sets of fingers to simulate parentheses.

'Oh Christ, Kate. Can't we just enjoy our meal without bringing that up again?'

'No. we can't. There's always some reason why we can't discuss it. You're too tired or it's too late or we're on holiday or something. We need to make a plan: either we're going down route A, or route B. That's it: simple.'

'But we've been over and over this. We can't afford another IVF session. We've tried everything Kate. Look. Why don't I pay for that spa weekend for you in Brighton? You can take Gill. It will relax you?'

'I don't want another fucking spa weekend Ed. There is only so much pummeling and hot stone massage I can handle. I want a child. That's it. End of.'

He looked around and lowered his head to the table. 'I want a child too Kate. As much as you do. Believe me.' He almost spat out the words.

And she heard the despair and the pain. But she wanted to hear it. She wanted to push him to this point – to be sure he felt what she felt. She knew he was not mentioning the two embryos put back two weeks ago and how they were getting on. He wasn't mentioning the blistering cost of the treatment or that they had no more embryos stored and that this was the last chance. She knows he had not mentioned these things because he loved her and she still wanted to push him to the edge, so he felt the despair she felt. Why was she doing this? When did she become so cruel? She took his hand.

'We could adopt. Look. Think about it at least. It's a possibility. A little girl from China or India.' Lila giggled as her father hoisted her onto his shoulders.

'Or Sri Lanka even? Is that why we're here? To window shop? Jesus Kate. Anyway we can't adopt. My parents would....'

'Ah. Now we have it. Of course. Your fucking parents. They wouldn't approve. But they're not the ones without a child, are they?' Kate pulled her pashmina tighter around her arms. Lila shrieked with joy as her father threw her up into the air and then caught her again.

'They have everything.' She nodded over to the thatched hut. 'Everything. Okay. I'm off. This is getting us nowhere.'

'Where are you going? You can't go back in the dark on your own?'

'Back to the guest house. Enjoy your beer...'

She wakes to the sounds of the shutters smashing. She checks her watch. It is 8.37 and Ed is lying next to her. She sits upright. The whole room appears to swell and creak. There is a low rumbling outside the window, the sound of shattering glass, of wood splintering. Her ring vibrates its way across the chest of drawers. Toiletries skitter across the sink. And then the proprietor shouts.

'Quickly. Everybody. Up to the top please. Quickly. To the top floor.'

She sticks her head round the door frame.

'Up to the top floor madam. Now please. It is too dangerous here.'

All the clients rush up to the roof of the building in various stages of undress: some in pyjamas, some in shorts. The proprietor's sons with mussed up hair and sleepy faces. Up to the top floor where the balcony has a stunning view of the ocean, where only this morning, Kate had eaten her breakfast. Through the metal fire door, Ed behind her, pushing her onto the tiled balcony. She hesitates. She draws a breath. God. Oh God. The breath catches in Kate's throat. The ocean has come to meet them. A swirling yellow river has replaced the road into town. Tuk-tuks revolving like Wurlitzers. The doors and windows of the shops beyond the road no longer visible. The beautiful garden of the guest house is totally submerged. The lights in the swallowed swimming pool cast an eerie green glow up through the water. The two benches floating around like gondolas. A terrified langur monkey screeches and howls as it tries to crawl along the telephone wires and then turns back as it notices the swirling eddies beneath. The birds swoop and wheel and all of nature seems to chorus: 'There is something wrong. Go back.' A shutter floats by with a stranded cat on top of it.

Eventually the water recedes and the next hours are taken up with clearing up. She makes hot chocolate for the proprietor's son who cries for his lost cat. The stinking water in the kitchen is bailed out. She finds Ed on the step outside the kitchen dragging on a cigarette butt. He tries to hide it behind his back.

'One won't hurt.' He says guiltily. 'Don't worry. It won't send my spermatozoa doing the back-stroke in the wrong direction.'

She is drawn to the thatched shack on the beach and while Ed is occupied with disinfecting the floors, she crosses the road to the path that leads to the beach-front. There is a boat, seemingly untouched, perched on top of two houses and a dog, tongue out, hanging upside down in a tree.

The scene reminds her of a trip to the Tate modern with Ed many moons ago. It had been a wet day. She hated modern art but they wanted some shelter and the café was good. They had trawled through all the rooms. All her preconceptions had been realised: every room full of pretentious crap: African scenes made from elephant dung, A naked female manikin with a condom pulled over its head. All pointless. And then desperate for a sit down, she had entered a gallery away from the others. It contained an exploded shed. The model was a shed in mid explosion. Every splinter, every shard of glass hung on a fibreglass string as fine as a hair. Breath-taking. Terrifyingly beautiful. And she got it. She really got it. She was enthralled. She could not tear herself away. Such beauty captured in a moment of devastation.

She curses her insubstantial flip-flops as she picks her way through broken glass, sticks, drawer fronts, plastic crates all stuck in the black silt thrown up from the bowels of the ocean. And everywhere bottles of all hues half-buried in the sand. The thatched hut is still standing but the beds, the Buddha statue, the barbecue are missing. Just an empty shell.

And then she spots them. The couple. Lila's parents. Sitting on a bench a little further along. She creeps up. She hopes. She prays. The sounds of the ocean lapping. The colours all become washed out. Just

Kate and her breathing in and out. Pulling in the air as best she can and pushing it out again. Opening and closing her mouth over and over again because that is all she can do. This moment that will make an imprint on her mind forever.

She knows they are dead before she sees their faces. They are just too still. They sit side by side on the bench covered in a fine layer of silt, their fingers touching. Their sightless eyes turned to the horizon.

She sits down near them and follows their gaze. She wonders about the last thing they saw. She thinks about the embryos floating inside her and how she has ten more days before she knows the outcome. She sees them drifting in their own amniotic ocean, swirling round like they were on the screen in the clinic. That day when she wanted to close her eyes tight and wish, but forced herself to look. The two of them lit up on a huge screen. She wonders whether they are drawn by the pull of the ocean or are they quiet and anchored. Have they clung on like the cat sitting on the shutter or floated down, drifted, been swallowed? She sees dark curls, a smile, a missing tooth.

She slips the leaf beetle ring from her middle finger and wraps it in an old till receipt from her back pocket. She pats her jacket pockets down and finds a blunt lip pencil. On the slip she writes: 'To Lila from Kate' followed by her mobile number. And then she folds it back up again and sticks both ring and paper into the mouth of an empty beer bottle and pushes this firmly into the sand outside the shack.

'Hello.' Ed touches her arm. 'I thought you'd be here.' Of course he knows where to find her – this man she knows better than anybody else in the world. Kate hands him a cigarette and lights it with trembling fingers. 'Here. Take it. One won't hurt.' They both sit cross-legged, backs against the bamboo screen, under a milky sun, hands clasped together in a fierce cold grip.

Bridges

Jacquie Franks

NYTV NEWS

Reports are coming in that Troll, pioneering model and TV personality, is dead at 31 after taking his own life – updates will be available when we know more. (Dave Roberts, Senior Lead)

***

WASHINGTON POST

Obituary

Troll, whose appearance as the first indie-model on the cover of L'Homme in November 2014 was an iconic moment for the We Are All Beautiful movement, died yesterday in Pittsburgh. He was 31. He had lived in Pittsburgh since the age of 19 after migrating from northern Scandinavia where he was born. A spokesman for the Pittsburgh police said Mr. Troll's death had been ruled a suicide.

Troll is sometimes referred to as the first indie supermodel. His agent Lynne Lorrimer stated 'He was a great ambassador for indie-people; he was continually trying to change cultural resistance. His ambition was to break down social barriers by encouraging us all to value differences, not to fear them.'

Troll often said his childhood experiences of inequality and prejudice had inspired him to strive to 'make a difference' at a time when there is a renewed stress on multi-racial pride, and cultural perceptions of trolls and all other indie-people are being challenged by the civil rights movement.

***

EXCLUSIVE - BE SURE TO BUY YOUR 'USA TODAY!' ALL NEXT MONTH AS WE BRING YOU PERSONAL MEMORIES OF TROLL BY THOSE WHO KNEW HIM – ALL IN THEIR OWN WORDS!

Reserve your copy now to make sure you read about Troll's life and times in three parts with cut and keep centre spread including never-seen-before pictures of his early years.

***

WEEK ONE:

(The following account has been translated by Jon Ek)

TROLL'S MOTHER TELLS OF EARLY DISAPPOINTMENT!

'Yes, he was my son. Born of me and my husband. He didn't behave like my son, though. Give him his due, he did try, I suppose. In the early years, at least.

His father blames me. It was winter. I was close to my due date, and should've stayed at home, safe, under our bridge. I was watching the river as it surged past me and I got restless. Climbed out to meet his father. But I was so bulky, I fell, and bore him outside the bridge. His father reckons that's why he never really bonded with us.

He didn't 'fit', somehow. His height was wrong, for one thing. Too tall. And he hated living under the bridge, kept complaining it was too damp and dark under there. 'Well of course it is – it's supposed to be,' I'd tell him. But he wasn't having any. As soon as he could, he'd wander out into the open. At that age! His father had to tie him to his bed at night.

Next, he wanted to go to school. Started following the schoolkids that crossed the bridge. They called him names, even threw stones at him. But he wouldn't give up. I told him to get used to it. 'People aren't safe. They're scared of us, always have been. Best stay away.' He didn't stop though, as soon as we turned our backs he was off again. 'I want to be like the other kids,' he'd cry. How do you tell your child that he will never be like the other kids?

In the end, the protection people stepped in. Bad luck for us it was, they arrived just after his father had tethered him under the bridge. Protection was horrified. We tried to explain that it was for Troll's own good, but they wouldn't listen. Placed him in a foster home. With humans. And after that, he changed. Worst of all, he started trying to change us. He'd suggest I do something – cleaning, say - the way humans and his precious Norrie, his foster mother, did things. Oh yes, he changed a lot after Norrie got her hands on him.'

FOSTER MOTHER NORRIE – TROLL WAS LIKE A PUPPY!

'I remember when the Barnevernet – the Child Protection Services – delivered him, he was so shy he couldn't look at me. But when he eventually did – well, I just melted. He reminded me of a lost puppy.

Timid, toffee-brown eyes peeking out from under all that coarse hair ... although I soon sorted the hair problem out for him.

He was such a curious little soul. Always asking me questions. 'Why do you do that?' 'What's this for?' 'How do you use it?' Bless me if he didn't think central heating was the best invention ever! He never could get enough of the warmth. Every opportunity he had, he'd sit with his back against a radiator. Begged me not to turn the heating off, even in the summer.

I don't know why he never made any friends at school, he was polite enough. The only difficult time I had with him was when the Barnevernet set up visits with his family. Bless him, he was so eager to see his mum again, he bought her a bouquet with his own pocket money. But he brought it back, all muddy it was. Said his mother had told him off for encouraging mankind's flower-murders. After a while, he began making excuses not to go. His parents didn't like the way he was living. Told him 'it wasn't natural for him to shave his body and that he was getting too clever for his own good'. The Barnevernet insisted he kept going – told him he needed to know his roots, so that he knew who he was. And he did go back to live there when he turned eighteen. and I couldn't legally foster him anymore. But I don't think he was happy. He made the decision to travel to America, soon after.'

***

WEEK TWO

CLASSMATE KRISTOFER TELLS OF TROLL'S DESPERATION TO LEARN!

'Not sure what I can tell you about him, to be honest. We used to call him 'Beast'. After Beauty and the Beast, you know? First times we saw him was when he kept following us to school. He'd hang around the gates and beg to come in. The authorities got involved. Next thing we knew, he was coming to our class. Our parents weren't happy at all. I mean, it isn't right, is it? Schools and education are for mankind. We invented the system, for goodness sake! What right did he have to think he could take advantage of it? No right. He had no right to try to be better than he was.

The girls were a bit frightened at first, in case he got angry and become dangerous – like that wild character from the X-Men films. Once he'd lost the hair he looked a bit more normal, I suppose. Apart from the nose.

We all thought he must be a bit crazy. I mean, no one begs to come in to school, do they? It's not as if he was an A grade student or anything – well, yes, he did get next best grades in the class, but not top. Alice, she was top. He wasn't top. I sometimes wondered if he'd cheated, how else could he have got the grades he did? It was a real shock to see he'd become famous, you know. Never expected him to get anywhere in life, him being a ... well, you know. One of them.'

TEACHER OLAF

'Sport? Well that was a bit of a shame. He was good, more than good – had the potential to be a great sportsman. He was stronger than any of the other kids. Fast, too. Great reactions. But none of the kids wanted him on their team. He was always picked last. He never said anything though, just got on with winning the game for whichever team he was in.

He was a bright guy too, not at all what I expected. Of course, university was totally out of the question, although he applied to quite a few. He was desperate to continue learning. But the rules don't allow, you see. It's a pity, but things are what they are. As I often said to him, you can't change centuries of rules and traditions overnight. 'Can't you?' he'd say. 'Why not?' And he'd point out that no one had ever thought that a black man would become president of the USA, and yet Obama did. I think that's why he emigrated. He looked across at the States and believed that they were more open minded over there. He had dreams, you see.'

FRIEND PHIL – WE WERE LIKE BROTHERS

'Oh yes, we both had dreams, it was our dreams which kept us going. Getting into America isn't easy, everyone knows that. I wanted to get a job, earn some money, get away from all those blasted bridges in Norway. I was born there, but I sure as eggs didn't want to die there, too!

Troll wanted more than that. 'A job and some money to start with,' he'd say. He hungered after something bigger. Although I don't think he knew what, exactly. Not then, anyway.

We bonded straight away. Well, hiding on a ship in an oil drum – that's what happens. We grew close. Stuck together. After we landed in America, we made for Pittsburgh. Turns out Pittsburgh is well named – it certainly was the 'pits' for us. People really hated us. 'Go home' was on everyone's lips. We hid under railway bridges for the first three months. Fought the foxes over takeaway remains thrown into bins. Took showers when it rained. Finally, we got a break. A publican took pity on us, gave us a couple of drinks, let us stay on after the local punters went home. We bonded at the bar. Turned out he was actually a wizard - in hiding from his own kind. 'How the hell have you managed to build a life here?' Troll asked. The guy shrugged. 'I pretend I'm the same as them.'

Troll, he heard that as a gospel truth. The wizard gave us jobs and

Troll worked all the hours under the sun to save enough money for plastic surgery. For his nose, see. He managed it too, but no surgeon would take him on as a client. Troll didn't talk much after that, just brooded. Then he started roaming around at night, going to places where no one was welcome. 'You got a death wish or something, mate?' I asked. But he kept going.

He wouldn't let me go with him, said he needed to be alone. I've never forgiven myself for not insisting. One night, he didn't come back. It was me that found him, in the end. Beaten up and left to die; a sign to other immigrants that we are not welcome in the US. God, he looked bad. His face! It looked like mashed potato – red mashed potato. I thought he was dead at first, but he grabbed my arm as I called the paramedics. 'Don't give any details, let them think ... please, Phil.' So, I didn't. And it worked. The doctors took it for granted he was a man with a mangled face and rebuilt his face along human lines.

He didn't forget me when he hit the big time, you know. As soon as he could, he got me a job as a runner for the agency he worked with. Later, when he became famous, he took me on as his personal bodyguard. Ironic, really, given that I wasn't with him the night he got beaten up. That's twice I wasn't there. I was away when he pulled that stupid 'This Is Me' stunt, too. Ah man, what was he thinking of? I dunno. I loved the guy like my own brother, but that stunt ... it ruined everything. He could have been a Martin Luther King for us Indies. Instead, every scrap of respect he'd begged from mankind was destroyed. Seems the world wasn't ready for the truth, after all.'

***

WEEK THREE

TROLL'S AGENT LYNNE LORRIMER SAYS TROLL WAS AN IDIOT!

'I know it's two years since the 'This Is Me' stunt but yes, I'm still angry with him. To throw it all away like that. The idiot!

It is every agent's dream, you know, to discover a 'someone'. Each of us lives and breathes in hope – forever scanning side-walks, malls, parking lots, for the next big 'look'. But I'd never expected to find a potential star in a pharmacy queue. God, if I hadn't been in desperate need of some aspirin for my headache we may never have met. There he was, this beautiful, long-limbed man, buying some aspirin too. I could tell immediately that he was photogenic. Better than that, he had an original look – sort of lost and lonely on one level, but full-on man underneath. I knew at once he had cross-gender appeal.

I didn't know about his background, not for a while. When he finally told me, I didn't consider it a problem. He was just a male model – Vogue, Tatler, L'Homme and so on – and clients are only interested in the photos. It was later, after he got a couple of TV gigs and people became interested in him, that I worried about a risk of negative publicity if we didn't manage the situation. My PR team created a background that played out with him, not against him. 'Get his story out there before the rumours start. Brand Troll as a 'true original'.'

Well, it worked! His career expanded. He became a public figure. He was superb at promoting indie rights. He didn't bluster and shout like some politicians – because that's where he was heading, I'm sure of it - he just kept planting seeds about fairness and equal rights. I don't think he set out to be a spokesman – whoops! 'spokesbody', Troll would have said! – it just started to come together once he had a voice through TV, radio, the press, etc. He thrived on what he was doing. When he fell for Anya – well, I think he thought that was it, he was going to change the world. And for a short while, I think he did.

It all started to go wrong when social media, particularly Twitter, really took off. You remember how some people became really abusive on the sites, and the press created the term 'Internet Trolls' for them? Troll was beside himself. He foresaw all his efforts to educate humankind and reduce their prejudices about indie people would be destroyed by the thoughtless use of that title. Of course, he fought back; every time he made a media appearance he'd ask people to reconsider the term and all that it meant. But then he became a 'trolling' target himself. He became obsessed with reading every word they said. He read them to me sometimes. They were all along the same lines. 'No one would listen if you had the honesty to be who you are.' 'You stand up for Indie Rights, but you left your home and changed your face.' 'Hypocrite.' 'Fake.'

Out of the blue he cancelled all his engagements for a month – of course, I know why, now. It was to let all his hair grow back! Hired his own PR and they released those awful 'This Is Me' photos. The campaign was totally misjudged. No one wanted to see what he really looked like! For goodness sake, every model is just a fusion of lighting, make up and digital re-imaging. The general public buy into an illusion, not the reality. They certainly couldn't cope with Troll's reality. The media offers and sponsorship stopped. He couldn't even get any work on the radio!

I had to let Troll go in the end. I couldn't risk losing any clients as a result of my association with him. I'm a business not a charity – and I believed Anya would look after him. If only she had!'

EX PARTNER ANYA DENIES RESPONSIBILITY FOR TROLL'S SUICIDE!

'It wasn't my fault! People keep pointing the finger at me – I've had to close all my social media accounts – it just isn't fair!

No one's given me the credit I deserve. After all, I stood by T all through the 'This Is Me' backlash. It wasn't easy. It was me who found him a psychiatrist you know, and I promised him all my support during his therapy.

I really regret that now, though. T got the idea that having a child together would spearhead a new equality across species and restore his campaign. T kept on and on about it. But I was scared! I mean, we needed to find out if it was biologically possible, first! T kept telling me of course it was, but he didn't really know. How could he? In the end I just wanted to be free, back in the real world. Yes, if you like, with my own kind again.

Of course I miss him, Of course I'm sad that he's dead, but we'd broken up when he did it! I'm not responsible for his actions! I know what my PA – my ex-PA now - said she heard, but it's clearly a stunt to make some money.

No, I will not confirm I said that. I told you, she's lying. I admit T and I had a few rows when he left, but my last words to Troll were not 'Go back under your bridge where you belong!' I can't remember exactly what I said, but it definitely was not that.

No, I couldn't speculate as to why T hung himself there. He always said he hated his time in Pittsburgh. And he hated the viaduct bridge at Silver Lake in particular, he always said it reminded him too much of his childhood.

No. No more questions, I tell you. No comment.'

The Outsider

Kevin David Joinville

Honourable Mention

The Union Square station smelled like it always did of fresh urine and rat. I followed the stench past an old dude playing Amazing Grace on his bagpipes and down the staircase to the uptown 4, 5, and 6 train. There was an express parked on the track, but before I could reach the platform, the doors closed with that familiar 'bing-bong' sound that made me give out a full on pissed off groan.

I pushed through several hundred of New York City's most disgruntled strap-hangers with my large, unruly backpack crashing into everyone attempting to exit. I caught an onslaught of dirty looks, bad attitudes, and a kick to the shins for all the effort I took to stop it from hitting them. People didn't understand that my school filled up my bag, not me.

I broke through the crowd and planted myself at the end of the platform. Faces blurred through the windows as the train sped off.

When the last car passed, the surrounding air picked up filling the vacuum the train left behind. It lifted my arms slightly towards the tracks and for a second, as the wind rushed past my ears, the entire station fell silent.

The junkie dug through a tall black garbage can. He wore a grimy jean jacket over a white t-shirt. Light brown hair covered his face and hid his features. Even hunched over, I could tell he towered me by a head. He had a pole thin frame; straight up and down without an ounce of muscle or fat.

He nodded off and his head lowered into the can. He woke up and nodded again. He repeated this dance over and over. That guy had probably spent his whole life stoned off his ass. I mean, I was a loser since I barely made it to the eleventh grade, but at least I didn't search the trash for food.

An old lady came down the stairs. She didn't move well and gripped the railing tight while taking it one step at a time. She waited for the train at the bottom of the steps. She planted herself right by the garbage can. She couldn't go much farther. She seemed like a nice grandmotherly type with her purse hanging from an arm too frail to fight back if the junkie tried to take it. She purposefully turned away from him.

I thought about standing next to her, to protect her, but I chickened out the moment the thought of being stabbed with a diseased needle popped into my head. It didn't feel like the manliest thing, but I decided to go, though it meant leaving the old lady defenseless. Before I could move, the junkie lifted up his head, turned, and walked away. With him gone, I gathered up my balls and stood next to the old lady, just in case.

Partially for safety and partially out of fascination, I kept my eyes on him. I wasn't the only one. Two dudes stood behind me talking about him,

'Look,' said one of the guys, ' it's some of the New York city wildlife.'

'What?' asked his friend. 'This city only has concrete. There's no wildlife here.'

'Sure there is. It's got pigeons, rats, roaches, alligators, and junkies.'

They both laughed. I wanted to laugh, but I thought better of it. The guy had failed at life, but he was still a person.

The junkie bobbed and weaved his way towards the far end of the platform taking a quick nap every few shuffles where he would do his heroin dance towards the floor. I hoped for him to make it all the way down, but he kept popping back up before hitting the ground. He fought sleep hard, although I couldn't imagine where he needed to be in that condition?

He bobbed his way over to the edge of the platform and stopped. His feet crossed over the yellow safety line.

I would've said something. I didn't want him to slip and be crushed on the tracks. But every time he nodded forward, a moment later he popped back up. So I figured he knew what he was doing. Even when I heard the loud screeches of the train coming, I didn't feel like I should say anything.

My foot crossed the yellow line as well, but I stepped back when the lights of the number 4 train appeared in the tunnel. The junkie didn't move his. He stayed at the edge. I inhaled deeply as he nodded forward right before the train reached him and I exhaled in relief as he moved backwards in time for the first car to safely pass him. He didn't fall on to the tracks.

I don't remember if it was a smack sound or a thud, but there was definitely a sound, because the next time the junkie nodded forward, his head smashed into the third car.

'Holy shit!' I yelled.

The man's face whipped to the side and vacant eyes looked back at me. Adrenaline rushed my stomach then leaped to my heart with such power that I jumped from the force of it. But the adrenaline didn't make me look away from the man or send me off in a safer direction. No, when I jumped, I jumped toward him.

I planned to run fast, to pick the man up, move him to safety, but that didn't happen. I didn't make it half a step before his feet slipped in between the train and the platform. His right side slammed to the ground. His head bounced. His hands flew out behind him as the train dragged his body toward me.

'Oh shit! Oh shit! Oh shit!' I started shouting. I searched for help. The old lady let out a scream. The two friends behind me ran away. I had no idea if I should follow them or what to do, so I stayed.

His body slipped further down the gap to his thighs. The train darted down the tracks. The man's arms flailed dead above his head not grabbing for anything. His eyes were closed and mouth silent. His only movements came from the train scraping him along the platform.

I decided that when the guy got closer to me, I would grab him under his armpits and lift him up.

So I waited.

I aimed for his arms, but I would've settled for anything, even his hair. But something else snagged his hair and his head got sucked under the train, his face squashed through the gap.

'Oh shit!' was the only thing I could say and I kept repeating it. I ran alongside the junkie until the train stopped. That car had a conductor with his window open. I ran up to him.

'Hey! Hey, man!' the conductor's head stuck out the window, but not facing me. He had his earplugs in and couldn't hear a thing. I tapped him on the shoulder. He turned around and freed an ear. 'Hey, man, you just ran over someone!'

'What?'

'You ran over this guy, look!' I pointed back in between the first door and the second, from mid-thigh to mid-chest was all that was visible of him. His head, upper torso, arms, and legs had all been sucked inside the gap. 'The guy's dead, man!' I didn't know that exactly, but he had to be. A chest jammed into a gap two inches wide couldn't house a heart that still beat.

The conductor's eyes widened, and he ducked his head back inside. I guessed to use the radio. I didn't know if telling him would be enough, so I ran upstairs.

I went back through the turnstile and stopped in front of the token booth where a clerk spoke to a buddy of his. I banged on the glass.

'Hey, somebody just run got over.' The guy either didn't hear me or didn't care. 'Are you listening?' I banged again, 'I said someone got run over!'

He wore the MTA uniform dark blue sweater and tie and was supposed to be a professional, but the big diamond earring in his ear told me something different.

'Which train?' he said then moved back from the microphone.

'The 4 train. The 4 train hit a guy.'

'Uptown or downtown?' he said calm and relaxed like he dealt with someone getting run over every day.

'The uptown.'

'Okay,' I don't know if he called 911 because I turned away. My pulse pounded in my head and my hands wouldn't stop shaking.

Someone left the station through the emergency exit. I still had to get home. I ignored the turnstile and slipped through the open gate.

I looked back at the clerk expecting him to say, Pay your fare! But he didn't. He continued with his conversation.

I walked down the steps pissed off and on wobbly legs. I reached the platform and backed up to the local side. The 4 train stood with its doors open and passengers emptied out of the cars. An announcement said it was out of service.

Most people didn't notice the dead man, but a few did. Mainly the ones who ran away after the hit. They came back like I did.

I squatted down to watch and hoped that somehow he survived. Two cops surrounded him, but all of the passengers' suits and feet blocked my view. The 6 local rolled in behind me. I didn't pay attention to it. I felt I needed to stay to give a statement or something.

A guy came down the stairs. He wore a badge around his neck that hung by a chain, but he didn't have a uniform on. He wore regular clothes, a thick flannel shirt, Yankees cap, and had a mustache. He must have been undercover because the other cops ignored him when he made his announcement,

'Okay everyone, listen up!' he shouted to the people on the platform and the others getting off the local, 'I need you all to either head upstairs or hop on this number 6 train. I need this area clear, so we can make room for Emergency Medical Services.'

He said it again. People hesitated then eventually did what the undercover guy said, but not me.

'Hey, son,' he said, 'Son, do you need medical attention?' I shook my head without looking at him, hoping he wouldn't tell me to leave. He came over and bent down, 'What's your name, kid?'

'Me? I'm Kevin.'

'Okay, Kevin. I need you to get on this train before it leaves, so I can make room.'

'But I can help.'

'Go ahead,' he said, 'you don't need to see this,' he picked me up and waved at the conductor to hold the door.

Me and another guy walked in to the local. The other guy was short and in his forties with a thick black beard. Hard looking, he wore an Army hat and jacket with blue jeans

'Here, you dropped this,' said the Army guy. He had my backpack in his hands. I didn't remember taking it off.

'Thanks,' I said and grabbed it from him as the doors closed behind us. I looked out the window. The platform had cleared except for the cops. They were shouting stuff at the dead man. He didn't respond.

'There's no blood,' the words came out weak.

'What?' said the Army guy.

Not a single drop.

'There's…' I let it go. It was a stupid thought. 'I tried to help him.'

'At least you did something,' he said, 'all those people out there, they didn't do jack. They saw a person get run over and they ran.'

'It wasn't enough,' I said.

He seemed like the kind of guy who liked to have answers, but he was failing at comforting me and knew it. It made him look hurt, or maybe he was sad for me. Without saying anything more, he pursed his lips and moved further into the car.

The train moved and I stared at the body until I lost sight of him. I turned and faced the other passengers. Why wasn't there any blood?

I stood in the car close enough to the last that there shouldn't have been such a crowd. And they were all smiling. They didn't witness a person get run over so they were smiling. I mean, they were giggling and laughing and having conversations. They were reading and listening to their headphones. They were relaxed and having too normal of a day. I didn't want to ride with them for the next nine stops. I hated them too much.

The train entered the tunnel. Out the window, darkness sped by, and blackened the glass. I watched the Army guy's reflection in it. Both of his arms were stretched out, grabbing the overhead bars on each side of him. His head slunk down and his body moved in rhythm with the train. I wanted to talk to him. He didn't call the guy a junkie. He called him a person. I hoped he'd catch me staring, but he never raised his eyes.

Parka Billy

Juliet Hill

Like a throwback to another century. That's how she'd have described it if she'd read about the incident in the days when she still bought newspapers. The Victorian-slum brutality of the dispossessed turning their rage against each other she'd have said, if she was feeling articulate and wanted to show off. She'd never have thought herself capable of such savagery, but that was then, before she became a non-person. By the time she found herself grateful for a dry shop doorway or a half-eaten slice of pizza, everything which had been anchoring her to her previous comfortable existence had long since evaporated.

Doug had always said she was the strong one. Even after he left her for a sulky hairdresser barely out of school uniform, he maintained it was he who was weak. He just couldn't help his feelings. She, on the other hand, would be fine, he was sure of it.

And she was for a while. She continued to work in the Town Hall until the redundancy; she continued to live in what had been their shared home until it was repossessed after months of uncertainty; she even continued to love her husband who she'd spy on from behind shelves of cereal in the supermarket, not quite believing that he was now happily shopping for three.

By then she was running out of sofas and friends and found she couldn't stop crying. So she just left.

She couldn't remember much about her first year on the street: cold and damp; smells that made her gag; names and faces merging into one endless dark night and freezing sunrise. The cold and damp never really left her but she soon became immune to the smells and the filth, and she survived. Begging, stealing, selling herself, selling others – you had to make the most of what you'd got or what you could get. She'd learned of the importance of making snap judgements about people: who to trust; who to ignore; who to approach. Whatever the transaction, it had to be fast; afterwards, their faces blurred into one barely remembered past encounter and it was time to move on.

But she couldn't forget Billy. His smile, the way he flirted with strangers and wheedled or coaxed money out of them, his mad sense of humour after a few cans. He wore a huge Parka coat with a fur-lined hood and endless inner pockets from which he would fish out random credit cards or smartphones, always ready to trade. He was one of the usual faces in the usual haunts – airless soup kitchens, intimidating night shelters – but few people spoke or if they did it was more to themselves than to others. That was the way it was. She'd learned to keep her mouth shut and avoid eye contact with the majority.

She spoke to Billy in her second year on the street. She didn't really know why. Maybe she was sick of having to trust strangers but keep her distance from a familiar face. Not that she tried to get too close or prise much information out of him. He never spoke of his past and she took her cue from that, skating over details of her own descent from respected professional to whatever it was she was now. What did it matter after all? Talking about something, putting it into words and saying it out loud only made it real again. She'd learnt to think of her past life as she would a series of vague childhood memories, never quite sure they'd happened. From now on she and Billy were what they were, and dwelling on the past was as pointless as thinking about the future. Sheltered by nothing more than a flattened cardboard box or a flimsy plastic sheet, she finally felt safe. There were ugly, frightening nights when they were spat on by rich drunks or kicked by poor ones but they had each other. She didn't have to be the strong one anymore.

But the night Billy died he'd decided to ignore one of their unspoken rules and look more than one day ahead. He'd been in great spirits all day, downing White Lightning and talking of whatever came into his head, making her laugh with nonsense about weddings and walking into the sunset. Maybe the booze had somehow convinced him that now was the time to make a serious gesture. They had a future in spite of the chaos and filth surrounding them.

'What do you reckon? Katerina?'

It wasn't her real name. Her real name was short and functional but she'd always liked Katerina.

'Kat, come on, we could do it. We could get off the street. I've got a bit of cash. It'd be like in the movies - a new life.'

And she tried to believe him. She downed a few more cans herself and willed herself to believe it. She looked at her surroundings: a dripping railway arch; a filthy mattress and stained blankets; the shopping trolley they'd used to transport their belongings from the last place. Surely there was a way out of this. They could put everything back in the trolley and move on to something better. Wasn't that how Doug felt when he left her?

But the grubby ring that Billy extracted from one of his hidden inner pockets was already hers. It was her wedding ring, the one she'd brought with her, thinking she could sell it. She looked at the tarnished gold, pretending to admire it, pretending to be drunkenly overwhelmed at his gesture but really checking the inside for the initials that she already knew would be there.

She remembered how it felt to wear it all the time, a constant reminder of her settled status and place in the world. She'd secretly liked Doug calling her the missus and even after the divorce she'd avoided taking the final step of removing it.

That night it had slipped off easily. There was no need for threats or violence; she could hardly function for terror and shock, let alone resist the two wiry men who appeared from nowhere and took everything she had. Was one of them Billy? She wasn't able to say.

Afterwards, she'd sat in a bus shelter, punching the reinforced plastic until her knuckles bled, still hitting it hours later as the streets filled with commuters. It was the last time she let her emotions get the upper hand. Since then she'd swallowed her anger and kept it comatose with cheap alcohol. It lay low, a tight mass somewhere in her gut, zipped in and held by strength of will.

But now Billy was staring at her, waiting. She looked again at the ring and didn't know whether to laugh or cry. Parka Billy was offering her a ring, her own stolen ring. The anger and fear of that first night pushed the breath from her lungs and she felt a prickling sensation in her scarred knuckles.

'Where did you get that?'

'What the hell does it matter? Some drunk bitch dropped it and now it's yours.'

Then he laughed.

She did nothing at first. She waited until the sun was beginning to rise and the cold was receding from her muscles before she made a move. Billy was lying on the mattress, still in his parka and clutching an empty can. From time to time his fingers gently stroked its smooth side and he would murmur something inaudible. I bet he's always been able to drop off anywhere, she thought.

There was a broken brick lying beside him as if daring her to pick it up. She'd seen it before. Now she held it and tested its weight, just to give herself a moment, but the tight mass of anger inside her had already been released. She could feel it scorching her intestines and rising in her throat and she knew she wouldn't be able to breathe if this poisonous sludge reached her mouth. So she swung her arm and used the momentum to hit the side of Billy's head.

There was no crack of broken bone, just a dull thud followed by the metallic sound of Billy's empty can rolling across the cobbles until it came to a standstill. She stood in silence for a moment and then lifted her arm to hit him again, only this time she found it much harder to see where she was aiming. The outline of Billy's head was beginning to blur into a composite of swirling faces, all of them bloody and snarling, and she stumbled backwards into the dripping wall and slid down it to land in a fetid puddle. Billy was still moving.

For weeks afterwards she could still see the brick, with blood and hair clotted onto the one sharp edge. She woke with it still in her hand and looked over at Billy's face. There was no surprise or pain, just contentment, peace even. The White Lightning had done its work long before she laid the first blow. She took the coat from his limp body, never one to waste anything, and waited for him to die, listening to his final breaths as carefully as if they were his final words.

After that she stopped speaking. It was her third year on the street.

She'd sit in Billy's coat with her cans and watch shoppers and commuters pass by as if she was seeing them on a screen, speeded-up silent movie inhabitants of a place she didn't live in anymore. People who she didn't always recognise urged her to search the coat, its inner lining and endless pockets, but she would shake her head in silence, unable to explain to herself let alone to others why she couldn't. Passers-by would wonder if this mad-looking bag lady was going to make it through another winter and they'd give her money while trying to avoid her vacant stare.

But Billy had friends, or people who claimed they were friends, and they hadn't forgotten him. They might not remember much but they weren't going to forget the possibilities of Billy's coat. So now she had to force herself to concentrate on places to avoid, people who might know of her, how she might be described or spoken of, even though she couldn't always remember why. She didn't really know what she looked like any more. One day she caught sight of herself in a shop window and didn't recognise the red-faced old woman with an empty expression and an oversized parka. That wasn't her. So she stopped looking.

But she always had the coat. At the back of her mind she had the idea that it wasn't hers, that she was looking after it for someone else but she couldn't remember who. In rare, lucid moments she would see herself stealing it from a dead man and shudder at her own brutality. Was that really her? But the memory would leave as quickly as it had arrived and she would stop caring. It didn't matter.

Billy's friends came for her on the coldest night of the year. She said nothing. What was the point of trying? She handed the parka over as quickly as she'd given away her wedding ring, but this time her anger seemed to have dissipated and she just felt an emptiness.

She didn't make it through another winter without Billy's parka.

Not Like Me But Just the Same

Taria Karillion

They weren't like me – the people who came out of the lake. I've never seen anyone like them, not even in pictures or holo-tales. I should have run home straight away, but I was curious – I wanted to see. My parents always say that curiosity killed the cat, and that's why they're extinct, but everything's a-a-a-always so samey in the Dome, so anything new or just different is cool, so I hid by a boulder and watched.

After the crash, when they waded ashore, they looked so small and bedraggled and weak, like the newly hatched chicks in the Habitat Dome - staggering, dizzy and dazed. I had to get closer – to get a good look. I couldn't see weapons, just frightened people – grown-ups, children and elders – and they all seemed as scared of me as I was of them.

The strangers came closer and started to talk, but not in a language I knew. I'm not supposed to talk to strangers, but some of them were hurt, and somebody had to help them, so I brought them back to the Dome - to the grown-ups in the Square.

My parents came – running! They took hold of my hands and squeezed them so tightly, scolding me for being outside with no suit. I think they were scared too, as if I was the one who'd been hurt.

We watched as the crowd of strangers grew. They were making odd noises and holding each other. We looked at them and they looked at us, and nobody knew what to do.

Then the Medics and Peacekeepers came in a big, loud hurry – with sirens and shouting and pointing, and took the Lake People away. Some of them were broken and bleeding, I think, but I wasn't allowed to look.

Soon, the Wise Elders came out and talked to the crowd about who the strangers might be, and where they could have come from. Everyone's eyes were wide. There were so many questions, but not many answers. Not at first. But soon 'They' were all people were talking about – mostly in whispers, in huddles, in corners, in each other's ears so we couldn't hear. But kids hear way more than grown-ups think, and I heard them muttering about the strangers' differentness, about what did they want and how many more, and what will happen now? Grown-ups all chattered at once - there were a lot of words I don't know. One word I heard a lot, but nobody would tell me what 'Invasion' means.

Our Teachers came and sat us down, and with serious faces and serious voices they said we mustn't be scared, but also that we shouldn't use the mean words that we were hearing in the crowd. They said the strangers are not Mutants, just Refugees, and they can't help the way they look because their families must have been poisoned by something and the poor things were probably born with those terrible defects.

The next day came and, at Recess, Raska Fisherson said out loud - reeeeally loud - that the Strangers SMELL funny and they're all far too PUNY to last very long, and even if they do, the WEIRD way they talk will get the freaky freeloaders chucked out of the Dome and good riddance, and he drew a finger across his throat and made a funny noise. I don't know what that all meant, but Raska was sent to the naughty corner.

The Capital Dome News came on and absolutely everyone stopped and was quiet and watched on the public viewscreens. The Announcer said that only a few hundred of the strangers had survived, and that 'public fears about resources being over-stretched are untrue, and rumours of protest riots are exaggerated.' But why would they say that after the shouting and chanting and banging at night-times? Don't they hear it too?

Then, even the President came out and gave us a speech – about all staying calm and remembering our duty to help those in crisis. But the President usually has two minders, and I definitely counted six. I didn't hear much of the next bit – there were lots of long words about segregation laws and detainment zones, but I forget what, coz that's when the scary protestors burst in and interrupted the broadcast. They were very loud and said some VERY bad words! They did a lot of angry pointing and shouting - that the refugees may look like us, but they're not! They're not just escaping immigrants, they're actual real-life aliens! That Divers found their ship, sunk outside the Habit Dome, but it's not a water ship, it's a space-ship, and the government are trying to cover it up!

When the Peacekeepers came, the protestors chanted - about charity starting at home, and 'Send them away', that 'we don't want them here'. As the protestor spoke, small blobs of spittle flew out from their mouth, like the pictures of predators in one of my books. They carried on sneering and shaking their fists until they were cuffed and taken away. I thought grown-ups knew the right way to behave, but that was like fights in our playground, but worse! I think they'll be put in the naughty corner for a very, very long time.

When dinnertime came, I asked my parents why some people don't want to share – the teachers all make us take turns and be fair. We have enough and they all have nothing. Like one of us having everyone's dinner all piled up on their plate – more than they need, just coz they want it - and the others at table having nothing. Why teach us 'be kind to people', but only if those people look the same as us. It doesn't make sense to me. PLUS, if we crashed somewhere far from our home and were frightened and hungry and hurt, wouldn't we want someone to help us? To be kind? To just be fair?

So, I came here, to talk to you, coz though I'm a child, this is Public Platform is for everyone, and my parents said that you need to hear the stuff I have to say. So, what I want to say is this...

If these strangers are aliens, and their home is all poisoned so they can't live there anymore, well our planet is ginormous, so surely, it's plenty big enough for everyone?! I don't understand why some grown-ups are scared of the New People, just coz they're not exactly the same as us. They didn't come here to hurt us – they came to escape a bad place where they might have died. They just want to be safe and together and not be bullied or go hungry. Just like us. Different doesn't mean bad!

We shouldn't care that they have two genders and no telepathy, and it shouldn't matter that they only have two arms - it's enough for their greeting. The new child in my class showed me. It's called a hug and it makes you feel nice, and I like it.

My Friend Ros

Jan Keegan

I was trying to remember when we had first met. Was it at the party at George's house perhaps? No, it couldn't have been then because I was still going out with Matt at the time and I knew that I had only met Ros when I became a singleton again. I don't know why that's stuck in my head as it has, but it has.

Then it all fell into place as it does when you remember something after a bit of thought. It was in the pub our group frequented. The 'Boot and Shoe'. I'd noticed her straightaway. It would have been difficult not to, what with her wild purple hair, the brilliant yellow trousers, vivid green top and oodles, simply oodles of beads. Then there were the orange boots. She kind of stood out.

I recall that, although she was in the middle of a crowd and was wearing really outrageous clothes, she still seemed to be alone. It felt odd at the time and it still does now. There was an air of loneliness about her, even though she was in a circle of chattering people, making comments now and again which generally resulted in hoots of laughter. This only served to make what happened later even more difficult to understand.

I had approached her with my best warm smile. I thought that she was definitely somebody worth getting to know. Someone who was her own person, who did what she wanted to, happy to be who she was. At least that what was what I thought she was like. I always gravitate to people like that. I'd really like to be like that myself, but I don't quite have the courage.

'Hi,' I said. 'My name's Esther. I love your outfit. You look fantastic. I don't think that we've met before have we?'

Ros had looked at me with interest. I noticed that she had brilliant blue eyes, really sparkling, eyes that held your attention when they looked at you. It was like being hypnotised.

'I'm Ros,' she'd replied. 'Good to meet you.'

We'd shaken hands in a very solemn way and then laughed at the absurdity of acting like a couple of middle-aged matrons meeting at the local Women's Institute.

'God, just look at us both. Like a couple of old farts!' she'd exclaimed, and I'd felt embarrassed at first, but then realised that Ros was quite right, and I laughed with her.

Have you ever met somebody with whom you hit it off right from the get-go? Ros and I were like that. We seemed to be able to understand each other and knew what the other one was thinking before she said anything. Others in the group thought that was a bit weird. Some of them didn't approve of her. Jill thought that she looked too outrageous and that she should tone it down. John didn't like it when she once told him that he was a 'stuck-up prick'. The fact is that he was, (still is actually), but perhaps it could have been put rather differently. Ros would not have got a job with the Diplomatic Service, to be honest. Even I thought that she sometimes went a little too far.

'Be careful Ros,' I counselled. 'You don't want to go around upsetting people.'

'Don't care,' she'd replied. 'People can take me or leave me. I'm my own woman.'

Anyway, over the next few months we became really good pals. We went on nights out, going to the clubs and seeing whether there were any men about who were worth the bother. Sometimes we hit lucky and other times we didn't, but we always had a good time. We laughed and laughed and were always getting into trouble for something or other.

There was the time that we decided to join a yoga class and we turned up and found everybody there was taking it all really seriously. So, we joined in at the back of the room, but Ros was totally unable to concentrate, and she kept putting me off. Then a woman in front of us farted really loudly. A real machine gun cacophony and that started us both off. I was trying not to look at Ros because I knew that if I did I would be totally unable to stop myself from dissolving into laughter. I could hear her snorting and sniggering and then, eventually, I couldn't stop myself. We both fell about laughing and stopped the class because we were in hysterics. The bloke taking the class asked us to leave. So that was the end of yoga.

I'm a primary school teacher. Not a great one if I'm honest but I enjoy it. I'd sort of drifted into it once I'd left university. Ros had been at uni too, but she'd not found her 'niche', as she described it. She had a couple of jobs, one in a coffee bar and one in a restaurant. She said that she would know when it was time to try to find her forte but, for now, all she wanted to do was to have a good time.

One day I was having my lunch when my phone rang, and I saw that it was Ros.

'Hiya,' I said. 'What's up?' I always answered my phone like that. I had no reason to think that anything was up, but it soon became clear that all was not well. Ros's voice was really quiet. I could hardly hear her.

'Can we meet after you finish work?' she asked. 'At the café?'

'Yeah, sure,' I said. 'Are you ok? Is something wrong?'

'I just need to talk to you about something,' she said. Then she hung up.

I couldn't concentrate for the rest of the afternoon. The kids were playing up and I let them. I was too busy thinking about Ros and worrying about her. I'd never heard her like that before. It really unsettled me.

Finally, after an interminable afternoon, the bell went, and I rushed to the café. I got there before Ros and I was sipping my latte when she arrived. I tried to be nonchalant, but I felt like I was failing miserably.

'Want a coffee?' I asked and she nodded, and I went and got her favourite. Americano with milk. I didn't need to check. I marched back to the table, plonked it down and then looked at her. I didn't know what to make of it. She looked totally miserable and couldn't even look at me. She was staring at the table, not moving a muscle.

'Ros,' I said, 'whatever is the matter? I don't think that I've ever seen you looking like this. Are you in trouble?'

She raised her head to look at me and there was a hint of a smile.

'I suppose that you could say that. I'm not sure what sort of trouble I'm in though. I'll have to wait for the test results.'

I felt a chill come over me. My stomach went into a knot and I began to feel sick.

'What do you mean? What tests?' I said.

'Two weeks ago, when I was in the shower, I found a lump in my left boob. I went to see my GP and he referred me to the hospital. I had scans today and they think that it might be cancerous, but they're not entirely sure. I've got to go in for an operation and they'll check it out. If it's cancer my breast will be removed. They'll check the lymph nodes as well to see if there's any chance that it might have spread.'

'Oh, bugger,' I whispered. It made Ros laugh a bit. Then I noticed a tear coming down her cheek.

'To be honest Est,' she said, 'I'm really scared. I'm only twenty-six. People at my age don't get cancer and die, do they?'

I didn't know what to say. I knew that anybody could get cancer at any time. It wasn't restricted to a particular age or group. That's why it's such a shitty disease. All sorts of cancers can kill all sorts of people. We both knew that and then I was scared for her. No time for that now though. I had to be positive.

'When have you got to go in?' I asked.

'Day after tomorrow,' Ros said. 'They're not hanging around. That's why I'm frightened really. They must think that its cancer. What am I going to look like with one tit? I'm gonna look a right freak Est. People will laugh at me. I'm never gonna get a fella looking like that.'

'Shut up Ros. You mustn't think like that. If it is the worst there's all sorts that they can do. Cosmetic surgery and the like. People won't even know. They do amazing stuff now. We'll find out about it and I'll help you. We can fight this together and we will.'

As I said the last thing I banged my hand down on the table and everybody in the café stopped speaking and looked at me. I stared back. Blow them, I was going to support my friend.

Later that night we went into 'The Boot' to meet up with the others. It was our usual Wednesday night ritual. I asked Ros what she wanted to do, and she said that she wanted to tell everybody. She didn't seem to think that there was any point in keeping quiet about it. She would be in and out having treatment, so why not tell people what was going on? I was worried about that bit. Some people can be a little bit funny about things like that. Turns out that I was right to be apprehensive.

Ros was trying to be light-hearted about it all as she told them her news.

'So,' she said, 'it looks like I've got cancer and I'm going to have an op and then probably chemo and radiotherapy. It'll be a few months but hopefully I'll be back soon.'

You could have heard a pin drop. Nobody said anything. Some didn't even look at her, whilst others simply stared at her as if she was an alien or something. There was coughing, shuffling of feet but nothing else. A couple of them found that they had suddenly forgotten a meeting somewhere and left in a hurry.

Eventually Jill spoke and said something like 'Oh, that's rotten luck'. I can't remember exactly what she said because by this time I was absolutely raging. What the hell was the matter with these people? They moved away and then started speaking to each other in low voices. It was quite obvious that nobody wanted to talk about it with Ros. Perhaps if they ignored it, they could pretend that it wasn't happening. Ros and I stood at the edge of the group, dumbfounded at their callous reaction. It felt as if we were carrying some infectious disease. I wanted to say something, tell them exactly what I thought of them, but Ros stopped me as I began to speak.

'Don't,' she said. 'At least we know who our friends are.'

'None of that bloody lot,' I replied. 'Well, that's that. They can all get lost. What the hell's the matter with them?'

Ros started her treatment. Her hair fell out and she looked really thin and pale. Sometimes she could laugh about things but sometimes she became very sad. A couple of times she was really angry, cursing the world and his wife. One day we were having a walk in a local park and she just started punching a tree, punch after punch, crying and cursing as she did so. I wasn't sure what to do. I just stood by and watched her for a bit but when her hand started to bleed I gently stepped in and held her and we both cried until we could cry no more.

I went with her to see the specialist and I was there as he told her that there was nothing more that he could do. The cancer was terminal. It was odd. Ros sat with a smile on her face, like he'd told her that she'd just won the lottery. I suppose that she had but it wasn't one that either of us particularly wanted to win.

We went to the pub and the old gang were there. One or two of them waved and a couple came over to ask Ros how she was. She shut them up very quickly.

'I'm dying,' she said. 'There's no further treatment.'

It was the same as last time. We were avoided as much as possible. I tried to understand. Perhaps it was all too hard for them to take in. They were young, they had their life in front of them. People such as we didn't die young. Not of disease anyway.

I stayed with Ros as she underwent treatment. She was estranged from her family and I said that maybe we should contact them, but Ros didn't want me to. They'd more or less kicked her out of the home whilst she was at uni and she hadn't forgiven them. She could be so stubborn at times. It didn't matter what I said, she just refused.

'I was too wild for them, but they wouldn't even try to understand. Just criticise, criticise all of the time. I don't want them around me now. You're supposed to be at peace when you die, right?' she'd said looking at me with those brilliant eyes of hers.

'Ok, I get that but they're going to have to know at some point. Wouldn't it be better to tell them?'

'I'll think about it,' she'd said. That was her way of ending any conversation which she didn't really want to have. I knew better than to argue with her when she was in that sort of mood.

I was with Ros watching the rain spatter the window. It was the half-term holidays, so I was able to be Head Nurse for a while. She'd had a bad week and had spent most of the time throwing up. She wasn't eating much, and spent a lot of the time asleep, curled up into a ball on her bed. She woke up with a bit of a start and looked at me. I had my 'are you ok' look on.

'I've just had the most peculiar dream,' she said. 'I saw my Granny and she was smiling at me and she had her arms open, like she was wanting to give me a hug. Granny died ten years ago. I adored her. We used to have such fun when I was little. Got up to all sorts. I know now that she's waiting for me.'

She spoke with a trace of wonder in her voice, as if she couldn't quite believe it.

'When I get to heaven,' she'd said, 'I'm going to find her. That's the first thing I'll do when I get there.'

Then she turned over and went back to sleep, but she had a little smile on her face, and she looked really contented.

I wasn't sure whether I had done the right thing, but I did contact her Mum later. I'd found a phone number in Ros's stuff and I decided to ring it. When I think about that call now it seems weird. Like an out of body experience. I explained what was happening to her daughter, but she sounded very cold about it all.

'Rosamund,' she said, 'Hasn't had anything to do with us for some time. I'm afraid that we disagreed rather seriously with her life choices and she decided to make her own way in the world. Thank you for letting me know. Do you need anything? Money or anything like that?'

'No thank you. She's getting good care, and everything is covered from that point of view.'

I couldn't believe what I was hearing. She'd treated me as if I was somebody trying to find out if she'd had an accident that wasn't her fault. So cold and icily polite. How do things get to be so bad that your own mother no longer wants anything to do with you, even when you're dying? I said that I'd keep in touch and let her know and then the call ended. I sat for a while staring at the mobile in my hand, pinching myself that what had happened had really happened. But that was that. Ros wasn't part of her family's world and, as far as her mother was concerned, she no longer existed.

It's been six months now and Ros is still hanging on in there. She has good days and bad days and some that are in-between. We both know that the outcome is inevitable, so, when I'm not at work, we spend our time reading and playing silly games. Sometimes, when she feels a little better, we totter out to the park or we go to see a film. We don't see much of the gang, although Jill did come round with some flowers a few days ago. She told us that they'd had a whip round and that everybody had contributed. A way of salving their conscience I suppose. She started to gossip about one of the other girls, but Ros stopped her short.

'You know, Jill, on the give a tossometer that rates as roughly minus five thousand.'

Jill reddened and changed the subject and I stifled a smile. Ros was never going to change and, I reasoned, why the hell should she? She would go out of the world in the same way as she'd come into it – shouting, kicking, looking red in the face and being true to herself. And as far as I was concerned, that was the best way to be.

Short Story Review 2020

When I Was a Boy

Colin Kerr

'I always wanted to jump out of an airplane,' said Mr. Tempest after a minute. 'The idea terrifies me, but my grandad was in the Paras in the war. I wanted to feel the way he felt. Falling. Live or die, it's up to me. Until I pull that chord, I'm free, nothing else matters. Because until I pull that cord there is nothing else. I want to experience what he felt.'

There was a pause. Mr. Tempest tried to look over his shoulder at Holly.

'Go on,' she said. The platform creaked as she moved her weight.

Mr. Tempest thought for another moment. 'I don't want to be shot at as I fall. But the rest of it I want to experience. And grandad jumped at night - I'd like to see what I'm falling towards. But the rest of it. That's something I always wanted to do. What has this got to do with carving a chair?' Mr. Tempest tried to look over his shoulder again. Through his clothes he could feel the light touch of Holly's hand at the nape of his neck and the base of his spine.

'I try to capture a little bit of you, of what makes you just you and nobody else, and let that guide the way I carve. Sometimes it guides the choice of wood. There you are, Mr. Tempest, measurements done,' said Holly, writing the length and breadth of Mr. Tempest's back in her notebook before folding her tape measure.

A cloud-freed flare of sunlight, broken by the window sash, cast beams through the workshop. They picked out dust floating lazily in the morning air. Instinctively Mr. Tempest waved his hand as if to wipe away the light.

'What happens now?' he asked, stepping down from the wooden platform Holly had him stand on for his fitting.

'Now I make a sketch of your chair. If you like the look of what I've drawn, you pay the balance, I make the chair. Takes a couple of months.'

'The balance is a lot of money.'

'For a made-to-measure, hand-carved rocking chair? It's a bargain, Mr. Tempest. You're buying a personalised work of art.'

Mr. Tempest took a few steps deeper into the workshop, letting his hand reach for, but not touch, the things around him. A half-finished owl cut from the top of a medium-thick length of trunk; a solid, high-backed wooden chair almost as tall as he was, the back and arms carved to resemble flames; a set of possibly salad spoons, their handles carved into spanners, but spanners with the texture of reptilian scales. Everywhere smelled of wood chips and sawdust. He could taste the wood in the air.

'I heard Sting has one of your chairs? It would be worth it if I can say Sting has one by the same artist,' said Mr. Tempest, licking his lips.

'You can say what you like, Mr. Tempest. I don't talk about my clients, just as I wouldn't talk about you,' said Holly. She ripped the measurements page out of her notebook and tucked it in a file on her desk. 'When you receive the sketch let me know if you want me to make the chair,' she said, her tone dismissive. She was already thinking of her next task.

Mr. Tempest opened his mouth to speak again but changed his mind. The workshop door shut behind him with a satisfyingly solid thunk followed by the after-tinkling of the broken bell.

Holly ignored his departure. She took a sheet of rough paper from a pile and a wooden box filled with sketching pencils from a drawer. She drew an open parachute, a parachutist after opening, and a sky diver in free fall. Using a second, heavier, pencil she picked out key lines from the form of each image. She crossed out the parachutist after opening and sketched a closed parachute next to it.

'Parachute seat, sky diver back, inverted open parachutes for the rockers?' she mused to herself. It didn't feel right. Was he lying? Is it not the freedom of free fall but the security of the parachute he likes? Should the back of the chair be the open parachute? She took a piece of clean paper from another drawer and started to sketch properly; with lines and curves, drawing the ghost of a chair still locked in wood. Her pencil strokes were, for a few minutes, the only sounds.

There was the thunk and after-tinkle of the door opening. A man Holly didn't recognise but who was of a familiar type – tall, middle-aged, lazy paunch, dressed casually with a regard only for the price of each item.

'Is this Two Trees Art?' he said.

Holly nodded.

'I have a return,' he said, and turned back to the door. Holly felt something inside her clench.

'Wait!' said Holly, standing. 'What do you mean, 'a return'?' But the man had not waited. She stood up and tucked her pencil into her hair.

A few minutes later he came back, holding the door open with his hip as he dragged in a large, heavy, two-seater bench inlaid with carvings of herbs and garden birds. One of the seats was slightly higher and more compact than the other, so if the person in that seat was small they would be at the same level as a person in the second seat if they were large. She recognised the piece.

When he had it inside he paused to catch his breath.

'That's Mrs. Birch's bench,' said Holly.

'Yes. I am returning it,' said the man. Holly stared at him, an eyebrow raised. 'I am her son,' the man added. 'Andrew,' he said, offering his hand to be shaken, but from across the workshop. Holly would have had to walk several steps to shake it. She did not.

'Why do you think you can return it?' said Holly. 'Is Mrs. Birch alright?'

'She's fine. She sits on it in the garden with tears in her eyes. It brings to mind my father, you see.' Only now did Andrew Birch lower his offered hand.

Holly nodded. 'She said that when we were designing it. That was why she wanted it made. What makes you think you can return it?'

'Well, it upsets her,' said Andrew Birch. Holly's eyebrow was still raised. 'I don't like to see her upset. So I am returning it.'

Holly's expression didn't change. 'I have no need for it. You'll need to dispose of it somewhere else.'

'No, I am returning it for a refund. A full refund.'

Holly's eyebrow lowered. Her face locked into a mask.

'No, you are not. Take it away when you leave,' she said. 'Thank you,' she added, as a piece of punctuation, nothing to do with thanks. Her stare had chisel-cut precision.

'I have rights, as a consumer!' said Andrew Birch.

'You do, but you haven't read them, have you? Mrs. Birch paid for my time to create a sketch and then to carve a bench. She also paid for a piece of sketch paper, some graphite, and an oak tree trunk. If you could return my time and the original tree trunk you might have a case to argue for a refund of the cost of each. But you can't. This is an individually commissioned piece of creative art, not a mass-produced office chair. Take it and go,' Holly said.

'I am a lawyer!' said Andrew Birch.

'No, you're not,' said Holly. She could tell by his reaction that she was right.

'It cost a lot of money! I want a refund!' His voice had risen a semi-tone, or possibly two.

'But you're not going to get one. Mrs. Birch knew the price before she decided to commission the piece. She was very happy with the design and the piece itself. Take it back to her.'

'She keeps sitting on it and thinking of my father,' said Andrew Birch.

'Which is why she had it made. Take it back to her.'

'But it was so expensive!'

They were standing a few feet apart, face to face, squared off, just inside the door to the workshop. A low, dark cloud had moved in front of the sun and the light through the windows was now vague and directionless. The dust particles seemed to have disappeared.

'You are wasting my time, which, as you know, I charge for,' said Holly. She crossed to the desk, picked up a pad. 'I am now writing you an invoice for my time from the moment you walked through my door to the moment you leave. Hang around as long as you want.'

Andrew stared at Holly as she took her watch off and put it on the notepad on her desk, then sat back down, patted her pockets sending out little clouds of sawdust, before remembering her pencil was tucked in her hair. She retrieved it and returned to work on the free-fall-or-parachute – should she draw both, let Mr. Tempest pick? - chair.

Andrew was not used to being ignored.

It took him a few seconds to realise Holly was going to continue to ignore him. He looked around the workshop at the carvings both complete and in progress. He was suddenly very aware of how solid, how definite, real wood can be. He swallowed. His mouth felt dry.

He took a few steps towards the owl-in-progress stump.

'How much is this one?' he asked.

Holly looked up from her sketches, staring at him over the top of the glasses she wasn't wearing.

'I work by commission, that piece belongs to a client.'

'What if I offered you more?' said Andrew Birch, running his hand over the owl's face.

'What?' said Holly.

'Offered you more than your client has agreed to pay.'

'I've told you already – my client owns that piece of wood and has bought my time to find a shape inside it. The owl is not mine to sell.'

'My wife loves owls. This would be quite a birthday present,' said Andrew Birch. 'Everything has its price,' he added.

'You actually think that?' said Holly as her head bowed and she went back to her sketching.

'Then can you make me another just like it?' said Andrew Birch. 'Or have it copied? You know, laser-scanned or something so that a machine can then cut copies of it. Mass-produce them.'

'No,' said Holly, a word delivered with the finality of an axe hitting a tree.

Her pencil made slight shhh noises as it added second dimension shadows to the image of the potential chairs before her.

Andrew was looking more closely at the owl.

'This owl is curious,' he said. 'What wood is this? It's very hard.'

'Yew,' said Holly, without looking up.

'Why is the owl curious?'

Holly stopped sketching. 'Because my client's biggest regret is she will never have time to read everything there is to read. The owl is both her love of owls and her desire to know all she can.'

'So the owl is her? Part of her? An image of her?' Andrew said, mostly to himself. 'The you within yew,' Andrew Birch added. Holly shuddered at those words, a mass market pun. She blinked to clear her mind and again went back to sketching.

'I could commission you to do something, then?' Andrew Birch said, wheels of inspiration creaking into gear. 'I could pay you to carve me something then I would own it and I could have copies made and the copyright would be mine?'

Andrew Birch's expression changed as if he thought he had said something he should not have. He looked askance at Holly, but she did not seem to be listening. He started walking round the workshop, looking at other pieces. He took out his phone, trying to hold it as if he was struggling to read something written on the screen, but really angling the built-in camera at the carving.

'Don't,' said Holly, without looking up.

'I'm sorry?' said Andrew Birch.

'Don't take any photographs. This is a workshop full of tools and I'd hate for one of them to accidentally damage your phone.' Holly said this whilst looking past Andrew at what turned out to be a small lump-hammer resting on a workbench.

'I –' Andrew Birch felt a whole speech form in his mind, a speech about rights, and how threats of violence could not be condoned, probably with a bit about how outraged he was at being talked to in this manner. But something stopped him.

He put the phone away. He put his hands in his pockets too, so as not to be led into temptation.

He was looking at a chair, a huge chair standing nearly two metres tall, carved of thick, heavy wood in the shape of living flames. His expression said there was something about it. That it impressed him. That he thought it would impress others.

'That's ten minutes so far. Twenty quid and counting. Will it be cash or card when you settle up?' said Holly.

Andrew Birch gave up and went back to the bench he had brought with him.

'Would you mind giving me a hand with this to the car?' he said.

'You seemed to get it in without any problem,' said Holly.

Andrew Birch pulled the bench to the door, opened it, held the door open with his foot, and manipulated the bench out.

'Before you get any bright ideas about getting that bench copied can I recommend reading the contract your mother signed?' Holly called after him. 'Shall I invoice you care of her?'

Thunk. After-tinkle.

Holly put down her pencil and stretched her finger, her arms, her back. She hated conflict, but she had learned the least unpleasant way of dealing with it was quickly. She rolled her shoulders, stretched her neck, looking as she did so at the two emergent sketches of Mr. Tempest's possible rocking chair. The one where the back was in the shape of an open parachute, the rest of the chair fairly conventional. The other where the back was reminiscent of a sky-diver in free fall; the rockers were the tops of two up-turned parachute shapes; the seat was an unopened, packed parachute. Two possible futures, nothing at all existed until one had been eliminated.

Holly was fairly certain Mr. Tempest would pick the first design. But until he did, she would nurture hope that he would pick the second. She took a lighter pencil from the box and went back to work. Outside the clouds had moved on and the sunlight through the windows was picking out the gently floating dust in the air once more.

The Initiate

Alan McClure

Honourable Mention

Sounds: footsteps crunching over broken glass; the buzz of an intercom, metallic crackle as the handset is lifted in an upstairs flat, but no speech; sharp click as the door is unlocked. He is guided into an echoing stairwell and urged, almost gently, towards the stairs. Sweat pricks his forehead under the blindfold and the smell of stale urine is sharp in his nostrils as he climbs, step by step.

One landing. Two. Three. And stop.

'This way.' He feels the breeze of an open window and hears dogs fighting below, then another door is opened and he is pushed through into sudden warmth and a carpet-muffled hubbub. A TV in a nearby room is silenced as the blindfold is pulled off and he finds himself blinking in a dim corridor. It's not what he'd pictured.

'Bring him through,' says a gruff voice from the room at the end of the corridor. Mike, who has guided him this far, rests a hand on his shoulder and answers his glance with a nod. They go through. They enter a room with large windows on two walls (corner flat, he thinks), tastefully decorated - furniture plain but good quality, lush patterned rug over deeply polished floorboards, pale walls interrupted here and there with art prints and mirrors. He notes the details, but these unremarkable surroundings serve only to frame the room's only occupant, who sits upright in a straight-backed chair, unnervingly still, hands bunched into fists on his knees.

'You the boy knows Connolly?' The voice is cold, the stare piercing.

'Aye.'

'The fuck you doing here?' This is an unexpected question. He had been summoned and so imagined the seated man must know the answer better than he did himself.

'Em, Mike says, you know, you might have a bit of work for me...?' He glances at Mike, who is staring fixedly out the window.

The seated man still hasn't moved, hasn't broken his stare. 'And why the fuck would one of Connolly's boys want to work for me?' This was closer to the script: Mike had warned him he might be asked something of the kind.

'I'm not one of Connolly's...'

'You're from Thornbank, aye?'

'Aye.'

'Well that make's you one of Connolly's, if you know it or not.' The blank eyes boring into him won't let him break the gaze, but he can sense other people in an adjoining room. He begins to worry.

'Listen, I've no fucking loyalty to Connolly, okay? The fucker sells coke outside the primary school. My wee nephew goes there, it's out of fucking order.' The seated man, John McAllister, stands up and walks towards him till he's nose to nose. Still staring - don't blink, don't flinch. A minute passes.

The war between the Thornbank team and the Hawsden Boys had

been escalating over the past year. Tensions had always existed, particularly in the border between the two territories - a border which a casual observer would miss completely but which was indelibly engraved in the minds of the protagonists. Of late, though, a number of attacks and reprisals had led to civilian casualties and a rising panic in the local press. The number of no-go areas had increased, leaving several families stranded, bewildered in the middle of a tide of vandalism, violence and petty crime. The most noteworthy incident had been the daylight shooting of Collum Dickie, McAllister's predecessor as the top boy in Hawsden. He had been a legendary hard man and a nasty piece of work, but the general impression was that Dod Connolly, the Thornbank boss, was the up and coming gangster and the man to watch and avoid. McAllister was as yet untested: so far, though, he seems pretty impressive.

'Okay.' He breathes again. 'Your name, son?'

'I'm Paul. Paul Wallace.' A flicker.

'You anything to do with Jenny Wallace?'

'Aye, Jenny's my big sister.' There's the flash of a smile on McAllister's face, quickly gone.

'Went to school with Jenny. Good lass. For Thornbank.' Paul doesn't know what to make of this so he waits. McAllister returns to his seat and beckons Paul to sit on the couch. As he does he notices Mike has gone - where did he go?

'Listen Paul. You're in big fucking trouble son. Just coming here, ho, that's you.' McAllister makes a cut-throat gesture. 'Curtains. And you know what? I don't mean Connolly. I mean me. You're double fucked son.'

Paul swallows. 'I don't...'

'You see,' says McAllister, ignoring the interruption, 'either you're here because Connolly sent you, in which case I'll kill you. Or you're here because you want to piss on his chips, and he'll kill you - or, if you don't manage to piss on his chips, I'll kill you. How does that sound?'

Paul is sweating now but this is nothing he hadn't expected. 'Look, Mr. McAllister, I'm not exactly sure what I can do for you. But I sure as fuck can't do anything for Dod Connolly. That lump of shite has turned Thornbank into a fucking war zone, and he's the last person to suffer for it. It's kids, man, kids in the streets are getting shot at. Anyone doesn't pay homage to the greasy wee shite, they're targeted. People's fucking grans are getting bricks through the window.' Paul is angry, genuinely angry, and part of him is pleased at how clearly this must be showing. Anyway, McAllister seems convinced.

'What makes you think I'm any different?' Now this was unexpected and Paul hasn't even asked himself that question. He thinks for a minute, growing surer that other ears are listening nearby.

'To be honest, I couldn't give a fuck. I don't live here. I live in Thornbank. Anybody can do anything to get that wee toerag off his high-horse, I'll be quite happy.' McAllister looks at him. Those are cold eyes, cold, hard eyes.

'Meaning, whatever it takes?'

Paul swallows again, nods. McAllister holds the gaze a second longer then turns to the open door leading into the adjoining room. 'Okay boys, in you come,' he says. Five men come in and stand behind Paul. Mike isn't one of them.

'Right boys. We've a new friend. Paul.' Short silence. 'Paul. We're not pissing about here. Things bad in Thornbank? Well, they're fucking dreadful in Hawsden. The place is a fucking mess, boy. That's Connolly too. So we're about to change things. Really, fucking, change things. This is endgame time.'

Paul shifts in his seat. No-one knows where he is, there are five heavy breathers standing behind him and the lean-faced man in front of him is looking slightly unhinged.

'Speaking of folks' grans. Connolly's gran. Know where she lives?'

'Listen, I...'

'Answer the fucking question.'

Dod Connolly's grandmother had been the subject of a particularly hysterical example of the recent spate of newspaper articles on the trouble. Some editor somewhere had clearly felt that Dod Connolly, drug baron, murderer and vicious piece of shit that he was, was insufficiently horrific on his own merits. The answer? To contrast his lifestyle with that of his one surviving relative, his grandmother. She led a life of disappointed respectability, appalled at her grandson's doings, in a terraced house on the west side. The human interest just leaped off the page.

'She was in the paper,' Paul says. He doesn't like the way this is going.

'She was in the paper. You're right.' The five figures behind him shift, apparently getting restive. 'So Connolly likes to involve people's grannies in his business, does he?' Paul doesn't answer. 'I've got a job for you.' Shit. Shit. 'A token of your goodwill, like!' This was a bad idea. What the fuck has he got into? 'Aye, a wee jaunt to the west end, I think. And listen son. Fuck this up? It'll be the last thing you ever do.'

***

One horrible hour later and he's standing between a rhododendron bush and a potted bay tree, finger on the doorbell. Whatever he had expected from his visit to Hawsden, this was worse. So much worse. The bell rings, an old fashioned ding dong.

For a minute nothing happens and he hopes beyond hope that there's no-one home. Not that that would save him. ('He's stuck now. Something Connolly wouldn't have the balls for in a fucking century.' McAllister had been standing again, gloating with his plan. 'That wee shite wouldn't have thought of this! This is going to change every-fucking-thing.')

Through the frosted glass of the front door, Paul sees movement. She's home. The movement is slow, punctuated. He guesses that each step necessitates the slow lifting of a zimmer frame. Her hunched shape looms closer. He wants to turn and run. He has nowhere to go.

Stick to the script. Choice is a thing of the past now. He knows what he has to do. McAllister was very, very clear about that.

The old woman is now close enough to make out a reddish shawl. She looks pixelated, like she's been blurred to protect her identity. Zimmer lifts, falls. She shuffles closer.

'Just a minute,' calls a wavery wee voice which sounds distressingly like his own grandmother's. (Stick to the script!) Four sparrows create a brief whirlwind of brown feathers as they chase each other round the foliage to his right. A vapour trail bisects the sky above him. He shakes.

Her hand reaches out, undoes the latch, chain and mortise lock in slow succession. Then she grasps the handle, pulls it down and the door swings open. Keen grey eyes look up at him and he can feel a trickle of sweat run down his back.

'Yes?' she says, politely inquiring. He knows what to say.

'Mrs. Connolly?'

'Yes?' As if she could be anyone else. He feels short of breath.

'Mrs. Connolly...' He can't do it! It won't work! What if he's seen?

'What can I do for you son?' asks the nice old woman before him. He braces himself. He really has no choice. There is only one outcome here. He follows the script.

***

Forty five minutes later, Paul Wallace is back at the old woman's house. The sparrows are still squabbling in the rhododendron. He doesn't ring the bell - he has the key now. He lets himself in. Through the vestibule, down the musty corridor. Into the kitchen. In a chair by the kitchen table is the figure of Mrs. Connolly - right where he left her.

He has been carrying two loaded bags of groceries and he lifts them onto the table. The old lady looks up.

'Here's your shopping, Mrs. Connolly,' he says.

***

Reprisals were slow in coming. It was generally assumed that the Thornbank Team had been slowed by their total disbelief. When the response came, however, it was spectacular.

In the dead of night, McAllister's entire street was attacked. Fences which had long lain broken and rusty were mended and painted. Dog-shit was cleared from grass verges and broken glass was disposed of carefully. The front door of McAllister's flat was sanded down and repainted and the graffiti stained walls were whitewashed. It was a humbling display of influence, and many of the Hawsden gang feared that a total loss of face had been inflicted.

John McAllister had other ideas. The very next day, the wasteground at the very heart of Thornbank was declared off limits as scores of dangerous men barred every entrance. Some were unabashedly armed. Any of Connolly's footsoldiers that came near were quickly sent packing. All they could report back was a great deal of noise coming from the wasteground, and a regular convoy of vans arriving and departing. When, at four in the morning, Connolly had finally assembled a retaliatory force big enough to evict the intruders they found them already gone, and in their wake, a staggering sight.

The wasteground was transformed. It had been flawlessly turfed. Saplings had been planted in winding avenues from the neighbouring streets to the centre of the ground, where there now stood a gleaming playground for kids - there were swings, slides, a climbing frame and a pirate ship. Park benches were sensitively placed around the new park, one bearing a brass plaque, the inscription reading, 'Dedicated to the people of Thornbank, with respect, from the Hawsden Boys'.

Dod Connolly was incandescent.

This new phase of the troubles was relentless. Stray dogs were taken from Hawsden, trained as guide dogs and donated to charities for the blind. A mobile library made ever-more daring forays into Thornbank, improving literacy levels among primary school children and serving as a meeting point for previously disaffected families. Broken streetlights in Hawsden were mended and decked out with colourful bunting, raising the spirits of all but the furious gangsters. Thornbank junkies were covertly contacted and taken to an excellent rehabilitation centre in Switzerland, at great expense. Many returned cured and reformed, and determined to make their community safe and prosperous. The pitted and broken roads and pavements of Hawsden were exquisitely resurfaced in the small hours of the morning. Teenagers from both sides were given travel grants by their antagonists, encouraged to go and see the world and do some voluntary work overseas. The police were nowhere to be seen.

Paul Wallace continued to get Mrs. Connolly's groceries, twice a week, despite regular written threats from her less-than-grateful grandson. McAllister had also employed a live-in carer for her, as well as a chef and a housekeeper. The old woman was very pleased, though rather mystified, at the way her life had changed of late. By the time the chauffeur-driven car appeared, she had almost come to expect such things.

When both territories had been forcibly improved to the point of being unrecognizable, there were few gestures left the gangs could make. Freshly washed cars sparkled on every street. Billboards displayed fine art. Gifted musicians provided live music from a proliferation of covertly-erected bandstands. Hawsden claimed the moral victory by being the first to hand all their weapons in to the police. Thornbank quickly followed suit, and trumped them by exposing all the main drug routes into the city and effectively bringing the trade to an end.

And, eventually, the border between the two territories disappeared completely. The war was over.

Short Story Review 2020

Breathing Backwards

Yasmine Lever

Mia sat on a blue cushion on the window ledge. Rodney paced nervously beside her, looking out at the purple Tisch School of The Arts flag hanging from the building across the street. They held plastic glasses of seltzer water with ice in their hand flavored with wedges of lemon. Vampire Weekend blared from the speakers.

They were at a party in Rodney's aunt Melora's NoHo loft, a raw space with exposed brick walks and glorious high ceilings. Melora had purchased the loft with money she made in her twenties and thirties starring in the soap opera, As the World Turns.

'Any news?' The question had been raging inside Rodney all evening.

Mia shook her head.

Rodney chewed on his thumbnail. 'Not even the slightest sign of...?'

'No.'

Outside pedestrians passed on the street below, hoodies and umbrellas protecting them from the drizzle.

'What if...' Mia interrupted his reverie.

'Don't even.'

'I'm just saying.'

'We can't think like that.'

Your thoughts become your reality. Hadn't this idea been drummed into their heads every single day for three months during the lecture following morning meditation? Mia threw him a dejected look.

Rodney and Mia had rocked up to Lifeskills on the same day. Lifeskills was a ninety-day Extended Care Program in Florida, a program which eased patients back into the real world following the safety of their thirty day stay battling their addiction in Primary. Rodney was an alcoholic. Mia favored smack.

Lifeskills was nothing like those ritzy programs in Malibu with daily yoga classes and personal chefs. At Lifeskills the patients worked part time. So, every day after group, Mia and Rodney grabbed a sandwich before changing into their brown polyester uniforms and rushing to the local Winn Dixie where they stood side by side stocking the supermarket shelves and flirting. At Lifeskills sexual contact was strictly forbidden. Sneaking around made it even more thrilling.

They graduated on the same day. They had been back in New York for six weeks. Rodney rented a basement from an African American family on Alexander Avenue in the Bronx. Mia lived in a sober female apartment on Broadway and 100th Street, a short ride from Rodney on the A train.

'I'm sorry.' Rodney came to sit beside Mia on the ledge.

'For what?'

'For being so careless.'

'It's not your fault.'

A couple of guests strode past. The woman, probably in her thirties, had dyed purple hair and wore a pink dress, bra strap showing underneath her short sleeves. She emitted a sharp scent. She held the hand of a blond boy in his twenties with a wide-open face wearing bottle green jeans and a white vest.

'Your outfits match,' the boy said in a light Southern accent.

'Not intentionally,' Rodney said.

The couple collapsed into a nearby love seat.

Rodney had been wearing a red tartan shirt when he came to pick Mia up from work. Mia had greeted him wearing a red tartan shirt-dress she bought after working her shift that day at Screaming Mimi's, the second hand store on The Bowery.

Mia leaned in. 'What if another week goes by and I still haven't got my period.'

'Please don't be so pessimistic.' Rodney swigged his seltzer. It wouldn't happen. It couldn't happen. The most drastic problem in their lives during this fragile stage in their early recovery needed to be accidentally wearing a similar outfit to a party.

Mia picked a dainty snack from a silver tray, and shoved it whole into her mouth. 'I pissed on a stick.'

Rodney could see smoked salmon and soggy bread mingling in her mouth.

'Actually, I pissed on three sticks,' Mia said. 'Clear plus every time.'

Rodney's breathing became jagged. 'Clear plus? What does that mean?'

'It means I'm pregnant.'

Rodney felt like a switch had been flicked in the back deck of his brain.

'How long have you known?'

'I took all three tests before breakfast.'

'Mia!'

'Yeah?' Her brown eyes widened.

A cocktail of tangled feelings gripped his insides. 'Clear plus every time?'

A cloud settled over her face.

Rodney grabbed a cheese ball and popped it in his mouth. Gooey cheese dripped out of a circle of dough and slid down his throat.

'This. You and me. It can't last right?' Mia's cherry lips twisted into a pout of feigned indifference, but her eyes dared hope as if her energy was simultaneously opening and closing.

'Yes.' Rodney hands grabbed his dark gelled hair. 'I mean no. No. It can't last.'

Mia fiddled with the amber pendant hanging from a piece of leather string around her neck. Rodney had bought the pendant from a street vendor in Soho, right before they attended their first twelve step meeting in the city.

'We're just too bored addicts in early recovery, right?' Mia gestured in a nonchalant fashion.

'Two bored addicts trying to escape our fucking boredom.'

He looked at Mia sitting, spine straight, legs crossed at the knee, a spirited twenty-two-year-old woman in the process of replacing the droopy shame-filled misfit who had first rocked up to Lifeskills.

'I mean we've had some fun,' she said.

'You've made every single day of mine a lot of fun,' he said.

Rodney wanted to stand up and move away from the ledge but he felt like someone had stapled his jeans to the cushion that he sat on. He looked out at the guests. People laughing, sparkling, flirting, accompanied by sexy music beats. Mia tapped a black stiletto ankle boot in time to the music. Rodney drummed on his jeans with his fingers. The guests sipped their cocktails, gorgeous colors shimmering in their glasses. Rodney turned away. He longed for the simplicity of Lifeskills. He missed standing in a circle singing 'Lean On Me' before the morning meditation every day. He missed sticking pins in the Feeling Map once he'd identified his feeling from the feeling chart. He especially missed ducking into the bathroom to have sex with Mia during the Saturday evening dances at Club Soda.

'You don't think...' The rest of the question suspended on his tongue tip.

'What?'

'I mean we shouldn't...' His words damming in his throat. He sipped his iced water.

David Bowie's voice gobbled the air.

Before going to rehab, Rodney had drummed in a promising indie rock band. They fired him because he got so drunk he would sometimes fall asleep on stage, drum sticks hovering in his hands.

Mia stared straight ahead. Guitar notes buzzed from the speakers into the space. 'What would you say, Rodney, if I told you that I'm not a fan of murder?'

Rodney spat a piece of ice straight back into his glass. 'Murder? That sounds so fucking moralistic.'

'I don't mean that in a moralistic sense. It's just that I had an abortion when I was seventeen. And it completely broke my heart.'

He could feel Mia's eyes on him watching his reaction. He attempted not to gape. He gazed into the party, his brain rattling. A woman in a dark linen dress leaned in close to another woman with greying cornbraids. A young woman wearing purple hip huggers lounged on the orange couch. A group of stylish types dove their hands into dishes of Doritos and mixed nuts.

Rodney caught sight of his Aunt Melora standing at the kitchen counter, her movements restricted in her white leather dress. She raised a thumb in his direction. He sensed the thumb was raised in question so he answered with two decisive raised thumbs back. He remembered Aunt Melora telling him that she had had an abortion when she was twenty-four even though her boyfriend begged her to keep the baby. Then, in her late thirties, the stress of trying and failing to get pregnant had ended her ten-year marriage to another man. Rodney was twenty-three now, one year older than Mia, one year younger than Melora had been when she got pregnant. But parents? Mia and himself? Didn't they need to spend every ounce of energy they had putting the lives they had trashed back together?

Since returning to the city, Rodney had found work as a housepainter, supplementing his income playing gigs as a paid drummer. Mia hoped that Screaming Mimi's would help train her eye to become a buyer. When feeling positive, Rodney liked to think their futures held a ton of promise. But when a cloud hovered, Rodney thought of himself as a hopeless fucking case.

He stared down at the dark needle imprints on the hard wood floor. The loft was in a converted sewing factory. 'I don't know if I can, Mia.'

'I'm not forcing you to do anything. I'm just saying that I've made my choice.'

Her choice? Rodney had always been a staunch supporter of a woman's right to choose what she did with her body. But he'd always considered the argument through the lens of the woman choosing termination. How crazy was he not to realize that a woman's right to choose might mean she would choose to keep the child?

He thought of his mother after his father had bolted from the family, coming home from work every night and collapsing on the couch with a bottle of gin, oblivious to Rodney and his older brother.

'Bringing up a baby, Mia. It's so hard.'

'I'll tough it out.'

Rodney imagined the soft curves of a gurgling baby in his arms. He heard the gurgling transforming into a howl. He envisioned himself failing to control his frustration and punching a wall when he couldn't take his baby's screaming any longer.

'I don't know if I can,' he said.

'I think you can.'

Rodney pictured himself and Mia putting furniture into a two-bedroom apartment in Queens then painting the baby's bedroom walls an aqua blue. He imagined himself coming home from work and sneaking a peak at his sleeping child. Then another feeling held him down, drowning out the peaceful scene he'd conjured. If he were back at Lifeskills staring at the Feeling Map he would stick his pin firmly into Terror.

'I don't have the guts, Mia.'

A young blond woman wearing a gaudy skirt and thigh length boots stalked past with a handsome man with heavy cheeks, hair greying at the temples. They left the apartment together.

'I mean I just can't.' Rodney felt mortified by his admission.

'Understood.' Mia's dismissive tone failed to camouflage the ache he caught in her eye.

'You're looking at me like I'm messing with your dream.'

'You're not shattering my...' Her voice wobbled. 'You're not messing with my...' She rose. 'I've got to go.'

'No! Wait!'

Mia put on her jacket 'I can't.'

'Can I come with you?'

'This is your aunt's party. It's rude if you leave.' Mia stormed towards the door.

Rodney rushed after her grabbing her arm. 'You make me really happy, Mia.'

'You make me really happy too.' Her mouth downturned, tears pooling then falling, smudging her eyeliner.

She shook her arm free and attempted to dodge past him but once again he blocked her.

'Me making you happy. That could change like that.' Rodney snapped his thumb and third finger.

'It won't.'

'You say that now.'

'I mean it.'

'In two years, Mia, you'll be sick of the sight of me. You'll be sick of the baby. In two years, you'll wake up every morning sick to death of every aspect of your motherfucking life. At first, you'll only fuck around a little bit. But then it will escalate.'

Mia's cheeks reddened. 'I'm not your dad!' She grabbed his shoulder, scrunching his shirt in her hands.

A woman sipping her drink through a straw turned to look them. Rodney twisted his lips into an agonized smile.

He turned back to Mia. His voice dropped to a whisper. 'Less than a year ago I was drinking a bottle of vodka before noon and robbing houses. And you were sleeping at your dealer's.'

'We're changing.'

'You can't wipe away our past just because you're pregnant. What if you start shooting up again? Or me? What if I go back to drinking? How would you like our kid to find their dad kneeling at the toilet every morning?'

'At least our kid will exist.'

Prince blared into the space. People danced, whoops of pleasure filling the air, Aunt Melora among the jostling throng. Aunt Melora waved. Rodney and Mia waved back. Rodney couldn't imagine anyone in this room dancing and singing along to 'Lean On Me' with the same passion.

'We'll be crap parents, Mia.'

'Stop it.' Mia shoved him away.

Mia turned to face the brick wall. She stretched her mouth wide then released it. She repeated this pattern several times pulling exaggerated smiles.

'Are you okay?'

She pulled another exaggerated smile. 'Micro Managing Michelle told me about this really crazy study.'

Micro Managing Michelle was the nickname given to one of the therapists, Michelle. She was the kind of control freak she brought a stopwatch into group to time all the patients' shares.

Mia spoke with difficulty as she continued to stretch and unstretch her mouth. ' In this crazy study, people with severe anxiety were forced to go through a completely artificial exercise of pretending to smile. After a while they felt better. So even though their brain was telling them they were depressed, because their facial muscles kept smiling...' She pulled another smile. 'They decided they didn't actually feel all that atrocious. It's called facial feedback hypothesis.'

Rodney watched Mia twisting her lips into grotesque grins. The last thing in the world he wanted to do was upset her. The last thing he wanted to do was leave Mia hanging in her torture.

'Babies cry, Mia. Babies cry a lot.'

'I know.'

'Babies cry all the fucking time.'

'I have seen a baby before.' She buttoned her jacket. 'I have to do this, Rodney. I have to. There's no room inside me for any more regret.' Mia careened towards the exit, stiletto boots digging into the floor, rejection trailing behind her.

Rodney felt a stunning sense of loneliness burning his stomach.

No room for any more regret? Mia's words howled inside his brain. He darted for the door like a clumsy puffin.

She stood in the narrow hallway waiting for the elevator, sobbing.

Rodney dropped to one knee. 'Mia.'

'Whoa.' Mia leapt backwards.

'Mia will you...'

'Oh shit.' Her hand covered her mouth.

'Mia will you marry me?'

'Shut up.'

'What?'

'Sorry. I mean no. I mean what era do you fucking think we're living in?'

The elevator dinged. The door creaked open and the blond girl in the garish skirt and the older man burst out of it stinking of cigarette smoke. Rodney still cowered on one knee. The couple darted along the corridor and back inside the party, the man throwing them an uncertain smile.

'Please get up, Rodney.'

'You're pregnant.'

'No shit.'

'I'm trying to save your ass.'

'You don't have to save my ass.'

'You need a ring.'

'I don't need a ring.'

'I need a ring.' His voice broke. He felt like he was breathing backwards.

'No, you don't.'

'Yes, I do. If we're going to do this then I need a ring.' Rodney leaned back against the wall turning his cheek trying to hide his tears.

Mia slid down against the wall to sit beside him. She placed her hand on the back of his neck. 'Something's happened to us both. Something huge. And it's totally screwed up the timing of...And screwed with our heads.'

Her hand felt soothing.

Rodney choked back sobs. 'What if the baby's part of second chances?'

'Yes. But the beautiful bits. Can't we take them one step at a time?'

The hallways smelled of something sweet. Maybe burned meringue?

Rodney kissed Mia. She tasted of fish and lemon.

'So... I dunno...What happens next?'

'I'm going to get stupid fat when this thing inside me grows. And I'm going to be moody as fuck. And I'm gonna crave all kinds of ridiculous foods like...eggs covered in maple syrup or broccoli and Cheetos. And I'm going to drink gallons and gallons of chocolate milk with salt. And then we're going to give birth to a tiny energetic stalker who is going to follow us everywhere we go.'

'That sounds terrifying.'

'I'm shitting massive bricks.'

Rodney rose and put his hand out to help Mia up. Arm in arm they reentered the party. Mia walked over to the window ledge and sat on the empty, blue cushion. Rodney hovered beside her. Outside the rain seemed to have stopped.

He could feel her breathing slowing down. He could feel his own breathing slowing also. He put a hand around her back. Her back felt warm.

His head made room for another dream.

Through a Keyhole

Katie Lewis

It took us about a year to realise the Goodies had disappeared. It should have taken longer, but we weren't known for sticking to their rules. We just had to be careful when straying from the colony was all: the Goodies liked their Kill on Sight policy.

But there. We'd noticed it was getting easier to stray but it wasn't till trackers went to the nearest Goodie village and found reports of a deadly disease that we realised what had happened. We were worried at first, but nobody got sick, and the Goodies didn't return. Then we were ecstatic.

Until someone pointed out that the bodies were missing. The Goodies were gone, but they weren't necessarily dead.

In the end, we decided to expand slowly. Our tribe went east, through the forest, till we found a city. It was eerily silent, as though not even ghosts ventured there. The size astonished me – it went on for miles. And the buildings were huge, with cars, computers, and even heating. At first, we spread ourselves out, but we were used to close quarters, so we took over a neighbourhood instead. And with all the tinned food, clothes, and bottled water we found, we knew we could stay for ages. It was our world now.

Everything changed after two months. The tribe sent us out scavenging. I liked it. Seeing how the Goodies had lived was fascinating: they'd had so much.

I was exploring a fancy house when I passed a sturdy door. I tried to open it but it was shut tight.

'Hello?'

I froze.

'Is someone there?'

I peeked through the keyhole. A brown eye peeked back. 'Hello?'

'How did you get out?'

'What?'

'You'll get sick.'

'I'll–' It clicked. 'You a Goodie?'

'A what?'

I grinned. 'You are. And you're stuck.'

'What? Who are you?'

'The daughter of people you sent to die in the colony.'

'Huh? Isn't it just criminals there? Kids get removed.'

'Sure. Shot on sight.'

'Really?' She sounded troubled. 'That … OK. But I don't understand. Can't you see the seeds?'

'The what?'

'They look like dandelion burrs.'

I looked around. 'Yeah. Why?'

'They carry the illness.'

I frowned. 'Well, I feel fine.'

'Really?'

'Yeah.' I grinned. 'Guess we're immune.'

'Why do you sound so happy?'

I shrugged, though she couldn't see. 'My sister died 'cause the Goodies wouldn't give us medicine. Nice to see the tables turned.' In the distance, Matty shouted my name. 'Anyway. I'm out of here.'

'Oh. OK.' A pause. 'But could you ... tell me what it's like out there?'

'Huh?'

'Just ... it's been so long. You don't have to. I'm sorry, this was stupid.'

I hesitated. 'It ... It's sunny. A few clouds in the sky, a light breeze. Not too hot or cold. I saw a cat nearby, half feral but it's doing alright.' Curiosity got the better of me. 'What are you eating in there?'

'Worried about the cat?'

I snorted, despite everything. 'Really?'

'No. They didn't come down. But lots of tins. Some stuff we've grown underground. There was a bunker here, readymade for the apocalypse apparently. We were waiting for a cure but even the people who went in full bodysuits didn't return. And nobody's brave enough to try again.'

'So, you'd rather die down there?'

'I ... I don't know.' A pause. 'I'm Efa, by the way.'

I hesitated. 'Callen. Cally. Dad killed someone in a burglary, Mum killed an abusive boyfriend.'

'Er. OK. My dad was a firefighter and Mum worked in a bank?'

I laughed, and Efa laughed too. 'Too much?'

'A little. How old are you anyway?'

'About twenty. You?'

'Same.'

'Cally. I've been yelling for ages. What are you doing?'

I turned. Matty was there, wearing some ridiculous Goodie outfit. 'I ... the Goodies are trapped. I was talking.'

'To a Goodie?'

'Why do you call us that?' We both looked at the door. 'Sorry. I didn't mean to interrupt.'

'They're stuck,' I said to Matty. 'The dandelions kill 'em. So, why not?' I turned to the door. 'It's a joke.'

'The dandelions?'

'No, calling you Goodies. Because our parents are the baddies, right?'

Matty shook his head. 'We should tell everyone.'

He was right. And I knew, if we told them, they'd probably destroy this house.

'It was nice to meet you, Cally,' Efa said. For the first time, I wondered what she looked like. 'If you have time, check out the park down the road. There's a great view at the top.' I could hear the faint smile in her voice as she said, 'Someone might as well see it.'

We told the tribe. Like I'd thought, people wanted to destroy the house. Nobody wanted the Goodies coming back.

But some called for mercy: the Goodies were clearly harmless now. We could arm ourselves. Move closer, catch them if they came out. Not be the monsters they said we were.

Usually, I stayed silent in these meetings. Non-originals weren't expected to give opinions, even though some newer originals were younger than us. But I couldn't help thinking of Efa, telling me to visit the park, laughing with me, asking about the world outside.

'Leave 'em.' When everyone looked at me, I shrugged. 'Killing 'em's easy. Let 'em die trapped, like they wanted for us. That's more fitting.'

People liked that. It satisfied those who wanted blood, and those who wanted mercy.

Besides. We didn't have any explosives.

Outside, Matty said, 'Didn't take you for a bleeding heart.'

'I'm not.'

He snorted. 'D'you even know if the girl's cute?' I clamped my hand over his mouth. He slung an arm around my shoulder. 'Relax,' he said. 'Nobody heard.'

'It's not your life on the line.'

He shrugged. 'Just have a brat, like everyone says. Near time anyway. And don't go back to the house. Colony won't like it.'

'No fear,' I said. 'I got better things to do.'

I returned to the house. In my defence, it was after I'd found the view in the park Efa had mentioned – on a hill that looked over the silent city, sparkling in the sunshine; a fountain in the middle, mountains on the horizon. It took my breath away. There was so much world outside the colony. If only the tribe would go there.

Efa was behind the door again, which surprised me. She sounded equally surprised that I'd returned.

'Is it just you there?' I asked.

A snort. 'No. There's a hundred of us.'

I whistled. 'Is it a centre point?'

'Uh. It was Jeff Galway's house.'

'Who?'

'He's rich.'

'Ah.' I sat, my back to the wall by the door. 'I went to the park. You ever go to the mountains?'

'Yes. Dad loved to hike. Wish I could go now. We don't have much space here. I've been jogging laps around tables.' I laughed at the image. 'Are there mountains by the colony?'

'No. We can see 'em but can't go to 'em.'

'Well, they really have their ups and downs.'

I paused. 'That was terrible.'

I heard laughter and couldn't help smiling. It seemed Efa had a sense of humour.

'Cally?'

'Yeah?'

'The fountain's pretty nice. If you have time, you should check it out.'

I went to the fountain with my parents.

'How did you find this place?'

'Saw it from a nearby park,' I said.

'It's pretty,' Dad said. 'But water's foul. Nothing to eat. Might be able to use the stone, I guess. Not sure what the point of the elephant is.'

Mum hummed agreement. I shrugged and agreed.

'Do they have schools in the colony?'

I was back in the house. On my second attempt, Efa had been by the door. I'd told her about the fountain, including its weathered elephant figure and the foul water. She'd seemed sad, so I'd asked if the elephant had meant anything.

'Yeah,' I said defensively. 'We learn what we need. Not stupid art stuff.'

'It's not stupid,' she said. 'Art helps you understand the world. It makes you feel.'

'Does it get you fed?'

'Not directly.'

'What's the point then?'

She sighed. 'Never mind. Anyway. The elephant is about strength and loyalty. How we all have to look out for each other. How together, we're stronger.'

'And Goodies believe that? After shooting us?'

'I ... well, it's true, isn't it?' I didn't answer. 'Never mind. I reckon it would have looked better with kittens anyway. Nobody argues about kittens.'

I laughed. 'Want me to smuggle one?'

'I wish. It would have seeds on it.'

'Then brush it. You Goodies, you're terrified of everything.'

'It's not that easy. We might die.'

'Everyone dies eventually.'

'Yeah. Eventually. I like living. Don't you?'

'Yeah,' I said, but for some reason, it didn't sound convincing.

'You ever go back to that house?' Matty said as we scavenged.

'No.'

'Liar.' He shook his head. 'It's pointless, Cally. You know that.'

'I know,' I said quietly.

After my fourth visit, she told me her schedule so I'd know when she'd be there. It was stupid. But I came anyway.

She liked simple things. She knew all the good views in the city. She wanted to travel. She'd never fought anyone. She could sing, properly sing, and made me sing despite my sounding like a strangled cat. She liked terrible jokes. The illness had killed her parents but her friends in the bunker kept her sane. She hated cooking. She'd been studying computers, and enjoyed indulging my curiosity about them. She liked to read, but had read all the books down there. Twice.

Sometimes, we argued. She thought the Goodies had their hearts in the right place; that some colonists deserved punishment. She thought it was better for individuals, not the community, to decide their roles. She wasn't sure the tribe always came before the person. She actually believed that people were good and someone would save them. She didn't think violence was ever justifiable.

'We're not savages,' I said when she said the colony sounded too violent for her. 'Deliberate murder gets you exiled.'

'Wonderful. What happens then?'

'Goodies shoot you.'

'Huh.' She was quiet for a bit. 'Have you ever …'

'Killed someone?' Silence. 'Yeah. Self-defence. Dad was proud, Mum was hysterical.'

'Huh.'

'Does that freak you?'

'I just can't imagine it,' she said. 'You're so sweet.' I blushed furiously but before I could put her right, she said, 'Anyway. Weather update. Go.'

I updated her.

'You're happy recently.'

I shrugged.

Matty shrugged too. 'Just good to see is all.'

I told her an anecdote about Matty. After a moment, she said, 'Is he your boyfriend?'

'Matty? No. Though we're an age to lie together. He'd be alright. I guess.'

'So … you want him to be your boyfriend?'

'No. But tribe needs me to lie with someone and get brats soon.

Might as well be him. He might make it not awful.'

'Oh.' A pause, while she digested things. 'That's terrible.'

'What?'

'You shouldn't have to sleep with him. It should be something you want.'

I sighed. We argued about this sort of thing often. 'Life isn't about want, Efa. It's about need.'

'It's about feeling. What's the point in living if you just survive? If you never get to be yourself?'

'Right,' I said. 'Because you're so active. Oh, wait. You're hiding because you're terrified of flowers.'

There was a long silence.

'Sometimes,' she said quietly, 'you can be really cruel.'

My stomach clenched. 'Efa …' I closed my eyes. 'I'm sorry. I didn't …' I looked at the ground. 'I really don't want to do it. But I have to. I have to.'

'Oh, Cally.' Her voice was sympathetic. 'I wish I could hug you. You sound like you need a hug.'

My arms wrapped around myself. 'You're sweet.'

'I bet you say that to all the girls.'

'Only the crazy ones.'

She laughed.

I kept visiting. I found books and read them to her; she told me stories from her childhood. She talked of places she wanted to visit; experiences she dreamed of having; family she wished she could see.

I talked of my sister dying; a man attacking me; a future I didn't want. Sometimes, we were quiet, talking only of our days. Others, we shouted and cried and laughed so loudly, it made my head spin.

The tribe said I was too distracted: I should stay back, help the women organise things. Matty defended me, but a feeling of dread built up. I didn't tell Efa though. I wanted to keep pretending, if only for a little longer.

I'd just finished a book, when she said, 'I wish I could be like that.'

'What d'you mean?'

'The heroes in those stories: they're not scared of anything. When I was a kid, I used to say I'd be like that. But I kept my head down. Never intervened in case it drew attention to me. Talking to you is the bravest thing I've ever done.'

'But you climb mountains. You moved to this city by yourself to study. You used to help the homeless. I reckon, if you had a gun, you'd be as good a fighter as anyone.'

She was quiet for a long time. 'Cally?' she said. 'Can I see you?'

It was weird. All this time and we'd never asked what we looked like.

I got up and stood in front of the keyhole. 'Go for it.'

Silence for some time, apart from occasional requests to move. Then: 'Those colours clash.'

I smirked. 'Thanks.'

'But you're really pretty.'

My heart stopped for a second. 'Efa ...' I coughed. 'Can I see you now?'

She assented so we repeated the exercise in reverse. From what I could see, she was slim, with pointed features, curly brown hair, and a wicked smile.

'So, what's the verdict?' she said as the keyhole cover slid shut.

'You're beautiful.'

I heard her breath hitch. 'Cally?' she said quietly.

'Yeah?'

'I'm really glad we met. I wouldn't change this for the world.'

'I would,' I said. ''cause then you'd be free.'

'We're heading back to the colony soon,' Dad said. He looked around. 'I'll miss this place.'

My stomach clenched. 'Why are we going?'

'Got to meet up. I heard Patrick's got his eye on you – maybe you should spend time with his tribe.'

I closed my eyes. 'I don't want-'

'He's a good man, Cally. It's for the best.'

'Then what?' I said. 'I lie there? Raise brats I don't want, to make everyone happy?'

'Huh?' He frowned. 'What's brought this on?'

'I ...' It was on the tip of my tongue. 'I don't like ...'

'Cally?'

'N-nothing.'

'What's wrong?' Efa said.

My voice trembled as I told her.

'Oh.'

'I'm sorry,' I said. My head was against the door. 'I don't want to go.'

'It's OK,' she said. 'The colony needs you.'

I dug the heels of my palms into my eyes. 'How do I save you?'

'Huh?'

'There must be something I can do.'

'I don't know,' Efa said quietly. 'Maybe we deserve this, for what we did to you.' I heard a snapping noise. Something poked through the keyhole and I drew it out carefully. A small elephant, from a charm bracelet. 'Like the fountain. To remind you of me.' She laughed suddenly. 'Crazy, isn't it? Everyone told me how scary the colony is and you …'

I took the tiny elephant. 'Thanks,' I said huskily. 'I'll treasure it always.' I swallowed as I stood. 'I guess this is it then.'

I heard a sniff. 'Have a good life,' she said. 'Just … be happy, OK?'

'I …' I squeezed the elephant tightly.

'It's OK,' she said softly. 'Just go.'

Back at the colony, joyful reunions began. People talked excitedly of the places they'd seen – sleek, modern, and empty. Several tribes had also found Goodie bunkers. Some had destroyed them. Others, like my tribe, had left them to rot.

'Funny thing,' someone said. 'Probably the palm weeds saved us. Don't grow elsewhere, do they? Disgusting but they come through for us again.'

Patrick who had his eye on me came over. He was strong.

Authoritative. He'd be a leader, one day. Our children would be strong.

My fist closed around the tiny elephant charm.

I looked at the weeds.

'Matty,' I whispered. 'Make me do it.'

'Cally-'

'I can't make myself.'

He closed his eyes. 'You're a bleeding heart.'

'What?'

'And maybe, if we were too, things would be better.' He looked at me. 'You do what you need to. We'll love you either way.'

I sniffed. 'Thanks, Matty.'

The door opened just as I got there.

For a moment, we both stared. Then the figure unzipped the head of their full bodysuit.

'Cally?'

'Efa?'

She blushed. 'I thought someone should try finding a cure.'

I hesitated. 'I might have one. Colony thinks it's this.' I took some weeds from my bag.

She stared. 'Cally?'

I thrust the weeds at her. 'Eat 'em. Please.'

She took them, chewed, grimaced, then swallowed. 'Is the colony …'

'I'm not welcome there now.'

She blinked, a strange look on her face. Then her arms wrapped around me. I hugged back, revelling in the feel of her, solid and there.

She stepped back. 'Let's take it slowly. If it works ...' Her expression was resolute. 'We say we'll cure the others if they make things better for the colony.'

'How did you know I had more?'

A hand touched my cheek. 'Because you're you.'

I closed my eyes. 'I need to save 'em both.'

'I know.'

'I don't know if the weeds work.'

'I know. But someone has to try. I ... I want to live, Cally. Even if just for a moment.'

'I know,' I said quietly.

'So ...'

'So, we go, I guess.'

She held her hand out and I took it. We took a deep breath. Then, together, we walked out into the sunshine.

And lived.

Volte-Face

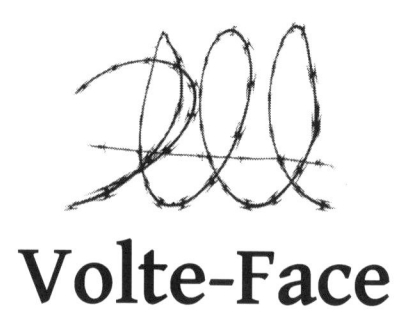

Alison Lock

Today my mother brings me wildflowers. I love the honeysuckle best; I like the taste of the pollen. She also brings Morello cherries plucked from the branches that grace the avenue. They are wrapped in a handkerchief, their red juice drips. Delicious. From their skin, their stalks, their stones, I can taste the earth, smell the grass, and feel the clear air that shoulders its way in from the mountains. How I long to run to the foothills, find the source of the rivulets, bound across streams, watch the bodies of the fish as they leap from the milky waters. I smell their salty flesh and taste the metallic essence of the white waters.

This town is built on the flatbed of the valley where a river meanders. Oxbows meet their own tails, forming curls of almost-islands. From my room, I see the rocks of Bear Heights that overlook the town and guard the pass to leads to an unnamed place. This building is made of metal mined from deep inside the earth, its sheets of thickened glass were smelted from the sands of the shallows that stretch into unfettered estuaries. It is built on the site of the first Longhall erected by the Humaners and has a plaque that commemorates the first arrival. The building is a statement to their power of invasion, a land claimed, named, and owned.

I am on the top floor, the place for the undiagnosed: the maligned, the carriers of a disease for which the White-Coats have no name. We dwell above the city, unseen by most. Our ululations come naturally at dawn and at dusk and must be muted. Our Keepers keep the windows shut, and they chide us when we begin our daily worship. If they could, they would stop us completely. We are allowed one visitor once a month, and they are not allowed to speak of us, or even mention our existence, outside of these walls. We are their secret. Our mothers, as it is usually they who visit, bring us gifts of cakes made of sweet milk. We are past the age needing our mother's milk now, but not before the Elders outlawed it for all us Bearfolk after the age of six months, when, if caught, the youngsters are taken away and placed in this vault in the sky.

It is believed that keeping us apart from the rest of the population is the only way to curb our strange habits, to mend our condition, to retrain us, and make us more like the Humaners. We are programmed to stand tall and walk without the use of roughened hands on floors. After we have passed their tests, our nails begin to grow, and our bodies lose their tell-tale hirsuteness, but we remain here. I have never known anyone to be released.

Sometimes, the Keepers are kind and tell us tales from the old times, stories that have been passed from one generation to the next. I suspect that many of the Keepers have a little of our blood in them, but they have learned to subsume their instincts, to placate the Humaners. My favourite tale is about the great rocks at the summit of Bear Heights.

It is said that there were once three rocks, the two that remain, and one other at the centre that is no longer there. These Stone Bears, as they were known, fell to their knees twice a day to praise the Gods of the forested heavens they had fallen from and said to be their ancestral home. They believed that one day they would return to the forests in the sky, where they would climb the trees, swing among the hammocked branches, eat the plentiful leaves. The story goes that there was one bear, named Vent, who had fallen out of favour with the Bear Gods and refused to worship them. The others were displeased with Vent for acting out of accord with their ways. He, in turn, was frustrated, and his pride would not allow him to compromise. He decided to leave, so the middle Stone Bear gathered his family and clambered all the way down through the slippery clouds until they reached the valley. There they found a land of barren deserts, and in the distance, they could see the treacherous seas. There was nothing that matched the plenitude of the heavenly forests. Nevertheless, Vent was stubborn and would not return.

So, the little family set off to explore the unmapped lands. But, the deserts were wider and longer than Vent could have imagined. He longed to see how far they stretched and when he saw the high mountain up ahead, he resolved to cross the deserts and see what lay ahead. His baby son was starving, and his wife had no more milk for her cub; she was exhausted and dehydrated. They arrived at the base of the mountain after days of sand storms that had stung their eyes. They climbed and climbed, and when they reached the highest rock, Vent lifted his young son onto his shoulders and turned to face every direction: north, south, east, and west. There was nothing to see, just more deserts and a horizon that stretched in an endless circle around them.

Vent became angry. He was a large bear, weighty and clumsy. As he stomped around on the summit, he dislodged several boulders, and the small bear on his shoulder bounced up and down until he was pitched forward from his father's neck. The little bear tumbled down the mountain with the boulders, rolling over and over until he came to rest on a stony ridge near the base where he lay, dead. All of his bones were broken, and after some time, and with the action of the wind and the sun, they began to crumble into white dust and mix with the small stones, the pebbles, the slaty shards, that lay on the valley bottom. Much of the larger debris was washed away, but these bone-crumbs that were swilled around in the soil, remained, enriching it until the valley became the dark and fertile place that it is today.

Like seeds that are embedded in the soil for decades, these particles lay dormant within their earthy cradles until one day, they felt the warmth of the sun and the moisture of the rain nudging them into life. It was enough to begin the process of germination of each fragment, which had been waiting for this moment to explode from embryonic life. By the following summer, these particles had grown into tiny balls of fur.

That was when the Humaners arrived. They found the hairy seed-heads, some already sprouted and defined into recognizable shapes with torsos and limbs, and they called them the Chitterlings. They took them into their homes and fed them along with their own children. These tiny creatures suckled along with the Humaners' own babies. The mothers produced ample milk, as the land became cultivated and bountiful. The Humaner children, once they could walk and run, left home every day with the fathers' who worked in the fields, but the Chitterlings preferred to stay at home. They were no trouble for the mothers, as unlike their own children, they were passive and quiet creatures. Their only utterances came at dawn and dusk when they fell to the ground, heads bowed, bodies prostrated, and they made strange ululations that echoed around the valley. Despite these differences, the mothers loved their Chitterlings as much as their own children, and for a long while, a few hundred years, in fact, everyone was happy: the mothers, the fathers, their natural offspring, and the Chitterlings.

It was only much later that the problems began. New Chitterlings continued to arrive each springtime as the fields were ploughed, and they rolled around, were pocketed, and carried into the homes of the mothers. By now, the menfolk had seen how fertile the valley was and the potential it contained--they became ambitious, wanting to make the most of every opportunity. They demanded that the women join them at their work in the fields and the mines so that they might double their yield. But they also wanted them to be the homemakers and the carers of the children.

The more the Humaners produced, the more they harvested, the deeper they mined, and the more they owned. Some began to accumulate more than others, and the supervisors' and managers' houses became larger than those of the field workers, with glass extensions that showed luxurious interiors for all to see, and gardens that evolved into paradisiacal places of colour and abundance with pools of warm water. These were places of calm and comfort, but before long, they needed tall fences to protect them and demarcate them from their poorer neighbours. For a while, there was a semblance of order that everyone accepted. But then the richer Humaners began to suffer from dreams and nightmares that took them to places of darkness. They started to fear each other and to worry about an attack from outsiders, although there had been no newcomers to the area for centuries. That was when they began to be suspicious of the Chitterlings.

The result of all this is that we Chitterlings have been taken away from our found homes. Our freedom is curtailed, and we have been placed in this building – this hold in the sky. We are here all the time, every day of our lives, suspended above the city, kept apart from the Humaners and forgotten by many. The mothers are allowed to visit us when they are able, and they bring us food, but otherwise, our only sustenance is a thin broth of desert weeds.

In the last couple of years, a new type of folk has arrived in the valley. They are the desert dwellers who existed for centuries in the caves of the shadowlands where they keep their goats on the dark sides of the mountains. But they have seen how rich and fertile our valley is, and they want to live here too. They began to arrive in ones and twos, wearing their rags and ushering their goats with high pitched calls. We could see them from here, shadows flitting between the buildings, and every night more and more would arrive. In the daytime, they kept to the areas on the edges, hovering around their fires of many colours, herding their goats back and forth along the desert margins. At first, the Humaners shunned them, pretended they did not exist. But late at night, when the skies are darkest, there are fights and killings.

More fences have been erected to keep out these newcomers, but that does not stop them from coming. They have grown bold, and they claim that the valley is part of the land of the deserts and, by rights, is theirs. Now, in the Humaners' factories, the metal that was used to frame the houses and the tools, is used in the mines or the fields is used for another purpose. A new factory has opened where metal is smelted and formed into hollow instruments through which small but solid balls are fired. But the incomers have their own means of attack, in the form of a suffocating smoke that is lurched high into the sky and falls silently over the city, expelling the Humaners from their luxury abodes, leaving the desert dwellers to walk into them and, take them as their homes.

From our eyrie, we see a pall of sulphurous smoke hanging over the valley. In desperation, the Humaners have turned to the Stone Bears on the mountain, and for the first time, they are prostrating themselves at dawn and dusk, in the way of our ancestors. We have had many more visitors lately, not ones we have seen before. They observe us, taking notes in their books, and recently we have been allowed to see our mothers every day and to receive more gifts, like the cherries and the flowers I was brought today. It is as though they believe that we hold a secret that will save them from invasion.

Right now, a Humcopter is tacking over the mountain, hovering around Bear Heights, and dipping in and out between the two great stones. I can see the pilot, and there is one other who is leaning over the side, a hand held out, letting out a rope that is snaking in the wind. There is something attached to the end of it that swings back and forth. The hairs on my back bristles. I worry that the rocks will be knocked, will loosen, and roll down to the edge of the city. But then I see a line of rope released through the air, and the package that is attached to the end falls onto the peak between the Two Bears. The Humcopter disappears over the far side of the mountain.

I fall in and out of sleep, and on waking up, I am still thinking about the Humcopter. I look out of my window, but it is not there. After a while, my eyes blur with the strain of peering at the Stone Bears. I must have been dreaming about the Humcopter and the package. Perhaps it was a bird, one of the great eagles that soar around the peaks dropping branches that will form the foundations of a nest.

When my Keeper arrives, I ask her to pull down the blind. I am restless. The rays of light from the setting sun pierce through the slats, and I cannot sleep.

'What is it?' she asks.

I point to the window, and she goes over to it, one hand on the pulley. For a moment, she twists it the wrong way, and the full view of the mountain is revealed: the orange sun behind, the rock that is purple in the foreground, and the distinct peaks that are familiar silhouettes. The mountain is as it always is.

'The Humcopter has gone now,' she says.

So it was real.

'Did it disturb you?'

She takes my paw and gently strokes it.

'It is nothing to worry about,' she says in her gentle, lulling voice.

I turn my head into my pillow. I do not believe her. I am still thinking about the package and the mountain and the Stone Bears.

'The Mayor wants to honour the Bears. Every day the Humcopters will drop a crate of fresh fish from the river as a gift to the Stone Bears.'

The sun is disappearing now, beyond the mountain, beyond the valley.

I slide out of my bed and prostrate myself onto the floor. Only when my vespers are complete, do I realise my Keeper has joined me.

What You Know

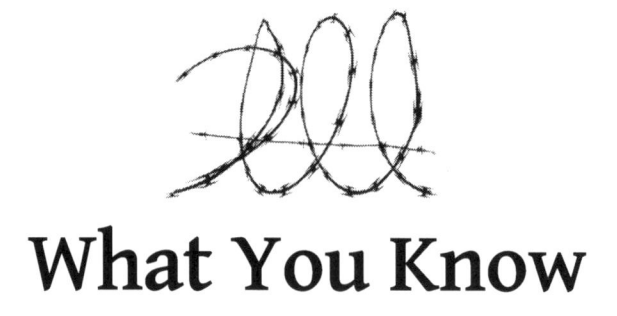

Melissa Paige Morrison

'Do you miss the heat of a real summer?'

The question hangs in the air as I consider the best way to answer.

I turn to my London-born-and-bred friend, who has only experienced the joys of a real summer on holidays on the continent for two weeks at a time.

I smile, take a sip of my wine. 'I guess I do, yeah. I mean, how could I not?'

She nods her head, as if she really understands.

***

Summer. When we played in the pool for hours on end, until our eyes stung and our skin no longer felt like our own. Sun-stroked, red-nosed, and constantly out of breath.

We would wear our hair with a slight tinge of green like a badge of honour. It was the chlorine, our mothers told us. They tried everything to run it out – all sorts of shampoos, tying it into a tight bun before we jumped in to the water, a simple deep condition afterwards. We didn't care. We liked how thin the strands became, sticking to our backs and smacking like cardboard whenever we somersaulted back into the water. And no curls! What a joy.

We were water-logged mermaids, limbs aching but buzzing on adrenaline, and we could never say no to an extra five minutes and another five after that – coaxed out only by the sharpest of tones from our parents, or tricked by a sausage in bread, fresh from the barbie and drizzled with tomato sauce.

Your biggest weakness, I remember, was the offer of home-brand crinkle cut salt and vinegar chips, even when they were placed on a table far from the pool, with access only granted if we toweled off first. We had to be quick though, the large plastic bowl could only handle so many little wet hands dipping in until the chips went soggy.

How we loved having the cousins over, because then we were allowed a small cup of pink sarsaparilla. The ultimate refreshment, so bubbly it burnt our throats – already hoarse from all the yelling during the pool games. When we pretended we were older than we were, like we were one of the big kids, even though were terrified of being pushed under for too long, stuck beneath the many floatable toys and boogie boards that littered the pool surface, like our mothers always warned us.

***

'There are things here though, that I never got to experience, and you did,' I say.

She laughs. 'Yeah, like what? A school with no grass? Wearing so many layers of clothes that you can barely walk?'

'What about snow? Or how close you are to Europe?'

She pauses, then continues to roll a cigarette. 'I guess I can give you the Europe bit. But it's not the most affordable family holiday. More likely you would have gone to Brighton, or Blackpool,' she sniggered. 'Then it would have been raining anyway, and you would have spent most of your time inside playing cards and getting into fights with your siblings or cousins.'

***

We made up stories, gave ourselves other lives. We were models on the catwalk, strutting our stuff up the length of the pool before making a spectacular dive. We were dancers, spending weeks and weeks learning routines and then playing them out for whoever was around.

Our mothers were there during those awkward years where the age gap between our older siblings and ourselves seemed to suddenly widen and become impenetrable. They gave us little tasks or ideas for play so that the hours in a weekend day would fly by until the older ones came home again.

I liked alternating between playing the Gameboy and writing stories in the 7 x 9-inch exercise books that were meant for school, but I remember you liked playing Harriet the Spy the best, stalking your neighbourhood by peeking out from the bushes in your front garden.

We were still kids while our siblings had things to do, people to go and see. We weren't old enough to ride to each other's houses alone yet.

Now, we're separated by tens of thousands of miles, of earth and sea.

Do you hold on to all those younger years, as I do? To turn to whenever in need of a quick pick-me-up? To quench a moment's hesitation, doubt, about how we got to be where we are?

Older now, the days would be lost as we lay in a stupor on our towel-covered plastic sunbeds, worn out over the many years they had been exposed to the sun, left neglected to face the elements over the winter. We roused ourselves from sun bathing with intermittent dips into the water, cooling off when the sweat got too much, our heads dizzy with dehydration. Still, we persevered, using coconut oil and sunscreen in equal measures. We alternated sides every fifteen minutes, made sure we weren't getting strap lines, moved positions whenever we noticed the earth had spun too far on its axis, skewing the angle of the sun's rays. Everything had to be even. It was a very serious operation.

We lay in the sun for hours at a time, I read books, you flicked through magazines.

We gossiped, giggled, wondered aloud where we would be in ten years' time, compared dreams, goals and family dramas. Until our mothers barked over the pool fence that we were getting burnt, that is, or that we should come inside to eat.

Other days we'd head to the beach, bags in tow, reveling in the tiny degree of independence being a teenager gave us. The hours would whizz by, the salt in the air sticking to our hair, our lips, the little invisible hairs on our cheeks. If our skin became tight and dry, we knew we had succeeded in getting some colour.

We'd leave when the wind started to pick up in the afternoons. We'd stop at the fish and chip shop on the way back, ask for 'extra extra chicken salt', and a small pot of gravy for dipping. We'd get a slushie from 7-Eleven – yours always raspberry flavoured – lose track of time as we strolled the streets and bumped into school friends, inevitably staying out too long watching the boys skate board or do wheelies on their bikes.

***

My friend shakes her head. Looks around despondently. 'I need to get out of this fucking country. Have you ever felt like that, like you shouldn't really be native to somewhere? That you belonged somewhere else, all this time?'

I push the thought that immediately comes to mind away, not allowing it a voice, I let it flitter back to the back of my consciousness, tucked away in a corner that I don't like to access too often.

I try to change the subject to something less tangential. I ask her where she got the wine from, it's so good.

But she's dissatisfied. She presses again: 'How did you make the decision to move here? Was it a light bulb moment? Or was it something you had been weighing up for a while, so when you decided it wasn't a shock for anyone?'

'God, I can't really remember, it's so long ago now.'

***

I found my diary of that year a little while ago. It shocked me how sad and uneventful it was.

Hints of frustration in every entry, a craving for something new, an achievement of any kind, a stable boyfriend. I had forgotten, but during that period I was simply cruising through each day. I had developed a routine: apply for graduate jobs, go out for coffee, catch up with friends or family, work at the pub, then go out with the girls. I vented in that diary about my social life, that I didn't want to go to certain parties, see this person, talk to that person. I was done with it all, but I still hadn't clicked what kind of change I wanted. I was still waiting for the perfect professional job to fall into my lap, that would prove my degree had all been worth it.

You, on the other hand, were embracing the stability of everyday suburban life. You had a man, a municipal job, you didn't mind living at home while you saved up cash.

We started having fights when we got too drunk. You told me I'd changed, that I was too full of myself with my higher education, that I always looked down on you, even though I hadn't realised I was doing it. I refused point blank to believe it, I said you were settling, that you shouldn't need to start saving for a house at 20, that now was the time to go traveling instead.

We were spreading apart, but we weren't ready for a clean break yet, so we clung on, for a bit longer than we should have, perhaps.

***

'Let's get out of here. Go to some obscure island in Asia somewhere. Take up surfing or something. How many holidays have you got left this year?' My friend asks.

I squint my eyes as I try to calculate. 'Probably just a few weeks.'

'I've been thinking about quitting my job anyway, might as well get on with it. I can go with you for the holiday part, then I'll backpack for a few months.'

I let out a laugh, then recover. 'Are you being serious?'

She takes a swig of her wine, flashes an out-of-control smile. 'Deadly.'

***

We never took overseas holidays, growing up. We stuck to the east coast of Australia, camping our way through the summer months. Hot, sweaty nights spent holed up in tents on stretcher bed sets shared with siblings. I always had to take the bottom bunk because I'd rolled off the top one too many times. We fell asleep to the pounding of rain on the tarp above our heads, the winds from the summer storms whipping against the makeshift walls, making them billow menacingly. The clang of rope against the metal pipes was a constant.

But by morning it was always clear skies. We filled our days with exploration, foraging across forgotten isolated beaches and through the surrounding bush. We hopped in boats and found mangroves, fished with our fathers, read books on sandy banks, stared out to sea as we perched on clusters of rocks. We made our way back to the campsite to help our parents prepare dinner, served on plastic plates, eaten at a plastic foldable square table. That table was with us for years, do you remember it? It was dark green with attached seats that had patterned bottoms, parts of which broke and became sharp over the years, pinching our bottoms if we moved too quickly. We washed our plasticware in another plastic tub, filled with water from the nearby tap. We showered at the toilet block in tiny dark cubicles, shared changing spaces with other campers, no mirrors to be seen anywhere.

We befriended the other kids at the site, took part in their wild, imagination-fuelled games, borne out of boredom and deliriousness from the sun. It was during those years that we really learnt how to stand up for ourselves, as we had to hold our ground against the bigger kids who thought they owned they place.

We stayed out late while our parents got stuck into the wine and beer, chatting deep into the night with other friends who had joined us on the trip that particular year, until one of them would suddenly remember they had children out there somewhere, track us down and send us to bed, where we would listen to the music and the gossip filtering through the mesh windows. Inevitably we lost the silent battle we waged against our exhaustion, succumbing to the sound of the summer storms as they returned, washing our memories clean so we could start it all again as soon as we woke up.

***

'Where in Asia, exactly?' I ask.

She shrugged, 'We could start in Thailand, snake our way to other countries from there. I've always wanted to do Vietnam. Bali too.'

I mulled it over for a few minutes, pretending to weigh the pros and cons, even though I already knew my answer. I got my first passport when I was nineteen, choosing Europe as my first overseas destination – I still haven't been anywhere in Asia, bucking the typical Australian trend.

I think of you. Of those photos I saw recently of your first big trip overseas as a family, baby in tow. You had chosen Fiji, where we always said we'd go for your hens. The hens that never got properly organized and was eventually abandoned.

'Sure, let's do it.'

'Really?' My friend looks ecstatic.

I nod; it's the easiest decision I've made in a long time.

A Fresh Start

Catherine Ogston

Honourable Mention

Your social worker turning up in the middle of the school day is never a good sign.

'Alright, Tom?' Iain announces, trying to sound breezy, but he's got that nervous twitch in the corner of his mouth that spells it out; trouble, meetings, end of the road.

My eyes find a stain on the carpet and I let them glue themselves to it. I don't want to see his face or hear his voice, softly explaining that it has not worked out and perhaps the next placement will be the one, my 'forever family'. Iain and I have performed this dance before; he delivers the bad news and I show him that I don't care. He doesn't call me out on my bullshit, but instead brings out his well-trodden speech about how all I need is a fresh start while I try to keep my face blank and smooth.

A Fresh Start is a social work favourite. In the last four years I've heard it enough times to start puking when it's cast up. Other favourite popular phrases include Managing Expectations, Getting it Right for Every Child and every foster carer's go-to motto, Tomorrow is Another Day. In this field of dreams, tomorrow is a land of infinite possibilities and all I have to do is wake up and grasp its potential. I'd like to hear Bloody Unfair, Cards Stacked Against Me and Life's a Bitch but no one's ever that honest.

I am tuning back in when Iain says, 'Did you take it?'

'Take what?' I say, my head bobbing up to meet his eyes.

'Janice says there's a hundred pounds missing from the money.' He's speaking carefully, like he's a bomb disposal officer and one wrong move could ignite an explosion. 'The money for the little girl with cancer, you know, the money Janice and her friends raised doing a sponsored walk.'

I know exactly what he's talking about. The money had been counted-- I helped her count it-- and put in a square margarine tub until Janice could get to the bank on Monday. There was a picture of a bald smiling girl on the front, Sophie I think she was called. She was nine years old and diagnosed with some rare childhood cancer that no one expects to get. The local area was fundraising left, right and centre for costs her parents were facing. Janice knew them, wanted to help and organised a sponsored run. A hundred folk in fancy dress filled the park, all happy to jog and amble about and then hand over their cash. Nearly four hundred and fifty pounds had been squashed into that tub, the notes sitting in satisfying piles, the loose coins jingling at the bottom.

'Did you take it?' repeats Iain the quizmaster who needs an answer.

'No,' I mutter and cringe as I hear the petulance oozing from me.

Iain sits back and I lean forward, staring at the carpet again like it's a puzzle I need to solve. I can't lift my head and I know Iain thinks this is guilt but he's wrong. It's my word against everyone else's though.

I had a nice home once. Mum worked in the local supermarket, Dad was a postie. Everything was normal until the day I woke up and Dad was gone. That's when the laughter left and something darker crept in, seeping into every nook and cranny. The cracks grew larger and wine and vodka appeared to be the glue Mum thought would stick all the pieces back together. Soon she was crying every night and hardly seemed to notice me. It wasn't long until she was drinking from lunchtime until bedtime and I was making my own dinner by the age of eight. By the age of ten it seemed normal to wash my own school clothes and lock the house behind me as Mum lay on the sofa sleeping off last night's Sauvignon Blanc before she started again. I would open the hall cupboard and find the hoover plus a stack of empty bottles staring back at me. More than a few times I had to climb out the kitchen window to get to school, the keys having disappeared somewhere mysterious. I guess my life would have remained the same if I hadn't mentioned all this to a friend's mum, who did that sucky-in-face and called the Social. Me and my big mouth.

    'This would be a lot easier if you told the truth,' says Iain and I despise him in that moment. I stare at his ridiculously large jumper and fight the urge to ask if he knitted it himself. He looks the type to do home-spun crafts and make his own bread. But I can't bear to look him in his eyes and plead for him to believe me.

    Janice's house was my fourth placement. The other three just hadn't worked out. Not my fault and yeah I know I'm the common factor in all this but really I tried my best. Said please and thank you, emptied the dishwasher, made my bed. Went to school, handed in homework, tried not to think about the future too much. The future was an unknown territory, like an alien planet or a desert I didn't have a map for. I didn't let my brain think about it too much so I just tried to move through each day, week, month. But three times now

Iain had come to get me, move me on, another Fresh Start. None of the explanations had sunk in so I can't even analyse them now.

I had arrived at Janice's on a Tuesday. She was a plain sort of woman, medium height with brown hair and a round face. Cheerful voice though and sort of bossy, the type of person who would organise tea and sandwiches in a crisis. The house was neat and tidy but with enough bits and pieces lying about that it didn't feel like a showhome. One of my placements had been like that – I worried about crumbs and mud on my football boots. But Janice put me at ease and had me set up in my room in no time, clothes in drawers, shelf in the bathroom for my stuff, house key installed in my pocket. It was all going great until Robbie got home.

'What's your name then?' he had said, in a tone that translated this into, 'What do you think you are doing in my house?' I'd come across his type before so I didn't worry until he had slammed my head against the newel post of the staircase and whispered, 'You'll not last long so don't even try.'

I look at Iain's face and realise it's too late to tell him any of this now.

'Janice is very upset. That money was for a sick child,' says Iain who seems to be choosing to forget that I'm innocent until proven guilty. I guess a fifteen year old lad in foster care doesn't get the benefit of the doubt. Cards Stacked Against Me.

'Am I out then?' I picture Janice packing up my bag, removing all traces of me from her house, erasing me.

Iain shifts uncomfortably in his seat. The room has a low round coffee table with chipped veneer, a scattering of chairs with fraying upholstery, squint faded posters pinned to the walls. Every school and social work office has a room like this; I've been in them all.

Eventually he clears his throat. 'Yes,' he says. 'I'm taking you to a new placement. I think you'll like it. A fresh start for you.'

'I don't need a fresh start,' I growl. 'Do I have to move school too?' I'd made a few friends and I'd sussed out the teachers who liked me, knew I wasn't a troublemaker. We were probably getting in the car in the next ten minutes; not enough time to say goodbye to anyone or collect my art project.

Iain nods and shuffles a cardboard folder. He's working up to one of his speeches so I cut him off. I haven't got anything to lose.

'It wasn't me. It was Robbie. He took the money.' I try to keep my voice steady.

Iain pauses for a second and then lays the folder down softly on the table. Linking his fingers together as if he is praying, he leans forward. 'Do you have any evidence?'

'No,' I say. 'But it's obvious. He hates me being there, doesn't want to share his mum with anyone. He took the cash. He must have because I didn't.'

Iain winces like I've just told a bad joke. 'Tom, you need evidence. You can't just accuse someone without some evidence.'

White-hot rage flows through me and my heart starts to thump painfully. 'Where's the evidence against me then?' I ask him.

I watch Iain open his mouth and shut it again. Then he repeats this action and it would be comical except this is my life that is being spun round like a roulette wheel.

'Janice feels you just can't stay with her anymore. It's best that you move on.'

'But where's the evidence that says I did it?' The white-hotness is still there but my voice is firm, like a lawyer in a film who knows they've got an irrefutable point to make.

'There were three of us there and I'm pretty sure Janice didn't take her own money. So that leaves Robbie and me. And I know I didn't do it.' I stare at Iain as he starts to sweat in his odd-shaped scratchy looking jumper.

'It's not that simple,' he starts to say.

'But why not?' The white-hotness is turning into something else, something I can't name yet.

Iain clears his throat and stares at my chest. He avoids my eye and I should feel happy that I've made my point but the rage is sliding into despair.

'It doesn't matter, does it?' My voice doesn't sound mine. 'It doesn't matter that I didn't do it. She'll always pick him.'

I think about my mum and the last time I saw her. She had been crying and the years of drinking had made her look like shit. Her voice had croaked and split as she had hugged me and told me she was sorry and that she'd let me down. Eleven years old and I'd been the one telling her it would be okay and not to worry and to look after herself.

'Everything's transient,' she'd said as I squeezed her hand as she was led out the room. I'd had to ask Iain what she'd meant. Lasting for a short time he'd told me. I guess she was trying to tell me things don't stay the same. Perhaps she'd thought she would snap out of her alcohol dependency, sober up for a few months and she would get me back. I was just a kid and even I had known nothing's that easy.

'I'm sorry Tom, it's time to go.' Iain picks up his folder and stands up.

I want to ask if he's sorry because I've been wrongly accused or because he's had enough of this meeting. Perhaps he's got a wife and kids and a loaf of homemade bread to get back to.

'I'm a transient,' I say.

'What did you say?' he asks.

'It's a noun as well as an adjective. A person who stays in a place for a short time.'

Iain looks at me, speechless. Then he pulls air into his lungs though his nostrils and he's about to give me platitudes I don't want to hear so I stride past him.

Tomorrow I'll be in a new room in a new house with a new family.

Tomorrow I'll be shown around a new school.

Tomorrow I'll be learning new rules and trying to fit in all over again.

I yank the door open and let it swing back until it slams behind me.

An Ordinary Life

Margaret Morey

It was just an ordinary day. Karen picked Jamie up from school as she always did. It had been a good day, according to the teacher. But the teacher reckoned every day had been a good day.

'Jamie has done you a drawing, haven't you, Jamie?'

She held the picture out to her. It looked the same as the one she had been given yesterday. And the day before. She would stick it on the fridge, the way she always did.

'We've had a great time today, haven't we?'

The teacher turned him gently to face his mother.

'He's not a bit of bother. We all love him, don't we, Jamie?'

Then she moved her hand in an exaggerated wave.

'See you tomorrow.'

Jamie made an ambiguous, absent-minded gesture with his hand, but his eyes were fixed on the ground, examining the stones around his feet. His scuffed trainers were no longer child-sized. Adolescence was approaching fast. Soon he would be bigger and stronger than his mother. This thought occurred to Karen more and more often. How would she cope with his meltdowns then? After all, she was on her own now, since Kevin moved out.

'I can't stand all this any longer,' he had said. 'I know it's selfish, but I just need an ordinary life.'

'Good boy, Jamie. See you tomorrow.'

The teacher gave another exaggerated wave, and went back into school.

Karen thought of her, going home to her normal world, with normal children, a husband. It was all very well to work with children like Jamie, but quite another thing to live with his condition. How would these professionals shape up in her shoes?

Jamie pulled at her hand, eager to examine the contents of the bin in the street outside. She allowed him to guide her, as she always did.

The car was parked round the corner, where she always parked. Jamie liked routine. He liked life to be predictable. A small group of kids came towards them from the local comp. Boys and girls, laughing and joking. Probably going to hang out together in the shopping centre, or slouch on sofas in front of the telly. Jamie showed no interest in them, and they flowed around him as though he were a boulder in their path. Their mothers would be still at work, making the dinner, or walking the dog. Later, they would all sit around a table, eating, discussing how their days had been. Another world.

****

She had once belonged to that mainstream world. They had all been new mothers together in the hospital, discussing sore breasts, nappies and sleeping patterns. All starting out together on a level playing field. Then there had been the coffee mornings. Comparing notes. Whose child was first to sleep through the night, cut a first tooth, walk, start eating solid food? It had never been Jamie. But that hadn't mattered. She wasn't competitive. And Jamie was the most beautiful child ever - angelic, other-worldly. Lots of people commented on his good looks. He was undemanding, able to entertain himself, no trouble to look after. He would do things in his own time, when he was good and ready.

Those mothers were still around. She bumped into them sometimes in the supermarket or in the street. They were full of stories of family holidays, school trips, exams, sporting successes. Soon it would be romances, part-time jobs, driving lessons, university applications.

'And how's Jamie?' they would ask, made suddenly uncomfortable by her silence.

'Just the same,' she would say. 'He's happy, on the whole. That's the main thing.'

It was best to say he was happy. She wasn't sure that it was true. He spent so much time being distressed. But she had learned that it was easier than trying to explain how it really was.

'That's great,' they would say, 'and does he speak yet?'

***

It was a particularly lovely summer afternoon. Warm, sleepy, suburban gardens lined the road where she had left the car. It made her think of another afternoon, long ago at the Chateau d' O. She'd read about it on the ferry, crossing the channel. So peaceful, the guide book said: the only sound, the plopping of frogs in the lake.

She'd shown the guide book to Kevin.

'Let's go there.'

He had smiled at her, his eyes full of happy anticipation. Their first holiday together as a family.

They'd picnicked under the trees. Not a care in the world, the perfect family. Cloudy Normandy cider, sun-softened brie, and a fluffy white baguette. Biting into ripe peaches, juice running down their arms. Then they'd carried six-month old Jamie on a guided tour of the chateau. He'd been as good as gold. Afterwards, someone had approached her, an older woman, and said Jamie was the most beautiful child she had ever seen…so quiet, so contented. Life had been perfect that day. Too perfect.

***

Karen realised she was not ready to go home yet. Not today. The weather was too nice. Jamie would insist that they went indoors and put the telly on. That would mean she would have to sit beside him on the sofa, to keep an eye on him. He would insist on drawing the curtains, to keep the sun out of his eyes. They would end up watching the same old cartoons for the hundredth time, trapped in darkness, while outside, all that afternoon sun and warmth would be going to waste.

'Jamie,' she said. 'Why don't we go for a walk?'

There was no response. You could never be sure how much he understood. She opened the car door, and he slid in, as he always did. It was only when she began to drive in a different direction and he realised they were not going home that he started to bite his hand, and make those unearthly noise which made her feel he was from another species.

'Would you like to go for a walk?' she asked again. 'Then we could have a drink or an ice cream.' She emphasised drink and ice cream. Those were the words he was most likely to understand. He was putting on weight because it was impossible to control his eating, and everyone offered him food as a bribe, just as she was doing now. But, just for today, why should it matter? They could sit in the sun together and enjoy quality time. Wasn't that what those professionals were always telling her to do? And the rest of the world could get on with its ordinary life. She and Jamie could have a good time, too.

She drove out of the town and headed towards the disused railway line, now a footpath. This was a good place for a stroll – flat, safe, with a pub half way along, where there would be drinks and ice creams, and seats in the sunshine. And the path went over a viaduct, so high it made her dizzy. She always wanted to hurry over it as fast as she could, but Jamie would linger there, looking over the rail, shrieking with delight, clapping his hands, jumping up and down. One of his favourite places.

***

They had had good times in the long-ago, before it had all

unraveled, like the sleeve of an old jumper. Bonding mother-and-child times. Friday mornings at the Music and Movement classes in the church hall. Cycling there and back with him on the child seat behind her. He loved to feel the breeze on his face, and watch the scenery go slowly past. At first she had enjoyed doing something with other mothers and toddlers. But then, small things had started to trouble her, like wrong notes in a symphony. An uneasy feeling that something was wrong was creeping up on her. He was in his own world, unearthly, detached when all the other toddlers were clinging to their mothers, and then shyly copying the actions, joining in with the songs. She had to hold Jamie firmly by the hand, or he would have run off into a corner to stare at a light that had started to flicker, or fiddle with a pair of taken-off shoes. The other mothers were starting to notice his strange ways. They were probably discussing him as they hung around together at the end of the sessions; they were probably going for coffee together, but not inviting her; they were probably apprehensive of how Jamie might behave in a café. The last time they cycled home together, he was humming one of the songs they had just been singing. He seemed to have some kind of strange musical ability, at odds with his slowness in other areas of development. She could hardly see for sudden, unstoppable tears.

'I can't go there anymore,' she told Kevin that night. 'It's too painful. And it makes me feel scared.'

She began to avoid the get-togethers of her hospital friends and their toddlers. Jamie's behaviour was becoming disruptive - chewing up toys and books, taking food from the other children's pudgy little fists. No-one had said anything, but Karen felt they were no longer welcome. She felt a wall growing up between the two of them and the rest of the world. And she could feel the wall growing higher every day.

***

Jamie sat in the back of the car, banging his head against her seat, biting his hand, making low, unhappy noises, like a dog growling. This was the first stage of something which could develop into a full-scale melt-down. His anxiety was mounting. He could lose control and become violent, and that was frightening. Perhaps she should drive home, forget the quality time. Jamie liked routine. He hated spontaneity. Calm would probably return once he was sitting in front of the TV watching Thomas the Tank Engine or Wallace and Gromit. After all, he didn't ask much.

She stopped the car.

'Jamie. I'm sorry. I thought you might like a walk in the sun, and an ice cream. We could go home…' Karen decided to play the trump card. She really wanted an hour in the sun, their quality time. '…but I thought you might like to go to the viaduct.'

He stopped biting his hand and looked at her hard through the hair which had flopped across his face. The mention of the viaduct changed everything. She would never understand how someone who couldn't dress himself knew what a viaduct was.

'OK, so you want to go to the viaduct? Then we could have a walk and an ice cream?'

He stopped banging his head and started to giggle and clap his hands.

It was as though she had switched one version of Jamie off, and another version on, just like that summer they had gone camping in France when he was two. That's when these big meltdowns had started.

'Must be the terrible twos,' Kevin had said the first time.

'I didn't realise the terrible twos were as terrible as this. When I've seen other kids kicking off, they seem to stop after a few minutes. But you can't distract Jamie once he's started. And it's hard to know what's caused it.'

There were several screamings a day, and each one lasted for at least an hour. It felt as though they were constant, and would never stop.

'Do you think he has a brain tumour?' she had asked Kevin one evening, when Jamie's screams had finally subsided into sleep, and they were sitting outside the tent as the sun went down. 'This screaming has got so much worse lately.'

'If you think that, perhaps we should go home and see a doctor.'

'That seems a bit drastic. I keep hoping it's just a phase and he'll stop. Perhaps we should wait and see how it is in a few days.'

'I think,' said Kevin, 'that it's something to do with the car. It seems to start when we try to get him out of it.'

Then, on a quiet lane in the middle of rural France, the car broke down. The engine failure was noisy and terminal. Another stroke of bad luck. A replacement car was delivered, and the screaming stopped.

'Good job we didn't go home,' she said the next night.

'I don't think we can come on holiday again,' Kevin had said. 'I don't think he likes it. It's all too strange for him. The car was the only familiar thing. That's why he didn't want to leave it. He's not attached to this new one. Not yet.'

'It's as though he likes the car more than he likes us. That's not usual for a two-year old.'

'Well, little boys can be very keen on cars and tractors and stuff I suppose.'

But Karen wasn't listening. She was imagining a future without holidays. Perhaps they just weren't like other families. Perhaps they never would be.

***

She stopped the car in the car park.

'Come on, Jamie. Let's go and see the viaduct. Then we'll get an ice cream.'

He hadn't completely got over his upset. It must be like getting over a really bad headache. He moved slowly, flicking his fingers, watching her out of the corner of his eye. He was still a bit fragile. The least thing could tip him back over the edge.

'First viaduct, then ice cream.'

This was how they had told her to speak to him. Short and to the point. No unnecessary words. Make clear exactly what was going to happen. Very slowly he undid his seat belt. Very slowly he eased himself out of the car. She locked it behind him. There was no going back now.

But by the time they got to the viaduct he was running, clapping his hands, laughing to himself. Karen hated standing on the viaduct. She hated the feeling it gave her in the pit of her stomach, even though, logically, she knew it was safe. She wouldn't have brought Jamie here otherwise. You couldn't accidentally fall off. You would have to climb over the railing. There was a notice telling people not to ride horses on the bridge, and another one with the phone number of the Samaritans. Karen imagined all the people who might have stood where she was standing now, punching those digits into mobile phones. All outsiders, all desperate, for whatever reason. For lots of different reasons, probably.

Jamie ran to the railing and looked over, his face full of joy. It was probably the same exhilaration he got from thrill rides at theme parks. Karen detested both heights and thrill rides. But he was in his element. He was completely happy.

'Jamie! Come here. Come away from the railing.'

He was oblivious of her, staring down into the void, strangely silent. Usually he chuckled with delight. She wanted to get closer to him, to grab him and pull him towards her, even though that that would set him off screaming again. She wanted to pull him back. But to what? To a world which didn't understand him, with adolescence looming. He could look forward to of becoming an adult with part of his brain still locked in childhood, and her not coping, growing old, giving him up to be cared for by people like his teacher, who professed love but didn't understand what it was to have given painful birth to someone so remote, so beyond their understanding. Jamie's life stretched ahead like morse code, the dashes of pain, the dots of pleasure. For Jamie, the problem was that the dashes would always last longer than the dots.

She looked around. Not a soul in sight. No one to help. But no one to hinder, either. Jamie was lifting his right leg over the railing.

'No, Jamie. Come back.'

He looked at her, hard and long. For a few seconds he sat, perfectly balanced, on top of the railing. She lunged to pull him back. He would have taken her with him, and, for a brief moment, she would have gone, but the railing stood in the way, and her feet stayed on the ground, while he fell away from her grasp.

She heard nothing but silence. She could not look down. She sat for a long time, propped against the railing, holding fragments of his tee-shirt between her fingers. Then, as the sun began to sink, she felt suddenly cold. She pulled out her mobile phone and began to type in the digits on the notice in front of her.

# Rewilding

Lucy Palmer

Early one Friday morning while he was out walking the dog on Brandon Hill, Marcus Mayhew thought he caught a glimpse of a wolf. Of course, it could simply have been a large dog (and their own dog – a Jack Russell-Chihuahua cross with an inflated sense of its own stature – was completely unperturbed), but Marcus had a distinct impression of a long, slim snout; alert ears; and cold amber eyes before the creature slunk between the bushes and was gone.

'You'll never guess what,' Marcus said to his wife when he got home that evening. 'On Brandon Hill this morning I could have sworn I saw a wolf.'

His wife, to his disappointment, expressed only the mildest surprise, or even interest.

'Darling, are you imagining things again? It can't have been a wolf. It must just have been a large dog.'

'That's what I thought,' said Marcus, 'but I'm pretty sure it was.'

For Marcus's wife, his fertile imagination was the end of the matter, and she went off to put the pizza in the oven. Marcus mulled over various other theories, all of which he doubted but googled anyway.

The internet made no mention of escaped zoo animals, a trend for unusual pets or the reintroduction of top predators in Bristol's parks. His wife was right: the creature must just have been a large dog, and Marcus dismissed it from his mind.

The following morning, on his Saturday run around the Downs, Marcus spotted a wild boar. It was some little distance off, among the dappled light and shadow of the trees, but there was no mistaking it: it was most definitely a wild boar. Marcus tried to calm his breathing and started moving stealthily in the beast's direction, but the boar raised its head and grunted crossly, then trotted off into the deeper shadows and could be seen no more. Marcus stood a while still trying to catch his breath and staring, unnerved, into the undergrowth. He briefly considered calling the police but then realised how absurd it would sound – and it hardly seemed worth bothering them for one solitary pig that was simply minding its own business. When he got home an hour or so later, his wife was catching up with some urgent emails and he decided not to bother her with it either.

On Monday morning, as Marcus crossed Queen Square, he thought he heard a cuckoo call. It certainly sounded like a cuckoo, but, of course, it could just have been someone's mobile phone. When he arrived at the office, Marcus opened the printed proposal he was reviewing and delicate hand-drawn tendrils began spiraling through the margins. He turned to the next page and tendrils wound their way between the lines, and in and out of words. Both enchanted and alarmed, Marcus closed the proposal and went to make a cup of tea. The act of making it was calming enough, but back at his desk Marcus sat for a long time unresolved, twiddling his pen nervously as his tea went cold. At last, gingerly, he lifted up the bottom corner of a page. The foliage was spreading and becoming more luxuriant, turning from hand-sketched drawings to living leaves. Marcus glanced about him. None of his colleagues seemed to have noticed. He picked the proposal up cautiously, as one might handle a wild animal, and placed it firmly below a pile of other papers on his desk. Then, complaining of a migraine, he took the day off work.

He headed at once for Brandon Hill and scoured the park for the wolf. So intent was he on his quest that he did not hear the hum of the traffic on Park Street or the roar of planes passing overhead. He did not see another soul, but nor did he catch sight or sound of the wolf, although he was listening out for an eerie howl. On his way home, Marcus passed parents and children coming back from school, sales people on their mobile phones, double-decker buses, and students going in and out of cafés. He arrived feeling so reassured as to the normality of the world that, yet again, he breathed nothing of the day's events to his wife.

On Tuesday morning, Marcus was nonetheless a little apprehensive about opening the proposal. His eye fell on the Oxford Dictionary of English beside his computer. Surely such an eminent publication could not be experiencing any botanical transformations. He opened it at random, and from the divide between 'flora' and 'floret' there shot out a tendril of honeysuckle. Marcus slammed the book shut with a clap that startled his colleagues and caused his line manager to turn in his direction.

'Is something the matter, Marcus?'

'Er, no, no. Never been better.' It was true that Marcus was feeling less sluggish than was usual on a weekday morning.

'Never been better?' His line manager raised a quizzical eyebrow.

'Well, no, that is to say – I don't quite know how to put it.' Marcus opened the dictionary a few inches, and between 'bramble' and 'branch' there sprang forth a thorny frond, quivering with fresh green leaves. He held it out silently to his boss by way of explanation.

The line manager remained non-plussed. She clearly could not see what Marcus saw; none of Marcus's colleagues could see it. Meanwhile, the bramble put forth flowers, and honeybees began hovering among them.

'Marcus,' said his manager gently, 'things have been tough here recently. Why don't you pop to see your doctor and take the rest of the week off work?'

Marcus left the dictionary sprouting brambles and went to sit in Queen Square. He did not call his doctor; he did not feel ill in the slightest. In fact, he felt remarkably fresh and alert – altogether more alive than ever before.

There definitely was a cuckoo, or rather a pair of a pair of cuckoos, calling to each other across the square, but look as he might, Marcus could not see them. Eventually, he made his way to Ashton Court and wandered around the deer park, reveling in the early summer sunshine. In the little copse at the top of the hill, he glimpsed a doe suckling a fawn before the two bounded off to join the rest of the herd. Marcus thought it charming but nothing more until he remembered that young deer were not normally introduced into the park until they were fully grown.

When Marcus got home that evening, tanned and exuberant, his wife noted the change in him.

'I got sent home from work,' he explained, 'and spent the day at Ashton Court.'

'Sent home from work? What for?'

'I wasn't feeling well,' said Marcus, unconvincingly, 'but I'm fine now. Gosh, that ficus has grown a lot recently,' he added.

'Grown? I keep forgetting to water it. Half the branches are completely withered – can't you see? Are you sure you're feeling better?'

All the houseplants seemed to Marcus to be feeling as well as he was. The ivy on the mantelpiece had spread all the way up the wall and was now starting to cross the ceiling. The bunch of flowers on the dining table had found a new lease of life, and there were buds once more where the previous day there had been dead heads.

'Darling, did you hear me? Are you sure you're feeling OK?'

'Well, it's very odd,' said Marcus and proceeded to recount the events of the past few days. As he talked, his wife looked increasingly horror-struck.

'Foliage?' she asked incredulously once he'd finished. 'Foliage and wild animals?'

'Yes,' said Marcus cheerily, 'that's it.'

The following morning his wife referred him to the friend of a friend who was an expert in stress-related illness. After a lengthy series of questions in which the psychiatrist established that Marcus liked his job well enough, was fond of his wife, got on well with his parents and had no traumatic childhood memories, she tried a Rorschach test.

'What do you see?' she asked, opening an ink blot in front of him.

'Foliage,' he answered, sparing her the details.

When Marcus returned home, the ficus in the living room had grown to twice its former height and the ivy covered the ceiling. He nodded at them approvingly and flung the windows wide open to let the air in.

It soon became clear that Marcus would not be going back to work the following week. Every book he opened sprouted greenery; on one television channel, a herd of deer was grazing in a woodland glade;

on another, a falcon hovered, and then plunged to seize its prey; when Marcus switched on the radio, all he heard between the white noise was birdsong.

He took to spending all day outside, in Bristol's parks and gardens, going home only when darkness fell. He scarcely saw his wife, and she, resentful, spent her early evenings mopping up the muddy prints of his bare feet.

At his wife's insistence, Marcus returned a few times to the psychiatrist, but it was abundantly clear that there was little she could do. She had never before treated anyone who hallucinated flora and fauna, and she could not go about curing a patient who insisted that he had never been so well.

After a couple of months, at the start of August, his wife raised the question of money. Marcus had little to say in response, but the next morning he walked barefoot to the office and gave his verbal resignation. While vetch wound its way up the chair legs, a colleague typed and printed a formal letter. Marcus signed between the fronds of ivy that began snaking their way across it, with a pen that turned from quill to butterfly then flitted out of the open window.

That evening, Marcus found his wife had left, taking her belongings and the Jack Russell-Chihuahua cross with her. On her side of the wardrobe, birch saplings were springing up; daisies were flowering in the bedroom carpet.

The following morning, Marcus went back to Ashton Court and got a job as a trainee gardener. On his return, the hall banisters had turned to living oak, and leaves were sprouting from the finials. From the forest of Marcus's bathroom, the Green Man gave a knowing wink, and Marcus winked back and grinned.

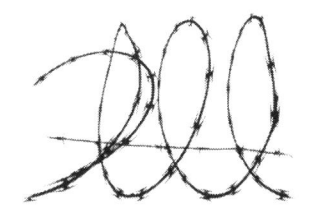

The Little House of Death

Ian Plenderleith

There was nothing much on Church Street besides the Little House of Death. On both occasions that Market Rasen briefly made the national news, it was down to this unremarkable, two-floor dwelling on the red-brick row behind Sheffield Manor School. The first time was when Anthony Marden murdered his wife Shirley in the kitchen after slamming her head several times on the counter-top. He then dragged her out on to the street, where she died while being ignored by a number of passers-by. Around one year later a gas explosion caused by a leaky pipe in that very same kitchen killed all three members of the Teale family, who'd paid for the house in cash using an envelope small enough for a birthday card.

For both events, Market Rasen Mail reporter Danny Selwood was sitting at the bar of The George just around the corner, the place he could always be found when not out and about taking pictures of school fêtes and coffee mornings. After Anthony Marden left poor Shirley battered and lifeless on Church Street, he walked in and sat down at the bar on a stool next to the reporter. It was a Tuesday lunchtime. After ordering a pint and lighting a cigarette, Anthony described in graphic detail exactly what he'd just done and why. Barman Matt Davey quietly called PC Wallingham, and Danny Selwood took mental notes. By the next day he was several hundred pounds richer, and the murder was lead story on page five of the Sun.

When the same house went up in flames because Mary Teale smelled gas and lit a match to find the source (or so the story went), Danny had a little more work to do. Upon hearing an explosion strong enough to send a ripple across the surface of his lager, he upped from his bar stool, then walked out of the pub and towards the smoke and the screams. He was eye-witness to nine-year-old Emma Teale staggering down Church Street on fire before she fell to the tarmac. Danny took off his jacket and flapped away at the flames, but he was too late. Her mum and dad, meanwhile, were identifiable only thanks to records kept by Dr. Boysen, the town's dentist. Danny's tabloid contacts in London were sceptical that death had now struck the same house twice in a town where nothing ever happened, but the reporter they sent up confirmed that it all checked out. Once again, the journalist was quids-in, making even more cash this time thanks to the dramatic eye-witness account of his self-styled heroics.

Lazy at the best of times, the gas explosion left Danny believing that he could best carry out his job without leaving the pub at all. The Little House of Death (the headline in both the Sun and the Rasen Mail), however, no longer yielded lucrative stories. What remained of the building was razed to its foundations, and Pete Salter built a modest car repair shop there instead. Danny waited for Pete to be crushed beneath the weight of a falling chassis, but the mechanic - who wasn't superstitious - was far too sober and careful to let a thing like that happen. Eventually, Danny gave up wandering by the garage just before noon and casually inviting Pete to join him for a few pints.

There were no more possible tabloid scoops until Pete's son Kevin, together with his best mate Graham Mead, claimed to have spotted a UFO on Walesby Road one early spring evening while walking back from the woods. At school, we were incredulous. It wasn't the part about the UFO. Disbelieving that part of the story was factored in. We just didn't believe anyone would seriously claim to have seen a spaceship flying over Market Rasen, population 2,600.

Danny had no hesitation in reporting the story at full length. He didn't hold many beliefs, but he did harbour an unproven conviction that things always come in threes. That Kevin Salter's dad now ran a car repair shop on the site of the Little House of Death was good enough for him, no matter how thin the connection (not to mention the story). And so our two school-mates, aged 12 and 13 respectively, appeared on the front page of the Rasen Mail looking dumbstruck and vacant into Danny's lens. The headline: 'Rasen lads claim to spot UFO.' That was pretty much the whole story. That a large carrier had been heading towards RAF Binbrook on the night in question was only mentioned at the end of the final paragraph, tucked away on an inside page.

Before that minor truth, the awe-smacked lads told of their sensational adventure. At twilight they'd been walking back towards town from the woods when the huge vessel had passed overhead, flying steady and low, and pocked with a medley of twinkling, coloured lights. The looming ship had given out a low rumble that had steadily increased in volume the closer it passed over Walesby Road. The boys had been scared, they confessed, but excited too. It could not have been an aeroplane, because aeroplanes flew so far above Lincolnshire that you could barely see them, only their soundless jet streams. It was obviously not a helicopter. Kevin and Graham weren't stupid enough to mistake a helicopter for a UFO. So, by a process of elimination, they concluded this was a visiting craft from another planet in a galaxy far, far away.

Danny had his front page story for that week and could head down to The George with his conscience clear. True or not, everyone was talking about it, and it made a change from 'Town Reserves win 3-1 at South Kelsey' or 'Claxby WI welcomes guest speaker from Barton.' According to Rick Carlton's sister, Suzy, who was Danny's assistant at the Mail, he called his usual contacts in London, but they were standoffish. Domestic slaughter and deadly explosions were one thing, but two school-kids claiming to spot a UFO? What was the real story? Danny conceded in the end that the mysterious craft 'might have' been a carrier headed for RAF Binbrook. 'But it's still a good story, right?'

'It's not true, though,' said the woman impatiently. 'We're only interested in stories that stand up.'

'Since when?' Danny asked, and she hung up on him.

The newsman's instinct was spot on, though. The issue sold out, no returns, which had not happened since the murder and the explosion. For Kevin and Graham, the news was not so good. The story was cut out and pinned up all over school, with pointy-headed aliens drawn in to the background. The two boys could not walk a yard without their fellow pupils pointing to the sky and exhorting them to look upwards. 'Ground control to Graham Mead,' the pupils sang. There was Life on Mars in abundance. We snickered about what the two had been getting up to in the woods.

After two days of this, they both stayed at home for a fortnight, and then came the Easter holidays. When they returned, the mockery had lost its momentum, and they only endured a few more weeks of fingers to the sky until we boys (it was only boys) tired of the taunting. The cruelty was revived for a week or two when Close Encounters of the Third Kind hit the cinema, and every time we passed Kevin or Graham we'd sing the five-note refrain that the fictitious aliens had used to communicate with mankind.

Kevin didn't respond to the catcalls, he would just look past you. Graham would - much to our delight - spit 'Fook off,' with genuine anger, even months after the sighting. Like the story really had been true. A UFO had flown over Market Rasen, and they'd been the only people aware enough to notice. One day, the aliens would land and hail Kevin and Graham like two of their own, then zap away the sceptics. We imagined them lying awake at night, peering through a gap in the curtains, ears alert to the return of that ascending rumble.

The two grew up without further fuss, and at some point they left school and bulked out. Kevin helped out in his dad's garage, and Graham shifted sacks of flour all day at the Old Mill. They stayed close friends and drank at The Aston, just around the corner from The George. Danny Selwood, meanwhile, hit less affluent times. There were no more murders, no more explosions, no more putative aliens. His shiny black hair was thinning too, while the paunch from too many hours at The George now hid the buckle of his belt. His bellicose tales of having 'a woman in every village' were less credible with each pint that passed his lying lips.

I'm not saying that Kevin and Graham did it. They were never involved in that hard-man nonsense you'd get in the market place and outside the Festival Hall disco on a Saturday night. They didn't try and stare you out when they'd had a few beers, although that's what we all deserved. They never spoke to anyone much, just to the bar staff and each other. They'd play a lot of pool, and would give you a nod of acknowledgment after the game, regardless of the result. Yet they somehow dominated the place with their gargantuan arms. It would have taken someone braver than me to go up after closing time, point to the night sky, and say, 'Look up there, mate, it's a fookin' UFO!' and break out into one of Bowie's songs from the 70s.

And so the rumour spread that Danny Selwood had limped into The George on Sunday lunchtime with several cuts and marks to his face. He'd had a bad fall, he said. No, he hadn't been drunk. It had happened at home, when he stood on a wobbly chair to change a light bulb. There was too much detail and way too many facial bruises for the story to make sense. The alternative version was spread by whispers. Kevin and Graham had followed him home to his flat on Waterloo Street the night before, while everyone else was rucking in the town car park. They'd waited until he was right in front of his flat, in a back alley, fumbling for his key after an all-day session. Wordlessly, they damaged him to their satisfaction and left him unconscious on his door step. A neighbour who'd heard noises poured water on the reporter, who'd then woken up and staggered in to bed.

That story never made it to The George, let alone the Market Rasen Mail. The rest of us wondered, 'What if that was just the start?' But there was no pattern of violence. Instead, people started buying drinks for the two lads, and invited them on to the pub's pool team. They joined, but they still played a wordless game, no better or worse than anyone else. When ET came out, there was not a single wisecrack.

Danny was still walking with a limp when he made a grand announcement a few months later, heard only by Matt Davey at the bar of The George. 'I'm off to the Spilsby Gazette,' he told him. 'Better pussy down there. This town's a dump.'

'You won't need to watch your back there either,' said Matt.

'What's that supposed to mean?'

Matt just shrugged and smiled. He wouldn't be sad to see Danny go, he'd been hearing his shagging brags and unfiltered opinions for over a decade. For once, the journalist went silent. When he finished his pint he said, 'You can all piss off,' got up from his bar stool for the last time, and hobbled out the door. A minute later he collapsed on Church Street, right in front of Pete Salter's car repair shop. Pete called an ambulance, but it was already too late. Danny had suffered a cardiac arrest and died on the spot.

At least, that's how Suzy Carlton wrote it up in the Market Rasen Mail.

Ferhana

Sam Szanto

I wake to a tightening in my belly. Could this be it?

Struggling because of my bulk, I get up before the others. I am, as always, tired and aching from sleeping with my head on my arm because there are no pillows. It is difficult to dress without hitting anyone in the face. There are twelve of us living in this iso-box that we built out of scrap wood. We clubbed together to pay for it after meeting on our first week here. It is uncomfortable, but I am grateful. Many without our luck sleep under tarpaulins or the stars themselves.

Clothed, I go outside to breathe in the crisp air, to enjoy the dawn quiet. It is so hard to find peace in this place: this is the golden hour.

When we have breakfasted on leftover food and cold drinks – there is no power to make tea or coffee – we sit outside the container in a circle, wrapped in blankets. To keep our spirits up, we make music. Some sing and others play instruments: Farsi love songs, classical Spanish guitar. Some of the young ones' voices are smooth as oil.

As the day wears on, the sensation in my belly comes and goes. It is like the worst period pains I have had. No one has taught me about birth, so I ask my friend Farah if this is how labour feels.

'Yes, you're having contractions. The baby will come soon. You should walk, Mariam.' Farah's face is alight with excitement.

We walk around the camp together. Every so often there is another pull, the baby reminding me that they are there. Excitement swirls into worry and back again, like the colours inside the kaleidoscope my mother bought me as a child. I wish my mother was here now, but she will not leave Afghanistan; I pray she and my father are safe. My husband should also be here. He was trying to get to Germany, where he planned to send for me and the baby, but I have not heard anything for weeks.

In the half-light, Farah and I pick around tents festooned with cables. Confetti-bright washing hangs on trees. Voices rise and fall; some angry, some gentle. Smoke billows from where Afghanis are baking flatbreads, a smell that brings my tongue alive. I'm surprised that despite the pains, I am hungry. But of course, I always am. The body remembers.

We pass the reeking toilets and the queues for them. It is the same with the showers. I have heard of ten-hour waits to wash in the freezing water.

The sheer volume of people makes the present feel very narrow. I smile at some of the faces I pass. Some smile back, mostly it looks like a mere contraction of the muscles. There is more fighting than smiling. More and more, more and more, every day: fighting in the queues, mainly. The more people there are: the more fights. Afghanis versus Syrians, usually. A war-zone, in a place we have come to escape war-zones.

Sunken-faced children drag their feet, as they slump behind their parents. Others, still full of life, eyes as large as the futures they deserve, clamber on piles of waste. One child offers us sunflower seeds. A man and woman carry a toddler between them in a cardboard box. I guess I will carry my baby all the time, unless I can find an old pram in the rubbish: unlikely. As much as I am longing to see my child, I am terrified of them living here. No child should look like these children, with their skin conditions; no child should sound like these children, with their breathing difficulties. Not all the children are like this, but this is what most of them become.

'Do not lose your hope, Mariam,' was the last thing my husband said, as I was leaving for the boat. 'I will find you, and Inshallah the three of us will have a wonderful new life.'

A contraction pulls me out of the rooms of my past. Farah says to rotate my belly. She knows what it is to have children, although her teenage boy and girl managed to escape to the UK. She cries every night that they are yateem: orphaned. But at the same time she is relieved they are safe, and not in our broken-boned country like her husband.

Suddenly, the dusty air is charged with expectation. Shouting, sirens, police. People are evacuating their shelters, moving to the boundary. Farah and I tread around piles of garbage and a wide pool of muddy water, past the military post, and reach the edge of the camp. It is surrounded by olive groves, scorched tree trunks. And, of course, semi-circles of barbed wire around the gates. Those who do not wish to use the gates go through a hole in the fence; on the other side is the Jungle, the area into which the camp exploded when thousands more people than it was built for arrived.

The darkness is creeping up. It is not good to be out late in winter: there has been no electricity for months. The night is when the violence comes alive. Farah and I stand by the fence and wait, shivering in the cold, until whatever has happened to involve the police has subsided.

The contractions are speeding-up; I occupy the pain for as long as it lasts. Farah times them in her head: they are about every five minutes.

'Should I go to the clinic?' I ask.

'I hope the clinic will not send us away. But the baby will come soon, Inshallah, you need help. Do you have your ausweis, Mariam?'

My ausweis are my police papers; I cannot go to the clinic after-hours without them. I have them tucked into the formerly loose-fitting pants that I'm wearing.

When people are walking and not running, we move too, past a pack of wild dogs barking. I keep stopping to move my hips, a crazy dance, yelling as the sensation tears through me. I scream curses at my husband; I cry that I need him. At least the pain takes my mind off the bone-chilling cold. When people come close, staring at me, Farah tells them to keep their distance as if I am one of the wild dogs. And then it is twice in five minutes, Farah says; she takes my arm to try to get to the clinic more quickly. I'm not sure how we will find it in the darkness that is like a mouth threatening to swallow us.

A group of men is dragging a blanket containing a screaming person along the ground. Whoever it is must either be wounded or have lost their mind.

'Where are you going?' Farah calls to the group, 'the clinic? Can we follow you?'

'If you can keep up, sister,' one of the men shouts over his shoulder. 'This brother is having an attack, he needs help now.'

We move heavily through the camp, past the olive tree burnt-out from a recent fire. Along the rivers of mud and rubbish we go, Farah and me holding each other's arms. Finally, we are at the clinic waiting for the gates to be opened.

The medics and translators wear head-torches. A young doctor asks about our conditions; the man in the blanket and I are colour-coded in triage. He is red; I'm green: less important. As our names are written on whiteboards, another contraction rocks through me; the pain is becoming unendurable.

Two young Syrian men stagger in. Stabbings: 'red', like their blood that has sprayed onto the floor and walls. One is swiftly moved to a bed, the other is not. Within minutes, the one left in the waiting area, whose face has the smoothness of childhood, is gargling and choking. It is dreadful to watch. A translator runs for the emergency doctor.

'I wish I had trained as a doctor,' Farah says. 'I was so proud when I graduated as a teacher, but what use am I at a time like this?'

'Teachers are always useful,' I say. 'The children need to learn.'

I've heard that, incredibly, there is a library being built in the camp. It will be a shack, but there will be books. The librarian is a man who gives classes under an olive tree. He does English, German, art, all kinds. I wish there had been ante-natal classes. At home, I would have attended them; I would have made friends with other soon-to-be mothers. I would have had some idea of what to expect.

'Well, nothing can really prepare you for labour,' Farah says, 'or parenthood.'

As the pain rips through me again, I shut my eyes, colours exploding behind the lids. I imagine my husband's skin against mine, his soothing voice telling me that we will all be fine. What would he say if he could see me near to birthing his child on this gravel floor, in this waiting room that is like a cage?

'When will they get me to a bed?' I yell.

'Really it is better without a bed,' Farah says, 'lying down is the wrong position. I had both my children on all fours, mooing like a cow.'

Things are happening. The medics have found an oxygen tank for the choking boy; there is another siren that I hope is an ambulance.

'Will you ask them to take me to hospital too?' I plead with Farah.

The medics push her back when she goes outside. The stabbed boys are more important than a pregnant lady. The boys are taken out on stretchers, lines feeding into them. I wonder what happened to the man in the blanket, whether he is receiving care.

'Worry only about yourself, Mariam,' Farah says, 'yourself, and your baby. Inshallah, she will be born safe and healthy. And born into a world where nothing is taken for granted: clean air, sunlight, fresh air, belonging to a country.'

Another contraction bends me double. As I am pushing myself upright, there is a whooshing in my insides and a torrent of brown water shoots out onto the floor.

'What's that?' I shriek.

Farah looks in concern at the puddle. I ask why she's worried, what it means, my voice shaking. She makes a motion in the air to brush my question away and hurries out again. I can't think that a doctor will come but one does, a white-skinned girl with a Western accent.

'Meconium in your waters,' she says briskly. The word means nothing to me. 'The baby could be in distress. We need to get you a bed, right now.'

The doctor measures my cervix. I am nine-and-a-half centimetres dilated. Farah says that means I am almost ready for the pushing stage. The doctor tells me that I was brave to have got to this point myself, but that I must not push until I am at ten centimetres. Farah asks whether I can be given gas and air, but there is nothing like that here.

When she has gone, Farah laughs.

'Try not to push, she says! That is like telling the waves in the sea not to move. I can guarantee that doctor-child has not had a baby.'

A translator, a middle-aged Iranian woman, comes in. She introduces herself as Anousheh and says the doctor sent her. Farah says she can go, as she herself speaks English, Persian and Pashto, but the translator explains that she works as a nurse at the clinic.

'I had my training watching the doctors and nurses here,' Anousheh says.

Is this kind-faced woman with no proper medical training going to deliver my baby?

A room with a bed in it becomes available. I walk there, leaning on Anousheh and Farah. There is blood on the walls and floor of the room. Anousheh and Farah clean it; they don't let me help. I rest my elbows and head on the bed. It has been weeks since I have even seen a bed and I would love to sleep on it, but the pain will not allow this.

The doctor strides in, measures me again; ten centimetres. She tells me I can push and goes out again. I push, feeling like I am being torn open.

I push and push, push and push, but nothing happens. It is as if the baby was sand slipping down the neck of an hourglass, and now that sand has got stuck near the bottom. I am exhausted.

'Farah,' I croak, my screaming having hurt my vocal chords, 'please don't stay up all night for me. Go and sleep.'

She shakes her head. 'I am not leaving you, Mariam. We refugees need to stick together.'

'I never imagined having a baby born as a refugee. They won't have a country: they will always be an outsider,' I say, tears flooding my face.

'Mariam, jaanaan, there is nothing wrong with being on the outside if you can see in. You cannot rely on a country. A country doesn't love you. It can, in the end, always let you down. You can only rely on another person, and on yourself.'

'Do you wish you had stayed in Afghanistan?'

'Sometimes I think that this camp is hell, there can be nowhere worse. But then I remember what the Taliban think of women: how they don't want us to read anything apart from the Koran. As a teacher, I could not let that happen to my clever daughter. She wants to be a doctor: she will be a doctor. I have to believe that I will see that happen. I have to believe that I will be reunited with my children. If this is hell, then that would be heaven.'

'There are different hells. My brother was killed in the Tehran attacks,' Anousheh says. 'We had no chance to say goodbye. At least we don't have suicide bombers here.'

The pain rips through me again: I don't feel I can bear this much longer.

'We need more doctors so much,' Anousheh says sadly. 'You know what happened yesterday? I was working in the clinic, doing dressings – the doctors can't do everything – and a young man fell through the doors with a knife in his back. I had to try and help him myself before the emergency doctor could come.'

'That young man is someone's son, someone will be grieving for him,' Farah says.

'They got him to hospital. But do you think refugees are a priority in Greek hospitals?'

Anousheh's is a rhetorical question. We are not a priority for anyone except each other; the ones of us who do not stab each other in the back: the ones as caring as Farah.

Pain and pain and pain. Although I am trying to push, I am growing weaker. I am afraid this could kill me, and my baby. Farah holds my head in both hands, as if it is a precious bowl.

'You know what, jaanaan,' she says softly, mother-like, 'when I got here and slept under the stars those first days with the coat and smelly blanket I was given, I stayed awake for hours. It was a clear night, and the stars were beautiful. We are all under the same stars, us and our families who love us.'

At last, the doctor comes back. She peers between my legs, tells me to stay strong, it will not be long. But my strength has almost deserted me.

'One more push,' Farah commands, squeezing my shoulders.

One more push – then one more – and the baby is in the world. A girl: a perfect girl. The cord is cut; the doctor cleans her and hands her to me.

My baby's eyes are bright as moons. She gazes at me solemnly then climbs to my breast to suckle; already, her knowledge is greater than mine. I call her Ferhana, 'one living a comfortable life'. Right now this is my sole hope for my daughter, but hope is its own miracle.

Born of Angels

Joan Taylor-Rowan

These wings are heavy. The muscles in my back are so huge now that I look like I've been necking steroids - which is no bad thing at 3 a.m. in Deptford. They're covered in real gold feathers and I hear a metallic tinnitus every time I fold them. Forget the harps, Gabriel always jokes, we're all about the Heavy Metal.

I'm in my favourite 24-hour supermarket - Housewives Cash and Carry - loading up with sugar and e-numbers. Gabriel says we are instruments of the Universe, and must treat our bodies like a Charlie Parker sax or a Miles Davis trumpet but I know he'll forgive me this once. I deserve a treat. Today I completed my first Visitation. I'm scanning the racks trying to find the Haribo sour cherries when a foot wearing a sparkly trainer stops my trolley.

'Fuck, it's you, isn't it!' she says.

I'm afraid to look up because my heart is flipping. Shania the Dropout; I've been thinking about her and here she is. I try to move the trolley but she's having none of it. I straighten up and my wings start their music. Dipping my face I allow my angel-gaze to settle on her. This usually causes weakness, dizziness and fainting in most women but Shania takes out her gum and crushes it hard onto the mesh of the trolley. She stares back at me with narrowed eyes, unflinching. Of course she does. But it wasn't always this way.

'So, you're still pulling this stunt then,' she says popping in a new stick. As she chews it, I see her pierced tongue writhing like a wounded animal. She's trying to undermine me; she can't help herself. That used to be our thing, snider-than-thou. She had matching T-shirts made for us that said I'm a chronic ironic. But irony seems like cowardice now.

'Give me a break and let me shop,' I say, faking world-weariness, although my blood is sprinting.

'Ooh let me shop,' she mewls. She peers into my trolley, picks up a baguette and points it at me. 'I thought man could not live by bread alone.' She smiles her crooked smile and I realise again how much I've missed her.

'Cool cloak by the way,' she says, looping her arm through mine as if it's been three hours not three years.

'It's my raiment,' I say, (yeah we have this special vocabulary). Its blue velvet with slits in the back for the wings and it's a bummer to get on and off, but it kind of completes the look. When I'm not at work, like tonight, I just drape it over my hump. I get glances, of course but round here they probably think I'm a performance artist from Goldsmiths', or a whacked-out weirdo who's best avoided. That works for me.

'You look like a Quasimodo drag queen,' she says. She unhooks her arm and sprints ahead pulling things off shelves then shoving them back again. I wonder if she's still using – she has that nervous twitchiness but I can't see her eyes for the fake lashes. I feel uncomfortable suddenly, watching her do the stuff we used to do. The supermarket security guard keeps his eye on her –he's a big, bored man with a soft waist and a name tag dangling on his chest.

His identity photo captures a moment when he had a vague hope that this job might go somewhere. I smile at him, shrug. I used to be like him once 'til I took to the streets with Shania. It beat the children's home or her money-grabbing foster mother.

We used to hang out in here in the old days; the aisles were our nightclub, the fruit section, our orchard. We would kiss under the fluorescent lights, their buzz and flicker the pulse of our passion. 'I will never leave you,' we said to each other, which was almost true. Madness, rain, morning fogs when we ran down Creek Road screaming and holding hands, stopping on the Halfpenny Hatch Bridge, feeding each other Skittle Sours as the Thames fled the city for the sea. She liked the green ones; I liked the yellow. We both hated the blues.

The security guard walks and watches. I grip the handle and stare into the trolley trying to hide my celestial luminosity. I'm waiting for her to come back to me and hoping she won't.

We were teenagers when we were chosen - when we chose - Gabriel likes us to take responsibility. We were on Comet Street, smoking our last bit of weed, eyes alert for someone with money. And along he came in a fancy suit, a black briefcase clutched to his chest, walking like he'd had one tequila too many. Gabriel was just too easy. So we stopped him, me and Shania, together.

'Got a light?' she said and he lifted his face and shone his countenance upon us. One gaze and that was it, a Maglite into the soul. I'd never thought about my soul before but I saw it then for what it was - a putrefied bit of potato peel, a puked-up hair ball. I covered my face. Shania tried to stare him down but even she crumpled in the end. We went with him.

She soon tired of the long hours though, the unceasing kindness and the discipline. I reveled in it. She never believed, like I did, that she could change. She missed our own bruised world of two. She missed the drugs. We'll be high on life, Gabriel said, and she sneered. They told us, you will be creators, spark-makers, but she thought it was all a scam, so she left before they told her what that really meant. I wouldn't leave and she couldn't stay. So we parted on the Halfpenny Bridge; her accusations were arrows in my back. I hated that she wanted me to choose but I had changed already, I could feel it.

What's in it for me?' she always said.

She says it now, looking into my trolley, 'What's in it for me?'

I offer her a bag of Doritos. And as my hand touches hers I feel the need in her flicker.

I put the Haribos back on the shelf. 'Come with me and I'll make you some real food.'

She doesn't refuse, which tells me a lot. I pay at the checkout and we walk out into the darkness.

It's silent even in the deep heart of the city. I can hear her footsteps trying to keep up with my silent seraphic ones. We walk past the new housing developments, the cranes, dissecting the old warehouses like surgeons.

'You still live round here then?' she says, 'I thought you must have moved, flown off.'

People talk a lot of crap about angels. We don't fly much anymore, we manifest. We appear from nowhere, radiant and shimmering. That sensation - here not here - is like a breath. Shania would have loved it. Breathing out on cold days, making the invisible visible…like kissing, she once said.

'I don't keep regular hours,' I say, 'and we don't fly, remember?'

'Very Extinction Rebellion,' she says. 'So how's life as an angel?' She flicks a smirk at me.

'It pays the rent,' I sigh dramatically, and we burst out laughing. I know I need to keep her at a distance but there's a part of me that yearns to hold her close.

The room I have now is in the top of St Paul's Church. I unlock a door that you'd never see unless you were looking.

'Will I be allowed in, given that I'm no angel?' She scoops up her green-blue hair and knots it into a scrunchie.

I'm wondering this myself. Strictly speaking this is a member's only club, and she did give Gabe the finger when she walked out.

'I don't think Gabe bears a grudge,' I say ushering her in. She stops and searches my face.

'What about you?' she says.

I shrug, and we continue up the grimy stairs to the loft rooms, my heart chugging.

Three angels are sitting on the couch watching 'Michael', starring John Travolta – it's one of our favourites. The smell of coriander and cumin pours out of the kitchen. Its manna, but it can take on any smell your stomach's hungry for. She looks surprised.

'We're still human...' I say '...mostly.'

I'm trying to think of a way to explain what happened to me today when Mattie walks out of the kitchen, wiping his hands on a red apron that shows a devil with a barbeque fork. 'I'm a helluva cook,' it says.

'Hey Bro, how'd it go!' he yells.

I nod, smile. The others turn from the TV.

'What happened?' Shania says.

I don't know how to begin and then I don't need to. Mattie, his arm resting across my shoulders, pinches my cheek.

'Today he created his first new life. Woo hoo!' He beams, and the other angels turn from the movie and clap. I blush and accept their congratulations.

Shania's face is a picture. 'Eughh' she says, 'too much information.' She looks away and chews on the inside of her flushing cheek.

'I need to explain,' I say.

Mattie does not spot the awkwardness at first and lumbers on like a big, stupid dog. 'Gabe warned me,' he says. 'There's fizz in the fridge, but only if you spill all to your Uncle Mattie!'

Shania is pouting, her arms folded around her chest. Mattie suddenly looks at Shania's contemptuous face and then at me, puzzled. I introduce them.

'This is Mattie, my Winger. Mattie, this is Shania, my... my friend- she's a Dropout.'

Mattie's luminosity dips a bit. 'Sorry to hear that, Shania.' But he can't wait, he turns to me, 'So come on then tell me how it went?'

He's desperate for details, some cock-up or a funny anecdote. For all his bluster and bravado, he hasn't graduated yet. I give him the basics of my Visitation and watch his big friendly face reflect the highs and lows of my story. Shania is unusually quiet but the sneer has turned into something else, regret, I hope.

My first Visitation was not what I'd imagined. We manifested, me and Gabe, in a car park, broken concrete, and abandoned cars resting on blocks. A fox stopped and stared at me, one paw raised.

Gabe whispered in my ear. 'We're in Sunderland.'

I shivered. I wasn't dressed for the north.

'See that woman?' He pointed over to the field of reeds. 'She works at the mechanic's as a receptionist. But she comes here every day and stares at the scummy clouds and the nesting birds and she yearns.' He squeezed my shoulder, and I felt my wings rustle like dry leaves.

'What do I do?' I whispered to Gabe, don't leave me!' He smiled and slowly de-manifested, like that cat in the Alice book.

The woman turned and gaped at me, her face round and pale as a plate. She crossed herself, her eyes darting from side-to-side. They call for you, but they never really believe you'll come. I turned away to calm my nerves. My wings caught the sun and flashed. The fox bolted into the reeds. The woman fell to the floor. Awful – I mean literally.

I knelt down beside her and she stared up at me, her moon face with its blond wispy hair a mixture of hope and terror. I smiled and offered her my hand. Then I did as Gabe had taught me. I lay my palm on her belly. I hoped she couldn't feel me shaking. We locked eyes. I saw the rusted cars reflected in her dark pupils, the reeds waving, then a carpeted room with an empty cot, a mobile of stars and moons, a secret drawer full of mittens and cardigans and scraps of paper with scrawled messages to Him. She gasped and I knew it had taken– a sharp heat, atomic lightning, a surge in my blood and bones like a fire catching.

'That's' amazing, Bro!' Mattie laughed and tipped back in his chair until his wings touched the ground. His eyes misted. 'What a blast! So man, you'll have to follow her now, check up on the child. A

Sparking's for life not just for Christmas.' He grinned.

Shania had been playing with zipper on her pink hoodie running it up and down faster and faster. 'So you're telling me that you've knocked up a girl and you're proud of it?' She bursts out.

Mattie's eyes widen and he begins to laugh and shake his head. I twist my mouth towards him, furrow my brow.

'No, thank the Godhead,' Mattie reassures her. He flicks open his cigarette lighter and rolls his thumb on the wheel until a flame pops up. 'He's just the Spark-maker. Humans do the mechanics – we do the rest….unless…' His face dims again, flickers like a neon sign on the blink.

'Unless what?' Shania says.

Mattie looks right at her. 'Angels get afraid too, sometimes.' A cloud crosses his face, passes. He rolls his chair back upright grabs the champagne with a big oafish grin and forces out the cork with his thumbs. It rockets off and Shania ducks. Foam pours down the glass.

Shania's leg is bobbing up and down under the table. I can feel the restlessness in her, the confusion.

She turns to me. 'Why would we have been chosen to do this? What did we have to make us special? We were just trash weren't we?' she says, 'Looked-after children. Yeah right.'

I study her angry little face, her knotted body and I want to cry. I know that stricken look. She has spent her life believing she's worthless; too worthless to take a hand when it was offered, too wary to give her own in return. When I 'graduated' today, Shania was the first person I wanted to tell, but Gabe advised against it. Now I realise why. Seeing her there, all spikes and wounds and wildness I feel a flash of that fierce love and yet I also know with unexpected certainty, that I chose the right path.

She massages her temples, as if shaping an important thought.

'Are we all conceived like this?' she whispers. 'Were we? What about the Ripper? Or Ted Bundy?'

I look to Mattie. He's so full of this miracle that he's gleaming at the edges. He opens his hands as if he holds a live beating heart in them and can hardly believe it.

'All of us. Even this useless lover of yours...' he flicks his head at me.

'Ex,' she snorts. Her chin quivers, her eyes bloom. 'Why doesn't someone, like, snapchat everyone about it?' she says. 'Why didn't someone tell me before I dropped out?' Suddenly, she is crying. 'If you'd told me... if I'd known. Look at me. Look what a fuck-up I am.' She pulls a tissue from her pocket and blows her nose loudly.

No-one turns from the TV. They're used to fuck-ups. I try to put my arm around her but she shrugs me off. Shania's heart only has the cynic settings.

'If my mum had seen an angel when I was conceived, you think she might have mentioned it,' she blubs. 'Chrissake.' She can't find a dry place on her tissue, so she wipes her nose on her sleeve. 'And if she did see one, how could she have, dumped me?'

Mattie looks at me and sighs. I lift one of Shania's fingers, with its chewed nails and home-made tattoos, WHAT on the right knuckles, EVER on the left. I wiggle her finger and she lifts her eyes to me.

'No one remembers it,' I tell her, 'and that's the saddest part. No-one remembers that we're all born of angels.'

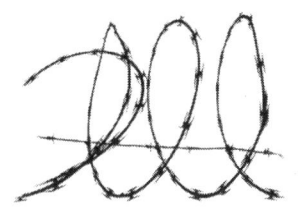

The Happiness Equation

Christine Powell

Honourable Mention

The doll had long, brown, curling hair and blue eyes that blinked. She came in a silver box with white ribbons and Amy wanted her so badly her chest ached. To win her, you had to pay ten pence (which went to school funds) and pick her name from a list. All the little girls giggled, pretending they couldn't decide, then ticked their own names when they thought no-one was looking.

One of the dinner ladies won the doll and gave it to her granddaughter.

'She was named after Saint Barbara, who lived in the third century,' said Sister Margaret. 'It is good to have a saint's name. Margaret is not my real name, I chose it. My saint is Margaret of Antioch, who is the patron saint of childbirth.' Amy and her best friend Claire pulled huge, shocked faces at each other behind the desk lids. Everyone knew that nuns were too bald and wrapped up like liquorice toffee to have babies.

On the first Friday at school it was fish, mash and cabbage for dinner. White fish, white mash and dark green cabbage that smelled like toilets. She pushed the fish carefully to one side of her plate.

Claire said: 'you have to eat fish on Fridays. God says so. It's the rule.'

Amy ate the potatoes. She held her nose and ate the cabbage, even though it made her feel sick. She stared at the fish. Everybody else was queuing for pudding. She couldn't not eat it because of the rule and because, obviously, God would be angry with her. She closed her eyes and shoveled it into her mouth really quickly, even though she knew it would make her ill.

Very soon, she came out in great big red spots. It was worth the itching because everyone was worried and thought she must have something extremely serious and infectious and Sister Margaret had to 'phone her mother to take her home.

On Tuesday, when she got back to school, Claire said: 'you'll never turn into a PROPER CATHOLIC if you're allergic to fish. And, by the way, there is no Saint Amy, I checked.'

Every Friday after that she had to sit in a classroom with one of the lay assistants. She got two Dairylea cheese triangles, some dry crackers and a green apple cut into quarters for lunch.

When Father Mulherne started taking the confirmation classes Amy, Claire, her sister, Pauline, and a girl with watery eyes called Rosemary had to go and do their maths homework with Sister Laurence because they were the wrong religion. One week, Sister Laurence was ill, so they had to squash into the back of the class with the others. The priest had grey hair and eyebrows like thunder clouds.

'This is a very important time in your lives. Now, who can tell me why that is?'

'Because Jesus is coming!'

'That's right. You will be visited by Jesus. You have only to open your heart, like opening the door to your home, and He, The Lord God will stay with you forever.'

Amy felt something hot and fluttery like butter melting down her chest. 'When's he coming? When did he say He was coming?'

Claire frowned and turned away.

Why hadn't anybody told her? Obviously everybody else knew, everybody else was ready, everybody else's mother had put the kettle on and tidied the spare bedroom.

Then even Claire deserted her. She found out one Thursday teatime. 'Unbelievable isn't it?' said her mother, 'those girls just nagged and nagged until their poor parents gave in.'

Amy's father turned to her, a fleck of egg white was stuck on his bottom lip. 'Don't ever let me catch you trying to pull that kind of stunt, young lady.'

'What's a stunt?'

'Turning Catholic. Never heard of anything so ridiculous.' And he stomped off to read his newspaper.

After that, she only ever seemed to see the rear view of Claire's long, black plait as she swung into the confirmation classes with her sister, leaving Amy to do battle alone with Rosemary, Sister Laurence, long division and equations on Friday afternoons. Life just seemed to be one inscrutable puzzle after another. Every time she tried to find some answers she just found more questions. So, one hot Friday she formulated the big question. Why is Hungriness like Saintliness?

She tried it out on Rosemary, who just narrowed her eyes and said, sarcastically, 'is that some kind of stupid riddle? Because, if it is, it's not very funny.'

Amy sighed. It clearly wasn't worth even trying to explain that it wasn't supposed to be funny. She comforted herself with the knowledge that Rosemary would never understand the plan. Rosemary would never discover how deliciously easy it is to lose a Dairylea cheese triangle down the side of a bench, or how many satisfyingly secret hiding places there are, little cracks and corners where nobody ever looks. So Rosemary, in spite of having a sanctimonious name, would never be saintly, except that her family did at least go to church on Sundays, whereas Amy's didn't.

But salvation, too, hides in strange places. When Angela from next door got married, Amy was a bridesmaid. She wore a pale blue satin frock and had yellow rosebuds in her hair. It was her first time in a real church. It was the wrong kind of church, but that didn't matter. She kneeled so hard she got bruises on her legs and she clenched her hands so tightly her fingernails left deep red gouges in her palms but it was worth it, just to feel good.

Angela's husband came from Canada. At the reception, which was in a big tent, he gave her a book of poems and wrote, 'For Amy. Thanks for helping us out on our special day, with love from Angela and Lowell,' on the flyleaf. Then he sat down beside her on the floor and said:

'What happened to your knees?'

'I've got stigmata.' Amy said, opening her hands.

'My! Are you sure?'

'Yes. It's important to know the correct name for things. Angela's lucky. She's named after the angels. There isn't a Saint Amy.'

'Amy comes from the French. To love. That's pretty good isn't it?'

He heaved himself to his feet, like one of those metal lamps unfolding.

'I have to go cut the cake now. You want me to keep you a bit with extra icing?'

Amy nodded and watched him all the way back to the top table, thinking how it was a shame he wasn't better looking. She tucked herself a bit further into her corner, so as to better observe all the grown-ups eating and drinking. There were flakes of pastry on the wooden boards, and a broken champagne glass. Angela's sister had lost her shoes. An unidentified pair of trousers crashed into the big flower arrangement next to the table with the gifts on, sending sprays of mimosa and white roses across the floor. Amy hugged her knees; now, more than ever, it was important to focus on the plan. And, slowly, everything became clearer. She could get away with not being named Mary or Agnes or Bernadette, with not going to the right church or any church, because her big question wasn't a riddle, but a simple equation: Goodness x Hungriness = Saintliness.

She wrapped her cake in one of the special wedding serviettes, snow white with a border of silver bells. Then, unnoticed, she slipped out of the tent and buried it underneath the ornamental gorse bush in Angela's parents' garden. It seemed a small price to pay.

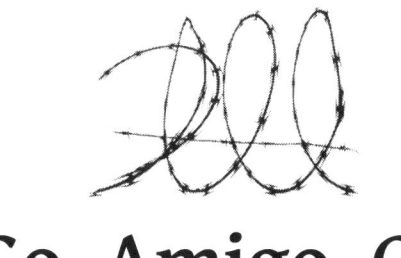

Go, Amigo, Go!

Joan Taylor-Rowan

Miguel drags the cart of boxed bananas behind him. He wants to stretch but his Eden-Super overall is constricting his chest. They didn't have one to fit him; he's too short and stocky. Got to lay off the burritos, amigo, Mike the Boss said. Mike is a numero uno asshole and Miguel would like to tell him to shove it.

He lugs the load past the deli counter with its sealed hot dogs, chicken sausages, and gleaming pink cylinders of ham. It isn't like the butcher's back home where the carcasses hang from steel hooks waiting to be chopped and wrapped. There he goes again. He's been trying to stop himself day-dreaming about it, but the memories ambush him. Everything reminds him that he's in a very different place, like the Trick or Treaters that cornered him on his first week in El Norte and asked him if he was dressed as a Narco.

He closes his eyes now and recalls the sour, iron tang of the carnicería, hears the thwack and grind of the butcher's cleaver separating bones from flesh. He opens his eyes again. Where is the wrinkled tripe, the wobbling crimson liver? They're afraid of it, these Norte-Americanos, afraid of the squish and drip of life.

Miguel comes to a stop in the vegetable aisle and swings the laden cart in front of him. Lettuces, radishes and onions sit in plastic trays. A row of angled mirrors above stretches them to infinity. Every few minutes they are bathed in a cool mist of water. They're perfect, like cartoon vegetables. Even the mangoes don't have that rotten-sweet smell that lingers in your nostrils; a sticker says when they are ripe and ready to eat. That's how they like things here, all surface, like the rich, fake ladies with the fat lips that look like they've been in a fight.

His curly hair keeps escaping its elastic so he pushes the strands back behind his ears. He glimpses the tattoo on the inside of his arm - a young girl wrapped in a Mexican flag. It's his little sister Martina. It's been six months since her death, but it seems like a century and then also like it was yesterday. He had the tattoo done in Pedro's place a week after the shooting. He wanted her image seared into his flesh, pain to mimic what his heart felt. He took in a photograph of her, the one he still keeps in his wallet. The needle was a relief even though it had made tears roll into his ears. It's the nerve endings make that happen, Pedro lied. Miguel strokes Martina's face with his thumb and feels his blood running through her. Today would've been her tenth birthday.

He begins to unpack the boxes. Chiquita bananas. The small hands of them laid out in rows look just like yellow baseball mitts. He stares into the box, floored. That's what Martina had been doing in the street when she got hit, crouching in her shorts, waiting for the pitch, Josefina about to send it skywards. He'd been sitting on a bench with his cousin Tiago watching the game. Then a sharp crack like a firework made him jump and duck. A car flashed white at the edge of his eye, a blast of pumping music. The bullet flew so close he'd heard its high-pitched whine. There was an instant of silence like God had hit the pause button then Josefina screamed and everyone ran like ants around a kicked-in nest. His sister lay on the ground, her white baseball shirt turning red and her glove still on her hand.

He'd been a father to her, the only father she'd ever known but like a fool, he'd tried to avenge her death, so he'd had to run. His friends used to talk of coming north but that had never been his dream.

'They look fresh; are they fresh in?' a large woman says to him even though she can see he's getting them out of the box. These gringos always say things they don't need to; use up words like they use up water, like they got so much of everything.

She pokes her hand into the box he's trying to unpack. She's looking for the best ones. He wants to tell her they're in his village market, not here in this box.

The screech she makes is a shrill burst like a cat being stepped on and then she's bobbing up and down, one hand on her chest the other fanning her face. People stop and stare at him, like he's done something. She's pointing to the box, her mouth opening and closing and then he sees it - two furry legs, creeping over the edge of the cardboard. He thinks of himself sneaking out from under the scrub oak, one arm at a time, his skin dark with dirt, his heart a wild drum, loud enough for the border patrol to hear.

Shoppers turn, alert to drama. The bolder ones come closer. An old guy sees the spider and gasps. A smile flits across Miguel's face. It's a banana spider and a big one too.

'S'okay,' Miguel says. He leans into the box preparing to pick it up.

'No!' the lady shouts.

He grabs a plastic bag from the dispenser by the apples. The spider tries to burrow under the bananas but Miguel lifts the bunch away. Cornered, it rears up, raising its red bristles. He feels an ache of sympathy for it.

'Someone got bitten?'

'I think it bit her on the right hand there.'

'Just kill it,' a teenager says.

'Where'd it come from?'

'Came in with the bananas.'

'Someone should build a wall.' The joker smiles at Miguel, like he should find it funny.

Murmuring soothing words in Spanish, Miguel puts his hand into the box, and places a finger and thumb on either side of the spider's abdomen. It can't jump when he has it like this. Its hairy body yields slightly to his touch like a ripe kiwi. He could crush it if he wanted. He holds it up to look more closely and the crowd draws back; there are cries of shock and some nervous laughter. He knows it's harmless but he can't think of the right words to tell them. He stares into its fierce and glittering eyes then places it in the bag and loosely knots the top. The spider, thwarted, shrinks into a corner.

A child is suddenly at his elbow squinting at the spider. 'He looks sad. You're not gonna kill 'im are you?' she says to Miguel, her eyes liquid.

He shakes his head. 'No, he is mi amigo, my friend,' he says, smiling down at her.

She peers in towards the spider, extending her finger.

'Careful,' Miguel says, bringing the spider a little closer.

A woman's hand comes out of the crowd and pulls the little girl back. She tries to shrug her mother off. He sees Martina suddenly, armed with a stick and halfway up a tree. I've found honey! she'd shouted down at him. He could hear the buzz of those bees five feet away. He'd threatened to turn the hose on her if she didn't come down. He sees her indignant face, her fearlessness and then he blinks her away.

A girl is heading towards them. She is wearing an Eden-Super overall too. It fits her well. She is carrying a First Aid box and quickly smoothing her fair hair.

'I heard a scream,' she says. 'Is someone hurt?'

She has round blue eyes edged with glittery green. Sky and lake, Miguel thinks. There is a lake like that near his home in Veracruz where Martina learned to swim. She was a slippery fish in his arms. Don't let go, Don't Let go! she'd squealed, while desperate to strike out on her own. He'd been trying to explain to her that people cannot sink.

'Excuse me, mam, clear the way there, I'm the first aider,' the girl says a bit too loudly and people move back. 'Oh wow!' she says, catching sight of the bagged spider.

She pats her chest, drawing a ragged breath and screws her fingers into a fist. She closes her eyes and her mouth shapes, 'One-two, one-two.' When she blinks them open people are staring at her, waiting. She clears her throat with a rasping sound. Bronchitis –Miguel thinks. It's what his mother died from. Then he remembers: this is the girl who has the oxygen machine, the one who sits at the checkout with the tube to her nose. Some of the guys have mean names for her.

She lifts her identification badge as if she has forgotten who she is. It occurs to Miguel that she hasn't done this before. He recalls signs on the staff noticeboard for first aid volunteers. He didn't expect to be working here long enough to volunteer for anything. He thought his fake social security number would have been found out by now.

'I'm Jenna,' she says. 'Now where is the injured person?' She stands on her tiptoes and cranes her neck. The crowd shuffles apart and she sees the crumpled woman slumped against the fruit display. Her ass is squashing the palisade peaches. She is whimpering and a man is squeezing her shoulder.

Jenna moves towards the woman with an air of efficiency. She's light on her feet despite her breathing. In the mirrors Miguel sees a flush on her skin the colour of the sweet potatoes, a map of her shyness slipping down her blouse. Jenna lifts a nurse's watch ostentatiously from her overall and checks the time. She should be checking this lady's pulse but Miguel says nothing.

'Mam, have you been bitten? Are you hurt?'

The woman shakes her head. 'It touched me! I can still feel it on my fingers. It was horrible!' She whimpers again but with less intensity.

'Hmm,' Jenna says. 'I've never heard of a spider incident in this store.' She opens the First Aid box and fusses with the contents then closes the lid again. 'But you're not injured so.... I think you're probably suffering from shock?' She catches Miguel's eye and he nods. She bites her lower lip, and glances away, a flush rising in her cheeks. She smooths her hair down again, first with one hand and then the other. She reaches out and pats the victim on the arm.

'H-enna?' Miguel says - he still can't get the hang of the 'j' sound. He smiles. 'The senora is okay now, and I need to take out the spider...' He lifts the bag by way of a gesture and the crowd ripples with disgust and delight, '... so someone needs to say to Mike, I go outside.'

Other workers have gathered to watch. They are holding ticketing machines and cartons of un-shelved juice, tinned tomatoes and dried soup. Their chat is punctuated by sideways looks, and darting glances towards the office. Miguel knows a couple of them; they have fake documents too. A long-faced girl called Cristina says she'll find Mike. Mike is probably in the office.

'I'll never eat another banana,' the fat lady says, shaking her head.

'I'll stick to apples. You know where you are with a apple.'

Jenna points her towards the pharmacy where she can get reassuring words from the man in the white coat.

The crowd is already dispersing. No-one has died and no-one is critically injured. They drift away, consumed once again by consumables.

The child's mother calls twice to her daughter who is hovering near Miguel. The child waves the spider goodbye. 'Can't we take him home, Mom? I could look after him.' The little voice fades away down the aisle of bar-b-que sauces and ketchups.

Now Miguel's alone with the spider and Jenna. He lifts the bag but the spider barely moves; perhaps it's in a state of shock. He needs to find a place for it.

Jenna clears her throat. 'Gracias... Miguel,' she says peering at his name badge.

Miguel's eyebrows lift. 'Hablas español?' he says, smiling.

She shakes her head. 'No. I watch the telenovelas sometimes but they speak too fast.'

'I seen you,' he says, nodding, 'in the tortilleria, next to Desert Liquor.'

She winces like she's been caught out.

'You like Mexican food?'

'Uh-huh. But my Mom don't...except Corona and Tequila.' She laughs awkwardly. 'She don't like nothing Mexican.' Jenna hesitates. 'She's the one sprays out the Spanish on the street signs.' She looks down at her feet, digs the toe of her tennis shoe into the floor, 'But I'm not like that.'

Miguel nods and wonders if her mother was the sharp-faced

woman with the 'Stump up for Trump' badge, who pushed a leaflet into his hand outside the post office. Something to read, she'd drawled, though it's in English.

Jenna breathes harder, as if she needs to suck more air from the room. 'Sorry,' she says, 'I love the mountains, but it's hard to breathe here.'

She gazes down the long clear aisle to the front entrance. 'Sometimes, in my dreams, I just run and run.'

He wants to reach out and touch her soft cheek. 'Maybe one day, you will,' he says. Jenna's smooth forehead puckers suddenly. Miguel turns his head. Mike is

Striding towards them swinging his arms. Shit.

'What the hell do you two think you're doing?'

'You,' he says to Jenna, 'Back to the checkout. Save your breath for the customers.'

Jenna's face burns and she scuttles off, leaving her first-aid kit in amongst the sweet potatoes. Miguel wants to punch him.

'Christ!' Mike shudders and draws back. 'Why are you still holding that thing? It's a friggin' health and safety hazard. Get rid of that fucker, and make sure its permanent.'

'I want to take him outside,' Miguel says holding the spider up, 'con permiso.' He bows extravagantly, anger pulsing through him.

The boss steps forward his eyes narrowed, and Miguel can see uncertainty flicker across his face. Mike, he realises, is not sure whether he is being mocked or if this is a Mexican thing. He jabs a finger at Miguel but at that moment the spider scrabbles and pokes a thick leg out through the top of the bag. Struck by the creature's boldness, Miguel feels a surge of joy flood through him. He thrusts the spider towards Mike's face.

'What the fuck! Christ!' Mike squeals, and his features crunch into a terrified grimace. He flaps his hands in front of his face, his wrists limp and childlike, until he gathers them into fists, 'You fuckin' bastard,' he spits.

Cradling the spider, Miguel stares into Mike's eyes, 'No poison,' Miguel says. 'Not all the spiders are bad.'

Mike's face is white. He opens his mouth to reply, but no words come out. He adjusts his glasses and wipes his forehead and stalks off back to his office, pulling his shirt from his shoulders and straightening his tie. Miguel punches the air with his free hand.

Holding the bag gently, he heads out of the store past Jenna who is hunched over her checkout, the plastic tube attached to her nose once more. He waves at her and she smiles and straightens up.

He strides out of Eden-Super, undoing the buttons of his overall. The mountains shimmer and the trees are the colour of cilantro and lime. Dust and gas fumes mix together over the hot tarmac. He pauses for a moment, the sun hot on his air-conditioned skin. The spider doesn't move in the bag, yet he feels its power and its life.

He walks around behind the store. The lot is dotted with needle grass and rocks and stretches to the road on one side and the river on the other. Miguel heads towards the water and stops near a tangle of shrubs. Squatting down, he undoes the bag and sets it on some kicked-up earth beside an old tree stump. After a moment or two the spider begins to uncurl then it hesitates.

Miguel jiggles the bag. 'Go home amigo, go,' he says, a lump swelling in his throat. The spider creeps out raising each leg, delicately probing the ground, wary but curious. Miguel follows its dogged progress, over stones, and twigs and clods of earth until finally it disappears down the slope and out of sight.

He leans back on his heels. The sun is on his face and the sound of the fast-running river blocks out the traffic. He picks up a handful of the dry red earth and lets it slip between his fingers. He thought he could run from sorrow but he'd been wrong. Martina's little coffin, the weight of it, was still there, like a hand pressing on his shoulder. He thinks all the time about going back, yet when he arrives at the end of his mind's journey, home is just a wasteland. But it's where he needs to be.

He takes in the wide arc of blue above him. A flock of geese sweeps overhead drawing patterns in the sky as they follow the high winds up and over the mountains.

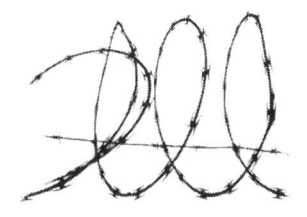

Charlene and the Fountain of Youth

Sarah Thomas

When Charlene decided to seek the fountain of youth, she was still what people would describe as young. Or 'youngish,' anyway. Charlene was thirty-nine when she found herself having strange urges, and wondering, for example, as she drove home from work, if her Jeep would make it over the barrier of the bridge that ran across the lake. And if it did, as she plunged in, and as her lungs filled up with water and her hair spread out around her face, weightless, would she think of her son's face?

Would she burst to the surface, changed? Or would she regret not drowning?

Thoughts like that.

She traced this daydream to an incident at a roadside donut shop one Sunday after church. Charlene was wearing a black wrap dress that framed her cleavage in an appealing 'V.' She felt this might balance out the silver wisps of hair that had begun to declare themselves amid the blonde.

The attendant at the donut window was a moonfaced teenager. Charlene was distracted by his fat, round nipples that shone through the thin shirt. She picked up her little boy to let him order, stammering, and when finished, he sprung from her arms to join her husband at one of the tables on the lawn of Astroturf.

'That's a cute little feller you got there,' the boy said.

'Well, thank you, honey.'

'Are you mama or grandmama?'

Charlene, unable to speak, had to concentrate intensely to will her shaking fingers to open the clasps of her change purse, feeling for the bills, reaching across the eternity of the red plastic counter to drop the money in his chubby white paw. She decided that if she never returned there, and she never repeated the episode to another soul, she might effectively blot it from existence.

But in truth, the boy's comment verbalized an increasing silence: silence in the place of whistles and car horns confirming her desirability. Charlene was so used to other people calling her 'beautiful' that she didn't know what she might call herself when that word no longer applied.

When she got home, Charlene went on a long, punishing run. She normally found her greatest pleasure in the power of her own body--solitary runs on country roads and swims in the lake. She had always been an athlete, thinking that those hundreds--thousands--of miles she had clocked effectively meted out distance between her and aging. Now she thought of the sun beating down on her freckled chest, gravity pulling her skin to the ground with each whack against the road. Beauty is truth, and truth beauty, she found her brain repeating, hatefully, as she exercised.

Charlene learned about the fountain of youth on a Tuesday. She was talking to a girl with a stud in the hollow of her cheek at a store called 'Blue Moon Books,' which her husband called, simply, 'the queer bookstore.' As Charlene was looking at travel books, the girl approached and asked if she had any upcoming travel plans outside of Pickney. Charlene wondered at her urge to tell the girl that she had studied abroad in Paris twenty years ago.

'My husband and I have been talking about a cruise,' Charlene said, 'But it's so hard for us to find time.' She thought of her husband watering the grass in his underwear.

'Perhaps you'd like the Bay Islands,' the girl said, and went on to describe a place in Honduras--a vaguely violent and brown country in Charlene's mind--so pleasantly. 'And If you're alone,' she added, 'You might enjoy a place called Boca del Fuente.'

The girl handed a booklet to Charlene, and her finger lingered for just a moment longer than was comfortable. Charlene felt the girl stroke the tuft of blonde hair on her forefinger, moving along lightly like the wing of a moth. The booklet appeared to have been produced at least twenty years ago--it had the look of an old Florida postcard: too bright, idyllic, and staged. Charlene pulled her hand away. The brochure had 'Boca del Fuente' emblazoned across the front.

'It's like a fountain of youth,' the girl said. 'Of course, you're too young to need that, but it's really just a place that beautiful people go to reenergize their auras, realign their chakras, and commune.'

This all made perfect sense to Charlene, though if pressed, she would have had a hard time describing exactly what activities would constitute such things, but she was stuck on phrases like 'too young' and 'beautiful people' and as she recalled tweezing a dark hair out of the periphery of her areola that morning, she said:

'Yes, exactly. That's what I need.'

By the time the plane had landed in Roatan, Charlene had consumed three Bacardi and Diet Cokes. She pressed through the heat of the airport, filled with odors and words she didn't recognize, as if possessed. She took a taxi to her motel, a white beachside building called Las Palmas. A pretty young woman with black hair led Charlene up to her room, which was spare and dated, with a radio and a window AC unit. She recommended that Charlene explore the town on the west end of the island.

When the girl left, Charlene turned on the radio, which played a scratchy song in Spanish that Charlene could tell was about a broken heart. She used the bathroom, showered, dressed, and upon leaving, she locked the door behind her. As she exited the lobby, an agitated man approached her.

'Excuse! Did you flush toilet paper, M'am?' he asked.

'I--yes, but nothing else,' Charlene whispered.

'Didn't you read the sign? No paper in the toilets here. Now I have a clog, and it's a Friday night.'

'Oh. I'm sorry,' Charlene said. 'Can I do anything?'

'Esta bien,' he growled and walked away.

The pretty girl walked up behind him and whispered 'Lo siento.'

Charlene walked away, already feeling out of place and if not young, certainly foolish. And then she thought of the girl trailing the manager, the apology from her lips, and she thought of how women are trained to apologize for the brutish nature of men, the world over it seemed, and she resolved to not apologize for men anymore. It felt so easy in that moment: I am finished with that, she thought, imagining moments that her husband got a little drunk, a little mean. Finished. And with this decided, she felt lighter--so much lighter, that she quickly forgot about the whole toilet paper episode.

In town, the sun was low, and the sky shone pink behind the stucco shops that flanked the beach. Passing teenage boys hissed things at her in a tongue she didn't know, but a tone she identified as obscene, and she was grateful. Charlene thought of Ricky and if he already had thoughts like this, if when he grabbed her breasts now it wasn't just a memory of nursing, but a divination of the future, a memory he hadn't had yet, of a woman. As she watched the boys careen on skateboards, she thought of what Ricky would look like at sixteen. And then, with gravel in her stomach, she realized that when he was sixteen, she would be fifty.

She wandered into a bar and ordered a beer. She felt someone touch her shoulder and turned to look into the unlined face of a tall, handsome boy with green eyes and a dragon tattoo creeping up his neck.

'What is a beautiful girl like you doing here alone?'

Charlene thought: I haven't been a girl in twenty years. Instead she said: 'I don't mind being alone,' realizing it was true.

'Ah, then we have that in common, beautiful.'

She looked away.

'What's your name?'

'Char,' she said.

'Char, like Cher? What are you looking for, my Cherie amour?' he smiled.

Nothing you have, she almost said, and instead said: 'A friend of mine told me about a fountain here--or a spring? I'm not sure.'

'She must have been talking about West Bay,' he said, 'you have to take a boat. Lucky for you, I am a water taxi driver.'

'It's too late,' Charlene said, 'I've got to be up--' and before she could conjure a lie, the boy put up his hands and backed away into the crowd.

'El Brujo,' the bartender said. 'That's what he's called.'

'What does that mean?'

He leaned in, and Charlene felt perhaps this boy wasn't just a boy, but something dangerous. 'It's like a witch.'

'And he drives a water taxi?'

The bartender laughed. 'Why not?'

Charlene woke without the pounding hangover she deserved and wondered why she didn't allow herself to drink more often. She was lying by the kidney shaped pool when she saw the pretty girl from yesterday. Charlene stopped her and handed her the brochure. The girl flipped through it and then said: 'La Ceiba. Las cascadas de La Ceiba.'

Charlene looked up 'las cascadas,' and she found that it meant 'waterfalls.' She made arrangements to travel to La Ceiba the next morning. She packed her small bag carefully and deliberately that night, smoothing the wrinkled brochure in her purse.

At 6 a.m., the airline kiosk was dark and abandoned. Charlene sat for three hours, and just as she began to cry, she was interrupted by the trill of a whistle. A man materialized holding a sign that read 'La Ceiba.' Charlene followed him, and she boarded the smallest plane she'd set foot on, which made a putputput noise like the rusted moped she drove around Paris all those years ago.

As they ascended toward the sun, Charlene saw the water below was terrified of careening into it. Her grip became slippery on the armrests, and she bargained with a God that she hadn't spoken to in years: that he might spare her life, even if it was unexceptional.

The taxi in La Ceiba took Charlene through what looked like miles of dirt parking lot, with goats and dogs and trash fires. A woman squatted by the road, urinating, and Charlene turned away. They drove up into the mountains on a road that seemed accidental, snaking into places a road shouldn't be, until a series of mismatched wooden chalets appeared ahead of them. Charlene was directed to her cabin by a boy that didn't speak.

She assessed the room with a cot and no mirror, and thought, What a blessing it must be to never look at yourself. Charlene searched her bag for the brochure and found it nowhere. She couldn't accept that she had left it back at the hotel--this having been the purpose of the whole trip--and thought of how out of character it was for her to lose things.

Since becoming a mother, Charlene was always prepared: her purse contained snacks and Band-Aids. But here, she had begun to lose things, and she thought of a poem she'd once read in college containing the line: The art of losing isn't hard to master, and she was pleased that she had managed, if not to find the brochure in her purse, a line of that poem in the recesses of her brain. When she said 'las cascadas' to a uniformed young woman, she replied 'Pico Bonito.' A nearby white couple, who were scrutinizing a map, said:

'Are you hiking to the waterfalls?'

They looked young and soft but had the added sophistication of their British accents.

'I suppose I am.'

The couple smiled to each other and invited her, explaining the directions.

'I'm Lucien,' the man said, extending his hand.

'Meg,' the woman said.

'Cher.'

Charlene followed the couple down a gravel road, to a sign that read 'Pico Bonito National Park.' She squinted, noticing only now she didn't have her reading glasses, and she saw that it said '15 kilometres,' and that seemed like a lot, but she wasn't confident with metric conversion.

Once on the trail, Lucien produced three chocolates in his hand. He said, 'Do you partake?'

'In chocolate?' Charlene asked.

'In special chocolate?' he said, winking at Meg.

'Not normally,' Charlene said, 'but I'm on vacation.' She took one.

'Great,' Meg said, 'Let's party.'

Charlene laughed, thinking that dessert must constitute a party to Brits, as buttoned up and glum as they could be in her limited experience, and she put the chocolate on her tongue, which tasted sweet and dark of cocoa, but also dusty, and earthy--like dirt. Charlene wondered how long they had stored these chocolates in a travel bag, but she didn't want to be rude, so she swallowed politely.

After an hour, they came to a massive ravine, at the bottom of which thundered a river. There was only a wood and rope footbridge stretching the expanse, and Charlene anticipated the panic she felt on the plane, but she felt none. As the breeze fluttered between her legs, and she looked down and had the thought: The wind is licking me with its tongue, and it was such a funny thought that she laughed. Lucien and Meg rather began to laugh too, and they held hands as they crossed the bridge. Charlene watched them walk over the great ravine on that tenuous bridge, hand in hand, and she thought: They think holding hands will save them, but if one of them fell, both would fall.

The trail became thin and reedy and the vegetation denser. Charlene noticed the veins on the leaves were a map of whole worlds unto themselves, and the veins on the back of Meg's pale calves were much like those on the leaves.

Then, the waterfall towered out of the dense jungle. It was deafening, terrifying and divine. Meg and Lucien took off their clothes, and they plunged into the pool at the foot of the waterfall, looking like amorphous beige gobs of gooseflesh. Charlene stripped off her clothes, too, not thinking to be ashamed. She dove under and opened her eyes in the dark, and swam around great boulders shaped like shoulders and breasts and human skulls. When she broke the surface, she heard the strange moaning of some dying beast, and she followed the sound, anticipating a scene of blood and viscera. But it was Meg and Lucien making love, and they looked like one thing, one creature that was dying or being born, pink and wet and pulsing. And Charlene watched silently, feeling entirely unlike a voyeur.

Charlene finally swam away. She put her clothes back on. She did not see Meg and Lucien. She followed the path again, as though she were in a trance, winding through the rotting smell, skipping over roots and stones. When she reached the bridge again, she raced over it like she was flying, unfettered, and she followed the road back.

By the time she had reached her cabin, the sky was full of stars, which appeared to Charlene like holes punched out of the universe, the bright eyes of God looking back through a million holes. As if God were an insect and insects were God. Her cabin felt claustrophobic, so she took her thin mattress outside and lay on the dirt, looking up at the stars.

Charlene awoke under a brutal sun, covered in mosquito bites. She stumbled to the outdoor shower and stood under the water for as long as it ran cold. She wondered what psychedelics they had given her, but with no experience for comparison, she decided that it was nothing. It was simply chocolate and the jungle unfolding around her. She packed hastily, scrubbing the memory of Meg and Lucien's lovemaking from her brain, like it was a particularly awful scene she had watched in a movie. But it wasn't awful.

She thought that: but it wasn't awful, as she rode back through the poor, dusty countryside, and as she boarded the tiny plane, unafraid, and as she returned to Las Palmas, and took a taxi downtown, and as she walked along the beach. She thought it as she spotted El Brujo smoking on his boat, and as she gave him her money, and he took her out of the bay, to another island many kilometers away, and when she said 'Boca del Fuente' to him, he put his mouth on hers, and swallowed the words. She tasted cigarettes and didn't mind it for the first time in her life. And they stopped on a beach somewhere, one with young people and bonfires, and rum that she drank in a steady stream. The night soared above them. The insect God looked down through a million eyes.

Charlene awoke alone in the darkness. Her cash and phone were gone. Her shoes, too. She felt foolish, that word again, but it was accompanied by another one: young. Young and foolish, she thought hotly, but the heat dissipated with each step, and she began to laugh. She walked barefoot, her toes pressing into the wet sand, her pockets empty, to twinkling lights along the beach, which took shape in the dark as a hotel. Charlene was both grateful and sad to hear voices and realize she was no longer alone. She found a water taxi, promising to pay the man when she reached the shore and apologizing when she had no money to produce.

He said: 'Lo siento. I am sorry you lost everything, Miss.'

Charlene said: 'The art of losing isn't hard to master.'

When Charlene made it back to her room, she located her passport. She put on a plain white dress--pious--she had thought when she'd packed it, but now it was only clean. She sat down on the bed and opened her atlas to the page on Honduras. She drew a star in the middle of the ocean and wrote 'Boca del Fuente.' She put the atlas in the drawer of the bedside table. She put her passport in her bra and left the rest.

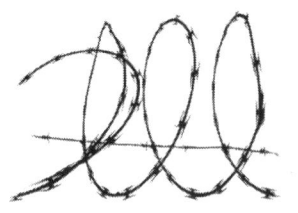

When a Caged-Bird Flies

Rima Totah

As I sat in the airplane aisle seat, 22F, I contemplated the unknown. This was the first time in my young existence that I traveled on a giant machine with wings. I've never been afforded the opportunity to venture out of the village where I was born, that was until now. I found myself on this daunting journey, flying with the birds, and traversing the boundless ocean called the Atlantic. My ears haven't grown accustomed to the airplane's pressure which made me feel a bit out of sorts. The symphony of the engine's grinding and humming sounds accompanied by constant vibrations at my feet wore heavily on my already frayed nerves. At intermittent times, the plane would jolt unexpectedly followed by a garbled and barely audible voice from overhead apologizing for something called turbulence. On my lap, I clutched tightly, a satchel that housed the identity of my past, present, future and very little money. I was eighteen years old and I had begun a seventeen-hour journey from India to a place called San Francisco to be with the 'husband'.

I didn't know this man that I am supposed to call 'husband.' He was distantly related to my auntie's husband and everyone, but me, decided it was my time to be married and he was declared the 'one'. However, I wasn't ready to be married, I wanted to go to university and become a teacher. Upon my eighteenth birthday a month ago, I was put on display like furniture for families of suitors to come and go, surveying the merchandise. My rights to decide were taken away from me the day my parents died in a car accident. I was fifteen years old at the time and my mother's sister reluctantly took me in. I was an only child and my parents didn't have much money to speak of, and what little they did manage to scrimp and save was taken by my auntie's husband; he justified his actions by the mere fact that he was now responsible for feeding me and keeping a roof over my head. Although, I didn't eat very much and barely had time to sleep since I had duties to attend to like cooking, cleaning and looking after their three younger children.

It's been forty-eight hours since the last week of my senior year in high school had come to an end. As part of a long-standing tradition, the girls wore green sarees for the graduation ceremony. I wasn't allowed to buy a new saree because there was no money, so I fashioned one myself from old curtains that use to hang in the sitting room. On the eve of the graduation, I returned home from school and found myself married by proxy and I was to leave the country almost immediately. The 'husband' was waiting for me and he doesn't like to be kept waiting, or so I'm told. I was not sure what he even looked like. My auntie gave me a tattered and torn picture of him when he was a child, he was now thirty-one years old.

'Indrani, who is that boy?' my auntie's ten-year old son, Ajay, came up next to me while I was scrutinizing the 'husband's' picture. I was in the process of preparing my things for the trip. I didn't have much to take with me because I didn't own many things.

'They tell me he is the 'husband', but I don't know him.'

'Then why did you marry him?' he asked innocently.

'Because I am to do what they tell me to do.'

'Why?'

'Because I don't have a mother and father.'

Ajay sat quietly processing what I had just explained to him.

'You can share my mother and father!' He excitedly offered me a solution. 'Then you don't have to do what you don't want to do!'

I smiled. 'I wish it were that simple. I really appreciate the offer, but I must finish packing. Now give me a big hug because I have to go away tomorrow.'

'Are you coming back?' His eyes welled up with tears.

'Maybe someday. Now promise me you will be a good boy and listen to your parents.'

Ajay gave me one more hug and then ran out of the room. He was the only one in this family who made me feel welcome.

Time sped by like a cheetah chasing a gazelle; three hours have passed since we took off and we're almost a quarter of the way there. I finally mustered up the courage to look around the airplane. Since boarding, I've kept my head lowered, I was afraid to make eye contact with anyone. The first thing I noticed and did not expect to see was a girl sitting in 21E dressed in a saree similar to mine. Her head was looking down and there were tears silently streaming down the side of her face. I tried to get 21E's attention, but she was too caught up in her emotions to notice anything or anyone around her. Although I so desperately wanted to make contact with her, I didn't want to create a scene if she didn't feel the same way; I decided to let things be for now.

Just then, a gurgling sound emerged from my stomach and I tried to ignore it. What an inopportune time, I lamented, because I just declined the food tray that was offered by the stewardess with the red hair. But then again, I couldn't help myself, the food tray didn't look very appetizing. Thankfully, I had the forethought to pack some naan last minute prior to leaving my auntie's house; I took the bread out of the satchel and enjoyed it. My stomach was satisfied, at least for the moment.

'Excuse me? Miss? You must wake up and buckle your seatbelt immediately. We will be landing shortly.' An unfamiliar voice with a British accent sounded in my left ear.

My eyes popped open to find red-hair standing over me with an annoyed expression on her face.

'Are we...are we... in San Francisco already?' I was disoriented and could barely get the words out; it felt so dry like there was cotton inside of it. I had no idea when I'd fallen asleep.

'I'm afraid not.' Red-hair answered in a terse tone. 'We have to make an unscheduled landing in Heathrow. There seems to be a mechanical issue with the plane.' Then she hastily continued down the aisle to avoid further questions.

I buckled my seatbelt and gathered my satchel in my lap. Although the airline requires that the items are to be placed under the seat in front of me, I wasn't about to let it go. It was too small, and I was afraid it could slip away at any time; my whole life and identity was in it. Fortunately, there was no one sitting in the seat next to mine to notice and expose me for breaking the rules. I looked out the round window into the dark sky. Everything always looks ominous at nighttime. I glanced at my wristwatch and calculated the time difference; it was half passed four o'clock in the morning.

I turned back to the interior of the plane and was surprised to find that 21E was staring at me like a deer in headlights. Her face was full of wrought emotions-fear, sadness, and perhaps relief that she wasn't alone.

She hesitated and then smiled shyly, and I reciprocated. Then she turned away again to continue staring at the back of the seat in front of her during the landing.

As we disembarked, I tried to keep track of 21E in the sea of passengers, but I quickly lost sight of her pink saree. Once in the terminal, I made my way to the customer service desk along with probably a seventy people who were already lined up ahead of me. While waiting, I scoured the gate area looking for 21E, but she was nowhere to be found.

It was finally my turn at the desk and the agent notified me that it will be approximately another four hours before they will resume the flight, or they could help me rebook on another airline and waive the additional cost. I opted to wait; I wasn't exactly in hurry to reach San Francisco.

The airline was kind enough to offer some refreshments. Not much was left by the time I got to the table; luckily not too many people were interested in the fruit items and I had my pick of apples, oranges, and bananas.

I managed to find an empty seat in the crowded gate area. I sat between an older gentleman in a dark suit with a matching derby and a middle-aged woman with an infant cradled in her lap. Sitting across the aisle was a younger man, probably in his late twenties, who winked and smiled at me; I ignored him, and thankfully, he got the hint. If my mother were around, she would have probably taken her shoe off and smacked him upside the head to protect my honor. It was disrespectful to show that kind of attention to someone's daughter, especially if, he was not formally courting her, with her parent's permission of course. My mother was a believer in old world traditions. I really missed her.

I was about to take a bite of my apple, when I looked across the terminal and two gates down, I saw 21E sitting there alone. My first thought was she might be confused and was waiting at the wrong gate or she just wanted to be left alone.

After a few minutes of debating in my head whether or not to go over to her, I threw caution to the wind and did just that.

I slowly made my way over to where 21E was waiting. I lowered myself into the seat directly across from her.

'Hello.' I spoke first and introduced myself. 'My name is Indrani.'

'Hello. I am Tripthi.' Finally, I know her name.

'How do you do, Tripthi. Very nice to meet you.'

'Likewise.' Tripthi replied and smiled, but her smile didn't reach her eyes. She looked apprehensive like she had to make a difficult decision and she didn't know how.

After a few minutes I asked, 'If it is alright, may I come and sit next to you?' Tripthi nodded.

'Is there is particular reason why you are sitting her all alone?' I asked.

'I'm trying to get the nerve to leave. I don't want to go to San Francisco.' Tripthi confessed.

'What's waiting for you in San Francisco?' I asked although I already knew that we were probably in the same predicament.

'A husband that I don't even know!' she exclaimed and then started to cry.

'Please don't cry. I know how you feel.' I tried to console her and showed her my satchel with the marriage papers.

After a few minutes, Tripthi composed herself and asked, 'How could you be so calm? Aren't you scared?'

'Petrified. But this is my destiny and I must accept it. I have no ties back home. Both of my parents are gone, and I have no siblings. It is obvious that my extended family could care less about me that they were willing to send me away without a second thought.'

Tripthi and I sat quietly in our own thoughts until she finally declared. 'Indrani, I am not getting on that plane.' Then she hesitated. 'But I'm too scared to stay here alone.'

For a split second, I thought Tripthi was out of her mind. However, it didn't take long for it sink in thoroughly and I started to give it some serious consideration myself.

'But what about the marriage papers?! They will come after us!' I protested. One of us had to be voice of reason.

'Those papers mean nothing, Indrani. Look at them. They do not have an official seal or anything!' She explained. 'If they are not legal in India, do you really think they would be in San Francisco?'

'How do you know so much about this? How old are you? You're probably my age, if not younger!'

'My father works as a clerk in a courthouse. When I was little, he would take me with him when he had no one to watch me. I picked up a few things here and there.'

My mind was racing with thoughts that were beyond my control. I felt like I was suffocating and started to hyperventilate.

'Oh, my goodness! Indrani! Are you okay?! Tripthi panicked and put her arm around my shoulders.

'Yes. Yes. Just give me a minute.' I responded in a breathless voice. Then a question came to mind and I was compelled to ask.

'Tripthi? I...I... apologize if I am being too forward in asking this. Why is it that you are being sent away to America?' Once the question came out, I regretted asking. 'I'm sorry, I shouldn't have said anything.'

'That's okay. I don't mind. My mother died a few years back and it's just been my father and I.' Tripthi responded, her voice trembling as she held back tears. 'My father is still relatively young, and just remarried. His new wife wasn't too keen on my being around and in the way...' Her voice trailed off and I could fill in the blanks.

'Ladies and gentlemen, we are pleased to announce that Flight #105 nonstop to San Francisco is ready for departure sooner than expected and we will start the boarding process now at gate 34B.' The voice boomed overhead.

Tripthi and I sat rooted in our seats as we watched the passengers for Flight #105 bound for San Francisco gather at the gate area for boarding. One by one each ticket was scanned until there was no one left in line.

'Final call for Flight #105.' The voice boomed once more and then almost immediately the door to the jetway was closed. At that point, it seemed that the personel just wanted to go home. It had been a long night and the dayshift would be starting soon.

Without saying a word, Tripthi and I stood up simultaneously and walked towards the large window for one final look.

Dawn was breaking in the distance as the airplane pulled away from the gate and quickly taxied towards the runway. According to my watch, Flight #105 took off at approximately five past seven AM. It's a new day, it's a new life.

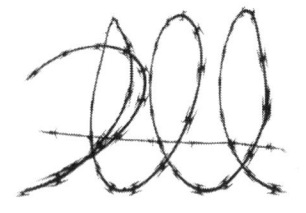

Everything That Means Anything

Maggie Veness

He spotted her from the opposite side of the pond in Richmond Park. Like a colorful bouquet, she was arranged on a wooden bench, watching the ducks. Dressed in a flower-print kaftan, she wore a fluoro-green sweatband low on her forehead, and her cherry-red hair in a high, messy knot. When Robert approached her all smiles with his hands behind his back, she eyed him suspiciously. He made small-talk about the warm spring days and cool nights and about duck breeds like the Mallard and Eider and Pekin; said he'd studied animal husbandry and was new in town; that he'd found casual work with a local Animal Hospital but was looking for something full-time. She told him her name was Jules and she worked in a shop called The Spirit Life Emporium, reading palms and tarot cards. After a while he sat beside her. Her perfume smelled fruity and reminded him of sweet marmalade. They were still talking an hour and a half later, and when Robert suggested a dinner date and she agreed, he was quietly hysterical. It was eight months since he'd dated. That was Helen. Helen was only two-thirds the size of Jules and smelled like wet newspaper. Jules was the biggest and most attractive woman he'd ever asked out.

***

The following Saturday night at the local hotel, after sour-cream and sweet chili corn-chips, and works burgers with fries, followed by a double choc-nut sundae next door at the ice-cream parlor, Robert took a chance and invited her back to his small, rented apartment.

'Thanks, but no. Sorry.'

'Oh. That's okay,' he said, and looked down at his tasseled, black loafers. Things seemed to be going so well and it was hard to disguise his disappointment.

'I would've, except I've got this rule about no sex on the first date. If you've got a guest-room, then maybe, but it definitely wouldn't be a romantic-type visit, so ...'

'I do have a spare room and I totally respect your rule. I'd love your company for longer Jules. I just don't want this date to finish.'

She reached across and knuckled his chest. 'That's really nice, Robby. Okay, count me in,' she said, two crescent dimples framing her bow-shaped mouth.

They entered his apartment, the chill air flooding in behind them. Robert hung her orange trench-coat behind the door then quickly flicked on the heating and the flat-screen. He sat on the edge of the sofa channel-surfing and found an old Tom Cruise movie. Tossing aside her fringed, leather shoulder bag, Jules slipped off her purple moccasins and sat beside him. Robert swallowed hard and reached for her hand, threaded his fingers between hers.

'So, what exactly is it you like about me?' she asked.

'You like ducks.'

'You know that's not what I mean,' she said, with a playful shoulder nudge.

He couldn't stop grinning. He'd spent most of the previous night thinking about their date, watching the luminous numbers change on his bedside clock and practice-talking to her in his head, and now, here she was. He clicked his tongue, imagined her head nestled in the crook of his shoulder, and said, 'Okay, let's see. You also smell good, like warm toast with orange marmalade.'

Jules considered this for a moment. Suddenly she was flinging his hand away, launching herself off the sofa, the sheer momentum propelling her to her feet at an impressive speed. He straightened up, unsure of what was happening. She stood with her back to him, yawning and stretching both arms above her head, then padded into his compact kitchen and flicked the light on. Relaxing back, Robert listened to every cupboard open and close. When she got to the fridge, the door stayed open.

'So, your turn,' he called. 'Tell me what you like about me.'

'Hmmmm. Let's see. You're hunky and tall and you work with injured animals. Vets are a lot like doctors,' she said, and slid a bottle of lemon soda out from the narrow top shelf.

'Umm, it's just a few hours a week helping out at the local clinic 'til I find something full-time,' he said, and chewed the inside of his cheek.

'Whatever. I love animals. And doctors.'

He heard the fridge door close and wondered if he'd ever be able to tell her he mainly swept floors and cleaned cages. There was that one time he kind of helped when a dog had to be euthanized. They were short staffed that day. Robert was asked to fetch a docile Pit Bull from one of the outdoor enclosures, then lift it into an airtight glass chamber. He didn't know what to expect and neither did the dog--a barrel-shaped, doe-eyed female with huge, tan paws. When the vet pressed the green button she started leaping about, trying to bark while the air was being sucked out of her. Robert had felt as though his own lungs were deflating and stumbled to the restroom to run cold water over the back of his neck.

Padding back to stand before him, Jules threw her head back and swigged noisily from the bottle. Robert decided hers was the most attractive, womanly neck he'd ever seen--so many soft, pink folds he hoped to one day properly explore. He asked about the unusual tattoo on the underside of her left forearm. It was a circle with colorful geometric shapes inside. She said it was her mandala and that she'd first seen it in a dream. He didn't even know what a mandala was. Not only was she smart and fun and beautiful, Jules was the most intriguing woman he'd ever met.

She sat down beside him and passed the lemon soda. He drank without taking his eyes off her then handed it back. Jules was eyeing him as well, as she drained the last few mouthfuls. The way his pulse was scrambling Robert suspected he was falling in love. She reached for her bag, produced a pack of coconut crusted caramels, fed him three, then took three for herself.

'Your skin looks really soft and smooth. That's another thing I like,' he said, moving the sweets around with his tongue.

Jules studied his face for a few moments while she chewed. 'Thanks Robbie. But there's something else. I've got a feeling it's important. Maybe you've never talked about it with anyone. You'll tell me when you're ready.'

'There might be nothing to tell,' he said, and cracked his knuckles.

'There is,' she said.

In that instant he was twelve years old, watching his sister's friend, Cassie, through a crack in the bathroom door. Cassie was eighteen and had a colossal build. He'd caught sight of her drying off after a shower, and was spellbound by her generous, pink body. She stepped from the shower and grabbed a towel. Balancing with one foot up on the bathtub, she took her time to pat herself dry, then gently dusted herself with talc. He was so excited he barely made it back into his room. Later, when he slipped back into the bathroom to rinse his underwear, the scent of her orange-blossom talc still hung in the air.

Realizing Jules was waiting for him to say something, he cleared his throat. 'Can I get you anything? A coffee maybe?' he said, hoping she wasn't psychic enough to pick up on what he'd been thinking.

'Ta but no. Bit late for coffee. I'd be awake all night. Actually, I've got a slight a headache. Probably too much sugar.'

He reached over and patted her knee. 'Be right back.'

Returning with two Aspirin and a tumbler of chilled water, he fetched a cushion for her head, helped her stretch out on the sofa, then sat with her calves across his lap.

They stayed like that for half an hour--her with her eyes closed, breathing noisily, him pretending to watch TV while massaging her feet, grateful just to be sharing his sofa with such an incredible woman. He recalled how lonely he'd been feeling before they met. Robert had decided not to stay in touch with his old buddies. He could just imagine them; the mockery. Now they wouldn't even know he'd had a date. He looked down at her untroubled face, and smiled.

When Jules eventually stirred, she told him she felt heaps better.

'You can play doctor with me any time,' she said, and reached for his hand. 'I'm a sucker for medical stuff. You don't have to be psychic to figure that one out. I mean, everything that means anything can be traced back to some key childhood experience.'

Robert was gently thumbing the velvety skin on the back of her hand. He wanted to know every last thing about her, and if this childhood medical thing was important to Jules he intended to understand why.

'Hmmm,' he said, and rubbed his stubbly chin. 'Well then young lady, you'd better tell Doctor Robert all about it.'

'Oh very cute ha-ha-ha, I love it! Okay then Doctor Robert. Let's see,' she said, and gazed at the ceiling. 'So, I'm a middle kid. Big brother, little sister. And it's well documented that middle kids don't get as much attention as the first born or the youngest, right?'

Robert blinked. 'Right,' he said, and quietly wondered what might be well documented about two-kid families like his.

'And so when I was eight or nine my brother's best buddy wandered into my bedroom and sat beside me on the bed. His name was Frank. He was somewhere 'round fifteen. I was playing with one of those little medical kits. Do you remember those? They came in a white plastic case with a big red cross on the lid. Anyhow, Frank was really tall with dark combed-back hair and gold-framed glasses. He stuck the plastic stethoscope in his ears and told me to lie back on the bed and relax.'

'Oh God! He didn't ...'

'No-no-no Robbie, it was all completely innocent. Come to think of it I was real lucky there. He just peered into my eyes and pretended to check my heart-beat, lifted my wrist and felt around for the pulse, held his palm against my forehead. That sort'a thing. Then he told me to sit up and took his time to gently wind the small crepe bandage 'round my wrist. After that he patted my shoulder and said well little girl, Doctor thinks you're gonna be just fine. You've been a very good patient. I'd like to see you again same time next week. End of story. He went back outside to sink more hoops with my brother. Anyhow that was the first time I remember being singled out and made to feel special. Explains the medical thing, see? But that's enough about me. Your turn. Something important happened to you when you were a kid. Something sexual involving an older female with a large build. Am I right?'

'Oh man! How could you possibly know all that?'

She slapped her chest and laughed. 'More observation and deduction than psychic ability, I assure you! So, do tell.'

Robert hesitated. He'd never told anyone about the Cassie thing. What if Jules took him for a creepy closet voyeur? She might never want to see him again. She was looking at him, waiting. His mouth had gone dry. 'Umm, well,' he said, and tried to wet his lips. 'She was eighteen and it was also totally innocent, but kind of different too and I don't wanna weird you out.'

'Oh. So, are you saying you did something weird with her?'

'Yeah. But not really, I mean, I didn't actually do anything with her. She didn't even know I was watching. It's just the stuff I saw.'

'A-haaaaaaaah. So, she was eighteen and how old were you?'

'Twelve.'

'Yep. That'll do it. Look Robbie, I doubt something you saw when you were twelve's gonna freak me out, and I'd kind'a like to know what happened 'cause it'd help me understand what makes you tick as an adult.' She gave his hand a reassuring waggle.

He bought her fingers to his lips, held them there for a few seconds, then took a deep breath. 'I was just a boy,' he said, then told her everything.

'Hey, thanks for sharing. S'pose that was kind of an unusual initiation. So, there you were, a good-lookin' school-boy going all through your teens surrounded by skinny Barbie-doll girls who didn't turn you on. Must'a been tough fighting 'em off! HE-HE-HE! As you can tell I'm not a bit freaked out. I mean, a hunky guy like you is happy to sit here holding hands with big ol' me on a Saturday night? I'd say that Cassie girl did me a favor,' she said, and made two more adorable dimples.

His throat and chest felt tight. 'I don't know what to say Jules. You're just so, well, you absolutely blow me away.'

'Yeah-yeah. Look, it's gotta be almost midnight. I'm beat. Might have to call it a night. How about you find me a toothbrush and something to sleep in and point me to the spare room?'

***

Around four a.m. something woke Robert from a deep sleep. Remembering his special house-guest, he sat up, blinking, just in time to see her greyish form mosey past his open door. When she reached the bathroom, light flooded the hallway. He saw the light diminish as though she'd left the door ajar. Not fully awake, he thought he heard the shower door rattle shut. Clambering out of bed, he went to stand outside his bedroom door to listen. The shower hissed to life, and suddenly that shard of light became an irresistible invitation.

Robert had never seen a more magnificent sight. Moving in and out of the water, Jules took her time adjusting the temperature, then used the bar of white soap to lather her curvaceous body. While he watched, dream-like, from the crack in the door, she slowly turned full circle, both hands sliding over and around every inch of her beautiful, feminine body. Robert stopped breathing. Eventually, she stepped out and reached for his striped bath towel. Lifting a foot onto the side of the tub, she proceeded to pat herself dry. By now he was so light-headed that he almost lost his footing.

Jules swung the door open and kissed his damp cheek. 'Bathroom's all yours handsome,' she whispered, then made her way to his room and crawled beneath the covers.

***

A couple of hours later, as they lay sprawled on the bed after making out for the second time, he said, 'I just realized you've broken your first date rule.'

'Yeah. Strange though. I don't feel a bit sorry,' she said, and gave a contented sigh.

Outside, wind buffeted the window. Reaching across to tuck his fingers under her arm and nuzzle her neck, he said, 'I still don't know very much about you. Will you tell me another story? I want to know everything.'

They were still talking when daylight started leaking through the venetian blind. Excusing herself for the bathroom, Jules rolled out of bed. Wearing nothing besides a purple sweatband low on her forehead, she padded over to peek through the blinds before heading toward the door. Robert felt like the luckiest man alive. Every woman he'd slept with 'til now had been self-conscious about her body. Jules didn't even try to cover up.

When she crawled back in beside him Robert kissed her mouth

then jack-knifed off the bed. 'My turn,' he said, and marched toward the bathroom with the stride of a drunken band-leader.

'Hurry back. Miss you already. Hey, you got a shift today?'

'Yeah, but I don't start until two,' he called over his shoulder.

'Perfect. Think I'll ring in sick.'

He returned via the kitchen, carrying a tray with chocolate milk and shortbread biscuits. Jules shimmied up to lean her shoulders against the padded, brown bed-head. They talked and laughed and talked some more and ended up with crumbs all through the bed.

***

Around mid-day, as Robert clung to her--his fingertips tracing an invisible mandala on the sweep of her outer thigh--he said, 'Look, I need to level with you. There's something I should've told you when we met the other day. Something very important.'

'Oh-oh. Lemme guess. You've got a wife and six kids.'

'Nah. Much worse than that. Thing is, Jules, I'm actually psychic as well. Yes, that's right. Obviously way more psychic than you otherwise you would've picked up on it. In fact, they tell me I'm gifted. And, hang on, I seem to be getting a vision through right now!'

Jules had started giggling.

'Wait. It's getting clearer. It seems to be about you. Waaaaait ...' He raised himself up onto one elbow. 'This is serious if you don't mind so try to pay attention.' He screwed his eyes shut, and touched an index finger to his brow.

'You crack me up! You're such an idiot!' she said, between fits of laughter.

'AH-HA! I see it all so clearly now. Yes! You are going to find a ring-box on your pillow. I see multicolored confetti raining from the sky. And wait. There's something else. I see something white. It might be a duck. Is it a Pekin? Or a Crested? No, hang on, it's not a duck. It's a man in a white coat. A doctor? Yes! Extremely handsome. He looks a lot like me. He's wearing gold-framed glasses and he's holding a plastic stethoscope to your pregnant belly.'

Jules stopped smiling and fell quiet for a few seconds. He wondered if he'd frightened her off.

'A baby, eh?' she said, and puffed out a noisy breath. 'You do realize I'm gonna stack on the weight.'

'Teaser,' he said.

Bog Biddy

MacKenzie Tastan

Honourable Mention

    The hag scrutinized her face in the bathroom mirror. She was old when the Celts had settled on the shores of her island. In the beginning, they had worshipped her in fitting ways. They had fed her the blood and flesh of their most beautiful maidens and comely youths. Even when Christianity came, they still feared her presence in the swamps and marshes, the liminal places where she dwelled. For many years she had been able to subsist on the fear of the travelers she led away from the bog paths, but eventually she had been forgotten. Occasionally her name was still whispered in stories to frighten children, but even the storytellers did not truly believe in her.

    She had resigned herself to quietly fading from existence when the child wandered into her hut in the swamp. The girl was small, but her eyes were old and weary. The hag looked into the child's heart and saw the despair there. Children were her favorite meal because they tasted like joy. This one was inedible and the hag told her so.

    The little girl did not scream or run away as other children would have. Instead she looked into the hag's terrible face, at her yellow eyes and sharp teeth, and did not flinch. 'I'm too old for fairy stories. I have responsibilities. I have to clean and cook and take care to be quiet. I'm not to bother my mother when she's ill and she's always ill.'

The hag looked at the girl's pathetic appearance and felt something she had never felt before, something entirely foreign to her. It was pity. The girl was too thin. Her ribs protruded from the ill-fitting material of her dirty t-shirt. It was far too cold in the swamp for shorts and sandals, but here she was. She smelled as though she hadn't bathed in several days and the hag could hear her stomach rumbling. No, this girl would not make a good meal. Something else must be done.

'Why have you come here, child?' she croaked, her voice rusty with disuse. 'This is not a place where you should wander alone at night.'

'She told me to leave. Sometimes when my mother has friends over, she says that I'm in the way. Even though I hide and don't make noise, she says that I bother them and I have to get out. I was walking and I ended up here.'

Something new occurred to the hag at that moment, something she had never thought about before. She decided she must see the new idea through.

'What is your name, child?' she asked.

'Danielle.'

'And where do you live?'

'I'm not sure which direction it is from here. It's easy to get turned around. It's the last house down the gravel road before you get to the swamp from the village.'

The hag nodded. She knew the place. It was a sad and lonely looking house, long in disrepair. It, too, smelled of despair, just like the girl. She began to shuffle around in her hut, sorting through her meager possessions until she found what she was looking for. She held the dirty piece of paper out to the child. She'd never understand how humans saw value in paper currency. 'Take this and go get something to eat. Surely your mother will be asleep by the time you return. If not, this path will remain open to you. You can find your way back here.'

The girl took the note, her eyes round with surprise. 'Thank you,' she whispered and then she was gone, as quickly and quietly as she had come. The hag began her preparations immediately. She had much work to do.

As she looked at her frightening face in the mirror, the hag thought about simply making herself look young and beautiful using a glamor. She still had the power, but she was wary of using magic now. Once, the prayers and offerings of thousands of suppliants had given her an unlimited supply. She had a direct line to the Otherworld and her powers were limitless. Now she felt disconnected from the source of that power. She had dwelled too long in the world of men. It had been years since she saw another creature from the time before their arrival. For all she knew, she was the last. Although her magic had never failed her, she nevertheless used it sparingly, in case men had corrupted its source, as they had so much else.

She redirected her attention to the mirror. This was not the time to daydream. She was used to letting her thoughts wander when she had nothing to do for years at a time. There would be plenty of time to ponder after it was done. She opened the small cosmetic bag and searched through its contents. She had purchased it along with the clothes and suitcase that sat neatly on the bed. She had even paid for the use of the hotel room with the strange paper money. She'd never had any use for it before.

She spread the contents of the bag on the bathroom counter. The hardest thing to deal with was the smell. The hag was a creature of the swamp. She was part of it and it was part of her. Scrubbing away the scent of her home with the strange scented liquid felt like sacrilege, but it had to be done. The stench of the swamp would offend the humans and they would not let her take the girl. When she was washed and dried, she ran the bone comb through her long white hair. Brushing it was the only vanity she allowed herself and the comb was an offering given generations ago.

Last of all, she squirted the white minty liquid onto the brush made for teeth. She cleaned them as best she could. Although they would never rot like human teeth, centuries of eating flesh had left her them permanently stained. She had done all she could do. She would have to use a little magic for the rest. As she stared into her reflection's eyes in the mirror, she snapped her fingers and watched it change. Her hair grew shorter and softer, twisting itself into a neat bun on the top of her head. She had seen several elderly women on her way here and she sought to emulate them as much as possible. Her frightening yellow eyes changed to a dull green and a pair of spectacles appeared on her nose. The sickly grey pallor of her skin changed until her complexion resembled the pale whiteness of most humans in the area. The sores which oozed and bubbled on her body disappeared, leaving only a blue patchwork of veins under the skin's surface. Yes, she would pass as one of them now.

She shuffled into the bedroom. She put on the trousers and blouse she had purchased at the market, thinking of how strange markets were now. Gone were the stalls where merchants bartered their wares. Now there was only a single building that sold everything, where every shadow was banished under unnatural bright lights. It had been harrowing, but she had gotten what she needed. Now she would fetch the girl.

The hag shuffled along the village sidewalks, past identically shabby buildings until she found the one she needed. She was careful to move like a human of great age. It would not do for her to take such time with her appearance only to move with energy of a spring maiden. She must be convincing. Although she did not understand why humans needed a building for social services, she entered it nonetheless. Were not all services social, since one person provided them to another? As she entered the small office on the second floor, she put her musings aside.

'Can I help you?' a plump middle-aged woman in a loud green frock greeted her.

'I'm here to petition for guardianship of my great niece. I found out today that she was recently taken into care.'

The woman shuffled through the papers on her desk without looking up, 'What's her name?'

'Danielle Braithwaite.'

The woman continued to shuffle papers and the hag breathed in her scent. She would make a nice meal. There was certainly enough of her, but she had vowed to curb her hunger on this visit. She would not foolishly arouse suspicion and have the authorities suddenly develop an interest in the girl. She would be patient. Finally locating the file for Danielle, the social worker looked up at the hag with disinterest, 'And who are you?'

'Jenny Greenteeth. Her grandfather was my older brother. I'm afraid I haven't had much contact with Danielle or her mother since his passing.'

The woman nodded, 'Can you prove that you have sufficient income and a safe residential environment for the child if you're named her temporary guardian? Her case is still under investigation, but she's been removed from her mother's care under suspicion of neglect.'

'Yes, I own a cottage where the two of us can reside comfortably and I have a fixed income from my retirement. I'm hardly wealthy, but we'll manage.'

'Very well,' the woman said. 'See the receptionist on your way out. She can provide you with the necessary forms. After you've filled them out, we'll make arrangements to have Danielle delivered to your residence.'

'I wouldn't want to cause you any more work,' the hag said. 'I can see that you're very busy. I can come and collect the girl myself as soon as it's convenient.'

'If you would prefer. Have a nice day,' the woman summarily dismissed her. The hag smiled, careful not to reveal her long pointy teeth. There was a time when she would have ripped out her still beating heart and eaten it for such insolence, but those days were long passed.

The next day, she returned to the social services office for the girl. She was cleaner and more warmly dressed, but still small and thin. Once again, she looked up at her with wide-eyed surprise. 'It's you,' she said simply. The hag smiled her careful smile as she led the girl out of the building with one hand on her shoulder. 'They said you were my great aunt. I told them I didn't have a great aunt, but they didn't believe me. Grown-ups never believe me.'

'Perhaps being believed isn't as important as knowing you're telling the truth,' the hag said. 'There are plenty who don't believe in me, but here I stand.'

'Are you going to eat me?' the girl asked. There was no fear in her voice, only curiosity.

'I've no plans to do so at present. It would have been easier when we first met at my home in the swamp. Now that people know you're staying with me, eating you would raise some inconvenient questions.'

'Am I going to stay with you?' The girl asked and the hag heard the hopeful note in her voice. It pulled at her cold black heart.

'Indeed you are, for the time being.'

'Why are you helping me?' asked the girl.

'The night we met you looked at me without fear. I've stopped the hearts of stout warriors at a single glance, but there you stood. You saw me in all my ugliness and were not afraid. That kind of bravery should be rewarded.'

'It wasn't bravery. I was just tired and hungry. Besides, you can't tell if someone wants to hurt you by looking at them. You have to talk to them and watch how they treat other people. There are real monsters in our closets and under our beds, but to other people they look just like all the other mothers. I'll never be stupid enough to think that someone must be cruel because they're ugly. Some of the worst people are the most beautiful.'

The hag left her hand on Danielle's shoulder, guiding her back to the shack in the woods. She saw the little girl's warrior spirit in her small underfed body. Perhaps one day she would eat the hearts of grown men for breakfast, but first there would be afternoon tea beside a warm fire and an elderly great aunt to read her bedtime stories and tuck her in at night.

'Will there be biscuits at home, Aunt?' Danielle asked.

'There most certainly will.'

Left Hanging

Natalie White

The young woman walking towards me was too thin.

It's difficult not to judge when you've been in a place this long. People often walk past me. But not this woman. This one headed straight for me.

She stopped and giggled, 'She really is a beauty, isn't she?'

The manager hadn't bothered to look up. She never did. But on hearing this, she actually smiled. Perhaps it was the woman's energy. She could barely keep still and kept walking around me, smoothing lengths of satin on her pale skin, and laughing.

Finally the manager came over. 'It's a vintage 1960's style. Exquisite detail. You won't find anything like it. Beautifully sequined. There's just a couple missing here and there; that's why it's such a bargain...'

I'd never heard her talk so highly of anything. Should I have felt proud, or did she just want the sale?

The woman giggled again - a twelve-year-old desperate to escape from a mid-twenties' body. 'Money, fortunately, isn't an issue. Daddy's helping us. It's just, I always said I wouldn't bother with a meringue dress. Only, this one – look at the colour. She's almost gold!'

The manager looked pleased, as though personally responsible. But we had a long way to go. When this waif tried me on it could all go to pieces. Literally. There'd be pieces of my material hanging off her.

Yet the manager said the dreaded words: 'Why don't you try it on?'

The woman's smile was wider than my hem. 'Oh, go on then!'

The manager handled me with uncommon care and lifted me from the mannequin. Hurrying to the cramped, damp changing room, the woman cradled me in her arms like a baby.

While she took her clothes off - she was even thinner than I thought - she spoke into the black curtain with such speed her words practically swallowed each other. 'It's a crazy situation, really, us not knowing each other even four months and suddenly he's on one knee proposing and I'm like, yes, this is the best and most natural feeling thing ever - and I used to think most men were wankers!'

The manager chipped in. 'I'm glad you've found one who isn't.'

Her husband worked in the tea rooms next door, and he was, as far as I'd seen, as miserable a bugger to his wife as she was to her customers.

But this cynical interlude did not bother the woman.

'We've just told our families and friends - well, he's going to fly over to Croatia and tell his! We're going to have the ceremony in his sister's back-garden! This is perfect! The skirt goes on forever – it's a gorgeous material – is it satin? And the way these sequins dance in the light! Wow! I love how there's no sleeves but it's not immodest - the waist doesn't fit but I can get that sorted, don't you think?'

I didn't fit at all, but she was right. With alterations we might be perfect together.

She stepped out of the changing room. My manager's face softened.

'Now that's the dress for you!' She said, and the girl curtsied - she transformed into a little girl, playing princess, excited to be rescued by her Prince.

For a good half an hour she tried on different shoes and jewelry. With a crystal tiara, long white gloves and gold high heels, she did look superb, even though there was space for two of her.

She spent a lot of money, the manager managed to be polite and I couldn't wait to leave.

Obviously in my new home (a spacious, modern flat) I had to be hidden away, far from a fiancé's prying, curious eyes, or the black cat's sharp claws. She wasn't sure at first where to put me, but decided on top of the oak wardrobe in the spare room. She climbed a stepladder and dusted, spraying something sweet there.

'You'll be safe here,' she whispered, stroking my neckline regretfully. 'I'd love to try you on again but Gabriel'll be home any minute!'

I settled myself down. It wasn't so bad, considering where I'd been, and anyway, I knew I wouldn't be left for long. We had to get ourselves fitted to each other. And she'd have to show me off. And then the special day!

After that – well – dresses like me, we try not to think about afterwards. The first time? It was a long time ago. Not such good luck. But I was being given a second chance.

My owner's name, I discovered, was Faith.

Faith came to get me one morning, and she cooed as she stroked the full length of my satin skirt as though I were a Persian cat, stopping to fondle my sequins, standing in front of the mirror and putting me against her hard body, sighing, smiling. She just wasn't quite as animated as before. She fitted me inside two white bin bags, whispered she'd get a proper cover after the fitting, and popped me in the boot of her car, carefully laying me out on a clean white sheet.

We parked outside what looked like someone's house. The open door revealed a set of winding stairs. She climbed them slowly, as though I was a weight she was dragging.

'Miss Wenlock?' Faith asked, as a lady appeared at the top of the stairs.

'Oh, call me Aurora, darling! Do come in!'

Aurora had a terribly posh accent. She was all bosom and flowers and smiles; as we followed, I noticed Faith could probably have fitted into her dress four times over.

As though reading my mind Aurora said, 'You're such a slight little thing! Goodness knows what you'll need doing to your dress. I could make you something new!'

Faith smiled. 'That's so kind of you – but this one, she's special. Let me show you.'

As she tried me on, I took in the spotless room. Its perfume was lilies, and there were many fresh flowers in vases. The wallpaper was red roses and silver leaves, and the plush carpet, pink. Somehow it was stylish.

Faith put on her new shoes, and two gold and pearl slides in her hair.

'Ooh! I see what you mean, darling!' schmoozed Aurora, as Faith twirled around a few times and even curtsied, some of the old flushness returning in her cheeks.

'Can you make her fit?' She held her breath, hoping, as I was.

'Of course! It won't even take me long! Now you just stand there looking pretty, and tell me all about the lucky husband to be, and I'll pop pins in here and there to make sure I get this done properly. You're going to look like a princess!'

Faith went back to the very beginning, how she and Gabriel had met on a river's edge in the middle of the summer; he'd been training to be a lifeguard.

'I fell for him there and then! I've always dated men who work in banks or offices. Here was someone who actually rescued people!'

Faith became more animated as she told the story.

But just as Aurora was putting the finishing touches to me, Faith started to cry. The sudden outburst made us both jump. Aurora even pricked herself with a pin. I was worried her blood would stain me.

'My darling girl! Whatever is the matter?'

Faith couldn't talk; she was all gasps and snot and tears and almost forgot to check none of her mess went on my satin. Aurora hastily handed her a handkerchief covered in flowers.

'I'm so sorry.' Faith finally said, in between sniffles. 'It all seemed so perfect, you know, but...'

'Pre-wedding nerves?' asked Aurora, nodding her head sympathetically.

'Oh no,' Faith shook her head. 'I'd never have had those, not with Gabriel! It's just, he's started to act really strange. The other day I found him in the garden trying to hang himself from a tree with the washing line.'

I felt Aurora stiffen. On such unchartered ground she was speechless.

Faith saw the fear in her face. 'God, I'm sorry. I shouldn't have said anything. Let me get out of my dress and I'll let you get on with it.'

Aurora stuttered for a second and then got her act together. 'Faith, darling. If your Gabriel is not – well, himself - then you must get help. You can't cope with this on your own.'

Faith nodded. 'I know. I know. I will. I have. I'm trying. I'm sorry again to burden you with this, Miss… Aurora. It's alright. It'll all be alright.'

Well, I didn't agree with her at all. But there I was, left at Aurora's shop, Faith on her way down the stairs, and that was that. I just had to wait and see what would happen.

***

Aurora was true to her word. She skillfully and neatly did all the alterations and replaced the missing sequins seamlessly.

When Faith came back to try me on, she cat-walked up and down, her eyes fixed on the two huge wall mirrors in front and behind her. 'I can't believe it; you've really made the dress mine!' and though a little pale, she kept smiling.

The two women made small talk throughout the fitting. But when Faith was paying by card, Aurora, avoiding her eye and busily tearing off her receipt asked, 'How is your young man?'.

Faith said softly, 'Oh, everything is okay now, don't worry.' She had stopped smiling.

Aurora nodded and wished them both the very best of luck on their special day.

'Do send me the photos of the wedding!' She called down the stairs as Faith hurriedly carried me out to her car.

'I will!' Faith called back, and then added under her breath, so softly

I could barely hear, 'if we ever fucking make it.'

Had it really come to that? Faith gave nothing away on the drive home.

And then back I was at my new address, and here Faith was, showing me off to one of her friends. Yet once again as she put me on, there was no laughter or glint of excitement, even when her friend said how beautiful we looked.

And when she turned to her friend and asked, 'But why did he cancel the engagement party? Who would do a thing like that?' I realised how the situation had worsened.

Her friend shook her head. 'But he hasn't cancelled the wedding?'

'Not yet!' Faith spat out. 'He keeps talking about the wedding! About what we're going to eat and the special uniform he's going to wear and where all the guests will stay – only...' Faith just kept shaking her head.

'Go on...' Her friend took her hand.

'I've not seen anything. No evidence he's done anything. He's not even working. He just keeps going to the Post Office and sending daddy's money to his family, says they're arranging everything there.'

'And you don't believe him?'

'Oh Christ!' Faith started wrenching herself out of me, almost popping my pearl buttons with the force of her despair. 'I don't know what to believe anymore! I managed to work out his passcode when he didn't know I was looking. I've been reduced to stealing his damn phone and checking all his calls and messages. There's no calls to Croatia, no messages, no mention of any wedding to anyone. Nothing. Which means what? My friends and family have all booked to go to a wedding which doesn't exist? What the hell do I do?'

Her friend sat down on the edge of the bed, motioning for Faith to sit next to her. For the first time ever, I was abandoned in a heap on the floor.

'Faith, you don't still love him?' There was an urgency in her tone.

Faith looked at her friend. 'For months now he's been saying he wants to kill himself. He's totally changed since we met. He cries at night. He doesn't sleep. He says he still loves me but the problem is, Amie... the real problem is... I just don't know who he is anymore.'

Amie stroked Faith's hand tenderly. 'You're going to hate me for saying this, but... well, he proposed so quickly - are you sure you ever did?'

Faith got up from the bed and picked me up off the floor, stroking me absentmindedly. And then I was left hanging in the wardrobe, inside the proper wedding dress cover she'd bought for me, as promised, a few weeks earlier.

Later that evening, or perhaps the middle of the night, I was disturbed by leaden footsteps. I told myself Faith had come to see me - she couldn't sleep and, in her excitement, wanted to try me on, as she had in the early days. But the footsteps were heavy, fierce. They came unnervingly close to the wardrobe. I could hear laboured breathing. The oak door was abruptly flung open, a small light gleamed and a glaring shadow engulfed the wardrobe. In the darkness I couldn't see the face. But I could hear sharp bursts of hissed words. It was Gabriel. His breath was rancid, his hands hot and vicious as he began blindly groping in plastic bags full of papers at the back of the wardrobe.

'If she finds it, that's it for me. Where the fuck is it?'

In his urgent clumsiness, one of the bags spewed its contents on the floor. He lunged for them, yanking my hem through the cover, then wrenching the entire base of my skirt. The small light blinded me.

'That's all I need! Her fucking wedding dress!'

His hands tightened around me, my material strangled by his rage. For one horrendous moment I thought he was going to rip me out my cover and drag me across the room, even tear me apart. But as quickly as it had started, it stopped. He let out a long sigh and sat down right there in the wardrobe, staring at the piece of paper he had found. And then a door slammed and the whole room lit up. He hurried from the wardrobe and left the room with Faith, their shrill voices piercing the darkness.

I was disturbed by a great deal of shouting not long after. Gabriel's voice was deep and rough, how I imagined concrete might sound if it talked, and poor Faith's like a tiny butterfly, trying to flit away from whatever he was screaming. There were doors slammed too, and I heard an engine rev, and then all was quiet. But I couldn't make out, from the depths of the oak wardrobe, any of the words.

What happened next was still worse. I heard Faith swearing and crying, pacing the flat, rummaging through rooms and drawers and throwing things, smashing things and ripping up paper, before the wardrobe door was opened and I was roughly, hurriedly taken out and bundled into one of the black bin bags strewn around the floor. Inside there were pieces of ripped cards, letters and photos. I could make out a few words here and there - 'I love you' and 'always yours' - and a smiling Faith standing with a smiling, stocky olive-skinned man, his hand clamped on her shoulder as though he owned her.

And then the bag was closed and darkness fell.

There was a short car journey and I was taken out, bag now open, faced with great big deep holes, everywhere, and deafening machines and people throwing in all sorts of rubbish, where crushing noises ricocheted around and seemed to grow in aggression before eventually fading away. Faith emptied all the cards and photos and letters into one. Endless stuff was emptied into others. I feared the worst. But as we reached the top of some yellow metal steps, Faith hesitated. She took me out of the bag, cradled my veil, stroked my soft satin and felt my full luscious softness in her tired hands.

She shook her head.

'Not you,' she whispered. 'Not you. I just can't do that.'

And down we climbed, back down those cold metal steps and back into the warm car.

And the next thing I know, we're right back at the shop where nearly a year before, Faith had fallen in love with me. This time she walked very slowly to the counter. This time her voice was as soft as a whisper and her tiny body seemed to float directionless.

'I'm so sorry to bother you,' she said to the stranger there. 'I wonder if you'd mind? This dress...'

She laid me out in front of her, letting my grace and beauty speak for themselves, 'I bought her here almost a year ago, because I was getting married. But I've just found out my fiancé is already married with another family.'

The woman behind the counter scrutinised Faith intensely.

'I don't want any money back and I haven't got the receipt anyway. I just want you to have the dress. Sell it to someone else. Give it another chance, would you? A new home? She's such a beautiful dress and I've really let her down.' Faith was fighting back tears.

I wished the damn saleswoman would do something, reach out and pat Faith or say something kind, but, just like the old bitch of a manager, she didn't express the slightest emotion. She just said,' We can't offer you any money and we're not really selling wedding dresses, but I'll pop it in the back room and see what we can do.' Then she vaguely smiled.

Faith also tried to smile. 'Thank you.' she said, turning away. 'Thank you very much. It's very kind of you.'

And as she just about managed to float emptily up the steps, out the front door, I heard her say to me, very softly, 'I hope you have better luck next time.'

I wish I could've replied, 'Right back at you, Faith.'

'Engrained' tells the story of Holly, a sculptor who whittles beauty from a piece of wood while manifesting her clients' greatest desires. She serves a highly personal, niche market that relies on both her technical skill and insight. While her pieces evoke great emotion, on this day she will encounter a customer who is highly agitated for the wrong reasons. A man who devalues individuality, he fails to recognize that what Holly exposes within the wood is unique, complicated, and personal. Human experience cannot be mass produced.

~ Meredith DePaolo, Momaya Judge

Engrained

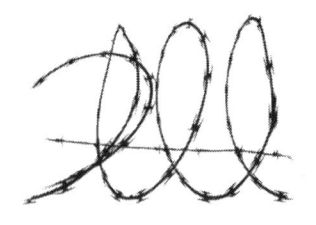

Antony Dunford

Third Place

'I always wanted to jump out of an airplane,' said Mr. Tempest after a minute. 'The idea terrifies me, but my grandad was in the Paras in the war. I wanted to feel the way he felt. Falling. Live or die, it's up to me. Until I pull that chord, I'm free, nothing else matters. Because until I pull that cord there is nothing else. I want to experience what he felt.'

There was a pause. Mr. Tempest tried to look over his shoulder at Holly.

'Go on,' she said. The platform creaked as she moved her weight.

Mr. Tempest thought for another moment. 'I don't want to be shot at as I fall. But the rest of it I want to experience. And grandad jumped at night - I'd like to see what I'm falling towards. But the rest of it. That's something I always wanted to do. What has this got to do with carving a chair?' Mr. Tempest tried to look over his shoulder again. Through his clothes he could feel the light touch of Holly's hand at the nape of his neck and the base of his spine.

'I try to capture a little bit of you, of what makes you just you and nobody else, and let that guide the way I carve. Sometimes it guides the choice of wood. There you are, Mr. Tempest, measurements done,' said Holly, writing the length and breadth of Mr. Tempest's back in her notebook before folding her tape measure.

A cloud-freed flare of sunlight, broken by the window sash, cast beams through the workshop. They picked out dust floating lazily in the morning air. Instinctively Mr. Tempest waved his hand as if to wipe away the light.

'What happens now?' he asked, stepping down from the wooden platform Holly had him stand on for his fitting.

'Now I make a sketch of your chair. If you like the look of what I've drawn, you pay the balance, I make the chair. Takes a couple of months.'

'The balance is a lot of money.'

'For a made-to-measure, hand-carved rocking chair? It's a bargain, Mr. Tempest. You're buying a personalised work of art.'

Mr. Tempest took a few steps deeper into the workshop, letting his hand reach for, but not touch, the things around him. A half-finished owl cut from the top of a medium-thick length of trunk; a solid, high-backed wooden chair almost as tall as he was, the back and arms carved to resemble flames; a set of possibly salad spoons, their handles carved into spanners, but spanners with the texture of reptilian scales. Everywhere smelled of wood chips and sawdust. He could taste the wood in the air.

'I heard Sting has one of your chairs? It would be worth it if I can say Sting has one by the same artist,' said Mr. Tempest, licking his lips.

'You can say what you like, Mr. Tempest. I don't talk about my clients, just as I wouldn't talk about you,' said Holly. She ripped the measurements page out of her notebook and tucked it in a file on her desk. 'When you receive the sketch let me know if you want me to make the chair,' she said, her tone dismissive. She was already thinking of her next task.

Mr. Tempest opened his mouth to speak again but changed his mind. The workshop door shut behind him with a satisfyingly solid thunk followed by the after-tinkling of the broken bell.

Holly ignored his departure. She took a sheet of rough paper from a pile and a wooden box filled with sketching pencils from a drawer. She drew an open parachute, a parachutist after opening, and a sky diver in free fall. Using a second, heavier, pencil she picked out key lines from the form of each image. She crossed out the parachutist after opening and sketched a closed parachute next to it.

'Parachute seat, sky diver back, inverted open parachutes for the rockers?' she mused to herself. It didn't feel right. Was he lying? Is it not the freedom of free fall but the security of the parachute he likes? Should the back of the chair be the open parachute? She took a piece of clean paper from another drawer and started to sketch properly; with lines and curves, drawing the ghost of a chair still locked in wood. Her pencil strokes were, for a few minutes, the only sounds.

There was the thunk and after-tinkle of the door opening. A man Holly didn't recognise but who was of a familiar type - tall, middle-aged, lazy paunch, dressed casually with a regard only for the price of each item.

'Is this Two Trees Art?' he said.

Holly nodded.

'I have a return,' he said, and turned back to the door. Holly felt something inside her clench.

'Wait!' said Holly, standing. 'What do you mean, 'a return'?' But the man had not waited. She stood up and tucked her pencil into her hair.

A few minutes later he came back, holding the door open with his hip as he dragged in a large, heavy, two-seater bench inlaid with carvings of herbs and garden birds. One of the seats was slightly higher and more compact than the other, so if the person in that seat was small they would be at the same level as a person in the second seat if they were large. She recognised the piece.

When he had it inside he paused to catch his breath.

'That's Mrs. Birch's bench,' said Holly.

'Yes. I am returning it,' said the man. Holly stared at him, an eyebrow raised. 'I am her son,' the man added. 'Andrew,' he said, offering his hand to be shaken, but from across the workshop. Holly would have had to walk several steps to shake it. She did not.

'Why do you think you can return it?' said Holly. 'Is Mrs. Birch alright?'

'She's fine. She sits on it in the garden with tears in her eyes. It brings to mind my father, you see.' Only now did Andrew Birch lower his offered hand.

Holly nodded. 'She said that when we were designing it. That was why she wanted it made. What makes you think you can return it?'

'Well, it upsets her,' said Andrew Birch. Holly's eyebrow was still raised. 'I don't like to see her upset. So I am returning it.'

Holly's expression didn't change. 'I have no need for it. You'll need to dispose of it somewhere else.'

'No, I am returning it for a refund. A full refund.'

Holly's eyebrow lowered. Her face locked into a mask.

'No, you are not. Take it away when you leave,' she said. 'Thank you,' she added, as a piece of punctuation, nothing to do with thanks. Her stare had chisel-cut precision.

'I have rights, as a consumer!' said Andrew Birch.

'You do, but you haven't read them, have you? Mrs. Birch paid for my time to create a sketch and then to carve a bench. She also paid for a piece of sketch paper, some graphite, and an oak tree trunk. If you could return my time and the original tree trunk you might have a case to argue for a refund of the cost of each. But you can't. This is an individually commissioned piece of creative art, not a mass-produced office chair. Take it and go,' Holly said.

'I am a lawyer!' said Andrew Birch.

'No, you're not,' said Holly. She could tell by his reaction that she was right.

'It cost a lot of money! I want a refund!' His voice had risen a semi-tone, or possibly two.

'But you're not going to get one. Mrs. Birch knew the price before she decided to commission the piece. She was very happy with the design and the piece itself. Take it back to her.'

'She keeps sitting on it and thinking of my father,' said Andrew Birch.

'Which is why she had it made. Take it back to her.'

'But it was so expensive!'

They were standing a few feet apart, face to face, squared off, just inside the door to the workshop. A low, dark cloud had moved in front of the sun and the light through the windows was now vague and directionless. The dust particles seemed to have disappeared.

'You are wasting my time, which, as you know, I charge for,' said Holly. She crossed to the desk, picked up a pad. 'I am now writing you an invoice for my time from the moment you walked through my door to the moment you leave. Hang around as long as you want.'

Andrew stared at Holly as she took her watch off and put it on the notepad on her desk, then sat back down, patted her pockets sending out little clouds of sawdust, before remembering her pencil was tucked in her hair. She retrieved it and returned to work on the free-fall-or-parachute – should she draw both, let Mr. Tempest pick? - chair.

Andrew was not used to being ignored.

It took him a few seconds to realise Holly was going to continue to ignore him. He looked around the workshop at the carvings both complete and in progress. He was suddenly very aware of how solid, how definite, real wood can be. He swallowed. His mouth felt dry.

He took a few steps towards the owl-in-progress stump.

'How much is this one?' he asked.

Holly looked up from her sketches, staring at him over the top of the glasses she wasn't wearing.

'I work by commission, that piece belongs to a client.'

'What if I offered you more?' said Andrew Birch, running his hand over the owl's face.

'What?' said Holly.

'Offered you more than your client has agreed to pay.'

'I've told you already – my client owns that piece of wood and has bought my time to find a shape inside it. The owl is not mine to sell.'

'My wife loves owls. This would be quite a birthday present,' said Andrew Birch. 'Everything has its price,' he added.

'You actually think that?' said Holly as her head bowed and she went back to her sketching.

'Then can you make me another just like it?' said Andrew Birch. 'Or have it copied? You know, laser-scanned or something so that a machine can then cut copies of it. Mass-produce them.'

'No,' said Holly, a word delivered with the finality of an axe hitting a tree.

Her pencil made slight shhh noises as it added second dimension shadows to the image of the potential chairs before her.

Andrew was looking more closely at the owl.

'This owl is curious,' he said. 'What wood is this? It's very hard.'

'Yew,' said Holly, without looking up.

'Why is the owl curious?'

Holly stopped sketching. 'Because my client's biggest regret is she will never have time to read everything there is to read. The owl is both her love of owls and her desire to know all she can.'

'So the owl is her? Part of her? An image of her?' Andrew said, mostly to himself. 'The you within yew,' Andrew Birch added. Holly shuddered at those words, a mass market pun. She blinked to clear her mind and again went back to sketching.

'I could commission you to do something, then?' Andrew Birch said, wheels of inspiration creaking into gear. 'I could pay you to carve me something then I would own it and I could have copies made and the copyright would be mine?'

Andrew Birch's expression changed as if he thought he had said something he should not have. He looked askance at Holly, but she did not seem to be listening. He started walking round the workshop, looking at other pieces. He took out his phone, trying to hold it as if he was struggling to read something written on the screen, but really angling the built-in camera at the carving.

'Don't,' said Holly, without looking up.

'I'm sorry?' said Andrew Birch.

'Don't take any photographs. This is a workshop full of tools and I'd hate for one of them to accidentally damage your phone.' Holly said this whilst looking past Andrew at what turned out to be a small lump-hammer resting on a workbench.

'I –' Andrew Birch felt a whole speech form in his mind, a speech about rights, and how threats of violence could not be condoned, probably with a bit about how outraged he was at being talked to in this manner. But something stopped him.

He put the phone away. He put his hands in his pockets too, so as not to be led into temptation.

He was looking at a chair, a huge chair standing nearly two metres tall, carved of thick, heavy wood in the shape of living flames. His expression said there was something about it. That it impressed him. That he thought it would impress others.

'That's ten minutes so far. Twenty quid and counting. Will it be cash or card when you settle up?' said Holly.

Andrew Birch gave up and went back to the bench he had brought with him.

'Would you mind giving me a hand with this to the car?' he said.

'You seemed to get it in without any problem,' said Holly.

Andrew Birch pulled the bench to the door, opened it, held the door open with his foot, and manipulated the bench out.

'Before you get any bright ideas about getting that bench copied can I recommend reading the contract your mother signed?' Holly called after him. 'Shall I invoice you care of her?'

Thunk. After-tinkle.

Holly put down her pencil and stretched her finger, her arms, her back. She hated conflict, but she had learned the least unpleasant way of dealing with it was quickly. She rolled her shoulders, stretched her neck, looking as she did so at the two emergent sketches of Mr. Tempest's possible rocking chair. The one where the back was in the shape of an open parachute, the rest of the chair fairly conventional. The other where the back was reminiscent of a sky-diver in free fall; the rockers were the tops of two up-turned parachute shapes; the seat was an unopened, packed parachute. Two possible futures, nothing at all existed until one had been eliminated.

Holly was fairly certain Mr. Tempest would pick the first design. But until he did she would nurture hope that he would pick the second. She took a lighter pencil from the box and went back to work. Outside the clouds had moved on and the sunlight through the windows was picking out the gently floating dust in the air once more.

Leftovers explores motherhood and memory in a way that feels fresh. We meet the main character, the mother, in the act of preparing her son's favourite food, an act that serves as ballast against the unkind and unsophisticated ways of his wife. What starts as a story of a mother who detests her daughter-in-law becomes a story of memory, and our ability to get stuck within it. As the act of preparing food shifts from an act of maternal superiority to a way of clinging onto love and memory, we witness the slighted mother and the despised daughter-in-law become redrawn into less simplistic characters and a fuller picture emerge.

~ Alice Shepherd, Momaya Judge

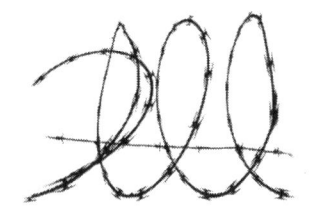

Leftovers

Kat Y. Tang

Second Place

I will never understand why my son decided to marry such a useless Woman. All she does day in and day out is sit at home, watching inane television shows while chewing popcorn with her mouth wide open, kernels falling to the couch and the floor around her like dandruff. The malnourished dog of theirs licks the popcorn off the floor--a qǐ wáwà they say, a qíguài wáwà is more like it: a queer doll with a scrawny body and giant head. No one in my village would have touched a sickly looking dog like that, even at the height of our starvation.

Today on the television four women with painted faces wave their hands around like harlots while sitting around a table talking. These are the Woman's role models. I turn off my hearing aid so that I do not have to listen to these women on TV quacking in their language--so harsh and grating with none of the melody and meaning of Mandarin. My back is bothering me more than usual today, but I cannot rest. If I do nothing, I will be just as bad as that lazy Woman. So I will cook a meal for my son when he returns from his demanding job as a bank manager. As I shuffle--slow damn slow--around the kitchen, I gather flour, egg, water, chives, dried shrimp, and ground pork. Jiǔcài hézi is my son's favorite. I remember the first time he ever ate one. He was 6 years old and it was the first time we could afford meat. It so upset his stomach that he threw it all up. Oh how angry I was then, all the money turned to bile! But now here we are, eating jiǔcài hézi so casually on a weekday night.

I hum as I mix the ingredients for the dough. This is perhaps the worst part of losing my hearing: not being able to even hear myself. I wonder at times what my voice sounds like when I dare to use it. I am afraid I sound simple, like Lu Hong from our village who was never the same after being beaten and raped by the Japanese. At least my son didn't marry a Japanese woman. Then I would have known for sure that he was trying to kill me.

The Woman is still sitting on the couch, but she has replaced one bag of popcorn with another without even bothering to discard the first. Disgusting. I place the kneaded dough in a bowl to rest and get to work on the fillings. As I finish mincing the chives, I turn and knock my carton of eggs on the ground. The Woman looks in my direction and hurries to the kitchen. She is saying something now as I can see her mouth working vigorously. She must have strong jaw muscles from all that chewing. She picks the carton and its few remaining unbroken eggs off the floor and starts putting it back in the fridge. I grab her arm.

'No!' I say, or think I say. 'Deen-ar for Xuyang.'

She shakes her head and says something loudly and slowly, her lips over exaggerating each syllable. I'm hard of hearing, not an idiot, I want to tell her, but she wouldn't understand. Finally she leans in close to my hearing aid and I can see the veins on her neck bulging.

'Pi-zza!' she yells. 'Pi-zza for dinner!'

This cursed Woman and her lazy ways. How many times can a man eat delivery before he dies of cancer or lack of love? No, my son deserves homemade food. I wrestle the carton back from the Woman's clutches and turn my back to her. I watch from the corner of my eye as she gives up and goes back to the couch in front of the TV, leaving the qǐ wáwà to lap up the eggy mess.

As I mix together ingredients for the filling with my hands, I chastise myself for wasting perfectly good eggs. One more reason she could use to convince Xuyang to send me out of the house and into some old persons' home. The little dried shrimps go into the mixture last. I can no longer see clearly their tiny black dots for eyes. At least I had not spilled those on the ground--it is an hour long bus ride to the nearest Chinese market and the bus drivers are not as patient with me as they used to be. Whenever my granddaughter comes home to visit, she makes the trips with me. No one else in this family does. When was the last time she came to visit? I can't seem to remember…

My granddaughter is simply wonderful, even though the Woman gave her a name I cannot pronounce in an effort to wrest her away from me. She may have given Eme-ri a name, but I gave her her eyes: sharp, watchful eyes. She once asked me why I pushed my way onto every bus, why I squeezed so closely to the person in front of me in line. What is a line? 'If you don't push,' I told her, 'you won't get anything. You always have to keep pushing forward or else your family will starve.' It seemed ridiculous to say in a supermarket that had 20 of everything, but I wanted to make sure that she understood this mentality. I was worried that she might have inherited some weak genes from her mother.

The dough, after having enough time to rest, has to be pulled and then chopped into small rounds. Each round gets rolled out into a circular, flat disk that then gets a good few spoonfuls of stuffing. I tried to explain this to the Woman when I first moved into the house, but she balked at the smell of the chives and scurried back to her spot on the couch. This was when I first realized the extent of her weakness. We used to eat charcoal to fill our stomachs, lick the remains off our fingers, and she can't stand the smell of chives? I make sure to put just enough stuffing into the center of the disks so that they are full, but not so full that they'll burst open like Xiao Pang's stomach when he died from finally eating a single bowl of rice.

Sharp filaments of pain ravage my lower back and are traveling up my spine, but I refuse to sit down. If I just focus on making dinner for Xuyang, I can ignore it. Pinch the two halves of the circle together to form a pocket and crimp the edges so the filling can stay inside and the two sides do not separate when cooked. When Xuyang got into graduate school in the US I was reluctant to let him go. We had suffered so much together, I felt our souls had fused as one. How could I let a piece of my soul fly across the ocean to a foreign land? 'Ma,' he'd said, gripping my tremulous shoulders, 'there are opportunities in America. When I make enough money, I will bring you with me and then we can live together.' 'But you don't even have a wife yet,' I'd said. 'Who will take care of you in America? You must find a wife first before you leave.' If only he'd listened! Then I would have someone who understood that elders must be respected instead of this Woman who doesn't even lift a finger when I come home carrying back breaking grocery bags.

My hands are unsteady as I pour oil into the frying pan. A bit of it splatters on my clothes, but these are merely the smallest of the indignities I now endure. Although I can no longer hear the sizzle of cold dough hitting hot grease, I can still feel it from my years and years working as a street vendor. What a luxurious job that seemed, after so many years of filling our mouths with nothing but dust. Back then, I could make a dozen ji ǔ cài hézi in a minute. My body still remembers the perfect time to flip the pocket for an ideal golden crust. I finish frying the 20th one just as Xuyang walks into the kitchen. He holds a giant cardboard pizza box in his hands: grease-carrying monstrosities, just awful things. The little q ī wáwà runs in pathetic circles around his feet. He comes up and puts a hand on my shoulder, shouts, 'Ma! I told you to stop doing this! Go sit down. I bought dinner.'

'Your favorite,' I say. 'It's not good to eat so much processed food.' His face looks swollen and his skin color is sallow. It is from eating food that has too much yǎng, too much hot energy. All American food has too much hot energy. Americans don't understand balance.

'Wendy doesn't like it, Ma. We've been over this so many times already, don't you remember?'

'Don't yell at me,' I mumble, though I know that if he didn't yell, I wouldn't be able to hear. But still, if my body had any moisture left I know there would be tears in my eyes. 'No one respects me in this house, not even my own son. Why did I leave China? To be treated worse than the dog?'

My son only sighs and sits down in front of the TV with his wife to eat their pizza. Cheese turns my stomach, I want to yell at him, you know that! Instead, I stand in front of my perfect jiǔcài hézis, biting into one that has just come off the stove, so hot that it would burn anyone's tongue but mine. I know, without even turning around, that they are looking at me, talking about me behind my back. Everyone talks, but no one talks to me anymore. I know what the horrible Woman is saying: that I'm a nuisance and wouldn't it be better if I were in a nursing home where I could spend my days with other people who are also on their way out of this life? I can only hope my son will defend me. My son, my only child. I curse him under my breath.

I bring the remaining jiǔcài hézis slowly toward the kitchen island, making a show of how heavy the plate is and how difficult it is for me to carry it, but neither my son nor the Woman look away from the TV. I consider dropping the plate, but it's unforgivable to waste food and I cannot do it. I am no longer hungry. Defeated, I dump the piping hot food into a bag and bring it to the freezer. Maybe Xuyang will come to his senses tomorrow and decide to eat better. They are almost just as good reheated. I strain to pull open the packed freezer drawer. What could possibly be in there? I tug with what little strength I now possess and the drawer flies open. I look down at bags and bags and bags of leftover jiǔcài hézi.

My heart pounds wildly. Did I make these? When? Last night? What happened last night? I can't remember. All I see is my baby sister's burial mound. Babies couldn't chew tree bark or digest dirt. I stuff this new bag into the freezer and shut it as fast as I can. Hide the evidence. Blame it on someone else. Kētóu to Chairman Mao. I'm going to be sent off to a place for crazy people. If I must go, send me home to my village, my village!

My mind is heavy and useless as melted metal. I must go to bed. In the downstairs bathroom, I giggle as I take out my teeth and place them in a glass like a little exhibit for old age. I step out of my day clothes and into the shower, and then out of the shower and into my pink and frilly nightgown, perfect for an old girl. Touching my bed, I realize the Woman is humiliating me yet again. She has placed some sort of plastic covering over the mattress underneath the bed sheet. As though I were an incontinent child who would wet the bed! I have suffered through bullets pockmarking the walls above where I lay sleeping and this is how I am treated? The anger that courses through me shakes my whole body and I am livid. How dare she? She will know the wrath of a woman who sold out her husband to save herself and her son. Son, don't cry, mother is here. When the Red

Guard took my husband away, he said nothing even though I was the one that had done wrong. It was I who burned Mao's picture for kindling. I cannot remember my husband's face, was it kind? It must have been...

  I think I fainted. But I am okay. It is 9 PM which is my bedtime and somehow I have already dressed myself for bed. I pull myself up off the ground and onto the bed and I can feel that the Woman has put some sort of plastic covering over my mattress, as though I were an incontinent child who would wet the bed! She's insufferable, but at least I still have my loving son and beautiful granddaughter. I have to protect them at all costs. I've lost so much else in my life. Tomorrow, I think I will make my son his favorite food.

In an oblique take on the theme of 'outsiders', D.R.D. Bruton tells the story of an orphaned lamb, raised by a family of sheep farmers, and in particular by the young son. It is his first real experience of new life and death, and the lamb's story is also part of the story of his growing up, as he learns that love and pain go hand in hand. His world expands to encompass different types of love: one refrain is that the young narrator loves 'mam and lil' Lucy, and meat in gravy with taters and peas' – but he also comes to love Annie, a girl at school, and of course the lamb, which is destined for the butcher's knife. 'A Lesson in Love and Hate' takes us into an unsentimental world reminiscent the one recorded by James Rebanks in The Shepherd's Life, although we are not in Cumbria, but in an unnamed country of a bygone era whose speech recalls the southern United States, but where shillings still circulate. The tale is told in a powerful voice, its syntax falling somewhere between the speech of a child and pure poetry, with hints of Biblical language. Echoes of Christianity imagery abound, but this new parable, that begins with the father blowing the miracle of life into the lamb, and ends with the shilling - the wages of betrayal - is one in which belief in God is explicitly rejected, making it a simple human tale of life on earth.

~ Gillian Pink, Momaya Judge

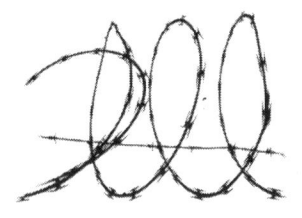

›
A Lesson in Love in Hate

D.R.D. Bruton

First Place

I was there, the night pa tugged the skittery critter out from the dying mother's slit belly, all slick and blood and snot, its body steaming like something cooked and its legs like broke sticks. Pa blew into its nose, like he blows when he wants a spark to start a fire, and he took a handful of straw and showed me how to wipe it clean and he was rough with what he did. In his jacket pocket he had a rubber-teated glass bottle of warmed milk for feeding it and he pulled open its pink mouth and taught it how to suck.

'Don't you go fallin' in love with it, now,' he said. 'Won't do no good but to break your heart, boy, when the day comes and it must be brought to the keen knife.'

I shook my head and I pushed the lamb away from me with my foot. I said it made no nevermind to me. 'Love,' I scoffed. 'I love mam and lil' Lucy, and meat in gravy with taters and peas.' And I swore to pa I'd not ever love the motherless lamb. But how could I not?

I told Mr. Mitchell about it the next day in school. I said as how it was a miracle what my pa had done, how he had given breath and life to the lamb, and the lamb standing in its stall was all the proof of that. I said as how it was as light as almost nothing and its eyes were dark as nights and it didn't have no mother to love it which was a crying shame. Then I told Mr. Mitchell I didn't believe in God no more and I think he understood.

I told the boys in the class, about the blood and the snot and everything slippy like slime. And it smelled of storm, I said, and the undersides of snails, and shit it smelled of, too. The boys said that was gross and what I was telling them was putting them off their lunch, but they said I was not to stop telling them.

And the girls, I told them that it was warm as beds that have been slept in and soft as feathers and small enough it could almost fit in a pocket. Annie sat a little closer to me then and she took my hand in hers and she said to tell it again.

The lamb was waiting for me when I came home from school, the air all bleat and bite and blow, and it was unsteady on its legs at first. Mam said she'd fed it on the hour, every hour, but she'd got the dinner to see to now, so I was to take over. She'd filled two bottles with milk and I sat with the wee lamb in the barn, fighting against its impatient butt and press, and laughing at the mess it made of itself and me, with milk everywhere. Afterwards, the sandpaper-lick of its tongue against my cheek and my neck, and it curled into me and slept on my lap.

'What should we call it?' I asked pa on that first full day. We were sat at the table and tea was finished and lil' Lucy was in her high chair making bubble noises with her milk. Pa was wiping his plate clean with a bit of bread.

He looked at me like he didn't know me, or like I was simple or daft.

'The lamb,' I said, 'it should have a name at least.'

Pa licked his fingers and then he wiped them on the leg of his trousers. He cleared his throat, as if he might have something important to say, and he said the lamb wouldn't fare long enough in this world to be carrying no name.

I called it Snot to show pa that I wasn't for loving it.

'You feed it up and there's a shiny shilling in it for you when Old Tom calls with his whetted knife and his enamel bucket for catching the blood.'

Inside, my stomach turned at that, but I didn't let pa see. I just nodded and looked at mam, looking quick in case I gave myself away.

The boys at school laughed when I said the lamb's name. The girls made crumpled faces. And Annie quietly said to tell her again what it was like, the soft and the warm that it was.

It got stronger, day by day, the lamb, and it looked for me coming home from school and it followed me round the barn and butted my legs and fell at my feet. I said it was no good what it was doing and that I never could love it, not if it was just going to break my heart. I love mam and lil' Lucy, I said, and meat in gravy with taters and peas. And I love a girl called Annie who sits beside me in school and holds my hand and she asks what a new-born lamb smells like. That's what I told Snot and I said it was a secret about Annie and pa wasn't to know and not mam neither.

The days crept at first, slow as drag and pull. And they seemed to have so many hours in them, hours when I was thinking of Snot and wishing for the clock in Mr. Mitchell's classroom to not hold on so tightly to the minutes. Then I don't know where the days went and they slipped like water through my hands and I did not notice them disappearing. One day was soon two and three, and they piled up like milk bottles that are soon emptied, and days became weeks and the weeks all in such a rush that they tripped over each other, or ran away from me without looking back.

And just when I turned my back and wasn't really looking, it was Spring, soon enough and suddenly. I think maybe it's called Spring because of all the fool lambs leaping in the fields and hares mad-dancing in the tall grass come March and the whole of the farm with a bounce in its step, even pa. Snot was no different, cavorting like a daft 'un when it got the run of the home-field, like someone filled up with happy – like the farm boy, Sonny, when he's had his hand under the skirt of Tilly the milk-maid and his fingers smell of fish and his lips are red from too much kissing and pa says the boy's just silly in love.

I'm silly in love, too, I reckon, but pa don't know that. Silly in love and with a small hard nut of hate bursting open at the dark very heart of me. Old Tom it is that I hate with his cheery 'good-day to you, boy' and his 'my, but you've grown lad and you're the spit of your pa and one day all this will be yours' the sweep of his hand taking in all of the farm. But mostly it's his knife wrapped in a bit of leather cloth that I hate, and it's sharp as a razor or glass.

Pa says Old Tom'll be visiting at the weekend and he reminds me of the shiny shilling that's waiting for me. I wipe my nose on the back of my sleeve and I don't let on that my heart's breaking somewhere inside of me. And when Snot comes running across the field cos he knows it's me, I kick it away with the hard toe of my boot, and love and hate becomes all mixed up together then.

On the day Old Tom is to call, Mam gives me extra meat in gravy and taters and peas on my plate. She says it'll give me strength for what's to come. I don't clean my plate, not like pa does with his bit of bread scraping the last of the gravy. I don't hardly make an impression on the meat and taters and peas and no one says anything about wasting good food and lil' Lucy keeps looking at me like she knows, which she can't, not really.

Pa don't say a word – I think maybe he knows. And he don't call me into the dry dark of the barn when Old Tom comes into the yard, not even when the farm dog nips and tucks Snot into its pen. I lie in the starless dark under my bed and I stick my fingers in my ears and I shut my eyes tight as pinches so they won't leak tears and I wait for Old Tom to be gone.

At school on Monday I don't tell Mr. Mitchell about miracles and life and breath and my pa being something tall and good. Instead, I say again how I don't believe in God and I say I don't see how I ever could. Mr. Mitchell just nods and presses his lips together and shakes his head.

The boys all want to know about Old Tom's knife cutting the throat and the blood spilling gobbet dark and thick as treacle, enough to fill a whole bucket, and Snot slung on a table, skinned as easy as undressing for bed, and cut into joints for the butcher to sell or for my mam to cook. I make it all up: Old Tom with silver spiders in his ears and his nose, his knife so sharp it can cut silence with a hiss, and the smell hanging in the air after, hanging so thick you can taste it and it tastes of metal, and blood steaming in a rusted enamel pail.

And Annie, she sits beside me same as before, pretty and quiet. She holds my hand like she's done more than a dozen times already, more than two dozen, and she whispers she doesn't believe in God neither, not if I don't. I can't look at her, not like before, just as I can't look at mam or lil' Lucy or pa. I pull my hand from Annie's and I slip a silver shilling into her palm. I tell her she should have it for it's the price of a broken heart. I don't know what I mean by that, but it feels like something true.

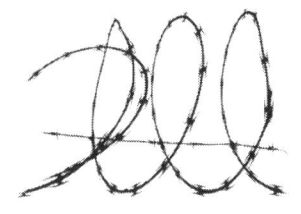

About the Authors

First Place

D.R.D.BRUTON has a novel published by Scotland Street Press called 'Mrs. Winchester's Gun Club'. He writes flash fiction and short stories too and has had some success in national and international competitions with these. He is retired from teaching and concentrates now on his writing.

What was the inspiration for your story?

The inspiration for this story has its roots in lots of things at once – vegetarianism, seeing new-born lambs in the fields each year, watching a programme where a farmer's son took on the job of bottle feeding a motherless lamb and the look on the boy's face said that he was pleased at doing something as important as keeping the lamb alive. The story came to me with the opening line, not as a fully formed thing but as something I wanted to explore and I wanted to know how it would end - which of course is obvious when you think about it.

What does it mean to you to be published by Momaya Press?

To be published by Momaya Press is always a thrill. The Momaya Review is a classy publication and to be included in its pages is such a lift.

What are your plans for writing in the future?

I had a novel published last year - 'Mrs. Winchester's Gun Club' (Scotland Street Press) - I have other full length work in the hands of an agent; with the success of this story I think it might be time for me to assemble a collection of my shorter fiction and to get it into print sometime soon.

Second Place

Kat Y. Tang is currently a first-year MFA student at Columbia and was recently nominated for the De Alba Fellowship. Kat attended the Summer Literary Seminar in Tbilisi, Georgia last summer, was also accepted into Disquiet (notable entry) and was long listed for Fish Publishing's short story contest.

What was the inspiration for your story?

I knew I wanted to write a story about unreliable memory and the way the distant past can intrude on the present. I had this in mind during the fall of 2019, when I spent some time with my boyfriend's family while his 90-year-old grandmother was visiting from China. She worked non-stop in the kitchen--chopping, kneading, washing – even though everyone told her to relax. Why did she constantly feel this need to keep *doing*, I wondered. What was she afraid of? These thoughts, combined with a strong first-person point of view inspired by Drive Your Plough Over the Bones of the Dead by Olga Tokarczuk, resulted in 'Leftovers.'

What does it mean to you to be published by Momaya Press?

This is my first print publication and I am incredibly honored to have been chosen by Momaya Press! I hope that the story will resonate with readers and that they will enjoy reading it as much as I enjoyed writing it.

What are your plans for writing in the future?

I am currently at Columbia for an MFA so my plan is to learn as much as possible about writing during my time in the program. I am also working on a collection of linked short stories ('Leftovers' is one of those stories) and will look to find an agent to help me publish the collection once it's finished.

Third Place

Antony Dunford was born and grew up in Yorkshire amidst hills and dales. He started reading before he can remember, and writing a little after that. He has had short stories win and be runner up in competitions, and one was published in an Australian online magazine. He has recently started work on novels.

What was the inspiration for your story?

'The Outsider' had me thinking about what they should be the outside of, in an increasingly homogeneous world that nevertheless remains made up of individuals. I wanted to celebrate the individual in the context of similarity. I remembered a table my parents had when I was growing up, hand-carved, heavy, distinct. Still functional, but it had a character - it was a tree that deigned to serve as a table, it was not a table that tried to pretend it had never been a tree. I remember eating meals at the table, and remember the table more than the meals. That prompted me to think of someone taking working with wood to a different level, to only work with wood when inspired by hopes, memories or dreams of the person who would take it into the small portion of the world they inhabited. And then I imagined the sort of person it would take to do that for a living. After that it fairly wrote itself.

What does it mean to you to be published by Momaya Press?

It's very exciting to be in print, and to be third is even more so. I have read three of the previous reviews, and the quality is always high, the variety of approaches to a single theme always fresh and surprising. To have a story considered alive enough to be included in that is very pleasing.

What are your plans for writing in the future?

To keep doing it. I have written a couple of novels that are close enough to be submitted for consideration for publication, I hope, and I have started a third.

Connie Ramsay Bott grew up in Michigan where many of her stories and poems take place. Her poems and short stories have been widely published in anthologies and journals. Her novel Girl Without Skin was published in 2017. She lives in Warwickshire, England.

What was the inspiration for your story?

I was born in Michigan and grew up there, but have lived my adult life in England. I've always been drawn to coming of age stories, young people are constantly needing to make sense of the world, so there is a wealth of material to draw from there. When I write fiction I often go back to my own childhood, remembered settings and the emotional extremes I experienced. When I was eight a girl at my school lost her teenaged sister in a boating accident. I didn't know her, but I tucked the incident away and tried to imagine how it would affect those around her.

What does it mean to you to be published by Momaya Press?

I am proud to be published by Momaya Press. I know I will be among a group of strong international writers, and I'll be happy to add Momaya Press to my list of publications.

What are your plans for writing in the future?

This story will be a chapter in my second novel. My first, *Girl Without Skin* (Cinnamon Press) is a collection of interwoven short stories. I find this way of putting a book together very satisfying.

Niall Buchanan has been writing short stories for some years. He is now working on a comic novel about an old man in Scotland who is trying to create a Gas Works Museum as a way of saving his town. The author was brought up in a remote location which has traces of the ancient buildings that feature in his story of the Stone Age People.

Michael G. Casey is an Irish national who has published several novels, a book of non-fiction and an award-winning chapbook of short stories. His poems and short stories have appeared in several international journals, and won awards.

What was the inspiration for your story?

The inspiration for it came from one of Edward Albee's plays where a man falls in love with a sheep--it was far more than a physical attraction. I began to wonder if this could happen between a lonely man and an inanimate object. (Apparently this is not unknown in Japan.)

What does it mean to you to be published by Momaya Press?

It means a great deal to be published in Momaya--a very impressive magazine with an international reach.

What are your plans for writing in the future?

For the future I intend to concentrate on poetry and short fiction.

Mona Dash is the author of *A Roll of the Dice : a story of loss, love and genetics*, *A Certain Way*, *Untamed Heart*, and *Dawndrops*. She holds a Masters in Creative Writing (with distinction) and her work has been listed in leading competitions such as SI Leeds Literary award, Fish, Bath, Bristol, Leicester Writes and Asian Writer. An engineer and MBA she works in a global tech company. She lives in London. www.monadash.net

Angela DiLella is a writer and artist. She graduated from the New School's MFA Creative Writing program in 2017, and continues to work on the graphic novel she began there. You can check out more of her work at the horror and folklore website Grave Reviews and on Twitter @Shanksspeare.

What was the inspiration for your story?

'The Rage' was inspired by a vacation I took a few years ago. The car ride was quite long and because I don't like driving, my boyfriend offered to drive the whole way. Fortunately, our relationship is nothing like the one in my story! But I still had a deep, uneasy feeling of unreality because I was going to a familiar place with someone unfamiliar to that place. Adding to that feeling was the radio going in and out while only receiving evangelical stations, and the fact that I forced myself to stay awake the whole time in order to help with directions. (I'm a champion at sleeping in the car!) Although the drive itself was completely mundane, my mind started wandering and I began imagining what it would be like if I really was trapped in the car, what could force me to stay inside of it, and so on.

What does it mean to you to be published by Momaya Press?

It is very exciting! Momaya Press has such a positive presence online and is open to diverse work and topics. I'm honored to join its community.

What are your plans for writing in the future?

I am currently working on a fantasy novel that includes graphic elements and I have a couple short stories in my drafts. Occasionally, when I'm feeling brave, I even try out poetry!

Madeleine Dunnigan is co-founder of Ladybeard magazine. She curates The Libreria Room, a series of writer and artist-led discussions and often hosts the Libreria Podcast. She is currently studying an MA in Creative and Life Writing at Goldsmiths, for which she has been awarded the Isaac Arthur Green Fellowship.

What was the inspiration for your story?

During lockdown I cooked and ate obsessively – to a point where it was no longer enjoyable. I was bloated and felt a little bit sick all the time. The story was inspired by this anxious gluttony, and the its deliciously disgusting consequences.

What does it mean to you to be published by Momaya Press?

It's hugely exciting! Especially to be amongst such a broad range of voices from around the world.

What are your plans for writing in the future?

I am currently working on a novel, taking breaks from this to write about other instances of disgusting expulsion: piss, shit and blood.

After leaving the glamorous world of accountancy, **Mary Fox** decided to try her hand at creative writing. She now lives in Epsom with her husband, 2 kids and a pair of hens named Pepsi and Shirley.

What was the inspiration for your story?

I was inspired to write my story after a holiday in Sri Lanka with my family. On one long car journey our lovely taxi driver recounted the story of friends of his, a couple, whose home was swallowed by the tsunami. They were found the next day, after the tsunami had abated, still holding hands, eyes turned towards the ocean. Very sadly, they had perished. It was such a hauntingly tragic image that I felt compelled to weave it into a story.

What does it mean to you to be published by Momaya Press?

I am thrilled to have my story appear in such an illustrious publication as The Momaya Press Review as the stories are of such high quality. I have received so many rejections in the past that this validation gives me the encouragement to continue with my scribblings.

What are your plans for writing in the future?

Like every writer I want to keep improving. However, I would love to have my own themed short story collection and I am working on three short stories at the moment.

Jacquie Franks live at the foot of the Mendip Hills in Somerset. She loves reading, particularly short fiction, and she can't remember a time when she didn't have a book in my hand. She has also always wanted to write but it wasn't until ten years ago that she finally put pen to paper and tried to create the sort of stories that she likes to read, mainly magical realism, and stories with a quirky style. She's been writing - and learning how to write better - ever since.

What was the inspiration for your story?

I was interested in exploring the theme of Outsiders, and particularly the idea that sometimes we can try so hard to 'fit in', that we become strangers to ourselves.

What does it mean to you to be published by Momaya Press?

One word – fabulous!

What are your plans for writing in the future?

I have just started a contemporary-fantasy short story collection; all the stories are connected by a common event and its impact on an island community. Plus I am in the last year of a distance learning degree in creative writing.

Most of the sentences **Russell George** writes are lost somewhere inside his mind, and only occasionally does he find them again. This is perhaps what living means. Beyond that, he helps to publish other people's scholarly books, and wonders at the fate of his football team.

What was the inspiration for your story?

Memory. It's based on a day now shrouded in the mists of time, but which somehow still resonates. But I also recently moved back to suburbia having previously lived in a city, and it's reminded me of growing up in all those pre-defined, narrow spaces which were, perhaps, also quite comforting.

What does it mean to you to be published by Momaya Press?

Well, this is the first time I've entered a piece of work so I'm thrilled that someone else has liked it! I've always been really bad at finishing things. If you don't send work off then it can always still be 'in draft'. But continually tweaking and rephrasing can, after a while, become destructive and you lose the energy of the original idea. To have a story published will give me the confidence to say 'enough – it's done'!

What are your plans for writing in the future?

I have several other stories in draft at the moment (see answer above), so I'd like to finish those. Ultimately, I'd just like to get better at the craft of short story writing. It's both a very satisfying and incredibly frustrating thing to do, and if I can somehow experience more of the former I'll be very happy. In terms of ambition, one day I'd like to have a collection that people who don't know me may read, and even like.

Juliet Hill worked as a theatre musician in the UK for twenty years before moving to Madrid where she started to write. She has written a number of short stories including *Laughing Boy*, a prize-winner in the Writer's Forum magazine competition; *Property is Theft*, shortlisted in the Fiction Desk Newcomer Prize 2015 and a runner-up in the Storgy Magazine's 2015 short story competition; *Parka Billy*, shortlisted in the Highlands and Islands Short Story competition 2015 and Commended in the Southport Writer's Circle Short Story

Competition 2016; *Onassis and Hoxha*, shortlisted in the Writer's Forum Competition 2016; and *The Psychiatrist and the Cleaner*, highly commended in the Segora Short Story competition 2016 and shortlisted in the Earyworks Press 2018 Competition; *Truth or Dare*, also shortlisted in the Earlyworks Press Competition.

What was the inspiration for your story?

I read a story in the newspaper about a homeless woman who was murdered by two teenagers, as if she and her life meant nothing. I wanted to explore the background to somebody ending up in that situation.

What does it mean to you to be published by Momaya Press?

I've entered quite a few stories for the Momaya Competition over the years, so it's extra-special to have one chosen for this anthology. Plus it proves that it's always worth persevering!

What are your plans for writing in the future?

I'm just in the process of finishing a novel and plan to write a collection of short stories all set in the same theatre.

Kevin David Joinville lives in a small town in Southern Illinois with his new wife and their dog Cheddar.

What was the inspiration for your story?

My inspiration for this story was the actual event itself and the feeling of overwhelming solitude it brought. Obviously, it's horrible for anyone who dies in such a way. Less talked about are the experiences of those who try to help like first responders and passersby who must live with having been unable to save someone's life and the loneliness that guilt brings. An event like this is so outside of everyday experience it's unrelatable to the majority of people. It scares others to hear such things happen to average people because that means it's something that could happen to them. The paradox is that in order to heal, people need to speak about their trauma, but the event itself is so isolating that speaking feels impossible.

What does it mean to you to be published by Momaya Press?

This is a great opportunity to get my story out to the world. I am truly honored and excited to be a part of the Momaya Short Story Review.

What are your plans for writing in the future?

I plan to continue writing short stories and hope to someday write a book or two.

Jan Keegan is a mother of four and grandmother of four (soon to be five). She lives in the north of England with her husband. She worked in public services until her retirement just over two years ago. Since then she's done nothing but write and diet. She aims to be successful in both projects!

What was the inspiration for your story?

I have an admiration for rebels, for those who do their own thing and live their life as they choose, (as long as they cause no harm to others of course). Ros is an independent, outwardly strong person but with hidden vulnerabilities.

I was diagnosed with cancer in 2013 and underwent treatment in terms of chemotherapy and then radiotherapy. As I was being treated I saw a number of young people (much younger than me) who were also undergoing treatment. I always thought it so unfair that these youngsters were experiencing this disease. They were young and should have been enjoying life, instead of being stuck on the end of a drip. Those thoughts have stayed with me and form the basis of my story. They were unable to enjoy the things that others of their age were enjoying and as such they were different, 'outsiders'.

What does it mean to you to be published by Momaya Press?

This is the first success that I have had since I began writing in a serious way, so it means everything. I've received such a boost since being told of my inclusion in the book.

What are your plans for writing in the future?

I write all of the time and I'm in the process of finishing my second book. I am looking to secure representation from a literary agent with a view to having my work published.

As the daughter of an antiquarian book dealer, **Taria Karillion** grew up surrounded by far more books than is probably healthy for one person. A Literature degree, a journalism course and some gratuitous vocabulary overuse later, her stories have appeared in a Hagrid-sized handful of anthologies and have won enough literary prizes to fill his other hand. Despite this, she has no need as yet for larger millinery.

Colin Kerr has been writing short stories for a couple of years. He has won one and been shortlisted for several more international competitions. He writes about the uniqueness and drama found in everyday situations and people.

Yasmine Lever is a playwright whose work has been produced all over New York and London. She received the James Kirkwood Literary Award, New Century Writing Award and an Honorable Mention in Zoetrope's Short Fiction Contest. Her story Most Especially You was published in Fiction Pool and her story Definitely Not will be published in an anthology later this year. She holds an MFA from New York University.

What does it mean to you to be published by Momaya Press?

I am very grateful to be published by Momaya Press.

What are your plans for writing in the future?

My plans for the future: I am currently pursuing my MFA where I am working on my first novel.

Katie Lewis is a tax lawyer, originally from rainy Wales but now living and working in London. When not working, Katie likes to write stories (short and long) and then evade her colleagues' questions as to where she found the time to do that. She has dreams of publishing a novel one day, ideally not about tax. In her spare time, Katie can often be found playing drums, reading, or travelling.

What was the inspiration for your story?

I went jogging down an unusually quiet road at the start of lockdown, and noticed more lights on in people's houses and flats than usual. I started wondering what it would be like if everyone currently inside was trapped due to the pandemic, but everyone outside was immune; in particular, what relationships could be built through locked doors, when all you could go on was each other's voices? Throw in having recently watched a film about a society where 'villains' had been banished to an island, and idly thinking that the relationship would be particularly awkward if the people outside hated the people inside, and the story spiraled from there.

What does it mean to you to be published by Momaya Press?

I'm thrilled. It's a great confidence boost and it's lovely to see my work in print. Given the story's quarantine theme, I'm also glad people weren't so sick of lockdown that they immediately binned it!

What are your plans for writing in the future?

I've been working on a trilogy for a couple of years. I suspect it's become a trilogy because I'm too terrified to try to get the first novel published, so I just keep going. Fingers crossed I don't stay so scared, it becomes a heptalogy. Other than that, I'd like to write some more short stories.

Alison Lock writes poetry, short fiction and creative non-fiction – the author of two short story collections, three collections of poetry, and a novella, as well as contributor to several anthologies. Her short fiction has won/been listed in a number of competitions: The London Magazine, The Sentinel Literary Quarterly, The Tillie Olsen Award, The Carve Esoteric Prize. She has an MA in Literature Studies from York St John University. Her work focuses on the relationship of humans and the environment, connecting an inner world with an exploration of land and sea, a love of nature, through poetry and prose. www.alisonlock.com

What was the inspiration for your story?

Being an outsider is something many of us experience on different levels. My story explores how we try to find our place in the world, and how our history, culture and belief systems can lead to increased feelings of alienation.

What does it mean to you to be published by Momaya Press?

The quality of writing chosen by Momaya Press is always excellent, so I'm delighted to have a story chosen for the anthology. Momaya gathers a community of writers, encouraging those who create their art as a solitary experience.

What are your plans for writing in the future?

I write poetry as well as fiction. My recent book _Lure _has only recently been published by Calder Valley Poetry, so right now I am feeling my way to working on a new project.

Alan McClure is a poet, songwriter, author and teacher based in Galloway, South West Scotland. His debut children's novel, 'Callum and the Mountain', was published by Beaten Track Publishing in August 2019. He lives with his wife, Michelle, his boys, Fergus and Robin, and his cat, Yoda.

Margaret Morey is a retired Careers Adviser, and English Teacher. She has always been interested in literature, and has a degree in English. She started to develop her interest in creative writing in retirement, and has achieved some small successes in entering competitions. She lives in the lovely Northumbrian village of Corbridge with her cat. She has three grown-up children, one of whom has severe and debilitating autism.

What was the inspiration for your story?

The basis of the story is that one of my children has severe autism and I have felt many times like an outsider in a crazy world which other people don't understand and which excludes you from a lot of social interaction with others.

What does it mean to you to be published by Momaya Press?

I am very excited to be included in your lovely publication with such talented writers, and pleased to reach out to people whom I don't know who may read my story. Recognition like this is a great motivator to keep writing!

What are your plans for writing in the future?

I just want to be a better writer, and to share my writing and learn from others.

Melissa Morrison has been writing stories since she was a kid growing up in Australia, taking shelter from the brutal sun wherever she could find shade, a pen and notebook always at hand. She currently lives in London with her husband, working as a journalist for the legal press.

What was the inspiration for your story?

I started writing this story after being asked the same question as my main character. It got me thinking about how quickly we can associate one word - 'summer' - with so many memories, how they flash through our minds even while we need to maintain a conversation. My character ended up becoming quite conflicted by her recollections - yearning for her childhood but also coming to terms with the fact that she'll always be a bit different to those she shared so much time with, not quite belonging here or there.

What does it mean to you to be published by Momaya Press?

This is my first published story so I'm very, very happy.

What are your plans for writing in the future?

I will continue scribbling away at short stories for many years to come, squeezing in as much creative writing time as I can around my day job as a journalist in London. I'm also working on a novel.

Catherine Ogston writes flash fiction, short stories and YA novels. Her YA manuscript has been long listed for the Exeter and Caledonia Novel Award. Her short stories have been published by New Writing Scotland and online journals. She has had flash fiction pieces short listed in the Bridport Prize and Bath Flash Fiction and will have pieces published in two flash fiction anthologies in 2020 and has also been selected for an anthology with Storgy.

What was the inspiration for your story?

I wanted to write about someone who, through no fault of their own, has all the odds against them and they are constantly struggling to fit in and be accepted. Their circumstances means the world treats them differently and they are always at a disadvantage. My story highlights a moment where my character's life changes again, at the whim of others, and I wanted to show his frustration that he feels so excluded from the life of stability he wants.

What does it mean to you to be published by Momaya Press?

Being selected for any collection or anthology means you must be doing something right! Writing is so solitary and to have others read and like your work makes the long hours at the keyboard worth it. I have read and enjoyed previous Momaya collections and hoped that one day I would make it in there.

What are your plans for writing in the future?

Currently I am redrafting my Young Adult novel, which was longlisted for the Caledonia Novel award last year, and I am hoping this may lead to getting an agent and publication. I am also always working on developing my skills in flash fiction and short stories and getting my work out there.

As a former teacher of English as a foreign language, **Lucy Palmer** takes comfort from the thought that EFL teaching was once J. K. Rowling's profession, and she has written two-and-a-half children's novels, which she hopes to get published one day, as well as a large number of short stories. Her first short story to appear in print, 'Epiphany', was published by Momaya. Lucy currently works as a proofreader for an educational publisher, and she writes fiction as an outlet for creativity and self-expression.

What was the inspiration for your story?

The idea came to me one glorious morning in early summer as I was sitting on a coach on the way to London, having spent all week sitting at a computer in an office in Bristol. I thought I glimpsed a deer from the coach window, and it struck me that all that mattered was to be outdoors, surrounded by nature.

What does it mean to you to be published by Momaya Press?

This is only the second story of mine to appear in print, and the first was also published by Momaya Press, over ten years ago. Appearing in this year's Review provides much-needed reassurance that my free time hasn't been spent in vain. Without a reader, writing can feel like a self-indulgent activity, and having a story published gives me hope that my subjective experience has been not just recorded but shared.

What are your plans for writing in the future?

I'm trying to put together some themed collections of short fiction: one of seasonal stories, another of stories based around music, and possibly a third of speculative fiction/eco-fiction. I'm also hoping to find a publisher for my two completed children's novels and to finish writing the third.

Christine Powell is a short story writer and playwright; she lives in rural County Durham in North East England. Many of her stories have been published in anthologies and magazines and won awards. They all deal with the fragility and absurdity of life from the outside looking in.

Ian Plenderleith is an EU-based, German Scottish freelance writer and journalist. His books include a collection of short fiction (For Whom the Ball Rolls, 2001) and a memoir (The Quiet Fan, 2018). As both a reader and a writer, short fiction is his favourite genre, and he has finished second or placed as a finalist in four international short story competitions. He is also a soccer referee – partly to stay fit, partly because it offers untold insight into the human condition.

What was the inspiration for your story?

In the small English east midlands town where I grew up, Market Rasen (population 2,600), we made the national news twice in the 1970s, and both times – bizarrely – it involved the same small house described in the story. Once because of a murder, the second time because of a gas explosion. The two teenage boys spotting an apparent UFO also made the front page of our local paper, as described in *The Little House of Death*. I took a minor leap of the imagination and linked all three incidents. I didn't write it with 'Outsiders' in mind, but when I saw that was Momaya's theme for the 2020 Review it was clear which story I'd be sending in.

What does it mean to you to be published by Momaya Press?

Writing fiction is a lonely job, so it's a good feeling to join fellow writers in a compendium and be part of a creative community, albeit a very distanced one. Still, I like to picture us all getting drunk in a pub together some day and swapping tales of insecurity, neuroses, writer's block, serial rejection slips and occasional euphoria.

What are your plans for writing in the future?

The Little House of Death is part of a dozen or so stories I'm working on that are all set in my home town of Market Rasen during my youth in the 1970s and early 80s. Small town America is very well represented in short fiction, small town England not so much, I feel. I'm also working on a post-Brexit, post-Pandemic dystopian novel set towards the end of the century. Which is granting me a lot of space to invent the hell out of the future and at the same time come over all melancholy and waste hours staring at the walls...

Sam Szanto lives in Twickenham with her husband, two young children and cat. Her short stories have been published online and in print. In 2020, one of her stories was shortlisted for the Henshaw Press Short Story Competition; another was highly commended in the Michael Terence Publishing Winter Short Story Competition and published in the anthology The Forgotten. In 2019, she was one of the winners of the Doris Gooderson Short Story Competition and her story 'Letting Go' will be published in the Wrekin Writers Anthology 2020. Sam also writes poetry, and her work has won and been shortlisted in a number of competitions. These include the First Writers International Poetry Competition (first prize); Hammond House International Poetry Competition (second prize and published in the Hammond House Anthology, Leaving; and the Grist Prize (shortlisted and published in their anthology Strife).

What was the inspiration for your story?

My story 'Ferhana' was inspired by the Moria refugee camp in Greece. Although the characters are fictional, everything that I describe is horrifyingly real. The camp was built to house 3,000 people; at the last count there were over 5,000 – the conditions have been described as like a 'living hell'. I wrote the story during April 2020, during lockdown; I found it a very creative time, which I didn't expect as I had my two young children and husband in the house with me twenty-four seven! It made me think about how although everyone was finding life suddenly very tough and unexpected, life in a camp like Moria is like being in lockdown all the time. No one expects to be there, and when they are there it is very difficult to leave. Everyone is an outsider, and yet extraordinary relationships can be forged. My grandparents were refugees, so I have a personal interest in the topic – I find it a rich source of inspiration. What I find most pertinent is that many people have a perception of refugees as permanent outsiders, and cannot imagine being in that situation themselves. Yet, of course, anyone can find their lives drastically changed: as we have all seen in 2020.

What does it mean to you to be published by Momaya Press?

I'm thrilled to be published by Momaya Press; it is wonderful for anything I write to be publicly recognised and praised. Writers have such fragile egos! Momaya feels like a very caring publisher, one with heart. It matters to me to have my work noticed by people who read it sensitively. It is a lovely thing to join the Momaya community.

What are your plans for writing in the future?

In the future, I will continue to write short stories and poems, and am working on a collection of stories on the theme of 'Overcoming' and poems with the theme of 'Leaving Home'.

MacKenzie Tastan grew up in Vandalia, Ohio. She currently lives in San Francisco with her husband and pet rabbit. Her work has appeared in The Momaya Press Short Story Review 2019, Illumen Magazine, and the Arizona Daily Sun.

What was the inspiration for your story?

I've always been fascinated by tales about Baba Yaga. I wanted to imagine what would happen if a lost child stumbled upon her house in the woods today.

What does it mean to you to be published by Momaya Press?

I'm thrilled to be published by Momaya Press again this year! It's been my dream to have a story published for a long time and I couldn't be more excited!

What are your plans for writing in the future?

I plan to keep on writing in the future. I've been most successful with short stories so far, but I hope to branch out and have more of my poetry and plays published as well.

Joan Taylor-Rowan writes literary fiction (short stories and a novel), inspired by art, nature and life's quirkiness. She is 60, half-Irish, one of three daughters, who grew up hearing many stories with her six Irish aunts and four nieces. You've got to have a good story and know how to tell it in her family. She recently moved from London to live by the sea. Places at the edge attract people on the edge. At the edges things spin faster, things get thrown off, ideas become far-flung, people become far-out and stories and endeavours become far-fetched. Joan likes to fetch them and write them down.

What was the inspiration for your stories?

Go Amigo Go:

On a recent visit to the U.S. I found myself watching a young Mexican teenager unloading bananas in a Colorado supermarket. His arms were tattooed with spiders. I asked about them in English but it was clear he only had the basics. Although I've visited Mexico often, my Spanish is a bit creaky, so we smiled and nodded in a friendly way. For some reason though, this young man stayed in my mind. Why was he in Colorado, how did he get there and how did he feel about it? Perhaps he longed to return home but had burned his bridges. We writers are exhorted to 'write about what you know' and I'm neither male nor Mexican but I decided to give him emotions that I knew about. Having recently left London for the coast and also lost a parent, I felt I could write authentically about grief and homesickness and trying to fit in. I took up the challenge and hope I did him justice.

Born of Angels:

This story was inspired by a Gauguin painting called Vision After the Sermon. The vision experienced by the Breton women in the foreground is the Bible story of Jacob wrestling with the angel. It was bold and radical (for the time) in colour and composition, but mysterious. I liked this mix of the ancient and the contemporary. I decided to write about angels in a rundown part of London that I know well. The 'wrestling' takes place between the angel who has just completed his first assignment and his ex-lover, a young woman who has dropped out of the training and is struggling with the emptiness and loss she feels.

What does it mean to you to be published by Momaya Press?

It's so hard to get your work noticed. There are many excellent writers out there competing for attention, so to have one story selected for Momaya Press Review was wonderful. The impressive panel of judges, and the high regard in which the Momaya Press competition is held, made me feel I'd achieved something substantial. To then discover that two of my stories had been selected was amazing! Having experienced judges see something special in what you've written is the dream of every writer. It will certainly be on every writing résumé I send out to agents and publishers.

What are your plans for writing in the future?

I plan to finish my Creative Writing M.A. this year and complete the first draft of a novel. A novel is a marathon. It's easy to lose heart and begin to flag. Having two stories selected for the Momaya Press Review has given me the extra fuel to keep going.

Sarah Thomas is a writer, editor, and educator living in Key West, Florida and Geneva, Switzerland. She holds a B.A. in English from Tulane University and an M.F.A. in Writing from Columbia University, where she also taught undergraduate writing. Sarah's published non-fiction spans interviews with rock stars and climate scientists, columns on Ernest Hemingway's love life, and op-eds about the social significance of public swimming pools. She has written for The Huffington Post, Al Jazeera America, xojane, Catapult, Apogee Journal, and Key West Weekly, where she also served as Editor.

What was the inspiration for your story?

The inspiration for my story was a teenager at a salad bar asking if my sister was my daughter! She's *older* than I am, but smaller, blonder, and with more money for Botox. Instead of dying of embarrassment, I thought 'Thank God I've cultivated a brain and a personality.' Then, I imagined a woman approaching middle age whose identity is intrinsically wrapped up in her (fading) beauty. Who might she become once society no longer considers her beautiful? Who might she become if she no longer considers society?

What does it mean to you to be published by Momaya Press?

I'll be so happy to see Charlene on the pages of Momaya, especially in international company. Since the story is about a woman leaving her corner of the world, I'm glad the story will do the same. I'm proud to be published by Momaya because I appreciate their vision of making publishing more accessible and diverse while continuing the great tradition of literary journals.

What are your plans for writing in the future?

I've recently finished a novel called *The Snowbird* that also follows another outsider trying to find herself by discovering another country. I'm currently seeking representation for it. My writing is available at www.sarahthomaswriter.com.

Rima Totah is an emerging fictional writer. In a prior life, she published several works (non-fiction) in peer-reviewed medical and pharmacy journals including Hematology, Journal of Oncology Pharmacy, Oncologist, and Southern Medical Journal. She is listed in the author section by her maiden name, Rima E. Tannous or R.E. Tannous. She has a Bachelor's degree in Biology from California State University, Northridge. In addition, Rima attended the University of Southern California and received two degrees from there including a Doctorate degree in Pharmacy and a Master's degree in Pharmaceutical Economics and Policy.

Events from the last few years have taken Rima on a new journey. She is happily married and raising two wonderful sons. With a little more time on her hands, she has found a passion for writing fictional stories with powerful messages inspired by the many people and their life-experiences that have crossed her path over the years. 'When a Caged-Bird Flies' was inspired by probably the most important person in Rima's life to whom she owes a huge debt of gratitude. Everything that is good in her life is because of her mother. She taught her to always believe in herself, be independent, and to never ever give up.

What was the inspiration for your story?

This story was inspired by my incredible mother, Lorance Tannous. She taught me to be independent, believe in myself always, and to never ever give up.

What does it mean to you to be published by Momaya Press?

It is a great honor and validation of my writing for it to be selected for publication. Thank you, Momaya Press, for recognizing my story and giving me a platform to share my work.

What are your plans for writing in the future?

I plan to continue writing and the hope is to turn this short story into a novel.

Maggie Veness realized years ago that fiction was a great way to disguise fact. Her stories get to the mad heart of things, which isn't always comfortable. Flash, short, and novella length--the vast majority print-published--her work has appeared in many countries in a range of eclectic literary journals and anthologies.

What was the inspiration for your story?

This story - like most of my fiction -

was inspired by my interest in atypical situations and relationships, and by attempting to understand how an individual's kink or quirk originated.

What does it mean to you to be published by Momaya Press?

I admire Momaya Press for continuing to print-publish their annual Review. Having entered without success in previous years, I'm delighted to have one of my stories make the list!

What are your plans for writing in the future?

Hopefully I'll continue to be curious about why people do what they do, because that will provide all the inspiration I need to keep writing.

Natalie White enjoys being an English teacher and loves to run in the Shropshire hills. Her first novel was longlisted for the Bridport prize in 2018, and this year she has already had two short stories published: 'Clear as glass' in 'Songs for the Elephant Man' by Mantle Lane Press and 'The Wall Around You' in 'Birmingham' published by Dostoyevsy Wannabe Cities. Being a member of the wonderful Tindal Street Fiction Group inspires her and has given her the courage to be the writer she wants to be. Spending time with her magical little boy reminds her every day to be grateful for everything.

What was the inspiration for your story?

The story is in fact about a real wedding dress. It was for sale in a vintage shop in a little town in Shropshire and was remarkably beautiful. It was bought for a wedding which was subsequently cancelled, and I wanted to tell this sad story from the point of view of the wedding dress itself.

What does it mean to you to be published by Momaya Press?

It gives me great pride to be published by an international publishing house which has such a wonderful reputation.

What are your plans for writing in the future?

My first novel was recently longlisted for the Bridport Prize, and I am looking for a publisher for it. I'm fortunate enough to have had a few short stories published in various anthologies as well – and I love to write short stories. I am also now working on my second novel.

Short Story Review 2020

About the Judges

Meredith DePaolo is a writer/director based in Kuala Lumpur, Malaysia. She got her TV start on the Emmy award-winning show HBO Real Sports with Bryant Gumbel. She's produced for CBS News, CBS College Sports, Bloomberg, WE, and Oxygen. Her documentary, Chasing the Dream: A Quarterback's Story, was selected as Sports Illustrated's 'What to Watch.' A Yale graduate, Meredith has lived and worked in Europe, the Middle East, and South East Asia. Her work tends to explore divisive themes in culture, religion, and race in a sometimes scary, always funny way. She collaborated with Ron Howard and Brian Grazer as an Imagine Impact Creator, she's a recipient of the Meryl Streep Writers Lab fellowship, and a Page Award finalist. Her feature, COUNTER KARMA, is in development with Imagine Entertainment.

Mikaela Pedlow is Assistant Editor at Harvill Secker, an imprint of the VINTAGE division at Penguin Random House UK. She studied English Literature, French and Fine Arts at the University of Pennsylvania. She loves to read stories from all over the world and works with many international authors, including Ismail Kadare, Ngũgĩ wa Thiong'o, Per Petterson and Enrique Vila-Matas. Mikaela is the coordinator of the annual Harvill Secker Young Translators' Prize. She lives in London.

Gillian Pink is Research Editor at the Voltaire Foundation (University of Oxford), where she has worked since 2007, producing the first critical edition of the French writer's complete works. Her book, Voltaire à l'ouvrage (CNRS Éditions), was published in 2018, and examines his marginalia. She has studied and taught literature from a wide range of styles and periods in the UK, France and Canada.

Alice Shepherd currently works as a copywriter within financial services. Prior to this, she spent a number of years working in within the editorial department of Penguin Random House and Headline Group.

Short Story Review 2020

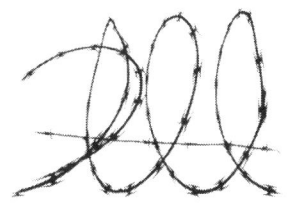

About Momaya Press

Maya Cointreau has twenty-five years of experience in publishing and graphic arts. She has written and published more than thirty books spanning the fiction, children's and non-fiction books genres. She was managing editor of *DCC Magazine*, a magazine with a circulation of more than 60,000 readers and is Director and Editor-in-Chief at Earth Lodge, a publisher of fantasy, youth and non-fiction books.

Monisha Saldanha earned her MBA at Harvard Business School in 2001 and has been working in publishing and digital product development ever since.. She is proud that Momaya Press is increasingly recognized as the premiere worldwide forum for short story writers.

How can YOU become an award-winning author?

There's really just one secret –
tell a great story and tell it well!

Submit your short stories and poems to
momayapress.com

Printed in Poland
by Amazon Fulfillment
Poland Sp. z o.o., Wrocław